Show Girl

Alyson Greaves

Chapter One

Yeah. I was screwed. And that meant the whole company was screwed. Perhaps terminally.

Mr Brewer, the email read, *I am sorry to inform you that several of our staff have been taken ill, and we are thus unable to provide three models as contracted for your upcoming event. Only one, Emily Swan, is currently available. I await confirmation that her services are still required.*

We will, naturally, invoice for a single model only. I would remind you that our models require regular breaks, and suggest that, if you decide to go ahead with the contract, you find her at least one other model as backup. A list of reputable firms is attached.

Regards, Frank Hammond.

"Fuck," I said to myself, rereading to make absolutely sure it said what I thought it said. Only one girl for the Consumer Electronics Expo, and almost no chance of acquiring anyone else: CEE was days away, and I'd found Hammond's firm only that week, after contacting every pro modelling agency I could find. Hammond's had been the sweet spot: the better firms were out of the price range I'd been given to work with; the cheaper ones had been booked up for weeks.

I shot off a few enquiries to the expensive firms, anyway, just in case, but it didn't take long to get a brace of apologetic replies.

"Fuck!" I said to myself again.

I'd have to tell James.

James McCain was an old family friend, and he'd taken me on at his startup after no-one else would take a chance on me. My unemployability was understandable, really; I was a kid fresh out of school with no experience, no degree, and thoroughly average A-levels. He was taking a risk on me, mitigated by the implicit suggestion that, should he have to let me go, our close ties would prevent me from making too much of a fuss. He was older than me, twenty-three to my nineteen, and in addition to having every physical attribute I wished for but didn't have — he was tall and well built; I was short and scrawny, and felt more so whenever I was around him — he was a software engineering genius.

And now I had to let him down.

The walk to his office was short enough that I didn't have much time to worry. McCain Applied Computing still had so few employees that we had no need for a lot of office space, so we leased half a floor in a reasonably nice building in a reasonably nice part of the city, spending James' father's money on location rather than square footage. He approved, apparently preferring that the McCain name be kept out of 'the poor parts' of London.

Yes. Gross.

Still, it meant that the two of us were often the only ones there. One of the engineers once asked me why we both persisted in coming to the office every day, every week, even though James required only a computer with an array of screens to do his job and I, as his do-everything gopher — his 'assistant', had we been a formal enough company to have real job titles — could have made do with a laptop, a phone, and a bottle of maximum-strength ibuprofen; I remember neither of us had an answer. If I'd been honest, I probably would have answered the question with a question of my own: what else was I supposed to do with my time? My home was a tiny, lonely apartment, I didn't have any hobbies to speak of, and my social and dating lives were uneven and unexciting enough that if I didn't come by the office I'd probably end up going weeks at a time without seeing another human face except at the supermarket.

His office door was open, as usual. I knocked, anyway.

"Alex?" he called from inside. I could picture him: he'd be lounging on his enormous leather chair, leg swinging lazily, one arm crooked behind his head. "Is that you?"

I poked my head around the door and discovered, to my surprise, that I'd caught James in a rare moment of extreme diligence. He was sitting forward at his desk, frowning at something on one of the monitors in front of him. We hadn't spent much time together today, what with me being so busy getting everything arranged for the expo, so this was about to be my first time seeing him since the night before, aside from a brief greeting this morning; I braced myself for the usual stab of jealousy in my gut. I had to get used to being around James, tall, handsome, toned and confident James, and every night I lost a bit of my resistance and had to build it back up through exposure. Today he was wearing a t-shirt that stretched itself a little too tight over his pectorals, and I had to exercise a spot of self-control to stop myself raising my hand to my own inadequate chest.

This was the man I was about to disappoint. The thought made me feel a little faint, and it took some concentration to make it to one of the chairs without slipping or tripping or otherwise making an idiot out of myself. I just couldn't get the images out of my mind: my impending unemployment; James returning to his father, chastened, horrifyingly expensive cap in hand. They were occupying the parts of my brain that apparently normally were used for standing upright.

His face broke out into the smile he always reserved for me, and then soured. "What's up?" he said. "You look— Shit, Alex, you look terrified."

I found my voice. "I just heard from Frank Hammond." His right eye crinkled, the way it did when I'd assumed some knowledge of him that he, naturally, could not be expected to possess, so I preempted him: "Of Hammond's, the booth babe people." None of the modelling agencies liked it when you called their girls 'booth babes' — or 'girls', for that matter

— and I'm sure the women in question felt the same, but in my short time in the tech industry I've been required to hang out with a lot of men, a lot of *blokes,* and I'd picked some things up. "They've got some girls out sick. Reading between the lines, it's impacted more clients than just us. The upshot: they can give us only one model for CEE."

James was quiet for a moment.

"James?" I said, when he didn't say anything. He was only ever 'Mr McCain' to me when we needed to look professional, which was practically never.

Okay, he was *also* 'Mr McCain' when I wanted to be cheeky. Not today.

"I'm thinking," he said, holding up a finger.

He sounded neither angry nor worried, which confused me. Booth babes were vitally important at trade shows for smaller companies — doubly so for startups like ours — because a large stage was both expensive and pointless when you didn't have the people or products to fill it out, and acquiring the floor space in which to put it and all associated signage was another, sometimes even larger, chunk of change, but hiring a handful of pretty girls and getting some eye-catching dresses made in the company colours was comparatively cheap, and about as good when it came to attracting attention. I complained about it when James first suggested it, but he had the numbers to prove that it, unfortunately, worked. As James' father, who made his insufferable presence known every so often when he wanted to remind James who provided the capital for the company in the first place, liked to say, "Technology is a sexist business, and the way to sell in a sexist business *ist* with *sex!*"

The expectant pause afterwards, for laughter we struggled to provide, was the worst part.

This week's Consumer Electronics Expo was likely to be make-or-break for McCain Applied Computing. We had a revolutionary product — a software solution to the hardware problem of putting a good-quality camera behind a phone display, without resorting to punching unsightly holes through the screen or vastly degrading the quality of the resultant

4

photograph — but the window we had to sell it in was unpredictable. All we knew was, if we couldn't at least make a start on getting some contracts at CEE, then by the time the next trade show rolled around, someone else might have solved the same problem; software and hardware engineers on every continent had to be working on it. Already some prototypes had been seen, albeit with awful quality; a mid-two-thousands feature phone could do better. We had other miracles in the works — James, like I said, is a genius — but nothing ready to show.

It had only been a week since we got it working at all. James and I spent from dawn to dusk and beyond in the office for months at a time, existing on expensed food delivery and caffeine. We'd set up adjacent desks and pushed ourselves as hard as we dared. When the other coders made their occasional visits to the office — for milestone meetings and gossip — they usually commented on how exhausted we both looked, all the time. But I never minded; it'd been fun. When finally we cracked it, we had no time left to celebrate; James immediately threw himself into courting the big manufacturers, and I set to work on logistics, signage, booth babes and dress design. At least, for that last week, we got a little more sleep.

I was proud of our software solution. None of it was my idea, and I mostly followed James' lead, but he'd been bought a top-notch education and I'd taught myself online and on the job; I was just glad I could keep up.

"Hammond says the girls need regular breaks," I said, "so just one isn't enough to cover a booth full time."

He nodded. "Can I see the email, please?"

I rooted my phone out of my pocket, unlocked it, and handed it over. He scanned the email quickly.

"These are all the emails you've exchanged with this Hammond guy?" he asked, holding the phone out where we could both see it and scrolling through the message history.

"Yeah."

"Okay," he said. "Okay. I've got an idea. I'm going to forward myself these messages and reply to Hammond personally. We'll use this Emily

Swan he's offering us, and I think I know where we can find another model. You think two girls will be enough?"

I shrugged. "We only had three booked, anyway. It means one of them will have to cover the booth while the other's taking a break, but it should work, especially with you and me and some of the engineers around to help out and talk tech."

He smiled and gave me back my phone. "Good. Go finish all the other preparations for Friday, and assume we'll have two girls. When are the dresses getting here?"

"They're not finalised yet. We'll have them Friday morning, if we pass on the measurements tonight."

"Okay, good," he said. "Now, go organise!" He shooed me out, picking up his phone with the other hand. The last thing I heard from him was, "Hi. It's James. I need a *big* favour…" before I rounded the corner, and the rest of his conversation was drowned out by noise from the street outside.

* * *

An hour or so later I started thinking about grabbing some lunch, so I headed to James' office to ask if he wanted me to pick something up for him and his visitor. The other man had arrived a little while back, trailing luggage and offering no name nor any explanation as to why James had called him, but he smiled at me and then marched off around the corner to James' office without asking for directions, so I assumed he'd been here before and just left them both to it.

I knocked on the closed office door, and James immediately called for me to come in.

"I was about to get some lunch—" I started, but he interrupted me.

"Alex!" He was in a good mood; I assumed his friend already found him a spare booth babe. "This is Ben, my roommate from university. Ben, Alex."

6

"Delighted," Ben said. I nodded, memories of James' tales of university life coming back to me. This was *that* Ben, then. A legend, and James' closest confidante.

"Alex," James said, adopting his serious voice, the one he put on to talk to real businesspeople, "shut the door and come sit down. I have a proposal for you. A... business proposition."

Confused but compliant, I did as he asked, settling into the chair next to Ben and putting on my attentive face, the one I used to receive and consider business propositions.

"What kind of proposition?" I asked. I was starting to get uncomfortable with the attention they were paying me. I welcomed it from James — he saved for me a smile that was barely a smile, just a curl in one corner of his mouth — but having a stranger regard me so intensely was unsettling.

James steepled his fingers. "I had a quick skim through your contacts for booth babes — trade show models, sorry — and couldn't find anyone who still had availability. Even the high-end places are booked up. You were *very* thorough."

"Thanks!" I said, perking up. Compliments from James were always welcome, however readily and often he offered them. It took me a moment to process the implications behind what he'd said, and when I finally did, I matched his frown. "Does that mean we *don't* have a second model, then?"

"That," James said, "is the question before the court."

I was confused, and said so.

"Ben here is an exceptional drag queen—"

"Performance artist in the medium of drag," Ben interrupted. I could almost hear the extra *e* in 'artist', and started wondering, as he and James shared a smile at the obvious in-joke, how much detail James had left out of his stories from university. Then, once again processing important information multiple seconds after receiving it, I realised what James was getting at.

"You want to use a drag queen?" I said.

They were both silent for a moment. I used the time to look Ben over. He was attractive, no doubt about it, with a deep, melodic voice, a carefully trimmed beard and, now that I could see him in the good light of James' office, the faintest suggestion of sparkling eyeshadow highlighting his dark skin. I imagined he was wonderful on stage.

At the expo, though, he'd make a statement louder than our product.

"Not me, darling," Ben said, smiling gently at me. I realised I'd been staring, and looked away. "James here wants to use *you.*"

My train of thought, already derailed, vanished into the scenery. I don't know exactly what my face looked like at that moment, but I'm pretty sure my mouth dropped open like I was a dead fish.

"Sorry, Alex," James said, and poked his friend. "I was *trying* to broach the subject more delicately."

Ben slapped his finger away. "You were dawdling, is what you were doing."

I remained silent.

"Look," James said, turning his attention back to me, "the thing is, you'd be doing me — that is, the company — a tremendous favour, and you'd be paid the modelling fee, too, so this'd be extra, on top of your salary. And it's not a bad sum, especially since *you* don't have to give any of it to an agent or manager like poor—" he glanced at his screen for a reminder, "—Emily Swan does."

I remained silent.

"Alex," he said, "I'm not asking you this as your boss, or even as your friend. Or maybe I'm asking you this as both? The fact is, *you* know this trade show is everything to us, and it needs to go perfectly. And *I* know that if your startup doesn't have some way to bring people in, some way to stand out, your startup will vanish from view amid all the other startups in your tiny corner of the trade show. And I *also* know that nothing gets attention like beautiful girls showing off your product. Girls *plural,* not just one who can talk to only one person at a time, and has to leave the stand empty when she takes a bathroom break."

I remained silent. James, later, would neither confirm nor deny that steam started coming out of my ears at this point.

"And you'd be *more* than just some agency worker we hired in for the day!" James continued, warming to his pitch. "You know the product better than anyone else except me. And you know about most of the other stuff we're working on, too; if a potential client talks to you, you can sell him on not just the product but the whole company! And, if it's just random members of the public, you can just, you know, turn on your inherent charm."

What charm? I asked myself, and then did my best to follow up my first coherent thought in a while with a handful more. "James," I said, speaking slowly and deliberately so I didn't lose control and start shrieking, "I don't understand why you're asking this. I don't know why one woman and one drag queen is your solution. I don't know why you think *I'd* make a good drag queen. And I don't know why you think potential clients — who, if they are the sort of people who like *booth babes* —" I emphasised the words derisively, "would relate just as well to a drag queen as they would to a woman, no matter how knowledgeable he is!"

I managed, just about, not to shout at my boss, long-time friend, and saviour. And his drag queen pal.

The drag queen pal burst out laughing.

"Hey!" I said, offended.

"I'm sorry," Ben said, "but you have grasped the *exact* wrong end of the stick here!"

"I don't want you to be a drag queen," James said, quietly, carefully. "I want you to be a *real* trade show model."

What?

"A booth babe," Ben added.

"A woman," James said. He didn't even have the good grace to look embarrassed about saying it, instead keeping his steady gaze locked on mine.

"Are you out of your mind?" I said, giving in and shrieking just a little. "Even if I agreed to do it, how would it even work? I mean, *look* at me!" I waved a hand towards my body, indicating the obvious — that there was absolutely no way someone as masculine as I could ever successfully masquerade as a woman — and glared at them in turn until one of them acknowledged it.

Ben's eyes softened, and he smiled. "Alex," he said quietly, gently, in the tone of voice you might use to get an injured kitten to drink its milk, "I've been looking at you since you walked in. You could do it."

"He's right," James said, diving into the pause created by my sudden exasperated disbelief. "I mean — and I really don't want to offend you, so I'm sorry in advance — you're not exactly tall, you're slim, you're delicate, you're — God, I'm *really* sorry about this — actually rather pretty..."

"I'm 'pretty'...?" I echoed in a whisper. It was all I could manage. The concept was absurd, even if, out of James' mouth, it was surprisingly flattering.

"You are," Ben said.

"When you don't cover your face with all that stubble," James muttered.

'Stubble' was giving it airs it didn't deserve; it was basically bumfluff. I *was* only nineteen, with plenty of time to grow a real beard, or so I kept telling myself. I covered my face with my hand, anyway, suddenly extremely self-conscious.

They were looking at me again, all analytical. I looked away, examined the wall instead, and wondered what they saw. I knew what *I* saw whenever I looked in the mirror: a mess.

"I just don't see how this could work," I said.

"Look," James said, "how about we all go to my place, where it's nice and private. Ben can work his magic on you, and if it doesn't work out—" he waved a noncommittal hand, as if there was no possible way it *wouldn't* work out, "—we have the rest of the day to come up with another idea."

"I don't know..." I said.

James waited in silence until I looked back up at him. When I finally did so, he trapped me with his deep brown eyes.

"Please?" he said softly. "Just give it a try?"

Something took control of my mouth and said, "Okay."

James' apartment was smaller than I expected. Larger than mine, sure, but I'd seen cupboards larger than my apartment; nicer, too. It was well fitted out — I couldn't remember the last time I'd seen a dishwasher — and clearly in several price brackets up from the hovel I grudgingly called home.

James had ushered me in through the front door first, as if to make sure I couldn't run away without having to go through him, Ben, and Ben's enormous suitcase; probably a wise move. Then, after giving me a moment to take in the splendour and the glamour of his couches, his enormous television, his open-plan kitchen and his pile of dirty socks, he sat me down and poured me a colourful drink from one of the glitzier-looking bottles on his bar. It only didn't look like a double because it looked like a triple.

"To relax you," he explained, handing me the glass.

I needed relaxing, so I downed it in a couple of gulps, preemptively wincing against the burn and then, when the burn didn't come, regaining the very stupid look on my face that had served me so well in James' office. It tasted fruity.

"You were expecting whiskey?" James asked, smiling. I nodded, feeling a little too foolish to speak. He patted me on the knee. "Sorry, I didn't want to scorch your throat."

"Thanks," I said weakly.

Ben clapped his hands. "Enough chatter!" he said. "Enough booze! Enough—" he gestured towards where James was crouched down next to me, "—whatever the hell *that* is! Let's get *on* with things; I've got a show to get ready for tonight."

As he wheeled his suitcase into what turned out to be James' bathroom, I turned back to James and tried to ask, with a mixture of silent gestures, if Ben performed drag with his immaculate beard intact. James nodded.

"Get in here!" Ben commanded, his voice echoing in the bathroom.

* * *

Getting your legs waxed sucks.

Ben insisted I be completely naked, waving aside my protests by confirming to me in a matter-of-fact tone that I didn't possess anything he hadn't seen and dined on before, and assuring me he wasn't into twinks, anyway. I kept up my objections for several valiant minutes before submitting to the inevitable.

It wasn't so much that I didn't want to be naked in front of Ben; I didn't want to be naked in front of *anybody.* So I think I can be excused for keeping my eyes firmly shut for the whole process. Prey animal logic: if you can't see them, they can't see you.

He did my legs and moved onto my crotch. The first strip shocked me too much to scream — yes, it was *that* painful — and while he was preparing the second strip I felt around the sink, found a washcloth draped over the side and jammed it in my mouth, so the only noises I made as he depilated the rest of my groin were some strained whimpering and the squishy, liquid sounds of a used flannel being destroyed by teeth. It tasted awful.

"You can open your eyes now," Ben said.

I compromised and opened one. Ben was holding out a mint; I spat out my washcloth and took it gratefully, and as I sucked away the aftertaste, he handed me a towel. "We're done with waxing, then?" I asked, as he tied me closed.

"Yes. Now we sort out that horrible little teenage beard thing you've got going on."

Before I could get too deeply into worrying about what arcane torture devices he might apply to my oh-so-manly chin fluff, he'd slathered me in paste. It was brown and smelled absolutely disgusting.

"Ugh," I commented.

"Count yourself lucky," Ben said. "This stuff will dissolve that fluff on your face without any trouble in just a few minutes. If you had a beard like me or James, we could leave it on for half an hour and all it would do is give you a rash." He looked annoyed when he said that, like he'd tried it on himself. I looked down at the tube and noticed it was half empty; obviously he had.

True to his word, when we washed it off it took most of my straggly hair with it. I took a razor to the rest. The end result wasn't much more fresh-faced than I usually looked after a close shave — although Ben insisted it should last a bit longer — and illustrated why I almost never shaved if I could help it: without the assistance of my unimpressive bumfluff, I struggled to look my age.

We were both startled by a light knock on the bathroom door.

"Everything okay in there?" James called.

"Yes!" Ben hissed. "Now go away! You can't rush perfection!"

"You need anything?"

"No!" Ben and I said at once. The prospect of walking out of the bathroom fully clothed (in a dress) was bad enough; I wasn't ready for James, of all people, to see me with the process half finished.

Ben kicked the bathroom door, for emphasis, and smirked at me. I was starting to like him.

With James' impatience and curiosity temporarily beaten, I relaxed again — for relative values of 'relaxed', anyway — and sat back on the edge of the bath, waving my legs in the air, entranced by the look of them. I had to admit, I looked better waxed. I'd never developed that thick coat of body hair you see on some men, and I'd definitely never had anything like James' tight little curls, which I'd seen once or twice, and which made him look sculpted and defined. My chest and arms were mostly downy, and my legs grew sad little patches of hair that stuck out at strange angles and served only to emphasise how scrawny I was. And my attempts to build muscle to compensate had gone poorly: I had a set of weights at home that I never used, because I was never at home to use them, and I was far too self-conscious to have used the little gym in our office basement more than once or twice, no matter how many times James invited me to join him. I got the bulk of my exercise walking from home to the office and back again, which had at least noticeably improved my stamina.

Ben handed me a tube of moisturiser and, in response to my confusion, rolled his eyes and mimed spreading it over my legs. Feeling playful, I stuck out my tongue at him and started massaging the stuff in, from ankle to crotch, rubbing my legs together when I was done and giggling at how frictionless they felt.

I think James' fruity drink was settling in.

"Finally having fun, are we?" Ben said.

I would have done anything to avoid blushing. "I'll never do this again," I replied, "so I might as well try to enjoy it." I wasn't lying, I realised. Encouraged by the alcohol, I returned his smile.

"Good!" Ben said, holding out a pair of what looked for all the world like disembodied breasts. "Because now the fun part begins."

* * *

They looked like breasts because they were, in a light colour that very nearly matched my pale skin. I bounced them up and down in my hands, entranced by the lifelike wobbling, and thus entirely missed Ben ambushing me from behind with a bra. I slotted the boobs into the cups as directed — cold! — and while they warmed from my body heat, I noted that they were smaller than I expected; Ben was *tall,* and I would have thought he'd wear something quite a bit larger.

"They're not *mine,*" he said, struggling to control his smile.

"They're not?" I asked, and just moments later felt like an idiot when he held his arm up to mine, dark brown against my sort of sour milk colour. He completed his point — not that he needed to — by pulling another breast out of the case to show me. It matched his complexion and was roughly the size of my head.

"It's a good thing you're pretty," he said, and tapped my forehead.

"Hey," I said, "I'm smart in... other ways."

He laughed, helped me up, and had me struggle into a couple of what he called foundation garments: a pair of knickers made of stretchy fabric which hid my junk completely, and which took a lot of courage to put on

14

after Ben's eye-watering demonstration of their function; and a ridiculous contraption which clung to my butt and upper thighs and looked like someone had welded squishy raw chicken to my undercarriage.

Sitting on it felt *odd,* and I said so.

"Tough it out," he told me, in a voice which brooked no disagreement. "You need a *butt.*" Meekly I let him sit me back down, and then he began to paint.

It had never occurred to me before that makeup would have a smell to it. I'd dated girls from time to time but never for very long, and I didn't have a sister, so I'd only encountered makeup pre-applied, as it were. The foundation Ben was applying, in florid little circles around my chin and left cheek, had a subtle floral scent; rather nice, really.

He handed me the sponge.

"Um," I said.

"Your turn," he said, clamping his free hand on top of my head and twisting me until I was looking at myself in the mirror. He tapped the half of my face that didn't yet have coverage.

"Why?"

"Because *if* you're going to do this trade show thing—"

"—I'm not—"

"—but if you *are* — and I think you can agree we should proceed with the best of intentions — then you're going to need to know how to touch up your makeup." He tapped my cheek again. "And you don't have a lot of time to become an expert online."

I sighed. James must have told him how I learned to code. Or possibly how I learned to do a proper necktie. "What do I do?"

He clamped my fingers around the sponge he gave me and guided my hand — and the sponge — around my cheekbone. "Like this," he said. "Gentle strokes. Gentle strokes..." He let go and nodded at me to continue.

I didn't. Not yet. Applying makeup myself felt different to having Ben do it; like doing it myself made it something I'd actively chosen to participate in, not just something my lovable arsehole of a boss/friend and his ex-roommate were doing *to* me.

Stupid, obviously. I'd chosen this. James asked and I accepted; denying that, at this point, seemed rather silly. No sense, after the bra, the boobs — which already felt disturbingly natural, now they'd warmed up — and the hairless body, in getting squeamish about a little makeup.

No sense at all.

Carefully, looking back at Ben to make sure I was doing it correctly, I stroked the sponge across my cheek.

* * *

We had to chase James off again. He hammered on the bathroom door just as we were nearing the end of our makeup routine. Ben told him that if he couldn't make his own entertainment for one or two measly hours he should go for a walk and, after some light threats, James grumpily agreed. We listened carefully for the front door and his feet on the stairs before we carried on.

And carry on we did: earlier, Ben had brushed my messy hair into something approaching order and then shoved it all under a wig cap, and now he added a long wig in dark blonde. He made me watch while he styled it, so I could fix my hair at the trade show.

"But I'm not *going* to the trade show," I insisted again.

"Nevertheless," he insisted back. I couldn't argue with that.

After the wig came the dress. I've left off describing it up to this point, even though it was hanging on the shower rail the whole time. There was just something too *real* about it. It was *so* blue and *so* short and *so* the capstone to this whole enterprise that I was becoming more and more dubious about it as the alcohol left my system.

It was even more real when I was wearing it.

It was tight. It hugged my fake curves like a second skin. It was short, reaching barely two-thirds of the way down my thighs; less when I sat down. And it was electric blue. I would have preferred a more muted colour, but Ben explained that he'd chosen my makeup to complement the dress, and he'd chosen the dress because it was the closest match he had to the colour of McCain Applied Computing's company logo, which was also the colour of the dresses we were going to have at the trade show.

The simple black shoes with the low heel were almost anti-climactic. I perched on the edge of the bath again and held my feet against his, asking the question without asking it.

"I bought them," Ben said. "Your reprobate boss owes me twenty-eight quid. And how *does* he know your shoe size?"

"Oh, right," I said, laughing. I twisted my fingers around each other as I remembered. "It's a silly story, really. There was a wedding — not his, a friend's; one of his friends, not mine; an ex-girlfriend, I think? — and he wanted me to come as his plus one, since he wasn't dating anyone at the time. And I didn't have any formal clothes, so he was going to rent me a suit, and he needed to know my shoe size... I didn't go, in the end. We hadn't known each other all that long, and I'm always at a loose end at weddings, and, well—" I hated this part of the memory; he'd been quite disappointed, "—I chickened out. Stayed here. In London. He was nice about it. 'Next time,' he said. He brought me back a piece of cake but it had gone stale, so we put it out for the pigeons." I should have gone. He *asked* me. "So, uh, that's how he knows my shoe size."

That's also how he knew I was a huge coward. Maybe this was an opportunity to show him otherwise?

Yeah, right.

The shoes, at least, fit perfectly. I stood, meaning to look at myself in the bathroom mirror, but Ben placed himself in the way.

"Do I look that bad?" I asked.

"Not at all!" Ben insisted.

"No, really. I look awful, right?"

"It's just bad light."

I would have forced my way past him at that moment if I thought I could possibly manage it, but he was bigger than me, he wasn't wearing heels, and he wasn't feeling like he was about to throw up (I assumed). I let him guide me instead, my hand in his, out of the bathroom and into James' bedroom. Ben let me go when we entered, and as I tottered unsteadily —

alcohol; shoes; terror — towards the full-length mirror by the wardrobe, Ben turned on the overhead light.

I gasped.

I was fucking *gorgeous.*

There was no way I could tell there was, well, a *me* under that dress, and that was with the considerable advantage of being able to look down at my own body and check.

"Girl," Ben said, "you wear that better'n I do." I think he phrased it that way on purpose, because I flinched, and he added, "And *that's* something you have to get used to right now. If you do *this*—" he threw his arms in the air in an exaggerated impression of my reaction, "—when someone calls you a girl, or a woman, or beautiful, or darling, or whatever, then you'll give the game away."

Oh God.

I looked at myself again: I couldn't get away from the woman in the mirror; she held on to me, kept me there. I realised a second later I was hugging myself.

I *stared.*

"Ben—" I said, and then forgot what I was about to say because I was still looking at myself as I spoke and the most ridiculous thing about all of this had suddenly, finally occurred to me. "What the *fuck,* Ben?" I burst out. "I may look the part — and Jesus Christ, do I look the part — but the moment I open my mouth, everyone's going to *know!*"

I was still hugging myself, only this time it was to keep the contents of my stomach in; my whole body had lurched when I saw the girl in the mirror talk like *that,* and I'd nearly covered James' bedroom floor with whatever remained of my breakfast.

Ben took a step towards me and put calming hands on my shoulders.

"I know a trick for that," he said.

"*What?*" I almost screeched. Making noises like that was becoming a bad habit.

"It wouldn't work for someone like James — not quickly enough, anyway; not in time for your trade show thingy — but your natural voice is high enough that you can probably get away with it. Come and sit with me."

He patted James' bed and, after taking a moment to calm myself — very much avoiding the mirror for now, lest I get stuck in my reflection again — I sat next to him. I was nothing but doubts, but I wanted to hear how he could possibly cover up my man's voice as easily as he covered up my man's body.

"This is something trans women learn," he said, "and impressionists, voice actors, and, yes, drag queens, sometimes, if they want to." The expression on his face said that he, personally, either did not or could not. "But the difference between men's and women's voices isn't just a matter of pitch. If you think about it, I'm sure you can come up with men with quite high voices and women with quite deep ones. There's a *huge* overlap in the middle, and your voice is right inside that overlap." He poked me to accentuate his last few words.

"Yes," I said, still acutely aware of my own voice, "but men with high voices still sound like men. I don't know why; they just do. Same with women, but the other way around."

He grinned at me. "*You* might not know why, but I do. When your voice broke, your Adam's apple — which I can't for the life of me actually see on you, but which I assume is in there somewhere — expanded, and that's why your voice got deeper and, if you'll pardon the technical term, more manly. But, if you know the trick, you can bypass that."

I sighed, still sceptical. "What's the trick?"

"Put a hand on your chest," he said, putting a hand on his own chest. "Right here."

I copied him, feeling the tops of the breast forms under my hand. An unusual sensation.

"Now, say something," he commanded.

Lost for words, I attempted, "Something."

"Something *longer,*" he said, exasperated. "Twit."

"Um," I said. A piece of doggerel popped into my brain: "The rain in Spain stays mainly on the plain."

19

Ben laughed. "Interesting choice. You feel your chest vibrate as you said that?" I nodded. "Okay, now what you want to do is say that *without* your chest vibrating." Before I could ask the obvious question, he continued, "Say 'aah'."

"Aah?"

"No, like you're at the dentist and he wants to look at your back teeth."

"Aaaaaaah."

"Good. Keep going." I kept going, and he kept talking. "Feel your chest. No vibrations?" I shook my head, which made my *aah* sound funny. "Now, without taking a breath, move your *aah* around in your mouth: first go from *aah*—" he said it like the vowel in *bath,* "—to *ahh.*" This one was like the vowel in *bat.* "And then go through all the other vowels. Move it *all* around your mouth."

I did so, waiting for my chest to start vibrating the way it had when I spoke before. It didn't.

"This is your 'head voice'. This is what you're going to talk in. It takes practice, and it'll sound a little reedy until you're good at it, but you *can* practise it and you *will* get good at it. And don't worry; it only becomes permanent if you never use your 'other' voice. You'll be able to switch back after the trade show."

"Switch back?" I said, in my normal voice. Ben slapped me, lightly, on the leg.

"Head voice!" he commanded. "If it helps, try going 'aah' again and then turning it into a humming sound without ever leaving your head voice."

I did as he suggested. It took a couple of goes to get it right. With his encouragement, I kept at it until I could do it every time.

"*Now* try and say something. Come at it from humming if it helps."

It did. "*Mmmmm*switch back?" I said, managing to stay in head voice.

"Well done. And yes, you'll be able to go back to your normal voice when this is all done with, but, for now, *don't.* I want you to talk like this until the trade show. The more you do so, the better you'll sound, and you need to get used to it, anyway."

"It's hard," I said, my voice almost cracking on the second word.

"Then we practise!" Ben said. I glanced at the bedroom door; Ben noticed. "I texted James and made him promise not to come back home until I say it's okay, so you *don't* have to worry about him walking in on us."

My relief must have been obvious, because he smiled at me.

"Okay," he said. "Let's just have a normal conversation, and you stay in head voice the whole time. I'll poke you if you drop out. Ready? What do you do at work?"

Work? I could talk about work until the cows came home. I loved working with James.

* * *

"Are you ready?" Ben asked.

"Absolutely not," I whispered.

"Well, you've got ten seconds to *get* ready."

I swallowed.

After an hour of talking, humming, *aah*ing, and otherwise making a minor fool of myself, Ben pronounced me 'better enough'. I was getting used to talking in head voice. It was, I explained to him, like riding a skateboard downhill: once you have the momentum, it's easier to keep going than it is to stop. We made a few recordings on my phone so I could hear myself and, true to Ben's word, I sounded like a woman. Kind of a tired woman with kind of a deep alto, for sure, but Ben promised me that, with time, I would get better at it, sound clearer, and my average pitch would also rise. He suggested I keep the recordings and use them as a reference to help me get back into the swing of things in the morning, and made me promise to use the voice for the rest of the day.

He'd been leaning on the assumption that I'd be doing this for more than just the next few hours, and I'd been studiously pretending not to notice. I fully intended, despite the voice work and despite my arresting reflection, to thank him very much for his time, make James pay him the £28 for the shoes, and glare hard at my contact list until it coughed up a viable alternative source for booth babes.

Ben texted James that it was time for him to come home, and dragged me into the living room to wait for him, in my shockingly light dress, heels, and wig. Real human hair, Ben swore.

I practised head voice. I checked for alternative exits. I snuck another double of the drink James poured me earlier. And I didn't know what to do with my hands without pockets, so when I finished my drink I clasped one hand in the other in front of my waist.

Next to Ben, next to even my image of my usual self, in hoodie and jeans, I felt very small.

A key turned in the front door lock.

"Is it too late to run screaming into the night?" I asked quietly, maintaining my head voice.

"If you run," Ben said, "after all the work I just put in, I'll chase you down myself. Remember, I've had a *lot* more practice than you at running in heels."

And then James was back.

It must have been raining outside, because his curly hair was matted and his coat was drenched. I think he was muttering, but the dark expression on his face evaporated when he looked at us.

"A— Alex?"

Okay, it's possible he was just looking at *me.* I gave him a little wave.

"Holy *shit,"* he said, and almost ran over to me, raising his arms as if to hug me, but Ben pushed him away.

"Absolutely not!" Ben scolded. "You're *soaking* wet. Go dry your hair and put on fresh clothes. She's been waiting hours for you; she can wait another few minutes."

There was that blush again. Ben had been calling me a woman and a girl repeatedly for the whole hour we'd been talking, enough that their impact had been blunted, but the pronoun hit me deep in the chest.

"I'll be quick," James promised, and immediately made a liar of himself by backstepping slowly away from me, looking me up and down.

When eventually he closed the bedroom door I almost fainted.

"I'd call that a success," Ben said.

I frowned. "What do you mean?"

"He knows exactly who you are and yet, if I know James, I'd say the rush of blood to his head just now was equalled only by the rush of blood to his cock." I opened my mouth to protest, out of loyalty to James — he wasn't like that! — but Ben cut me off. "And if you can do *that* to *him,* no straight man at the trade show is going to be able to resist your charms. They're *all* going to be buying your... whatever it is you're selling." He took me by my upper arms and very nearly lifted me off the ground. It was like he was displaying me to the world. "You'll be a smoking hot booth babe, Alex."

The alcohol made me giggle. "Hey," I said, when he put me down, "if *you* get to be a performance artiste in the medium of drag—" I inserted the *e* in 'artist' with the rudest grin I could muster, "—then *I* get to be a trade show model."

"So, you're going to do it, then?" he asked, suddenly serious.

"I don't know," I admitted. Seeing James respond the way he did had shaken my resolve. "You really think my voice will be okay?"

"I think *with practice* your voice will be okay," he said. "So *don't stop practising!*"

I redid my *aah*s and my hums.

* * *

James took his bloody time. Ben and I were still comfortably chatting and helping ourselves to James' home bar, and James was *still* in his room, when Ben's phone chimed.

"Shit," he said. "Sorry, Alex, but I can't stay here forever; I have a show tonight."

My heart nearly crashed out through my chest. "You're going to leave me here? With him? Alone? Like *this?*" I gestured down at myself, encompassing with my frantic flapping the dress, the shoes, the hip pads, breasts #1 and #2; everything. Suddenly it wasn't a fun game I was playing with a new friend, one who'd made it very clear he wasn't into me no matter what clothes or makeup I might or might not choose to wear; suddenly I was going to be stranded, dressed up as a girl, with my boss, in his apartment. I thought back to Ben's comments about the rush of blood to James' dick, and blushed. And panicked again. Panic-blushed.

"You'll be fine!" Ben said.

"How do I even take all this off?" I said, taking a moment after to realise I hadn't dropped out of head voice even under duress, and being mildly impressed at myself, despite everything.

Ben looked at me like I was an idiot. Again. He might have had a point. "Just undress and get in the shower," he said.

Yeah. He had a point. The transformation he'd guided me through felt so total that it hadn't even occurred to me that I could just remove the bum pads, the wig and the boobs, and shower off the makeup. It could all just... come off.

Strange feeling.

"Gotta go!" Ben said, and kissed me gently on the forehead. While I'd been having a moment of self-discovery re my own idiocy, he'd been gathering up his things: he had a couple of heavy duty plastic bags slung over his shoulder. "I'll leave the trunk," he added, nodding at the luggage, out of which he'd extracted all the torture devices he used on me, and which contained more clothes and makeup and other drag accessories. It looked emptier than before, and when one of the bags shifted as he moved I snorted in amusement: the outline of his large prosthetic breasts, pressed against the side of a Sainsbury's bag, had become rather obvious. "Yes, yes," he said, grinning at me. "They'll make for an interesting conversation with the Uber driver. I do like to keep them on their toes. You've got everything you need?"

I nodded, and he was out of the front door in a whirl.

And I was alone. In James' apartment. In a dress.

And it was getting dark outside.

I needed another drink.

* * *

I knocked back more of the unlabelled liquor — which, I decided, after much contemplation, was mostly cherry flavoured and entirely delicious — and succumbed to slightly drunken boredom. I hunted around the apartment for my phone, expecting to find it in a pile with what might charitably be called my work clothes, but instead I found it, my wallet and my keys on the table by the front door.

James was still a no-show.

"You okay?" I called through his bedroom door, managing to stay in head voice.

"Yes," he replied. I thought I could detect a slight hesitation. I wondered what he was doing in there.

"Ben's gone to his drag show," I said, leaning against the door so I didn't sway on the high heels, "so you need to come out and keep me company."

"Two minutes," he called back.

I shrugged and returned to the couch, listening to the sound of my heels on the wooden floor. The steady *click-clack* was something I'd always associated with women; novel to be responsible for it myself. I sat back down, leaned into the cushions, and experimentally tried crossing my legs. It was uncomfortable to cross them at the thighs — I could feel my cock getting crushed inside the stretchy knickers Ben made me wear, and felt perversely like the reminder of its presence wasn't helping with the role I was trying to get into — so I settled for crossing them at the ankles, and relaxed.

I was midway through replying to my third work-related email when James' door finally, *finally* opened.

25

He'd changed into slightly nicer stuff than he usually wore at the office, although I, a fashion novice at best, struggled to pinpoint what it was about it that was nicer, specifically.

"Hi," I said, smiling. "What took you so long?"

"I just—" he started, then interrupted himself. "What happened to your voice?"

I frowned. "You only just noticed? I was yelling at you through your bedroom door."

He looked nonplussed. "I, uh, didn't put two and two together," he admitted. "I was kind of preoccupied. Shit, Alex! Ben said he could do *something* about your voice, but you sound like a *girl!* How do you do it?"

"With effort," I said. "But it's getting easier. Ben taught me."

"But you can go back, right?"

So concerned. "So he promises me," I said. I could tell he expected me to have dropped into my old voice to prove that I could, so I added, "I'm trying to keep it up. As practice. If I'm going to do the trade show, I need to get *good.*"

"You're really going to do it?" he said, walking over to the sofa. I shuffled over a little so he could sit next to me without being uncomfortably close; he sat uncomfortably close anyway. Thighs touching. But he fidgeted: hands in his lap, tapping his nails together.

"Maybe," I said. I'd been giving it serious thought while I wrote emails on autopilot. And I'd examined myself a few more times in the small mirror hung by the front door, just to remind myself what I looked like. "There's no way we can get someone else. We were insanely lucky to get the three Hammond girls, and now we're down to one, so either it's her and me, or it's just her." I held up a finger to forestall his excitement. "I'm *not* saying I'm definitely going to do it. But I'm less terrified about the prospect than I was."

"How much less terrified?" James asked.

I held up finger and thumb, millimetres apart. "I'll see how it goes," I said, "for the next couple of hours. If I don't completely freak out, it's a solid maybe." I shook myself. "I need to lay off the alcohol; can't rely on being tipsy at the expo."

He frowned. "You're drunk? Alex, I—"

I silenced him with a finger to his lips, and then wondered why I was touching him so casually. Alcohol, obviously. I put my finger away. He watched it, in case I did something else unexpected with it.

"Only enough to make my inner voice less screamy," I said. A lie: my inner voice was having a bit of fun with how self-conscious James was being. He was normally so controlled, so together! In all our time together I'd never had the upper hand like this.

"Well, what do you want to do for the next couple of hours, while you sober up?"

Push him! my inner voice said. *See just how uncomfortable you can make him!*

"Why don't we go out to dinner?" I said.

Chapter Two

We looked over the contents of Ben's case, spread out on James' bed like a neon pride flag made of tacky dresses. Laid flat, I thought they were kind of ugly, but I bet he made them work. He left James' flat in a fitted and flattering but muted and unshowy outfit; about now would be the time he'd be climbing into something in bright colours and interesting cuts.

I wanted to see his act.

Still, none of the clothes he left me were suitable for a quiet night out. My womanhood might have been disposable and very recently acquired, but I was already forming some quite firm opinions on the sort of clothes the girl version of me — I decided to call her Girl Alex, for now — would *not* want to wear out of the house, and all of Ben's dresses fell into that category. And James and I both agreed there was no way I could go out in the electric blue dress I was already wearing; I looked like a colour-inverted traffic cone. (At least Ben's preference for the gaudy meant he'd been able to find a close match for the company colour without leaving his wardrobe, with the only major effort required being to buy a pair of shoes in size 8. Which reminded me: I needed to tell James to pay Ben £28.)

I looked up from the kaleidoscope on top of the duvet and caught another glimpse of myself in James' full-length mirror. A glimpse that turned into a gawk. Just when I thought I was getting used to all the new experiences this afternoon was bringing — speaking in this voice, wearing these clothes, being all shoved into unfamiliar and not entirely comfortable underwear — there'd be something that bowled me over again. When we were sitting down on the sofa together, warmly drunk, thighs touching, that *something* had been the view of my bare legs poking out of a dress that didn't reach my knees.

Not just that, being honest. It had been the contrast: my legs, waxed and moisturised and looking and feeling like they never had before, next to James' loose and fashionably frayed jeans. A clear visual signifier of the gender divide Ben had helped me hop over.

The feeling of the fabric of James' trousers brushing against my calves had been *electric.*

And now I was once again staring at myself, reflected in the mirror in James' bedroom. I looked for all the world like a normal woman, albeit one with questionable taste in clothes. And, like every other time I'd looked at myself since I put the dress on, I struggled to tear my eyes away. I watched myself breathe, mesmerised. When we went out, I'd have to make sure to steer clear of reflective surfaces or we'd never reach our destination.

James said something, but I missed it. I was too bewitched by this apparition in the mirror, this beautiful woman who, I was suddenly perversely afraid, might vanish without warning.

"You know what's weird?" I said, aware as I did so that I sounded slightly dazed. "I actually kinda look my age. I've *never* looked my age before. I've always looked younger than I am. People always tell me that."

James said something else that I didn't catch. I ran a finger along my cheekbone and down my jawline, frowning. Despite the horrible goop Ben had covered me in, my jaw still had a little of that strangely smooth feeling you found on men's faces after they'd had a close shave. I'd have to remember not to let anyone who wasn't in on the secret touch me there.

James' hands closed over my bare shoulders, and I jumped, and would have turned around except he was holding me in place. I turned my head instead and almost headbutted him; he was so close!

"Alex?" he said. "Are you okay?" That smile of his again. Turned up at the corner.

"Yeah, I think so," I said. *Head voice, head voice, head voice,* I recited to myself. I'd almost cracked on that first word.

"We don't have to go out if you don't want to." His voice was gentle.

Did I want to? Sternly I interrogated myself, trying to push aside the alcohol that was still warming me from the inside out, trying to ignore the heat of James' hands on my shoulders.

What did I want? I wanted our software to find a buyer, to get either a single big contract or a bunch of little guys who could help get our name out there. I wanted our company to succeed. I wanted James to be proud of me. That last one was a bigger contributing factor than I might have thought, back before I started working for him, because, even with the contributions I'd made to the codebases of various projects, I'd never felt quite like I belonged among the engineering staff: they all, James included, had qualifications, degrees, experience. I was the kid hired straight out of school, who fell into a good job because my family knew the boss' family, and it was just luck that I turned out to have a knack for coding. Whenever I worked with someone other than James, there was a part of me that felt like a fraud. I could almost see the judgements pass through their minds, and it made me self-conscious, which made me, in the moment, worse at my job. Maybe that's why I threw myself into the organisational stuff so much; I was better at talking to people than most of our skeleton staff, and that felt more like something I could do that was genuinely useful to the company, something I brought to the table that no-one else did — bar James, who was still, damn him, far more charismatic than I.

What did I have to do to get what I wanted? Right now, what the company needed was to draw attention to ourselves at a crowded trade show and, in that environment, if a large, impressive stand wasn't practical, pretty girls in eye-catching colours did the trick at least as well; at least, that's what James said, and unlike me, he'd been to one of these things before. And since the number of girls available to us had just collapsed to one…

I snorted as I reached the end of the logic chain. I was going to have to be a booth babe. A trade show model. It was something I was, seemingly and utterly inexplicably, suited for, in a way no-one else we could get our hands on at such short notice was. In the mirror, I confirmed again that I looked good enough to fool myself.

The only questions remaining were: was I good enough to fool everyone else? And *could* I go out in public like this without freaking out?

"Let's go out," I said. "Let's go to dinner." I patted one of his hands and shrugged to prompt him to remove them from my shoulders. "We need to know if I can handle this around other people, and we need to know if other people see a perfectly normal woman when they look at me. If it's a negative in either column, we need to come up with a new idea, so the sooner we know, the better."

"You're really okay with this?"

"Yes," I said, nodding emphatically. I tried to sound confident, and it helped a little; with every affirmation I was making myself a little bit more certain I could do this.

"Okay," James said. "Should we come up with a safe word?"

"A safe word?"

"Pomegranate," he decided. "If you get too uncomfortable and need to get somewhere safe, just say 'pomegranate'."

I laughed. "We'll be out in public. If I say 'pomegranate' and then we both leave without a word, that's going to look pretty weird. If I need to come home, I'll just say so."

* * *

In the Uber, I realised I was sobering up: the nice warm feeling cushioning my anxiety had all but dissipated, and now my belly was filling up with ice cubes. Worse, I needed a piss, and the suspension on the rideshare car was terrible. Have you ever combined a full bladder with tight, restricting underwear and poorly maintained London roads? I do not recommend it.

I'd managed to recalibrate James from his automatic assumption that 'going out to dinner' meant a posh restaurant for rich bastards and not, for example, a *Pizza Express*, and as soon as he got the message it was like a light bulb turned on over his head. He dug in some drawers and found a few casual items that an old girlfriend left behind, unsuitable for a reservation at Le Fucke Maison or wherever the hell (languages are not my strong point; adding an unnecessary extra *e* to unsuspecting English words apparently is) but probably fine for a meal for two at a classier-than-McDonald's-but-don't-go-nuts chain restaurant, and definitely appropriate to my very nascent ideas about what Girl Alex would wear out of the house.

Naturally, his ex-girlfriend hadn't left behind any trousers for me to wear.

So there I was in the Uber in a dark blue maxi dress (I'd had no prior notion of what a 'maxi dress' was, but I was together enough to read the label on the inside) and the heels Ben got me (which didn't 100% work with the dress, but I was fine with that), worrying about how I was going to take a piss without giving the game away. I had visions of walking into the women's loos at Pizza Express and being laid suddenly bare in the harsh lighting: stubble visible, body the wrong shape, wig obvious; generally suspicious as hell. I pictured myself held down by restaurant staff while a panicked customer called the police.

At least this dress covered my shoulders *and* my knees.

We were headed to another part of the city, away from our usual stomping grounds, on the theory that if it all went tits up (pun not intended), we could run like hell and never show our faces there again. I hoped it wouldn't come to that, though; I'd never run in heels before, and didn't want to ask James to carry me.

"You kids having a nice night out, yeah?" the driver said, shaking me out of my thoughts and distracting me from my bladder.

I looked over at James, who was lost in his own world, staring out of the window at the rain. I tried using my mind powers to jolt him out of his introspection and make him respond to the driver, but I was unfortunately no more psychic than I had been at age ten — when I got a little overexcited after an *X-Men* movie marathon and tried to catch crockery without touching it — and James remained unresponsive. It was up to me.

I swallowed a few times to lubricate my throat; I was going to have to go straight into girl voice, and the thought of fucking it up had turned my mouth into the Sahara.

"Yes," I said.

It came out okay! Not my best work, sure — I sounded more like I had when I first started working on it, eight hundred million years ago this afternoon — but good enough. I followed up with a smile, hoping the man would be satisfied.

"A date?" he asked, with his eyebrows as well as his mouth.

"Yes," I said, and directed what I hoped was an infatuated smile at James; I was horrified at the idea that the driver might try his luck with me if he thought I was available. "First date," I clarified. I didn't want to have to pull off a girlfriend-and-boyfriend-in-love act, not with James completely checked out and me struggling to keep my nerves and my bladder under control.

"You two have a good time, yeah?" the driver said, and returned his attention to the road.

I sighed in relief and nudged James with my foot.

No response. Damn. When we got to the restaurant, was he just going to keep sitting there? Would I have to lamp him with my shoe to wake him up? I hooked my ankle around his foot — there, again, was the interesting sensation of his trouser on my bare leg — and yanked on him as subtly as I could. As if waking from a dream, James came alive. He blinked at me.

I indicated, using a complex system of frowns and glares, that he should pay some fucking attention. He frowned, realised what I was on about, and mouthed, *Sorry.*

I should think so too! I mouthed back at him. He wasn't the one in the dress.

It wasn't long after that we finally got to the restaurant. The driver parked over the road, told us we were lovely passengers and wished us a wonderful evening. I whipped my phone out of the handbag slung over my shoulder (borrowed from the same ex-girlfriend, and I could see why she didn't bother asking for it back: it was battered, and the side pockets flapped loose inside the main compartment) and gave him a five-star review. He hadn't tried to hit on me, nor had he beaten the crap out of me for being a man in a dress; he hit all my gold standards for good service.

I hopped out of the car, landed awkwardly on my heels — *you* try getting used to them in just one afternoon! — and then had to dive for the shelter of an overhanging shopfront. Still raining! And me in just a dress! James' inconsiderate ex hadn't abandoned any jackets for me to borrow, and we were both too distracted to have picked up an umbrella, so my options were limited. I stood under the veranda and shivered, wrapped my arms around my belly for warmth, and wondered how I was going to make it across the road to Pizza Express without the rain plastering my dress to my body.

James announced his arrival with a bit of splashing and some loud swearing, which I thought was on point. At least *he* had a couple of layers on and wasn't in danger of getting soaked to the bone. I looked up, ready to ask if he had anything more useful to contribute, but he was already removing his jacket. He gestured for me to turn around, and when I did, he hung it around my shoulders.

Now, I'd never thought of myself as small; underdeveloped, sure, but that was mainly because other men seemed to think it important they tell me. At length. And not just back at school, where I'd grown to expect that kind of thing from boys, but in my adult life, too. James was always trying to get me to come with him to the mini-gym in the office basement, to get in a spot of exercise before work, and since my ability to resist him had never been spectacular — witness the dress! — he eventually succeeded. And at first it was okay. Kind of fun. But then he got a call from a client and had to run upstairs to talk to them, which left me alone with my ill-fitting gym clothes, my inferiority complex, and some guy from the office on the ground floor. James had been gone for barely thirty seconds when the guy stopped the treadmill, looked me up and down with a patronising grin, said I had 'potential', and offered to be my personal trainer.

I didn't even make my excuses; I just left. I legged it back up the stairs, dumped the borrowed tank top and joggers in James' office, and spent the rest of the morning sulking and trying not to remember what the other boys used to say to me in the changing room after PE. James, bless him, brought me a Pepsi and an apology when he returned.

So, yeah, I knew I was scrawny and insufficiently masculine in basically all possible ways, but they sold my size in the men's section of the department store, didn't they? There *were* other men shaped like me, even if we had to flick to the very back of the rack when we wanted to buy new jeans. And James, yes, was larger than me in every direction, but we were still basically the same shape, I thought.

But when James hung his jacket over my shoulders, I realised that had never been true. It bloody *engulfed* me. I felt like a teenage girl in one of those American coming-of-age movies, borrowing her footballer boyfriend's blazer to show off their attachment around school. James completed the image by putting an arm around me and leaning over slightly, so he could use his body to shield me from the rain. Deciding I had ample time later to be embarrassed about this, I leaned into him and hugged him tightly.

As one, we crossed the street.

* * *

If you'd raised the topic with me six months ago — hell, if you'd asked me yesterday — I would have said the idea of going into the women's toilets in a public place was extremely low on my bucket list, somewhere around 'get shot', but by the time we got to the restaurant I was too desperate even to hesitate. I dived for the ladies' room as soon as we were inside, side-stepping around a pair of older women who were just leaving. They looked from me to James and back again and smiled at us both. I interpreted that as a vote of confidence in both my appearance and my choice of dinner companion, smiled in return, and locked myself inside the closest cubicle. I still had to take off the stupid bum pads and pull my knickers down, which yanked my penis out of its tuck with rather more violence than I (and it) would have preferred, but when I was finally ready to piss, it was everything I'd been dreaming of and more.

When my brain came back online, somewhere around halfway through, I heard someone peeing in the cubicle next to mine and I realised that that was *all* I could hear. Paranoia made me reach down and push my dick back a little, just enough that the stream went straight into the bowl with a reassuringly loud tinkle. My poor abused penis was alarmingly sore to the touch, but I kept my finger in place; I didn't want to give my neighbour any reason to be suspicious. *I'm an ordinary woman here,* I thought at her, giving my psychic powers another hopeful go. *Just having a piss, same as you. Nothing strange about me at all. Please leave?*

I dawdled in my cubicle, cleaning myself and reupholstering my undercarriage with the maximum of lethargy, taking enough time that the other woman — whoops; *the* woman — was well into washing her hands before I was fully dressed again. I learned from past mistakes and put the bum pads on first and the knickers second. They seemed like they wouldn't give quite as tight a tuck that way, but I was wearing a loose dress, not leggings, and it meant that next time I needed to piss in a semi-public place I wouldn't have to get quite so horrifyingly naked.

Next time. Dammit. Today, tomorrow, and the three days of the expo meant I had five days of this farce ahead of me. *If* I agreed to it, that is! God, I'd gotten so used to folding the instant James asked anything of me I was preempting my own capitulation.

I made sure I was presentable — penis definitely not sticking out of dress, dress definitely not tucked into knickers — and left the cubicle. The place was blessedly empty except for me, which gave me some time to calm down. It was strange, watching myself in the mirror, my mascaraed eyes blinking in a manner that seemed exaggerated, my artificial chest responding to my breathing. So many little differences!

Critically examining myself, I thought perhaps Ben's makeup job, which was for sure eye-catching and masterfully done, was a little over the top for the clothes and the environment I found myself in; he'd dressed and painted me for a day at an expo in a dress you could see for miles, not an evening at a chain restaurant in a hand-me-down. I rubbed experimentally at my eyelids, trying to reduce the amount of colour there while being careful to avoid spoiling the mascara, but didn't have much luck until I brought a damp paper towel into play.

Better! I checked myself out again — looking at myself in the mirror while done up this way was becoming quite routine quite quickly; another thing I filed away to think about later — and decided I looked a little top-heavy: all the drinks I'd had back at James' had taken their toll on the lip colour Ben had applied, and the effect was as if a pro makeup artist had started work on me but got called away by an emergency while they were halfway down my face. I rummaged through the hastily assembled assortment of makeup I'd dumped in the handbag, extracted what I hoped was a lipgloss and swiped it across my lips. I smacked them together afterwards, the way I'd seen women do on TV, and then surreptitiously rubbed the excess off with the back of my hand.

I didn't want to look too showy.

The bathroom was still blessedly empty, so I took advantage: I ran through my voice exercises again. I stood facing the mirror as I did it, both to check that I wasn't breathing with my shoulders and to fix in my mind the idea of myself as a woman, to make it habitual, mundane. That was important: if I was going to look natural in public, I couldn't very well flinch every time I passed a reflective surface.

I felt very stupid — saying, "Lady lady lady lady lady lady," in a variety of pitches will do that to you — but when I played myself back on my phone I sounded fine, better even than I had at the apartment, so I exited the loos with a swing in my step and found James still hovering nervously outside.

"Weren't you getting us a table?" I asked.

"I was worried," he said.

"You're very sweet," I said, picking my words carefully to make sure I wasn't about to say something that would make any lurking toilet detectives regard me with hostility. "But you don't need to worry about me."

That just made him frown. I controlled the urge to sigh — the risks we were taking, being out like this, were perhaps ninety percent on my head and only ten on his, and yet I was the one acting like I belonged while he was the one glancing around the place as if scanning for improvised explosives and hidden snipers — and took his hand. He barely responded, so I gave up on trying to loop my fingers through his and simply clasped it as one might grasp a lead pipe, and pulled on him impatiently. I was getting irritated at the way he kept bouncing from being perfectly normal when we were alone together to being a wreck when we were around other people.

"Come *on*," I said. "Let's find a nice, quiet table in the back somewhere."

I dragged him to the small queue of people standing near the entrance and deposited us at the end. He was shaking a little, so, while we waited to be served, I stroked the back of his hand gently with my fingernails.

* * *

The waitress led us to a table at the rear of the restaurant, dropped off some menus and left us to it. I rolled my eyes as I watched a confused James vacillate between being a guy on a date with a girl and a boss out for dinner with his (male) subordinate, and batted away the hand that tried belatedly to pull out my chair for me. I sat down, made sure I wasn't wrinkling my borrowed dress, found a place for my bag and fiddled with the table settings, trying to pretend to myself that I wasn't putting off the moment when I'd have to meet his eyes again. After all, I'd held his hand, led him through the restaurant, and generally acted *highly* inappropriately; touching him the way I had felt, looking back on it, far too intimate. But when I finally looked, he didn't seem annoyed with me, just stiff and scared, although he wasn't looking back at me, not yet.

What the hell is he *scared of, anyway?*

"For fuck's sake, James!" I hissed. "What's going *on* with you? You're shitting yourself, but *I'm* the one who has to wear this stuff!"

He briskly nodded his understanding and forced himself to relax, practically shuddering as he unhunched his shoulders and unclenched his fists. "I'm sorry," he said. "I thought I'd be cool with this, but it's hard."

"What do you mean, 'this'?" I was pretty sure I knew what he meant; I wanted him to say it.

"You know... You, all dressed up. I mean, don't take this the wrong way, Alex..."

When he trailed off, I made *please continue* gestures that hopefully also indicated I wasn't planning on taking whatever it was the wrong way.

"...But you're gorgeous," he finished, and looked at me at last.

It was like being slapped.

He should have said I was freaking him out! He should have said my wig was wonky or my knees were knobbly. He should have said he was ashamed to be seen in public with someone who wore a dress with the same inelegant awkwardness as, say, Godzilla might. A compliment, let alone one delivered with such sincerity, was emphatically not in the possibility space I'd mapped out. I think I hid my reaction pretty well, though; I just blinked and swallowed and kept running the subroutine in the back of my mind that was suppressing my urge to run away.

I was 'gorgeous', was I? I'd had the thought myself, but it was more *real* from him. There'd always been the chance, minute though it was, that every mirror had been lying to me, that I'd deluded myself, that back at the flat it had been Ben's dress (which I'd replaced) and Ben's makeup (which I'd mostly rubbed off) doing the work of making me look presentable, but now...

I thought of the way he called me pretty, back in his office, and the memory cut through what remained of my irritation and pushed a smile out of me so broad and genuine that James couldn't help but return it.

"So," I said, in a low voice, "that's all? You're not scared people will find out?" Even whispers sounded different in head voice. Very odd.

He laughed at me. "Not a chance," he said. "I mean, look at you!"

"Yeah. I've been looking. It's... weird." I propped my chin on a knuckle. "So what is it, if it's not that? Why're you being so antsy?"

He thought for a moment. "When it's just us," he said, "it's normal. You're... Alex, even if you look different. It's, I don't know, comfortable. It's you and me, like always. I can be myself around you, and I think you can around me. Doesn't matter what you're wearing." I nodded. We had an easy chemistry; it's why we worked so well together, how we could spend whole weeks seeing no-one but each other and still not go feral. Looking back, though, I didn't think we'd ever actually talked about it before. Strange, the things that go unsaid. "But when we're around other people, it's suddenly *real*."

Relatable. "Real how?" I asked, and bit absently at my lip.

"You're a *girl* — or you're supposed to be, for now — and I'm a man, and when we're together in a car, or in a restaurant, it's, you know, loaded? I get tripped up, not knowing how to behave around you. I know what people *expect* to see, with a man and a woman at dinner like this, and I keep catching myself almost going along with it. Which, I mean, I don't want to freak you out, or offend you, or—"

"James," I said, interrupting, because I had a feeling the poor boy would just keep going forever if I didn't pull the brakes on his train of thought, "please, for the duration of this — whatever 'this' is — I want you to stop worrying about that. I know what we look like together, and I'm actively trying to act the part. I'm *not* going to get offended or weirded out if you play along." His brows knotted, and I kind of wanted to hurt him for being so dense, but that could wait until the expo was over and I could drop character and really go to town on him with one of the heavier office keyboards. "In fact, it's *best* for you to act like a..." I almost couldn't say the next words, but I coughed, swallowed, and tried again. "Like a guy on a date with a girl. It means I'm less likely to have a problem."

"'A problem'?" he echoed.

"Yes," I said, "a problem. Like, people kicking the shit out of me, for example?" I was fixated on the idea that people were going to hurt me. Couldn't imagine why.

He blinked at me. "Alex," he said, "you have *no* worries on that front." He looked around, and continued in a whisper, "You look like you've always been a girl! You even walk right."

I tried not to deal with the first part of that sentiment and zeroed in on the second. "It's the shoes." I squirmed in my seat, suddenly very aware of all the things I was wearing under my dress. "And all this padding. I couldn't walk like I normally do, even if I wanted to."

We were silent for a few moments. He fiddled with the napkin on the table; I swung my leg around under it and accidentally kicked him in the shin. Whoops.

"So!" I said quickly, unsure whether to apologise, like a girl on a date, or laugh at him for flinching, like I would at the office. "If that's *all* it is..." I trailed off, trying to prompt him into being a bit more helpful. I was starting to miss the old James, the unflappable guy with the infectious confidence. This lost little lamb act was almost as discomfiting as the public crossdressing.

He looked pained. "That's *not* all it is," he said. "If I do as you ask, behave like I always would in this situation... you *know* what that means, Alex!"

"Actually, I don't. You don't take me with you on your dates, usually."

That forced a nervous laugh out of him. "I think you can imagine, though," he said, and I fervently hoped what remained of Ben's foundation covered the rising heat in my cheeks, because I definitely *could* imagine. My dates had a tendency toward disaster, but I'd seen James around women, seen the effect he had on them, and I could just picture one of his old girlfriends, sitting opposite him like I was — although probably wearing nicer clothes — unable to stop herself from reaching out for him, taking his hand. "Half of me wants to end this right now," he continued, startling me out of my thoughts, "for us both to go our separate ways home, but, Jesus, Alex, the *other* half—"

"Are you ready to order?"

The lurking waitress startled us both. Just our luck to end up at the only Pizza Express where the waitstaff were trained for stealth combat operations. But I quickly replayed our conversation in my head and, unless she'd been hiding around the corner and listening in for a good few minutes, we were in the clear.

The least helpful part of my brain wandered off on an unimportant tangent. *What about the other half of him?* it wanted to know. *The half that* doesn't *want to end this right now? What does* it *want?*

I put the thought aside and focused on ordering. Figuring I'd better watch my waistline for the next few days, I picked something light. I didn't think about my diet most of the time — I ate whatever found its way in front of me, generally once a day, sometimes twice — so it was possible a pasta bowl and salad was overkill (underkill?) for the weight-conscious woman I was pretending to be, but at least I wouldn't be uncomfortably full by the end of the evening. James ordered a pizza, obviously — I resolved to steal a couple of pepperoni slices — and a bottle of white wine for the table.

Wine? Is that such a good idea? I asked him with my eyebrows. He understood, of course, and when the waitress returned to her stealth fortress, replied out loud, "I need a drink. Like, I *really* need a drink. It seems like it helped *you* out."

"Aw," I said. "Having trouble relaxing?"

I think he wanted to kick me for the grin I directed his way; his lips twitched, as did his fingers. After a moment, though, he just said, "Yes."

"I could probably do with another drink, too," I said honestly, as I considered my situation. "I burned off all the alcohol I had earlier, and I'm running on pure adrenaline. I don't know how long it'll carry me before I just sort of—" I mimed dropping head-first onto the table, "—crash and burn."

He nodded at me, satisfied and starting to seem more like himself. Something had changed between us. Perhaps because we successfully ordered food and wine without consequence? Whatever; his confidence was back, and it made me happy to see it. He smiled and said, in the smooth, slick manner I was used to, "Then the wine was a *great* choice. You'll like it, I think; not a bad pick for a chain restaurant."

Rich boys! "Snob," I said, and wrinkled my nose at him.

"Peasant," he said back. An old joke. I contained my snort of amusement — it would have been unladylike! — and blew him a kiss instead; it seemed more in the spirit of our respective roles.

Like the guy in a cheesy rom-com, he pretended to catch it.

I frowned. The other part of my brain, the unhelpful one, wouldn't shut up. "What were you saying before?" I asked. "About... um...?" I pretended not to remember; I wanted him to pick it up, to finish the thought he'd started, and the less prompting it took from me, the better. *What does the other half of you want, James?*

"I don't remember," he said.

Well, shit. I thought about pressing him further, but realised I was on the verge of getting obsessive, so, frowning inwardly at myself, I dropped it. I didn't know why I cared so much: we were proving we could handle this, so what else mattered?

The waitress returned a few minutes later with the wine, made a show of pouring some out so James could taste it — I was glad she didn't ask me to do so, since my palate was so inexperienced I was willing to go only fifty/fifty on being able to identify it as wine — and then left us to get tipsy while we waited for our food.

* * *

We polished off the first bottle in record time and ordered a second to arrive with our food. By halfway through — me, with my pile of pasta and greens; James, with his gargantuan pizza (minus a few pepperoni slices) — I was nicely relaxed and enjoying myself.

So many things about being out in public as a woman were interestingly different. The waitress smiled at me, but not in quite the way I was used to. The other women in the restaurant were sort of neutral-friendly towards me, rather than neutral-indifferent, and when I was idly scanning the room, passing some alone time picking at my salad while James visited the men's, a young woman at a nearby table gave me a serious-looking nod; I didn't know what to do with that at all, so I smiled at her and attempted a serious nod in return. She smiled back, so I don't think I screwed up.

The men? They mostly just stared when they thought I wasn't looking. A handful of them kept it up when I caught them at it, too. Unsettling.

I wondered if I'd ever done that. If I'd ever sat in a public place and made some poor woman uncomfortable with my unwanted attention. I didn't *think* so. I'd never much been in the habit of noticing people, and preferred in public to keep my attention on my phone, on the horizon, or, in extremis, on an interesting paving slab. The few girls I'd somehow managed to date had been the ones to make the approach; more or less out of the blue, as far as I was concerned. Apparently, I looked 'cute' and 'interesting'.

Unfortunately, I was also 'distant', 'busy' and, although this one was more subtext than outright stated, 'sexually inadequate', and so the subsequent relationships tended to be short.

I tucked my hair back — it had slipped a bit while I was looking around the room — and smiled to myself: playing with my hair like that was an unconscious behaviour, a bit of rediscovered muscle memory. I'd had long hair for most of my teen years, and dealing with it became second nature. It hadn't been a fashion choice; I was never especially interested in how I looked, but Mum said she liked my hair long, and that was all the justification I needed to let it grow as it wished, with just the occasional trim at home, to fix split ends. I had it cut short only twice: once to try and get the boys at school off my back (it didn't work; they kept bullying me), and once before my interview with James, as part of an attempt to look professional (it didn't work; I had the cut two days before and swiftly discovered I didn't know how to care for short hair).

So I was used to having long hair, and the wig was almost comforting because of that. But it was also more styled and cared-for than my real hair ever had been under my own hand. I ran the light waves of the wig through my fingers, amused that I'd paid more attention to my appearance in the last few hours than I had, cumulatively, over the last few *years,* and felt curiously ashamed of my past self. I resolved to do better in the future, and smiled at the idea that spending time as a woman would make me a better man.

At the very least, I could take better care of my hair. Maybe grow it out again, but on purpose this time.

"What are you thinking about?" James asked. I jumped; I hadn't noticed him return to the table. I looked up from my near-empty plate to see him smiling curiously at me.

"Just about all this," I said. "About how different it is. From, you know, *usual.*"

His smile widened, and he leaned forward, shoving his empty plate to the side. "Tell me."

I made a show of glancing around the restaurant. Business had picked up a lot since we arrived, and there was a family sitting directly behind him. The boy of the family had been looking at me a lot; I wouldn't put it past the cheeky little shit to be listening, too.

"Ask me again later?" I said.

"I will. So, do you think you can do it?" He leaned farther forward, lowering his voice to a whisper. "The expo?"

I thought about it. The purpose of coming out to the restaurant had been to test for failure, and so far no-one had screamed or hit me or called the police or given any other indication they'd discovered I was not what I appeared to be; I, for my part, had pretty much gotten over my earlier nerves. People were just... treating me normally.

But I had to be sure.

"How do *you* think I'm doing?" I asked. "Do I seem like a—" I matched his whisper, and leaned in to meet him, "—a normal woman? Or do I come across as someone who doesn't know what the fuck he— *she's* doing?" The pronoun nearly got me. I'd have to watch out for that.

"Honestly?" James said. "You're doing great. I wouldn't know you were having a hard time at all if you hadn't had a go at me earlier."

"God," I commented, "I don't even think I *am* having a hard time any more." I sat back, popped one of my few remaining pasta shells into my mouth, and looked around. A nice little restaurant. Good food. Good company. A slightly baffling nod from a woman at another table. And the dress gave me room to move my legs, even kick off my heels and tuck my feet under my bottom, if I wanted. I grinned at him, suddenly confident. "I can do it," I said. "And I *will* do it."

James echoed my grin and grabbed my hand, squeezing it. I got the feeling he would have leapt over the table and hugged me if we weren't in relatively polite company.

"Thank you *so* much, Alex," he said. "Your modelling fee is going to be *insane.*"

I liked the sound of that. And then a thought that had been travelling slowly around the back of my brain for the last several minutes asserted itself. "Shit," I said, as the thought settled unpleasantly on the part of me that controlled my mouth.

"What?" James said warily.

"We need to get the measurements to the tailoring company tonight, right?" I held up my phone. "It's nearly eight!"

James' expression crashed into mine. "Fuck," he said.

"Right?"

"You get us an Uber back to my place," James said, and started looking around for the stealth waitress. "I'll get the bill."

* * *

It was the same Uber driver. I climbed into his back seat, draped once again in James' jacket, and wondered how many embarrassing experiences it would take finally to kill me. He smiled and winked at me and I decided that, yes, that wink might well turn out to be enough to take me to the embarrassment LD50 threshold. Goodbye, cruel world, etc.

And then I pushed it all aside. Fuck it! He was just one guy! And I was riding too high to care. I'd shot off a quick email to the tailors, who came back instantly — workaholics surrounded me on all sides — and confirmed that they wouldn't start work on the dresses until morning, so we had all night to get them the measurements. Crisis averted: all I had to do was measure myself, get Emily Swan's measurements off her file, pass everything along to the tailors and then I could succumb joyfully to the pleasant alcoholic glow that suffused me from top to toe. In the face of such relief, a mere wink from a man who thought I was another man's girlfriend couldn't make much of a dent.

Besides, James owned his own company! I giggled to myself; if I *had* to be someone's girlfriend, he was the best option for miles.

I sank into the seat cushions and felt very content.

"Did you have a good night, then?" the driver said.

James spoke up before I could. "Yes, thanks," he said. "We had a business proposition to discuss, and it went well."

"Weren't you two on a date?" the driver said.

I winced, and thought quickly. "We were," I said, "but we only just started going out, and I work for him, so it's awkward. And has the potential to get a bit legal." Stuff a kernel of truth into your sack of lies, as they say.

"She's my secretary," James said, grinning at me.

My relief that he got the pronoun right — right for tonight — was eclipsed by my annoyance. His secretary? The sexist little arse.

"I'm his personal assistant," I corrected, and kicked him, out of sight.

James stuck his tongue out at me. I almost reached over to give him a playful slap before I remembered about the driver, who was watching us in the rear-view with obvious amusement, so I bottled it. When the driver looked away again, I raised a fist and brandished it where only James could see, a dire warning of future terrible punishments.

His answering grin was impossibly wide.

* * *

I locked myself in the bathroom and immediately disrobed, taking great pleasure in hanging the dress up on the shower rail and theatrically turning my back on it. It wasn't that it was a bad dress, or that I disliked the idea of wearing dresses — over the last few hours, the stunning revelation that they were just tubes of fabric like everything else I'd worn my entire life, except with the holes in different places, had sunk in so gently that I barely noticed until I'd gotten naked — but while wearing it I felt strangely vulnerable. Especially when I was alone with James. I couldn't stop thinking about what he said in the restaurant, about what came naturally for him in these situations, and I could have sworn, once or twice, that he looked at me like I wasn't *Alex* any more. And that had been *before* he opened the door to his apartment for me, offered me another drink, and sat expectantly on the sofa with his arm draped along the top of the cushions.

At least he'd looked startled when I boggled at him and bolted for the bathroom.

"It's not you!" I whispered to myself, unravelling the cloth tape measure. "He's just drunk and running on autopilot!"

I might have made a more convincing argument, but shortly afterwards I fell in the bath while trying to get my inside leg measurement.

The next few minutes didn't go much better. I almost dropped my phone in the toilet, I nearly brained myself on the sink, and I failed utterly to get a single useful number off the tape measure. Either I wasn't bendy enough to do this on my own, or it was a two-person job.

Great.

Even with the bum pads and the alarmingly tight knickers covering up all my traditionally naked parts — and a couple of extra naked parts I'd borrowed from Ben — I still *felt* naked, and I very much did not want to be naked in front of James. Hell, if he was going to keep reverting to type, I wasn't sure I wanted to be around him at all.

No choice, though. I threw the dress back on and unlocked the bathroom door. James, thankfully, had relocated to the kitchen table and was working away on his laptop. It didn't seem like his heart was in it — he looked sleepy — but at least when he smiled at me it was as my friend

James, not as a man trying to flirt with a woman. I joined him, pulling out a stool from the other end of the kitchen table and sitting cross-legged on it.

"All done?" he asked.

"Not yet," I said hesitantly. "I, um, need to ask you for a favour."

"Considering what you're doing for me — for our company — I'll grant you any favour you like."

I blushed so hard I could feel it in my feet, and I knew he could see it; there was no way any amount of foundation could conceal that level of embarrassment. "I need you to measure me," I whispered. "All over. I can't do it on my own."

He thought for a moment, looking hard at me. And then he smiled with the corner of his mouth and nodded to himself, as if one side of him had just won an argument against the other side.

"Okay," he said.

I silently pushed my unlocked phone across the kitchen table, and he checked over the tailor's web app. It guided you through the process from start to end and showed a woman's silhouette with all the required measurements marked against her body.

Some of them were in very delicate areas. I'm pretty sure I watched him realise this.

"Do you mind if I rifle through your ex's stuff again?" I asked. "This dress is long enough that it'll get in the way of some of the..." I trailed off. Some of the dot dot dot indeed.

He nodded, still frowning at my phone, so I escaped to his bedroom and quietly died for a minute.

Once I was done with my crisis, I rifled through his drawers and found a crumpled-up nightie. It was a little bit cute and, when I tried it on, a little bit tight; tighter than the maxi dress I'd borrowed, so either this woman had been mis-sold on one of them, or the drawer contained the leavings of more than one ex.

"How many girlfriends has he had...?" I muttered irritably, as I examined my reflection. It *was* tight, but not uncomfortably so. It was short enough that the thigh and leg measurements ought not to be a problem, and the material was thin enough that the measurements around my waist and chest ought to be doable without me having to disrobe. The very bottom of my padded butt stuck out below the hem, which made me grateful I'd approved knee-length dresses for the girls at the expo.

Even with the protruding pads, though, I still looked... *good*.

Far too good. I wondered if Ben could even recreate such a miracle, if this was a one-night-only deal, if all this would vanish come the morning, never to return.

Flattering, Alex, I told myself. *You're a pumpkin carriage. Possibly a mouse horse.*

"Shit, though," I whispered to myself. The girl in the mirror really was enchanting.

It felt strange, walking out of my boss' bedroom in just a nightie, and I could tell he had the exact same reaction as soon as he saw me, because his eyes widened and he made a little noise in his throat. How many other girls had he seen, dressed like this, walking out of this door?

Not a helpful thought, Alex.

I took another deep breath as I rounded the table and made my way to the middle of the room. He'd turned off the main light, I noticed, darkening the whole place. The only sources of illumination now were the spotlight above the stove, the work light on the kitchen table and the little lamp by the television on the other side of the room.

Too intimate. Nothing I could really do about that, though, unless I wanted to make things awkward — *more* awkward — by actually *talking* about it.

"I'm ready," I said.

He took a few seconds to get moving, so I raised my arms into what seemed like a handy measure-me position. T-pose to assert dominance.

"You'll tell me if I make you uncomfortable at any point, yeah?" he said.

I laughed, a little hysterical. "If that's the criterion, back away now," I said. "But, yeah, if I need a break, I'll say. What was the word?

Pomegranate. I'll say pomegranate." I'd doubtless make *some* kind of noise, anyway.

He dragged a stool over from the kitchen and placed his laptop carefully on top. He took another step towards me and unrolled the cloth tape with an apologetic look on his face.

"From the top?" he asked, and I nodded.

With a nervous but theatrical flourish, he held the tape up in front of me and let it unroll until the other end hit the floor. Then he stepped around behind me, and I could do nothing but guess at what was coming next, until I felt his toe against my ankle, holding the tape taut as he ran it the length of my body to the top of my head.

Safely out of his sight, I bit my lip, almost hard enough to break the skin. His hand was on my back, smoothing out the tape, his fingers were running up my spine from my coccyx to my neck, and I had to do *something* to fight the impulse to shiver.

I couldn't remember the last time anyone touched me like that.

"One-seventy centimetres," he whispered, and left me on my own for a moment, almost quivering, while he recorded the number on his laptop.

"I don't need to know every number," I said, struggling to maintain both head voice and composure. His fingers were so *warm*. I'd never been so aware of someone's presence.

"Stay still," he said, smiling and holding up a finger. I braced myself — I've never liked the feel of things pressing on my neck; fortunately for me, I went into software engineering, a field mostly allergic to neckties — and thus did not flinch when he pressed it against my throat. He wrapped the tape around my neck, captured his finger inside, and pulled it tight. "Small..." he muttered.

"And you're so big?" I said, trying to keep the mood light.

"Bigger than you."

I think we both realised the accidental innuendo at the same time. He looked away from me — I wondered if he was blushing, if his cheeks would feel hot if I reached out and touched them — and took my arm and shoulder measurements from behind me.

After typing them into the laptop, he paused, tense, with his back to me. "I need to go around your chest," he said. "Around your, uh…"

"It's okay," I said, resuming my T-pose when he turned around. "It's not like they're *mine*." I repeated the phrase in my head a couple more times.

He nodded and stepped up to me. Still warm. He held the end of the tape against one of my nipples — well, against the fake nipple on the tip of the fake breast — and, apparently unable to control his schoolboy nature, pushed against it, compressing the soft, fleshy material against me.

"It feels so real," he said.

"Have a lot of experience in that area, do you?" I said, sounding slightly more annoyed than I intended.

He smiled apologetically. "Some. Do you mind if I—?"

I had no idea what he was asking, so I just nodded. He reached up with his other hand and cupped my breast in his palm, weighing it like a newborn kitten.

"Weird," he said.

"Yeah," I said, feeling a little faint. I didn't like his frown. "They're weird." I could feel his hand against my chest, my *real* chest, and the way he was taking the weight of the breast, manipulating it, sending ripples through it, was having an interesting effect on my nipple, buried somewhere under there. I never thought nipples could be sensitive like that. At least, not the ones on me. I supposed I'd never really prodded at them before.

"No," he said, "I mean, it's weird that it's *not* weird." He shook his head, and repeated, "It feels so *real.*"

I waved my arms slightly; they were getting tired. "Could you do the measurement so I can lower my arms?"

"Oh. Sure."

He let go of my breast — *the* breast — and wrapped the tape around my torso, pulling it tight. As soon as he took a step backwards to record the result, I gratefully let my arms drop.

He nudged my wrist. "I still need your arms up a little," he said. "I need to find the narrowest part of your waist."

"It'll be somewhere above the pads," I said. Before today, before acquiring the uncomfortable new accessories Ben loaned me, I'd been more or less a straight line up and down, like a pencil that was good with people but didn't get a lot of third dates. Now I went in and out in all the appropriate places.

James crouched down, which brought his head roughly level with my navel, and wrapped the cloth tape around my waist. He frowned, pinched the fabric of the nightie so it was as tight as it could get, and then pulled on the tape again. I stood there for what seemed like an hour while he fussed, apparently having some difficulty locating the exact narrowest part of my body. He had a palm flat on my belly, which was extremely distracting and probably had something to do with me losing track of time. When he finally let me go, I swayed a little, overcompensating for not having his steadying hand on my stomach any more.

"Sorry," he said. "Should have warned you."

I smiled, and felt my blush, which had been getting to know parts of my face it'd never visited before, deepen further. "Not your fault," I replied in a near-whisper. "I kind of zoned out."

He turned away to record whatever number he'd finally come up with on the computer, and I put a hand over the warm spot on my belly, crinkling the fabric of the nightgown in my fingers. If you'd asked me, right then, what I was feeling, I couldn't have answered. I'd never felt it before.

Waist-to-neck and waist-to-floor were straightforward and didn't induce any confusing sensations. I was grateful for the breather.

"You doing okay?" James asked, standing in front of me and stretching a leg. I felt bad for him, doing all the work, and then I remembered which one of us was in the nightie.

"I think so," I said. I was feeling wrung out; I'd had a decent quantity of wine on top of the liquor from earlier, and the alcohol was starting to seep out through my pores, leaving behind tired and dehydrated flesh. I wanted nothing more than to steal a bottle from James' mineral water stash, down it in one, and fall asleep in a dark, warm hole. And not only were we not yet done with the measurements, but I would also have to undress, shower, and get an Uber back to my personal dark, warm hole before I could sleep. Depressing.

"You sure?" He looked concerned, and reached out to me, grasping my upper arm in a gentle hand. I closed my other hand over his and smiled.

"I'm sure. Just tired."

He grinned and squeezed my arm. "Me too," he said. "I feel like if I blink for too long right now, I might never open my eyes again. Long day, huh?"

"Long day," I agreed. "Now stop stalling and do your job!"

I had a go at injecting some levity, but when he crouched down in front of me again, when he put his hand on my hip, it was like someone hit me with defib paddles. He wasn't even touching me, had his hand instead on the pads I was wearing around my hip and butt, but that didn't seem to matter. Just the pressure was enough.

Enough for *what,* I didn't yet know. Sweat was sticking the nightgown to my back, and I hoped he wouldn't notice.

He wound the tape around me, and I did my best to stay still.

"Two to go," he whispered. Still crouching, he lifted the hem of my nightgown just a little and wound the tape around my thigh. His fingers met, pinching the tape tight, and I could feel the pressure of both his hands between my thighs.

Warm.

I wanted to squeeze my thighs together to keep him there. I felt my cock tighten in anticipation. Trapped as it was inside those horrible knickers, it was an only slightly unpleasant mixture of pleasure and pain.

What exactly am I anticipating here? I asked myself.

He leaned away to use his computer and I squirmed as subtly as I could, unable to calm myself, caught in the throes of nascent arousal as the most sensitive part of my body started to push against the tight tucking underwear.

"Last one," he said, turning back to me and crouching down by my feet. "Um, lower your feet, please?"

I hadn't even realised I was standing on tiptoes. I forced myself to rest, and felt the end of the tape under my heel.

Even after the thigh, I wasn't prepared for what came next. James ran the tape slowly up my leg, pressing it against the inside of my calf and then my knee, smoothing it as he went. He slowed as he approached my thigh. His thumb glided over my bare, newly hairless skin, all the way up to my crotch, and I shivered. He held the tape there with one hand, and with the other he gently raised my foot so he could retrieve the other end. He pulled the tape taut, leaning in as he did so, his head resting on my hip, his breath warming the top of my thigh, the back of his hand pressing against my crotch.

It was just too much. My cock stiffened again and I suppressed a gasp. I had no idea if he felt it move under his hand, if a sensation that felt seismic to me was even perceptible to him. I tried to freeze, to lock my body into place, but hot waves were cresting all over my body and the tides were dragging me down at the knees. I put out a hand to steady myself, aiming for his shoulder but shaking so much I landed on his head instead, and pressed it harder into my hip.

"Sorry," I said, letting go of him and knotting my hands together behind my back. "I'm getting a bit wobbly."

"S'okay," he whispered.

He released me and wound up the tape, sitting back on his ankles and granting me relief from the sensations that were battering me. He still had one hand on my thigh, and he gave me a reassuring squeeze before he stood up. He took his laptop back over to the kitchen table, presumably to enter the last measurement and email the tailor. It was over.

Overwhelmed, I collapsed onto the nearest piece of furniture available and sank into the sofa cushions. My crotch throbbed, my jaw ached from clenching it and my blood was boiling all over, so I just lay there for a minute, too exhausted, too confused, too fucking *hot* to pretend to myself or to James that something hadn't just happened to me.

Why was I responding this way? Why now? And why with James? I'd never been so aroused, not with anyone, and I knew with a certainty that shook me to my core that if, when his hand was on my crotch, he'd pulled my underwear aside and touched me more intimately, I would have let him. Where it would have gone from there, I didn't know; I also didn't care. I wanted it.

It was getting painful down there. Trapped in the tucking underwear and unable to become erect, my cock was rubbing against the fabric, and wriggling my hips to try to free it only made things worse. I had to clap a hand over my mouth to quiet the sound that tried to escape me.

Perhaps the only thing to do was to reach down with my other hand, and—

James came over. He looked down at me, all six foot of him, a silhouette against the glow from the lamp by the television.

"You okay?" he said.

I quickly redirected my hands, one to my belly and the other behind my head, and forced a smile onto my face. "You ask that a lot," I said.

He returned my smile, crouching down next to me, joining me in the little circle of light. He reached out with his hand as if intending to take mine, but redirected at the last moment, acting like he meant to steady himself on the sofa all along.

"I think it a lot," he said.

Just looking at him was helping calm me down. His face was probably, after my mother's, the face I knew best, having seen it every weekday and some weekends since I started working for him. He was *James*. And I was Alex. And these feelings that had come over me, this inexplicable heat, made no sense.

Butterflies in my belly, though. Still.

"I'll survive," I said. "Too much to drink, too much time all strapped up in this underwear, and too little sleep, I think."

He tapped the cushion twice and stood. "Speaking of... I'm going to pour myself something. You want to join me?"

I almost agreed, but now that I was regaining control of myself, I knew the thing to do was to get out of his apartment, go home, and spend some quality time not thinking about things. Maybe screaming a little into a pillow.

"I can't," I said. "I need my bed. And I still have to take all this crap off, first."

For a moment, a look of disappointment might have crossed his face, but it was likely my imagination. I wouldn't have been surprised if I'd started seeing pixies in the corner of the room, I was so tired. Besides, standing, he was half in shadow again, and more difficult to read.

He nodded, walked over to his bar and poured himself something, setting the glass down on the coffee table.

"Before you sit down," I said quickly, "can you help me up?"

"Sure!" he said, reaching out for me. I pulled against his arm, and together we manoeuvred me into a standing position. I almost fell into him, but he caught me, and for a second we stood together, my arm looped around his.

He steadied me with his other hand. A little spot of warmth in the small of my back. A little reminder.

"Thanks," I said, and pushed him gently away. Again: the flash of an expression I couldn't quite read. It was enough to make me feel guilty, though, so I stepped back into him, grabbed at his arm and pulled it back around me. "Really," I said, "thank you for doing that. I nearly broke my brain against the sink trying to do it on my own. And thanks for dinner, too." I butted my head affectionately against his shoulder — he was about six foot and so not unusually tall, but he'd always felt that way to me; without my £28 high heels on he had five inches on me — and added, "*And* for not making this really, really weird thing I'm doing any weirder than it already has to be."

He laughed and hugged me back, and I luxuriated in the embrace. James was a relatively touchy guy, but we still didn't hug all that much. I tried to think of the last time we had, and almost came up blank before the memory of a drunken Christmas party returned to me. James had thrown it to thank us all for helping grow the business from a wild idea into something viable. We were all to get a bonus with our December pay, and some of us — the two women we'd had on contract, and me — got ambushed under the mistletoe on the way out.

James had been startled to be told that one of the people he'd kissed that evening was me; he'd had rather a lot to drink. I said he shouldn't worry, that it was my fault for not getting away in time, and he laughed for a little too long. "You're right!" he said. "You *are* slow!" And then he caught me in a hug to prove his point.

God, I hoped he hadn't noticed anything tonight. Whatever the reason for my unexpected arousal, I wanted to keep it to myself. I didn't want him to know that I'd gotten turned on in his presence. Not that James could *possibly* have a problem with gay people, not after rooming with Ben and spending so much of his university social life around gay men. And not that I was gay! But...

Go home, Alex, I told myself. I was too tired to think straight.

I tapped him on the back, a signal to release me, and stepped away with a smile when he did so. "Shower," I said, pointing my thumb at the bathroom door. He nodded, sat down on the sofa, and retrieved his glass. The last thing I saw as I shut the bathroom door was him knocking back his drink in one.

I hitched up the nightie, pulled down the knickers and sat heavily on the toilet. I stared vacantly around the bathroom while I put a thumb up to where the wig met my head, and thus I discovered Ben had glued the damn thing on at the exact same moment I realised the clothes I'd gone to work in that day were nowhere to be seen.

* * *

Ten minutes later, I was still in the bathroom, still on the toilet, thinking. I wasn't convinced I could get the wig off without horribly damaging either it or my scalp, and I didn't want to catch an Uber, looking like this.

59

I'd have to ask James if I could sleep over. I washed up, smoothed down the nightgown and left the bathroom to find him, only to discover he was sound asleep on the couch. His glass was mostly empty, but at some point he'd fetched whatever bottle he was working on, so he had to have had at least one more drink from it that I hadn't seen. It sat unstoppered on the coffee table.

I walked over to the sofa and crouched down next to him.

"Hey," I said quietly. "James?" He didn't respond. "I can't get the wig off and I can't go home alone like this. I need to stay the night." He still didn't respond.

Drat. I couldn't leave him that way, but there was no way in hell I was going to try to undress him and drag him to bed; I'd need some sort of pulley and winch system just to get him up off the couch. I sighed, stood back up, went to his bedroom and searched around for something approximating a linen closet. Eventually I found where he kept the spare blankets and carried one out to where he was still asleep, snoring lightly. I draped it over him, feet to chest, and folded his free arm over it to keep it in place.

Touching him seemed to rouse him a little.

"Hi," he said.

"Hi," I said, returning his smile. "I need to stay the night. Is that okay?"

James' smile broadened. "O'course," he said, slurring a little. "Stay as long as you need."

I patted him on the shoulder and was about to stand up when he suddenly grabbed my hand. Before I could react, he'd leaned up and kissed me wetly on the mouth, his half-open eyes looking directly into mine. Then, just as quickly, he let me go and fell back onto the sofa, eyes closing.

"G'night, beautiful," he muttered.

I wondered who he thought I was. A lost love? One of the girls whose clothes I'd been wearing? *Someone* beautiful, at any rate. Someone decidedly not me.

I needed a distraction, quickly, and found one in the mess he'd left on the table. I stoppered his bottle and replaced it on the bar, and then I busied myself with other tasks: I checked his emails to make sure he'd sent the measurements to the tailor; I shut down his laptop; I rinsed the dirty glasses and placed them upside down in the sink; I made sure the front door was locked; I turned out the lights.

It was hard to just leave him there. Shouldn't I at least have woken him properly, made him clean his teeth? But, as I lingered at the door to his bedroom, listening to his breathing deepen as he slept, I decided I'd imposed enough.

"Goodnight," I whispered, and shut the door behind me.

The fatigue that bit at every limb made me stagger and I fell haphazardly onto his bed. I didn't even try to remove the bra or the padding, I just crawled up the mattress and pawed at the covers until I'd pulled them over me, and before I could think another coherent thought I'd drifted off, my head deep in James' pillow, surrounded by his smell.

Chapter Three

I was back in the restaurant with James, but we were alone, our table in the centre of a pool of light, encompassing the entire universe in a handful of square metres. I was wearing the dark blue maxi dress again — I didn't remember putting it back on — and James was wearing a suit. It was a fitted suit in textured charcoal, worn with an off-white shirt and a maroon tie, and I'd seen him wear it before, usually when he wanted to impress important people. Here, he was wearing it for me.

There was no food on the table, just wine, and he had his glass raised, waiting for me. He was looking at me, smiling, and I felt myself smile back, felt it in the warmth of my cheeks and the softness of my belly, and that was the instant he came alive. He reached across the table with his spare hand, and I gratefully took it in mine, encircling his wrist with my fingers.

"Are you having a good night?" he asked me.

I didn't answer right away. I drained my glass first, maintaining eye contact with him. The alcohol spread through my body, numbed my limbs; weightless, I stretched out under the table to anchor myself. My ankle grazed his, just like it had in the car, a shock of static where our skin made contact, and lazily I kicked off my heel. I gently touched his leg, under his trousers, and slowly ran my foot the length of his shin. His leg hair tickled my toes.

"I am," I said.

My empty wine glass was gone, or it just didn't matter, but it was okay because his was, too. I leaned forward on the table, close enough that he could reach out and touch my face if he wanted to. He made me wait a few seconds — he was teasing me, the bastard; I wanted to pull on the hand I held, to force him to come to me — before he finally caressed my cheek. I leaned into it, rubbed myself against him.

And then his fingers were in my hair — my *real* hair, not that awful wig — and he ran them through the length of it, from the top of my head down past my shoulders. He played with the strands that danced around my breasts, and for a moment I closed my eyes, releasing the hand I held in mine in an instant of complete contentment.

I felt a tension in my neck and I realised he'd cupped my jaw in his hand and was guiding me forward, towards him. I let myself be led. He leaned forward, and the last thing he said before he kissed me was, "Hello, beautiful."

I kissed him back.

His hand lowered from my neck to the small of my back, drawing me closer, and I arched my back to meet him, stretched up on tiptoes so we could keep kissing as we stood. He leaned down and the disparity between our heights was so great that he nearly dipped me. The table and the restaurant were gone, might never have existed; it was just us, in the light, kissing, holding each other, falling as if in slow-motion into his bed.

As we fell, I peeled his jacket from his shoulders, undid his tie, and started to unbutton his shirt. He waited until I was done and then lifted my dress over my head and discarded it. He shrugged off his shirt; I removed his belt; he unclasped my bra and let it fall away. He was underneath me now, haloed in silk sheets, kicking away his trousers and gently sliding my underwear down my legs. As he looked up at me, his hand returned to the small of my back and he pulled me down with him.

We kissed again, bodies pressed together, and he stroked my face while his other hand traced its path from my back, across my buttocks, around my hip, down to my crotch. I bit his lip as his fingers entered me, and I woke.

* * *

The first thing I was aware of, before I even opened my eyes, was James' smell. The whole bed smelled like him — I wondered sourly how often he changed his sheets — and while it was far from unpleasant, it was a little overwhelming. Still, I was warm and comfortable, lying on my side, curled up under the covers, my right arm tucked under a voluminous pillow.

I could stay here a while, I decided. I felt dried out, almost desiccated, with that faint afterglow of pain that means you got lucky and burned off most of your hangover while you were sleeping. I'd have to get up and deal with that eventually, but there was no immediate need to move.

My left wrist twitched; it felt a little sore. I recalibrated my senses and stretched the fingers on that hand. They wetly tickled the insides of my thighs.

It took a few more seconds for me to finish fully spooling up to something approaching full consciousness.

Slowly, carefully, trying not to wipe it against the sheets, I extricated my left hand from between my legs and inspected it. It was damp, but it didn't smell like I'd wet myself; it actually smelled like—

I don't think I've ever got out of bed faster in my life. I flung the covers away and heard a plastic crash that suggested they'd knocked something off the other bedside table. I didn't look to see what I'd broken; I didn't care. I couldn't take my eyes off my wet fingers. Couldn't stop thinking about what they might signify. I reached down slowly with my clean hand and pressed it tentatively against my crotch.

Yeah. My underwear was soaked.

My cock might well have been pinned tight against me all night, and it definitely hadn't been able to get hard, but that hadn't stopped it from ejaculating. I'd probably ruined Ben's awful fucking knickers.

At least there was a bright side.

I sat down heavily on the bed and regarded myself in the mirror: the hair; the tits; the nightgown. What had felt kind of glamorous last night, once I'd (mostly) got over my fear of discovery, now just looked... stupid. Ugly. Like a collage, artlessly pasted together. What was I doing?

I groaned as I realised I was committed to another four days of this shit.

Which made me think about the Consumer Electronics Expo. Which made me think about the dresses they'd probably already started working on, and which I'd have to wear. Which made me think about the measurements I'd made James take, working over my as-far-as-I-was-concerned nearly naked body from a distance of inches. Which made me think about the way he'd touched my stomach, my inner thigh; the way he'd grazed my crotch with the backs of his fingers.

Which made me think about the dream, and of falling asleep, intoxicated by the smell of him.

What the *fuck* was I doing?

* * *

Alex: Ben, you horrible man, why didn't you TELL me you glued the bloody wig on? I didn't know how to get it off without ripping it so I'm still wearing the damn thing and I have to work!!!

I threw my phone down on James' bed and glared at it. I wasn't normally a three-exclamation-point guy, but it'd been that kind of morning. My vague hope that the wig had been loosened by a night spent tossing and turning, writhing and moaning and wishing for James to—

Calm down and start again, Alex.

Whatever. What mattered was that the wig was still firmly attached to my forehead. If we didn't need it for the trade show, and if I didn't want to owe Ben the cost of replacing it, I would already have used James' toenail clippers to hack off the stupid lacy front bit and shred the itchy cap underneath.

I couldn't stop thinking about the dream. Rather, I couldn't stop *not* thinking about the dream. It crowded my thoughts, made it impossible to concentrate on anything else. It'd been a while since my last girlfriend, sure, but I hadn't thought I was *that* desperate.

It was the dress. It had to be. I'd spent half a day dressed as a woman and a whole evening on a date (of sorts) with James; that'd mess with anyone's head. And his behaviour hadn't helped: he'd kissed me! He'd leaned up from the couch and bloody kissed me. The kiss must have planted something in my subconscious that then played out in my dreams.

It had been a nice thing to take to bed, to be sure, but that was only because it was nice to feel desired. I'd basically never had a successful relationship, never had a girl hang around long enough to kiss me before bed, not the way James had. Not in a way that implied casual, loving intimacy.

Never lusted after someone enough to dream about them, either, Girl Alex pointed out, unhelpfully. I ignored her. It was the kiss; it was the way he'd called me beautiful; it was the way he'd looked at me. And even if all of it had been as fake as my tits, even if James had thought I was one of his exes, the experience had been real enough for my lonely, touch-starved brain to latch onto.

James didn't want me. I didn't want him. I just wanted to be wanted. There was no other explanation that made sense.

My phone buzzed. Grateful for the distraction, I practically leapt on it.

Ben: Okay so thing one, WHY are you worrying about going to work, isn't your boss literally JAMES, wouldn't he let YOU do more or less anything???? ESPECIALLY considering what you're doing for him!!!!

Ben: Thing two, James has told me over and over how smart you are but I don't believe him because YOU'RE VERY DUMB. The wig glue is WATER BASED! Soap and water is all you need. Just get

your fingers or a paper towel all soapy and rub gently under the lace until it comes off, didn't you find the instructions in the case????

I couldn't help but feel he was making fun of me with the multiple question marks.

Alex: Oh. Right. Water-based glue. I suppose that makes sense. I didn't see any instructions, though!

Ben: I only used a little glue, a hot shower with a shower cap on should have done the trick if it wasn't ready to just pull off, didn't you FIND the shower cap I left you in the bathroom????

I sighed at my own stupidity, and replied, **Didn't see that, either.**

Ben: OH COME ON

Alex: It's my first time crossdressing! Okay, so that, strictly speaking, was a lie, but what Ben didn't know couldn't be used to make fun of me. I added, to underline my point, **I can't be expected to just KNOW this stuff!**

Ben: You didn't think to, I don't know, GOOGLE IT????

Alex: Is EVERYTHING you text a question????

Ben: Not with people who aren't dumbasses, no, and that means you didn't google it, did you????

Alex: No. I was really tired and still kind of drunk when we got back in.

Ben: ...

Ben: YOU WENT OUT TOGETHER????

I decided, as a matter of urgency, to develop better habits when it came to just saying stuff.

Alex: **Please forget I said that.**

Ben's reply was so fast I didn't even see the '...' typing indicator: **Never.**

Alex: Oh hey, while we're at it, where are my clothes????

I really felt like that one had earned the four question marks.

Ben: Okay I'm actually sorry about that, James asked me to take them, immersion therapy type thing. I'll bring them when I swing by the office later. I've even washed them! You're welcome.

Alex: What am I supposed to wear to go to work? I have nothing else here.

Ben: You're telling me THAT was your best outfit???? I feel so bad for you right now. I'm taking you shopping. Block out a day next week to take off work. James will understand. I'll tell him it's an emergency.

I started work on the snarkiest and most unpleasant response I could generate without the assistance of coffee, but Ben replied before I could finish, and as his replies stacked up I realised I was, once again, screwed.

Ben: WAIT

Ben: ALEX

Ben: ALEX!!!!

Ben: Do you mean to tell me YOU STAYED THE NIGHT AT HIS PLACE???????

Ben: Tell me EVERYTHING!!!!!!!!

I fell back into the pillows, hoping against hope that they might swallow me. My phone buzzed a couple more times, but I ignored it, resolving instead to find out where James' rich family kept their inevitable survival bunker and go live in it for a few years, until all this blew over.

* * *

I examined myself in the mirror. It was becoming a habit. I'd taken off the bra, the nightie and the knickers, but hadn't yet tried my luck with the wig. My legs and crotch were still smooth, as was my face, and the overall effect was sort of androgynous. For the hell of it, I posed like a model for a few seconds, but the lingering remnants of my overnight hangover made me unsteady on my feet, and I got dizzy.

I turned away from the mirror and looked for a bathrobe. Better to occupy myself than keep staring.

James, unsurprisingly, was still asleep. He tended to take alcohol pretty hard, especially in the quantities he generally imbibed, so I didn't feel like I needed to creep too carefully around the flat. I checked on him, to make sure his blanket hadn't fallen off, and there he was, snoozing quietly. I smiled at how peaceful he looked, before remembering that this was the guy who'd stolen my clothes and dressed me as a woman and taken me out and kissed me and had, therefore, committed a terrible crime against my equilibrium.

Unsatisfied with just the dream, my subconscious started working away again as I looked down at him, so I turned quickly away and got on with my morning.

I rummaged in Ben's trunk for the proper wig-removing soap or solvent or a pair of garden shears or something but found nothing of the sort. I also didn't find the wig-removal instructions he'd sworn were in there, so I added that to my list of grievances. In the end I settled for a bit of dishwashing soap on a sponge and headed back to the bedroom to get the damn wig off.

It was insultingly easy to remove.

I charged out of the bedroom and into the bathroom, locked the door, and started the shower water heating up while I dealt with my full bladder. I was done and wiping myself before I realised I'd sat on the toilet again, instead of standing.

I really didn't need *that* to become a habit.

* * *

"Off to the gym this morning?" the Uber driver asked, jolting me out of my early morning daze. I was never at my best before coffee even when I'd had a decent sleep, and thus far, I'd had neither; my night had hardly been what I'd call restful, and James' coffee maker was so stained and full of sludge it looked like he was using it to create life, or possibly engine oil. I was actually quite proud of my brain for keeping my vital functions going *and* getting me to the rideshare car without tripping over my own feet.

I almost asked him why he thought I was going to the gym, and then I realised it was the most sensible option, given that I was wearing a borrowed set of James' exercise clothes. They were the only things I could find at his place (other than the dress) that fit me, and even then I'd had to pull the drawstring on the jogging trousers as tight as it would go, and I could have pitched the hoodie as a tent.

I opened my mouth to correct him, to tell him I was just going to work, and didn't get out a single syllable before I had a coughing fit. I was *incredibly* dehydrated. Ordinarily after that much alcohol I would have had a pint of water before bed and another after waking up. I supposed the part of my brain that made the sensible decisions had been otherwise occupied.

"Oops, sorry love," he said, smiling at me in the rear-view. "Just making conversation. If you're in a bad way, don't worry about it."

'Love'? What did he mean by that? There was no way I still looked like a girl! I tried to sneak a look at myself in the car window, suddenly afraid that I hadn't taken the wig off after all, or that it had chased after me and latched back on like a face-hugger from *Alien*, but the glass was too misted up to see myself clearly. I surreptitiously reached up and felt around the back of my head, unable to dispel the notion that I might have absent-mindedly reattached the wig somehow, but there was only my usual shaggy mess of hair. I was ordinary, everyday Alex, exactly as ignorable as always, just wearing gym clothes.

I'd probably misheard him. That was all it was. It made no sense for him to gender me that way. Still, I decided, there was no sense risking it by talking and collapsing the wave function, so I smiled at him instead, tried not to look as nervous as I felt, and tapped my neck to indicate that I had a sore throat.

He nodded. "Understood," he said, returning his attention to the traffic jam. "Sorry you're not feeling well."

I gave this guy a five-star review as well.

* * *

The office was blissfully free of James-shaped distractions. I'd tersely informed him via text, from my Uber, that I was headed to the office alone. I even added the angry face emoji. And then my guilty conscience got the better of me, and I sent a much nicer follow-up text advising him to drink lots of water, to take painkillers and to be careful when coming in this morning.

I looked at the phone for a long time after I put it down. I could just call him...

No.

I shook my head — the image of James asleep on the sofa was hard to shake — and set to work. There was still a lot of organisational detritus to deal with before the expo the next day, and meticulously and thoroughly dealing with every little bit of it served pretty well to distract me from James, from the dream, and from the fact that the expo was *the next day!* I was less than twenty-four hours away from having to do the booth babe gig for real! What had I been *thinking,* agreeing to this?

I drained my water bottle and worked out some of my feelings on the poor, defenceless computer keyboard. It was tough, though, and it could handle it: James was a mechanical keyboard nerd and had outfitted every PC in the office with these clacky things that were built like tanks. Fortunately for me, they were all identical; on the off chance that my mood made it all the way through the keyboard and out the other side, I could just swap it out with one from another desk and it'd be six months before anyone noticed, which was long enough even for someone who felt as much like shit as I did to make an escape.

It was only when the phone rang, and I answered it with the tortured wail of an early adolescent whose voice was breaking, that I remembered I was supposed to be practising my head voice. I struggled through the call, tried throughout to maintain something close to my normal voice, and was deeply irritated when the caller signed off with, "Thanks, er, mate."

I hated that guy so much. I slammed the phone back in its cradle, closed my eyes, and went through my warmup exercises. My vowels went okay, and my humming was fine, but when I tried to transition to a real, spoken sentence, the teenage squawking returned. Frustrated, I called up the voice recorder app on my phone and recorded myself, then listened to the recordings Ben and I made during our practice session. Then I listened to myself from just now again.

I sounded worse!

The phone rang again. I let it ring, glaring at it until it stopped; I'd pick up the voicemail when I was done freaking out.

James arrived about half an hour later, when I was finally getting back to something approaching the voice I'd had when I first started practising. I was worried that it had been the alcohol that had got me as far as I had the day before, that without it I couldn't relax my vocal cords enough. I'd imagined I could develop the head voice enough that I could drop easily in and out of it, and that once I had it down, I could speak normally until we got to the expo, but that looked impossible now; I couldn't get through a sentence of head voice without fucking up.

By the time James sauntered in, I was in an absolutely terrible mood.

"Good morning!" he said, smiling at me, obnoxiously cheerful.

"It absolutely is not," I said, glaring at him and losing my voice on the last word. "Fuck!" I hit the desk with the flat of my hand.

"Alex, are you okay?" James said, walking over to me as I was massaging my hand; that had *hurt*.

I couldn't take it any more. "No, I am *not* okay, and would you please stop fucking *asking* me that?" His wounded expression made me want to attack him with a stapler. "I'm scared half to death! I'm going to have to be a fucking booth babe for three whole days, I'm going to have to wear those stupid fucking underpants Ben forced on me the *whole* damn time, and I'm going to have to do the voice the whole time, too, except right now I can't even do *that* right!" I blinked, turning away. I didn't want to cry in front of him, no matter how inevitable it felt. "I'm fucking *useless!*"

"Alex—" He put a gentle hand on me, but I swatted it away.

"Don't *touch* me!" I yelled, without really meaning to.

He raised both hands in the air and stepped back, looking like I'd slapped him. I deflated, feeling like an arsehole, and before he could apologise, I stood up and put on my best approximation of a smile, to establish that even though I was about to walk back most of what I just said, we weren't going to hug it out or anything.

"Sorry," I said. "I had a crappy night—" a lie, mostly, "—and I *am* scared, and I'm *definitely* having trouble getting the voice back. I'm sure you can tell." I sounded *wrong*. Even as I was talking to him I sounded awful, and the fear that I might be unable to fulfil my obligation made it even harder to talk properly. I was practically strangling myself with anxiety. And every time I dipped back into it, my natural voice sounded harsher; uglier. "It's all a bit much, but it's *not* your fault. I agreed to this. It's just... there's so much at stake! Your future; this company's future; mine. It's all on the line, and I'm supposed to sound like a girl and I just..." I couldn't finish the sentence. Couldn't put the thought out there between us. I just sagged.

"Alex," he said (he was saying my name a lot, lately), "nothing that's at stake is as important as you. *Your* health; *your* safety." He took a deep breath. "We can still cancel. Or we can go ahead with just one model. Now that I say that, it doesn't even sound that bad of an—"

"No," I interrupted. "I'll do it. We need this to work. I need this to work. No half-measures or compromises. I'm just— I'm going to need some space. Personal space, you know?" I swallowed, and hoped what I was about to say wasn't too revealing. "I can't do the kind of thing we did last night again. The dinner, the stuff after. I thought it was okay at the time—" I smiled briefly, unable to help it, "—but it kind of messed with my head, after."

A sympathetic look shuffled onto James' face. "Nightmares?"

"Just dreams."

"Look, Alex," he said, taking a hesitant step towards me and then stepping back again when he realised what he was doing, "take my office. Go relax in there, get your voice sorted; chill. I'll take your desk and deal with anything that's still left over to do."

"Are you sure? There's a lot—"

"I'll be fine."

"There's a *lot.*"

He smiled. "You didn't always work with me, you know. I had to get things all on my own. It was horrible—" the smile turned into a teasing grin that I unwillingly returned, "—but I managed."

Still, I couldn't stop myself from being a little concerned. The details weren't really his thing; he was a big picture kind of guy. "You're really sure?"

"Go!" He made shooing gestures. "Go to my office, practise, play some games, stream some movies, do whatever. I'll bring some coffee through in a minute. I've *got* this. And so do you."

* * *

I finally got my voice back. Well, Girl Alex's voice, and I was happy enough when it clicked that I figured *she* was happy, too.

I'd started to think of her as a semi-separate entity, someone with her own preferences and, yes, her own voice. She was someone I kept... slipping into; someone I would attempt deliberately to inhabit for a whole long weekend. And it made sense, didn't it, if I were to imagine an alternate version of myself, a twin sister I'd never had, that she might be a little pervasive? She'd have opinions about the clothes I picked; she'd behave a certain way around people. She'd dream of kissing some guy, and indulge herself in the way that was natural to her, right?

And the way people were treating me, the way I was responding to James... this whole *afterglow* was just *her* spilling over into the rest of me.

I imagined a room in my head for her to live in when I didn't need her, firmly shut the door, redrew the boundaries between James and me, and continued with my exercises; having regained my voice — *her* voice — I didn't want to lose it again. I was pleased and a little surprised I'd managed it without the relaxing influence of alcohol, because Girl Alex seemed to like a drink more than boring old regular Alex and I really didn't want to encourage her.

I hadn't had much else to do while I voice trained — aside from firmly suppressing Girl Alex — so I'd been mucking around online, at first just getting caught up with the news and then searching for instructional videos that might help me this weekend. I had to click around a bit to find things that seemed both relevant and helpful, though: I watched videos on basic makeup techniques, and then on basic makeup techniques for drag queens, and *then* on basic makeup techniques for trans women, and *then* on proper cleaning and maintenance of your home defence arsenal, and *then* — after a quick search to check on the correct way to pronounce *détente* — on voice training for trans women, and it was those last ones that gave me the extra push I'd needed.

On the instruction of one of the videos, I'd been singing in my head voice, and it wasn't bad! My voice was getting stronger and clearer as I found my limits and stretched them. I'd always liked to sing, and I'd never had much of an issue singing along with the women's parts, but I'd obviously always sounded like a guy when I did it. It was a little easier now to hit higher notes clearly, bouncing them off the top of my mouth instead of struggling to raise them out of my throat; it wasn't so much that my range was expanding, though it was a bit, but my singing voice had always gone to shit if I went much above middle C unless I flipped into falsetto. Well, not any more! Recording myself and listening back, I wasn't going to give Adele anything to worry about, but I sounded much more androgynous than I used to. If it had been someone else on the recording, you could have told me they were a woman or a man and I would have believed either.

If nothing else, I was going to come out of this a better singer.

While I was having fun singing along with a YouTuber who was performing both the male and female parts of *A Whole New World,* James happened to walk by the glass door to his office and looked in. I instinctively cringed a little, embarrassed to be caught singing, still kind of embarrassed to be seen by him at all after last night — *please, Alex, stop thinking about the kiss* — but he gave me a grin and a thumbs-up and I smiled back at him. I felt like I owed him another apology; he was doing his best to help me, and I'd been acting kind of weird around him. He'd never been anything but good to me, as long as we'd known each other.

He made swigging motions through the glass, and I nodded. He returned a minute or so later with a bottle of water.

"I got the voice back," I told him, in the voice.

"I heard!" he said, passing the water over. "You sound great! Exactly like you, um, should." I opened the bottle and downed half in one go; I was still tremendously thirsty, and the coffee from earlier hadn't lasted long. God, it felt good. "Actually," he added, a little hesitantly, "you still look kind of like—"

"I know," I interrupted, grimacing and running a hand through my hair. Even though I'd only worn the bloody wig for a single night, it felt a minor novelty to have shorter hair again. Not that my hair was all *that* short; it fell in my eyes sometimes, especially in the shower, but it wasn't actually messy, so I mostly ignored it. The natural wave helped, gave it body, made it look more like something intentional rather than something I neglected, even though it wasn't remotely fashionable: the haircut I'd gotten for the interview with James had been one of those generic short-back-and-sides cuts barbers give you when you sit in the chair and shrug, and those probably aren't intended to be grown out to the extent I'd let mine.

I looked at myself in the semi-reflective surface of one of James' computer screens, and snorted; yeah, I looked like a bloody fifteen-year-old again, and that was being generous. "This is why I don't shave," I said, stroking my jaw with the back of my hand. "I look like I'm bunking off school."

"It's not that bad!" James protested. "You don't look like a kid, anyway, not *really;* you look more like..." He trailed off, frowning, so I prompted him by waggling my water bottle at him. "You *don't* look like a kid," he repeated.

"Thanks." I decided to take some solace in that. Even being taken for a woman — like the driver this morning had — was better than being seen as a kid again.

"Oh, hey," he said, "I cancelled the extra rooms at the hotel since we have two fewer models now. And I followed up with the tailors; one of us can pick up the dresses on the way out of town in the morning. There'll be six; three each, one per day, right?" I nodded. He listed the other tasks, major and minor, that he'd taken off my hands that morning, and I confirmed he'd done the right thing for each of them, or close enough to the right thing that I could fix it on the day. I was almost proud.

"So," he finished, "with all that done, we can both rest up for a bit."

"*You* can," I said, smirking. "I've been resting for the last two hours. Actually," I added, remembering something I wanted to bug him about, "why did you tell Ben to take my clothes last night?"

He looked sheepish. "Oh, sorry," he said, but he didn't sound apologetic at all; more like I'd caught him out. "I just thought it'd help to, you know, stay in character."

I fixed him with a stern glare. "That's your first and last warning for taking my agency away," I said.

"I promise not to do anything like that again," he said, managing to seem contrite this time. I nodded, somewhat mollified. "Say," he added, looking thoughtful, "do you want to grab some lunch together?"

I *was* hungry. "Sure," I said, but then realised: "I can't. I've got to keep practising this voice, and I look like *this* right now." I gestured with my nearly empty water bottle at *this*. "Like, you know, a man. Or a teenage boy, I guess. So I'd have to drop it and start all over again after lunch."

"Well, actually—"

I held up a finger. "Whatever plan you're hatching: no." James looked like he was about to say something else, probably something deeply cheeky, but his desk phone started ringing. Keeping my warning finger in place, I hit the speaker button with my elbow.

"McCain Applied Computing," James said, leaning over the desk and pushing my finger aside. Then he grinned and hooked his finger around mine, holding it in place. "This is James McCain."

"Hi!" said an unfamiliar woman on the line. "This is Emily Swan, from Hammond's? I'm supposed to come over this afternoon to go over the promotional details, and I wanted to confirm the address."

Fuck, we both mouthed at each other.

"Absolutely, Miss Swan," James said, putting on his friendly phone voice. He looked at me, narrowed one eye like he was assessing me, and continued, "I'll pass you over to Alex Brewer, my assistant. She'll be running our booth with you this weekend." He mouthed, *I'm sorry,* and I was momentarily too stunned to do anything unpleasant to him in return.

Only momentarily. I extricated my warning finger from James' grip and raised a much ruder one. I swigged the last of my water, rolled it around in my mouth, swallowed, and hoped like hell I was about to call on Girl Alex's voice and not the adolescent caterwaul from this morning; incipient terror was constricting my throat. "Hi," I said, sounding basically fine. On the other side of the desk, James breathed an exaggerated sigh of relief, and I would have kicked him if my legs were longer. "This is Alex Brewer. How are you, Miss Swan?"

"I'm fine," she said, and paused. "I'm sorry, but, um... I was expecting a man."

Shit. *Shit!*

My chest seized up for a moment, and I thumped on it a couple of times to unfreeze myself. When I looked up again at James, he was making confusing gestures at me. "Don't worry about it," I said, to stall her, and mouthed, *What?* at him.

"Look at your emails!" he hissed. "The ones with Hammond!"

Oh. Of course. He'd been miming *take your phone out of your pocket.* I quickly checked and got the gist of what he was saying pretty quickly. In every email I identified myself as 'Alex Brewer', or just as 'Alex'; the only time anyone used 'Mr' was when Frank Hammond had been writing back. I scrolled through again, just to be certain, and, sure, if you were forwarded the whole conversation, you'd come away with the *impression* I was a man — and what an impression; what a man! — but, crucially, I'd never claimed the identity myself.

James rolled his eyes at me, and I remembered forwarding him all the emails yesterday; this must have occurred to him long before the phone rang. In fact, he probably would already have supplied a new name for me if the old one was attached to some guy.

Well, now I felt stupid *and* panicky.

"Hello?" Emily Swan said, hesitantly. "I didn't mean to—"

"It's okay," I said quickly, and ran the bullshit generator in the back of my brain — the one that bamboozled difficult clients with made-up technical terminology — harder and faster than I ever had before. "I'm not offended. I'm thinking your boss told you to expect a man? Men do that a lot." Did they ever. Although not so much lately. "If I'm never going to meet them in person, it usually goes more smoothly if I just don't correct them. *Especially* in this business," I added, letting some of my genuine exasperation seep through.

"I get it," she said, relieved. "Can I confirm your address?" I rattled it off, and she promised to be no more than two hours.

"Fuck *me*," I said, after she hung up.

"Later," James said, and I really did try to kick him that time. "Look, you just need to get changed into your stuff. Two hours is enough, right? It'll be a dry run for the weekend."

"'Stuff'?" I snapped. "What 'stuff'? I didn't bring any of it with me! And I didn't become an instant makeup expert overnight, *and,* even if I had brought it, do you *remember* what Ben's dress selection was like? 'Hi, Miss Swan,'—" I mimed holding out a friendly hand, "—'welcome to McCain Applied Computing! Why, yes, I *do* like to do business in hot pink rubber! Isn't it chic? Coffee? Oh, don't worry about spilling any on me; the dress wipes clean.'"

He hesitated. "Okay," he muttered, whipping his phone out of his pocket. He dashed off a text and then marched over to the small safe in the corner of his office. "Ben was going to come over later, anyway," he said, as he fiddled with the combination, "to go through our plans for the expo." I gave his back a piercing look, which he obviously detected, because he explained, "He'll be your makeup artist and general gopher for the whole trip. I decided it'd be better to keep Sophie out of the loop." Sophie was James' cousin, and our original makeup artist for the expo. I guess I was glad I wouldn't have to explain to her what I was doing in a dress; to be honest, in all the excitement, I'd forgotten she'd been involved at all.

James handed me a tiny leather wallet, which contained what turned out to be the company credit card. I took it and let my eyebrows ask the question.

"Assuming Ben agrees," James said, "which he ought to for what we're paying him, he'll meet you at my place, do you up, and you can both go buy something suitable. You're going to need *something* to wear this weekend when you're not in the booth babe getup, anyway."

He was right: I'd need to be Girl Alex off the clock. Even if I planned to go straight from the show floor to my hotel room and lock myself in with movies and minibar every night, it would be prudent to provide for other eventualities. Otherwise, in the event of, say, a fire alarm, I'd have to squeeze back into the expo dress to go stand on the pavement outside. At least I'd be brightly coloured; easy for the person driving the fire truck to see at night.

I'd always thought of myself as a pretty smart guy — and maybe I was, when I was in my comfort zone and not in, say, a dress — but the last day or so kept coming at me with things I just hadn't considered.

"Okay," I said, sighing and extricating myself from James' wonderfully comfortable (and expensive) office chair. "It's a good plan. I'll get moving." What choice did I have?

"A moment," James said, and fumbled in his pocket. He pulled out his keys, removed one of them from the ring, and handed it to me. "You can keep it," he insisted. "It's spare."

The key to James' flat! Girl Alex squealed, from somewhere inside me.

"Oh," I said, giving Girl Alex a look.

I was saved from having to say anything more intelligent than that by the phone. James waved me out of the office and picked it up with his other hand.

"Ben!" he said. "We have a slight Alex emergency. Can you meet her at my place? She needs to look 'office smart'..."

The barrage of pronouns was all the incentive I needed to escape the room.

The Uber driver *definitely* thought I was a woman, which was convenient because I'd forgotten to drop the voice. I didn't know what else it meant but I decided, for the duration of this mini-crisis, to put all those worries in my pocket to think about later. Talking to him with no wig or makeup on, in jogging clothes, and being seen as a woman anyway just because of the voice was a pretty timely confidence-booster, so I gave him a five-star review.

Chapter Four

When I got back to James' place, I spent a useful and highly satisfying minute praising my past self for remembering to throw the horrible stretchy underwear I'd made such a mess of in the washing machine before I left for work. The dry cycle hadn't been done all that long by the time I skipped happily over to the machine and extracted the sordid little knickers, and I had to steady myself against the kitchen counter as I realised it had been only a bit more than three hours since I'd woken up in my boss' bed, after spending the night dreaming about him.

It wasn't even midday yet. It used to be that whole *weeks* passed me by in a flash; suddenly, my life was happening in bizarre, slow-motion, technicolour detail.

I counted breaths again with a hand on my stomach, in a foolish attempt to control myself that achieved precisely the opposite: I remembered breathing hard in a restaurant restroom, watching my borrowed breasts rise and fall on my chest; I remembered James' hand where mine was now, steadying me, with his other hand circling me from belly to back; I remembered the dream.

Careful, Alex.

Something to concentrate on. That's what I needed. I looked around the place and found that with the blinds all open — James must have let the light in when he woke up — the flat was revealed in all its glory as a complete and utter tip. What my mum always called a 'boy's house'. I rolled my eyes at the state of the place, pretended I wasn't grateful to be handed a task to occupy me, and dodged a pile of crusty underwear as I headed into James' bedroom to get dressed. I slung on the bra, bum pads and knickers, inserted the fake boobs — cold! — and put on the heels from last night; a little extra practise couldn't hurt. I stared at the wig and Ben's collection of makeup for a little too long, before deciding against trying to do anything with either, lest my amateur fumblings do irreparable harm to the wig and/or my face.

Then I started on the washing up.

James got through an awful lot of takeout meals, which was kind of sad, and he left the remains glued to various plates and bowls (and the boxes and bags in a pile in the corner), which was less sad and more gross. I dealt with most of the more recent detritus and left everything else to soak in soapy water; some of it had to be over a week old! I found an (untouched) roll of trash bags on top of the microwave, unrolled one and set to work, demolishing the pile of takeout boxes and exhuming the sinkside teabag graveyard, then marched around the rest of the apartment, looking for more trash to add to my grim collection.

Back in his bedroom, after scooping up a couple of empty tubes of moisturising lotion, I saw myself in his mirror again and laughed: I was in heels and underwear, carrying a trash bag, scurrying around my boss' flat like I was his bloody maid! I grinned at myself and mock-curtseyed in the bedroom mirror, like I'm sure no maid in history ever has, then dropped the bag and retrieved the bathrobe I'd borrowed earlier. If there was one thing I didn't need, it was snarky commentary, whether from my own hindbrain or from Ben.

And where *was* Ben?

I took the trash bag out into the main room and dumped it by the front door, sprayed down the empty surfaces in the kitchen as one might direct a flamethrower at an invading alien army, then returned to the bedroom to fix the mess of sheets I'd left behind that morning and rescue the alarm clock I'd apparently knocked onto the floor at some point. I was rounding up dirty underwear to fill the washing machine when I heard a key turn in the lock and rushed back out, almost falling over in the heels I'd almost forgotten I was wearing.

It was Ben, and considering I was sure he'd been out later than we had last night, he looked remarkably together. He hadn't shaved, but the stubble coming in around his carefully trimmed beard rather suited him.

"Alex!" he said, sounding happy to see me.

"Ben!" I replied, echoing the sentiment. But then I saw the suitcase he'd manhandled through the front door — even bigger than the one he'd left here! — and a percentage of my goodwill evaporated. "More torture devices?"

"Hm? Oh, that? That's for the weekend, sweetie. In case I don't have another chance before tomorrow. And, I promise, no torture devices." I narrowed my eyes at him and he placed an affronted hand over his heart. "I swear! But there *is* something I want to talk to you about. Something James and I think might be helpful."

So far, James and Ben's definition of 'helpful' had been variable. "What is it?"

He looked pained. "I'm not sure if you're going to like it," he said. "It's sort of good and bad. From your perspective, I mean."

"Just tell me," I said impatiently.

* * *

Hair extensions! I couldn't believe I was doing this.

Ben gave me the choice of getting extensions or glueing that bloody wig to my head for the whole weekend, and when he put it like that it didn't take me long to pick. The wig cap had been uncomfortable and hot and itchy and a constant reminder that the hair falling into my mouth was not actually mine, and I'd already been apprehensive about putting up

85

with that for days on end; in addition, I'd started to imagine unlikely but possible disaster scenarios — things like, what if I caught a strand of wig hair on a door handle and had the whole thing yanked off my head? — which extensions, from my brief assessment, would mostly avoid.

All the same, the step into the hairdressers wasn't one I'd ever imagined taking, even after I started my dubious new career as James' dress-up doll. It was on me, though; I agreed to do the job on the assumption that it would be a strictly daytime thing, that I could just slap on a wig and some makeup and a dress, stand around for a while, and then take it all off back at the hotel. I *really* should have thought a little harder about the practicalities before I said yes, but something about the night before had bewitched me, and now here I was, on the verge of a total makeover. But I'd had time enough in the Uber over to think about the plan — extensions; new clothes — and I'd come up with several solid, practical reasons why it was a good one, and mere emotional reasons why it wasn't.

I still wanted to talk to James about it all, though. I'd started worrying, hopefully uncharitably, that part of the justification for the extra expense was that he was planning to ask me to do this all over again whenever we had something new to sell, for as long as we could get away with it, which was probably a good few years, given the slow pace of my masculine development. So, as I sat in the salon chair, I started marshalling arguments in my head that would keep me out of dresses in the future. It was good to be prepared; recent experience had shown me that if I just walked back into the office without a properly rehearsed litany against crossdressing ("I will face my dress. I will not permit it to pass over me. I will throw it in the trash and run away to watch sport with people who sweat a lot.") he'd turn those awful rich-boy puppy-dog eyes on me and I'd find it hard to say no.

The whole process was due to take about two-and-a-half hours, which nearly had me back out of the chair again and down the street, if only because I'd be stuck here when the girl from the agency arrived. James talked me down over the phone, insisting he was perfectly able to talk her through most of the stuff she needed to know, and that it was important we didn't rush my preparations. He told me he wanted me to be as discovery-proof as possible during the trade show, and, like always, I folded. I still didn't like the idea of James talking to the model on his own, but I couldn't really point to why. I imagined them both running off together, marketing materials unstudied, and adding her clothes to James' ex-girlfriend drawer at some undetermined point in the future.

So he made his point, my paranoia backed him up, and between them they had me dropping into the salon chair and agreeing to whatever Ben thought was best.

They colour-matched my hair, after praising how thick and wavy it was — I resisted the temptation to make the obvious joke; "Thanks, I grew it myself," probably got old after the first hundred times — and two of the staff, a guy called Warren with short, dark hair, delicate fingers and very pale skin, and a woman, Selina, started work. I tried not to blush under their attention, failed, and settled for avoiding my reflection and listening in on Ben's phone calls. Since the extensions were to eat all our remaining time, we weren't going to be able to go shopping together, much to Ben's irritation and my mild relief; instead, he was describing our needs to a personal shopper he knew. He also gave them my measurements, passed on by James, which led unavoidably to me squirming in my seat at the thought of what it took to get them. Warren had to whap me on the forehead to get me to sit still, and Ben took his phone to the other end of the salon. Probably wise, considering I was having things heat-bonded to my head and ought not to be eavesdropping on conversations that might distress me. I decided, when eventually Ben sat down again, not to bug him about it. I was the ball in the Rube Goldberg machine, bouncing from apartment to hair salon to personal shopper to office, and the most helpful things I could do at this point were to shut up and keep tucking.

Besides, having my hair worked on was relaxing. Even the heat bonding, about which I'd been mildly alarmed, seemed routine; Warren and Selina were clearly as skilled in their own field as Ben and James were in the field of making my simple life incredibly complicated and embarrassing, and chatted happily as they worked.

I took the opportunity to catch up on some sleep.

I didn't dream this time, thank God. I was woken up by Selina lecturing Ben on how to style keratin extensions. I realised they were talking about me at the exact moment I remembered why I was here, and had one of the unpleasant rapid bootups that had quickly become a core feature of my life.

They'd done an incredible job. My hair, which before had tickled the middle of my ear at its longest point, now covered the top half of my chest — the memory of a dream inserted itself; I dismissed it — and the highlights were a nice touch. It wasn't styled, particularly, but I assumed either that they didn't have time, or that there was a waiting period before you could play with the new hair too much.

I kinked my head from side to side in the mirror. Difficult not to be at least a little entranced...

"She's awake!" Warren said, grasping me by the shoulders.

Yes, that pronoun again. It was weird how fast I was getting used to it. Weirder still that I had no idea if the salon staff knew what my actual gender was — I'd come in wearing my real (shortish and untidy) hair, but with a full face of makeup and the maxi dress Ben had taken an instant dislike to — but I'd decided before I fell asleep that they were unlikely to care, so why should I? It was that sort of salon; I was likely not even the most unusual person currently in the building. The thought had been comforting: it was nice, despite my dress, to feel both safe and relatively ordinary.

The dress itself was less comforting. I looked down at it, remembering how hard it had been to put it on again, after the dream that — I whacked the back of my head against the seat — I couldn't seem to stop thinking about.

"Sorry," I said, to Warren's suddenly worried face. "Just waking myself up."

"Unconventional, honey," he said. "So, what do you think?"

I smiled at him, leaned forward in the chair, and ran my fingers through some of the hair that hung around my chin. "It looks *fantastic*," I said, doing my best to show enthusiasm and appreciation, to take the sting out of the next bit. "How do I take it all out?"

It didn't work; he looked disappointed. "You want rid of them already?"

"They're only for the weekend," I said. "For a job."

Selina reached forward and pried Warren's fingers off my shoulders. "Just massage the keratin bonds with olive oil," she said to me. "It'll take a while and it's a bit fiddly. Ben gave me your number; I'll send you a link. It'd be better if you came back to us, though. We can do it properly, and we can talk about your future styling needs."

"Seems like a waste," Warren said.

"Yes, yes, it's a tragedy," Ben said, breaking up our little gathering and tapping at a non-existent watch on his wrist. "Alex, we have to go!"

I remembered to grab the battered handbag as I stood up. "Thank you *so* much, both of you," I said, directing my broadest smile towards the slightly downcast Warren. "Ben, did we pay already?"

"Yes, we've done terrible violence to the company credit card; let's *go!*"

I let Ben drag me out of the salon, waving to Warren and Selina. When we got out onto the street, the wind picked up my hair and blew it about like I was in a shampoo commercial, and I watched it in the salon window, fascinated. Perhaps it *would* be a waste to get rid of it straight after the expo; they'd gone to such lengths.

* * *

In the Uber back to James' place I noticed some sneaky bastard had put acrylic nails on me while I napped (I had a vague memory of waking briefly to find someone buffing at my fingers but had dismissed it as a hairdressing-induced fever dream). They weren't huge talons or anything, just rounded little things perhaps a quarter centimetre longer than my real nails and painted a colour that looked translucent but wasn't, and I supposed they did cover up my slightly ragged real ones. The driver told me I looked nice, though, and she was so friendly that I almost forgot about the nails while we chatted. I gave her a five-star review, which was tricky because I had to use my phone screen with the flat of my finger instead of the tip.

* * *

Ben tried to hide the logo on the carrier bags that populated the hall outside James' apartment door, but he wasn't a particularly wide person and I have the advanced pattern-recognition skills of the professional coder and problem solver: it wasn't hard to infer the missing letters between *HAR* and *OLS*.

"Your personal shopper friend works at *Harvey Nichols?*" I yelled, doing the high-pitched screech again. I'd be attracting dogs soon; I decided in advance to set them on Ben. "Do you *know* how expensive they are?"

He gave me a look like I'd asked him about his third arm. "Of course *I* know," he said, dropping some bags by the sofa. I dumped the rest of them in the same spot. "I'm surprised *you* know."

I didn't know, not personally, not precisely, but Harvey Nicks was up there with Harrod's in the don't-even-think-about-it category. I was a Primark guy who stepped up to Next if I needed something posh for, say, a wedding I ultimately didn't go to. My entire interaction with the place up until that day had been glancing at it on my way through Knightsbridge and thinking, *Huh, it's that posh shop off the telly.* Money aside, I'd never seen the point of nice clothes, anyway; they didn't ever look good on me, so why *not* buy cheap crap?

Ben nipped into James' bedroom and came back with a couple of clean sheets. He laid one over the sofa and the other over the kitchen table, and started unpacking the shopping bags onto them.

Gosh, there were a lot of clothes.

He continued to unpack.

A *lot* of clothes.

I think I gasped, or screamed, or died temporarily, because when Ben got done laying out one of the outfits, he turned a glare on me. "Look," he said, "we *really* don't have much time, so if you're going to have a panic attack, can you please try to do something useful while you're at it?"

"Define useful," I said, feeling stubborn.

He reached into one of his cases, pulled out a small plastic bottle with a pump attached and threw it at me. It turned out to be an adhesive. "Heads up!" he said, and I looked up to find another bottle flying toward me at head height. I caught it awkwardly. It was isopropyl alcohol, which, in combination with the adhesive, meant... absolutely nothing to me. I shrugged at him, glue in one hand, alcohol in the other, and he sighed.

"Take your tits out," he said, belabouring every word, like he was talking a child through their fiftieth failed attempt at tying their shoelaces, "wipe your chest and the back of the tits with the alcohol, then spray glue on the tits and put them back on."

"This is tit glue?" I said, trying hard to keep my voice neutral. "Is it... permanent?"

He laughed at me and returned to sorting through clothes. "You think I carry industrial-strength superglue in my drag kit? I just thought it would be nice if, for example, you had to bend down to pick something up and your tits didn't fall out."

I had visions of chasing an errant breast out of the apartment like it was a cat who'd stolen my dinner, and laughed with him. I stepped out of my dress, took the breasts out of my bra and laid them on the kitchen counter, thanking providence I'd cleaned it that morning. "Bra on or off?" I asked.

"On. It'll help you position the forms. The last thing you want is wonky tits."

I snorted. "I think, actually, this whole thing is the last thing I want."

"Crybaby."

I set to work, cleaning my chest and my chest accessories with the alcohol solution.

"Just reassure me I'm not a perv for doing this," I said a short while later as I held a tit in place and waited for the glue to set.

"*I've* done it," he said, pretending to be offended. "Am I a perv?" At least, I thought he was pretending.

"No," I said hurriedly, waving the hand that wasn't busy with a fake tit, "not at all! But you're, you know, *gay.*"

"And you're n—?" he started, but interrupted himself and changed tack, too quickly for me to focus on what he almost said. "Drag queens do this; trans women who haven't started HRT yet do this; B-list Hollywood stars making a play for Best Supporting Actor do this, usually terribly; even cis women do this sometimes, if they've had a mastectomy."

I frowned, and switched tit, since the first one seemed like it was pretty firmly attached. "What's a 'cis' woman?"

Ben looked up at the ceiling. "And to think, I'm not legally allowed to murder her," he muttered. I deliberated over which part of the sentiment to be more offended by. "A cis woman is a woman who isn't trans; a trans woman is a woman who isn't cis." My face clearly did that thing again, because he continued, "Okay. A cis person is someone who has no desire or need to switch away from their gender assigned at birth." I opened my mouth to ask a question about that, but he preempted me. "Jesus Christ, Alex; have you never been on the internet, like, ever? Kids today!"

"Hey," I said, pouting, "aren't you only a couple of years older than me?"

He raised an eyebrow at me, ignored my question, and continued, "Let's make it really simple: if you are a boy—" he used the child-lecturing tone again, "—and you are happy being a boy, or at least not miserable enough to *do* anything about it, you are cis. If you are a boy, but inside you're *actually* a girl, then you're trans."

I'd like to say that realisation dawned, but mostly it was a desire to end an increasingly awkward and patronising conversation. I nodded anyway and said, "Okay. I get it." I thought I sort of did, anyway.

"Thank *all* the heavens. Just remember, I gave you the simplified version. Don't try and explain it to anyone else until you've done the background reading." He smiled at me momentarily, and then looked me up and down. "*Are you not moisturising your legs?*" he exclaimed, borrowing my dog-attracting screech.

"What?" I said, looking down at them, as if that would help. "Am I supposed to?"

"Oh my God," he said. "You're a world-class idiot. We waxed them *yesterday*. Do you *want* to get a rash?"

I wanted to protest at the 'we' part of that but settled for defending myself. "Hey! I've only been doing this for a day. Just let me have that one."

"Fix it," he ordered. "But not with anything you find around here; James buys crap moisturiser. I don't know why, because he's richer than God, but he has, like, supermarket own-brand stuff. It might as well be mayonnaise. I had to borrow some once and it's... well, it's just awful. For people like us, who were AMAB'd, if we want good skin, we need to go the extra mile."

"'Ah-mabbed'?" I hazarded.

"It means— Never mind." He shook his head at me. "It'd be like showing a quantum physics textbook to a poodle," he muttered, and then shooed me. "Look in the smaller case for the blue bottle. Go." He shooed me again. "Go!"

I disappeared into the bathroom, good moisturiser in one hand, phone in the other, and decided that now was the appropriate time for some of that thinking I'd been putting off. It was money, right now, that was foremost in my mind; the cost of all this just kept climbing! I'd had some concerns in that direction back at the salon, but getting extensions put in at a decent hairdresser had *nothing* on Harvey Nichols. At this rate James would have to keep me in skirts for a decade to justify the expense; he'd have to make me come into work every day in a new outfit, and—

Yeah. Okay. Unhelpful line of thought.

I nipped to the Harvey Nicks website and scrolled through some of their stuff, and unless Ben's personal shopper friend worked out of some unadvertised bargain basement, we'd splashed out considerably more than a thousand pounds on clothes alone. I scrolled some more and found a skirt — a simple loop of black fabric! — that cost over four hundred quid, and tripled my estimate.

Shit. With that kind of cash, I probably could have found *some* agency to supply us with models. I might have been able to hire us a minor royal or a disgraced Tory MP! So why was James choosing *now* to throw company money around? I prepared my list of questions for him as I rubbed moisturiser onto my legs. Which did, I had to admit, feel pretty good.

* * *

Ben joined me in the bathroom with a present: a new contraption that looked sort of like a micro-miniskirt in flesh tone (my flesh tone, anyway; it was several shades too light for either James or Ben). Before I had a chance to complain about it, he told me it was the replacement for the horrid bum pads; it would give me essentially the same measurements, while also being considerably more comfortable and essentially invisible under a dress. The flat front would give the stretchy knickers a hand when it came to hiding my junk, and I wouldn't even need to take it off to use the loo, just slide it up my body. A *definite* upgrade! I almost hugged him, until he pointed out I'd need to take the bum pads with me anyway, in case I wanted to wear trousers, and I felt a little less good about him.

Then he made me wash off my makeup and hunted across my face for stray hairs; it turned out we'd missed a few with yesterday's goop-and-shave session. He plucked at me for a few minutes — first my jaw, then around my eyebrows — and slathered me in more moisturiser. Calling me done 'for now', he dragged me out into the living room to face the array of incredibly expensive clothes that awaited me.

The remainder of my charitable feelings vanished when it turned out he'd hidden my maxi dress. "No fallbacks!" he said. "If last night was about showing you how to look like a girl, *today* is about showing you how to be beautiful."

I avoided commenting that James seemed to think I was plenty beautiful when we were in the restaurant together — Ben would get the wrong idea — and instead gravitated towards one of the more modest outfits Ben had laid out: a reassuringly calf-length blue skirt and a shimmery top that looked loose and billowy. Ben blocked me, standing in front of it and wagging a finger.

"That's *casualwear,*" he said. Absurd; casualwear was jeans and a sweatshirt, not anything that still required me to wax my legs. There actually was a pair of jeans in the mix, draped over a chair on the other side of the room, but by the time I noticed it Ben already had his hand on my back and was guiding me towards the clothes he'd laid out on the sofa.

I was surprised at how relaxed I'd become, being essentially naked around Ben. It helped to know he wasn't interested in me, but I'd never really felt comfortable naked around *anyone* before; not men, not women. I'd always carried with me a quiet sense of shame about my scrawny, shapeless little body. I never slept in the nude even while home alone, and I didn't look at myself in the mirror after showering until I had a robe on. And yet here I was, in bra and knickers around someone who had, up until yesterday, been a stranger.

Perhaps it was because, as Girl Alex, it was like I was playing a character; it wasn't really *me* who was standing around in her underwear.

"Is there any reason," I said, when he brought me face to fabric with the outfit he'd selected, "why I *can't* just wear jeans?"

"You'd have to put the old arse pads back on," he said, grinning nastily at me.

"I... could deal with that."

"Alex, you are *not* wearing casualwear to the office!"

"But I *feel* casual!"

He put his hands on his hips. "You'll feel anything *but* casual when you get there and find James alone with Emily the model."

I twitched a bit. "I told you," I insisted, "I stayed the night, yes, but we weren't *together.* Separate rooms!" I added, refusing to yield. "He can be alone with Emily all he wants." I definitely didn't stumble over that last vowel.

"I'm sure. All the same, how will you feel if you're slobbing around and she's looking like a million dollars?"

"I'll feel very comfortable," I said. So convincing!

"Be quiet and put that on," he said.

That turned out to be a black skirt with gold horizontal bands and a black top with an asymmetrical neckline. I liked that the top covered my arms all the way to the wrists; I didn't like that the skirt covered only half my thighs. I had to admit they fit well, though; Ben's posh personal shopper knew what they were doing. He directed me to a pair of black ankle boots with a two-inch heel that fit better and more snugly than any shoes I'd ever owned, and while I was admiring how comfortable they were, Ben turfed all my stuff out of my handbag and into a much smaller and less battered one.

"Now, sit," he said, pointing at one of the kitchen stools. I did so and he turned on a lamp, which he must have brought with him because I didn't remember it from last night. The damn thing shone right in my face, but he immediately apologised and taped a bit of greaseproof paper over the front. It softened the light, so it was no less bright but more diffuse, and I blinked as my eyes got used to seeing colours and shapes again. "Your hair needs barely any work, so there's only really makeup to go," he said, and opened his kit. "I'm going to do you up in gold around the eyes. It'll go with the skirt and make your eyes look bluer. Is... that okay?"

Wow. Asking for consent! What a novelty. I nodded.

"Good. It's only a shame we didn't have time to pierce your ears."

"You are *not* piercing my ears," I said firmly. There were some lines I wasn't ready to cross. Increasingly few, apparently, but still.

"I'm not piercing your ears," he promised. "Imagine if they got infected in that dirty conference hall!" He shuddered.

I relaxed. It turned out we had a limit, after all. When all this was over with, the extensions could be taken out, the clothes could be sold or donated, and the bum pads and tucking underwear could be loaded into a trebuchet and launched into the sea. We weren't piercing my ears.

I closed my eyes and let Ben paint me.

We rode to the office in a taxi. An honest-to-God taxi, unattached to any predatory rideshare service! The last time I rode in a real taxi, I was twelve and stuck in the middle of my parents' difficult divorce. Real taxis had kind of had bad associations for me since then, but I was able to put them out of my mind; I had so many other awful things on which to concentrate.

In the back seat, knees together (short skirt) and ankles strangely elevated (higher heels than I was used to), I focused on controlling my breathing, thinking through how I would approach Emily Swan and preparing for my biggest challenge yet: meeting a perfectly normal woman. Ben held my hand when he realised I was shaking, which was sweet. It was a shame he wasn't going to be available for me to lean on or hide behind this afternoon; there were a few more things he needed to round up for tomorrow, he'd said. I shuddered when I imagined what terrible equipment he could acquire with a few hours at his disposal. How many more things could possibly be strapped to my undercarriage or glued to my chest?

When we arrived, I got out and I dithered. I stood there on the pavement, looking around, fiddling with the strap of my new handbag, shifting my weight from one foot to the other as I continued trying to get used to the taller heels. I kept the building pointedly behind me, partially so I couldn't be identified by anyone looking out, but mostly because I didn't want to think about it yet. Ben must have asked the taxi driver to wait, because he startled me out of my thoughts with a gentle tap on my elbow, and once he had my attention looked me square in the eye.

"You can *do* this," he said.

I looked back at him, unsure. Yesterday had been an experiment, and kind of fun, but today... today we were *trying*. I was wearing a *stunningly* expensive and — even to my uneducated eye — absolutely gorgeous outfit, and Ben's makeup job was twice as effortful; I looked incredible. Which put the problem squarely on me, the person under the skirt and the foundation and the hair extensions, wobbling around in ankle boots and distinctly unprepared for what lay ahead of me.

"I don't know," I said.

"Alex, you *can* do this. Remember: you're capable, you're beautiful, you're charming..."

"I am?"

"Yes, yes and yes. You helped design the software you're showing off tomorrow, you have *killer* legs and — I promise you — when you and James are in the room together, he *only* has eyes for you."

I felt that. Right in the heart. I wanted to protest, to tell Ben that I didn't care about that, that I wasn't interested in James that way, but I had a feeling he would remain sceptical on that front. Anyway, all dressed up as Girl Alex, it was hard to deny that she, at least, was... paying attention to James. What that meant for me — the rest of me; Boy Alex — I hadn't even begun to deal with.

Still, though, the idea that James returned my interest was a non-starter: we'd known each other for a while, and I'd never seen him express any interest in guys at all. It was just Ben misreading James' lack of obvious discomfort around me, that was all. The guy's best friend was a drag queen! Of course he wasn't put out by a bit of crossdressing! But did that mean he was into me? No.

I accepted Ben's praise and his reassurance, anyway. There were parts of me that, apparently, wanted James, wanted to be seen by him, and they were only getting an outing for the long weekend, so why not let them have their fun?

Ben steadied me; I must have swayed on my heels. So I smiled at him in thanks and stepped back, putting James out of my mind and trying to focus solely on being Alex Brewer, knowledgeable coder, good organiser, and McCain Applied Computing employee of the month fourteen months running; but, like, the girl version.

There. Found her.

"Thanks, Ben," I said.

"Just remember," he said, grinning back at me, "stay in character!"

Before he could climb back in the taxi, I stepped forward and hugged him, keeping my arms low so I didn't crumple the new clothes or smudge my makeup. "Thank you, really," I said. "I'm sorry if I've been kind of a..."

"Bitch?"

"Yeah."

"You're welcome. Now, go be amazing!"

He pushed against me, trying to disengage from the hug, but he wasn't exactly James — despite the pleasingly firm belly I had my arms around — and I wasn't overpowered so easily. Before I let go, I nipped in and kissed him on the cheek.

It felt like something Girl Alex would do.

* * *

James was in the lobby, fighting with the coffee vending machine, and I was glad he had his back to the front doors because it meant he didn't see my sharp intake of breath; I'd expected to have at least the elevator ride to finish preparing myself!

Okay. I had to be honest with myself: at least part of my gasp was because he was bending over to peer at the buttons on the machine and it pulled his dark jeans tight around his arse. Rather difficult not to notice a thing like that. Or a *pair* of things like that, straining against the denim. Maybe it *had* been a good idea for Ben to dress me up...

I swallowed, straightened my sleeves and assessed the situation. Obviously, James was playing the good host for Emily Swan — *Don't sulk, Girl Alex!* — and he'd come down to use the coffee machine in the lobby because we'd run out of those stupid little pods for the office machine. Which was *definitely* a good thing, because it meant I'd have a chance to reintroduce myself to him, unsupervised. So why did I feel like I'd just been ambushed?

Breathe, Alex. Breathe.

I needed something to focus on. I fiddled with my restrictive clothes and envied him his. And it was more than a little annoying that he'd dressed so casually today, despite his flattering jeans. He had a t-shirt on that I knew for a fact cost £6 because I'd been in the office when he came back from lunch clutching two three-packs from Marks & Spencer; I'd made fun of him for shopping at the supermarket for aspirational grannies. He looked comfortable! And the worst thing he'd have to wear this weekend would be a tailored suit! I, meanwhile, was wearing a grand's-worth of Harvey Nicks swag and had to remember to keep my knees together when I sat down. Look at him! The bastard hadn't even had to wax his legs!

Perhaps being irritated with him was the best way to cope with Girl Alex's increasingly urgent crush. Perfect. All he had to do was keep annoying me and, luckily, if James hadn't been able to make it in business, he could have been an obliviously aggravating bastard on an internationally competitive level. There were probably grants for it, and you probably got them almost by accident, simply by being in the right place at the right time, just to make the whole exercise even more annoying for everyone around you.

I watched him take out his phone and mess with it, which yanked a smile out of me. I decided he was tweeting something like, I can't even make coffee without Alex to do it for me, I'm so terrible at life. And then he kicked the vending machine, and I shook myself. Time to intervene before something — the vending machine; James; my delicate feelings — got hurt.

"You forgot to select cup size again, didn't you?" I said. Nailed the voice, first time. It had started to feel quite natural.

He turned around, took one look at me and dropped his phone. It was a good thing the lounge area around the vending machines was carpeted or I was sure he would have guilted me about his smashed phone screen for the difficult couple of hours he'd have to put up with it for, before a new one arrived from wherever rich people just effortlessly get stuff from. He opened his mouth to say something but seemed briefly to forget how to speak. He shut his mouth and looked me up and down, a muscle in his jaw tensing as he did so.

"What?" I said to his frown. I didn't *think* I looked weird, but I gave myself a quick once-over, just to be certain: I hadn't broken an ankle in the boots, my skirt hadn't ridden up, my bag wasn't spilling its contents onto the floor and neither of my tits had made a break for the horizon. I was momentarily puzzled by his reaction, but then I remembered the way he looked at me when he saw me like this for the first time, returning to his flat after Ben dressed me up. Then, like now, he was trying to square my appearance with the knowledge that it was *me* under all this, and probably getting a headache. So I decided to tease him, just a little. "Never seen a pretty woman before?"

"Al— Alex?" he said, eventually.

"Yep, and still so good they named me twice," I replied, grinning. I'd tried it in the mirror a few times and knew how striking my smile could be when I had lipstick on. One of the small things it'd be a shame to lose, after this was all over.

"Hi?" James said, still blinking slowly at me.

I stepped forward, bent down carefully — knees together; God, the skirt was tight! — retrieved his phone, and placed it in his limp hand. I had to close his fingers around it so it didn't fall right back out; he seemed much more interested in gaping at me than in paying attention to anything important.

"I thought you said you could cope without me," I said, "but, here you are, defeated by the vending machine. Again."

"Oh," he said. "Um. Yeah."

I still had my hand on his — making sure he wasn't going to drop his phone — so I squeezed it, released him, nudged him aside with my hip, and cleared the half-finished order off the machine. I had no idea where all this confidence was coming from, nor why it had replaced the nerves I'd been so consumed by in the taxi, but I wanted to bottle it so I could have some whenever I liked. Being Girl Alex around James was intoxicating!

"How does she take her coffee?" I asked.

"Um," James remarked, and then seemed finally to get himself back together. He even pocketed his phone! "Black. No sugar."

101

Same as me; I liked her already. I dialled up a black, no sugar, and handed him the paper cup when it was done. He took it but continued to stare at me. He was acting a bit like he had in the restaurant, before time and wine forced him to relax, but for some reason I was finding it funny now, and perhaps even a little charming.

I did worry that this suggested he was going to need a good run up like this *every* time I put on a skirt, which suggested he'd be spending every morning at the expo walking around in a confused daze, but that was a problem for him and the pillars he'd be walking into, not me.

I poked him and pointed to the compartment which had just popped open on the other side of the machine. "Lid!" I prompted.

Clumsily, he retrieved and applied the plastic lid for Emily's coffee, and while he was making a meal of that task, I sorted out a cup for me (also black, no sugar) and a cup for James (full cream, a squirt of syrup and a sprinkle of chocolate flakes; he always claimed it was Ben who got him on fancy coffee). I made him carry both his and Emily's, and redirected him from the stairs he automatically headed for, steering him towards the elevator in the corner.

"It's only a couple of flights," he complained. He was the kind of well-off fitness dork who had a gym membership, a private pool membership, blew off steam in the objectively terrible mini-gym in the office basement and never took the elevator as a point of pride, which was presumably how he was able to drink coffee that was mostly sugar without compromising his impressive physique. (I was the kind of skint loser who stayed thin largely because of forgetting to eat at most mealtimes; I lost track of stuff if I didn't set reminders. I suspected I got so good at organising other people because first I had to learn to organise myself, and in doing so overcome the greatest obstacle ever faced in the history of human efficiency: me.)

I nudged him with my boot and laughed when he jumped a little. Still so tense!

"These things—" I waggled a foot at him and was rather proud I didn't tip over with just the one heel on which to balance, "—are at *least* two inches and, in case you forgot, I'm kinda new at walking in them. If I try taking the stairs right now, I might break my neck! Worse: I might spill coffee all over this expensive outfit." And while the NHS would repair me for free, dry cleaning this skirt would probably be pricey as all hell.

"Fine," he said, surrendering.

I tapped the button for the elevator. "So, what's she like?" I asked, to fill the silence.

"Who?"

Okay. He was starting to cross the line from *slightly behind events* to *fully absent.* Less charming. "Emily Swan?" I said. "The model we hired? I assume she's up there; you're carrying her coffee, after all."

"Oh," he said, looking around nervously, as if she might suddenly appear from behind the vending machines, "uh, yeah."

"So...?"

"Right. Yes." He cleared his throat and seemed to come back to his senses. "She's smart, actually. Asked a lot of good questions. Surprised me. I think you'll like her."

"Great!" We'd hired a booth babe, and all we technically required of her was that she look pretty and avoid punching any of the attendees, but if she was all that — attractive; non-violent — and smart, too, we might well have found ourselves a repeat booking.

The elevator doors opened to admit us, and I stepped in, taking small, careful steps, aware that I had heels on and very much not wanting to get one stuck in the gap.

"No," James said, "I mean, I think you'll *like* her." He sounded a lot more like his old self, which had its pluses and minuses. I kind of liked having him at least a little off kilter. "She's your type," he added, nudging me with an elbow.

Naturally, part of James being back to his old self meant he was back to trying to set me up with women ludicrously out of my league. He didn't want me to be lonely, he said, over and over, no matter how much I insisted that I was fine, that I had my work and my health and my one (1) friend.

"You mean, someone who'll stop texting after three weeks? Someone who'll cheat on me with some guy she met at a club? Someone who'll flirt with *you* in front of me?"

"It's not *that* bad—"

"It is and you know it," I said, my buoyant mood well and truly sunk.

My history with women was dire, and he knew exactly *how* dire, because he'd had to pick me back up every time I got dumped. I'd never understood what I didn't have that other men did that made them capable of real, lasting relationships with women! All I knew was that I wanted it, and seeing James with women made me want it all the more.

And fuck him for reminding me, actually! Fuck him for bringing me right back to my shitty, everyday life, just when I was starting to feel almost confident! I felt stupid: suddenly a skinny boy in a skirt he didn't know how to wear, with heels he barely knew how to walk in and hair he didn't know how to care for. Reduced to Alex, out of his depth.

I closed my eyes, tried to block everything out, tried to resummon whatever had possessed me in the lobby. Call it confidence or Girl Alex or the high of taking a vacation from my life; whatever it was, I needed it back.

"Sorry," he said. He didn't sound sorry; he *did* sound abrasively loud in the tiny space. "I just think you'll like her. She's smart, she's pretty, she's down to earth. You should ask her out. You *should!* You've got to meet the right girl sooner or later. It's just a matter of time and persistence, like I keep telling you."

I opened my eyes to glare at him, which was pointless because he'd delivered his little speech while looking resolutely into the corner of the lift. "James!" I snapped, trying to demand his attention. "Do you think I can afford to ask a girl out when I'm like *this?*" I watched his jaw twitch, but otherwise he didn't move. "Look at me, James!"

"What?" he said, but he looked at me anyway, and his pupils dilated. I think he'd forgotten how I was dressed. Or had been deliberately trying to forget it, or something. He was behaving like a parody of his old, blokish, jocular self, more like he'd been in my first few months at the company, when he'd been encouraging me (rather crudely, sometimes) to keep seeing the girls who approached me, even though it went wrong time after time.

Well, no. He didn't get to be that guy. Not while *I* was being *this* guy. Girl. Whatever. I grabbed his face with my free hand, to make sure he couldn't look away, not without jerking out of my grip. I wasn't normally so physical — I couldn't believe I was being so bold, actually! — but I was, in that moment, so mad at him, so mad at his casual masculinity, his easy charm, even his fucking *smell!* I was mad at everything that made him James, everything the lack of which made me Alex. For the longest time I'd had to watch him be *the guy,* the aspirational figure from the cover of the lifestyle magazine, the handsome man with the charisma and the thick wallet, while I'd had to be the skinny little hanger-on who got his job through charity and who was destined to be forgotten once this phase of James' life was over, and, well, I'd been someone else for a while. Only for a few minutes, really, but I'd felt *good* and I'd been having fun and then James, accidentally or not, had put me right back in my place.

Looking at it with clear eyes, I kind of hated my place.

The elevator doors opened and I took a sideways step, interposing my leg between them so the sensor wouldn't let them close, all the while keeping a good firm grip on James' face.

"If you're going to make fun of me, James," I hissed, "then you're going to get out of this elevator *alone* and go round the corner to the office *alone,* and I'm going to go the *fuck* home, burn these *stupid* clothes, and you can wear a dress to the expo yourself!" I knew I was overreacting — or I thought I did; perhaps I simply doubted that I had a right to my anger — but I was too heated to stop myself.

"I'm sorry!" he said. His voice was comically distorted by my grip on his cheeks, so I let him go. "I didn't mean anything. I promise. I was just... I didn't mean anything."

"Okay. But remember how freaked out I was, this morning?" He nodded. "None of that has magically gone away. I'm staying on top of it — or I *was* — but it's really, *really* hard, so, if you please, leave my tragic love life alone, and try, just *try,* to bloody well *help!*"

"God, I will, yes," he said, flustered, looking away again.

"Right," I said, exiting the elevator.

Behind me, I heard James mutter, "When did you become such a bitch?"

I almost stopped. Almost. The word felt so different in his mouth, in this context, than it had when Ben said it, and I wanted nothing more than to turn around and kick him somewhere sensitive.

Instead, I took a deep breath, opened the office door, and prepared to meet Emily Swan.

Chapter Five

Wow. Emily Swan was *gorgeous*. I knew that already, having seen her headshot in the packet from the agency (along with pictures of the two other models who were now off sick and thus presumably getting a lot of sleep and watching TV in their pyjamas; no, I wasn't jealous, not at all), but photos never really sell someone properly; there's always something missing. In this case, that something was that she was *tall:* she had a good two inches on me, even with me in heels and her in trainers.

Oh yeah, that's the other thing she was: wearing casual clothing. Jeans and a tank top. Here I was in a skirt that didn't reach my knees even when I tugged on it, in a whole outfit that cost more than my rent, and the professional model in front of me looked like she was about to interrupt a cosy evening in front of the telly for a quick trip to the corner shop to buy tea bags. My plans to murder Ben, which I'd put on hold in the taxi over, started ticking over again.

She was standing by my desk, leafing through some of our technical documents, and looked up when I marched in. She smiled at me, but also raised her eyebrows a little, which led me to wonder what kind of impression I made; with her and James both in jeans, I was the most overdressed person in the office by a factor of twenty. And definitely the one with the least comfortable feet.

Okay. Show time.

"Miss Swan," I said, pushing my voice off the top of my mouth as hard as I dared, for a warm, clear tone. "I'm Alex Brewer."

"Miss Brewer, hi," she said, holding out a hand. I shook it, remembering not to do the stupid guy thing where you pump someone's hand like you're trying to loosen an overtightened screw; I was always terrible at that, anyway, just like every other bonding ritual which required me to assert my strength and confidence. I perched on the back of the next desk over, taking some of the weight off my feet. I would have sat down, but then I would have felt even shorter compared to her.

"Call me Alex, please," I said, depositing the coffee cup on the desk. The phrase *Miss Brewer was my father* jumped into my head before I could stop it, and I turned the grin into a welcoming smile.

"Then you can call me Emily," she responded. "Mr McCain was just talking me through some of your other projects." Ah, so it was 'Mr McCain', was it? I cursed my traitorous brain for picking up on that and making favourable deductions about the level of intimacy they'd reached. "He said he was just killing time until you got back, though, and that you'd be better placed to go over what we'll be presenting on the show floor tomorrow."

I nodded, holding in a moment of panic at the reminder that the trade show did, in fact, start *tomorrow*. At least the bright office lights were a decent enough preview of conditions on the show floor; no intimate restaurant lighting to help me, here, and Emily Swan had yet to ask me about my stubble, my foundation garments or my penis. Perhaps she was just being polite.

I was flailing over how to respond — still analysing every movement of her eyes, every twitch of the muscles in her face, trying to decide whether she'd worked me out — when James backed through the office door, coffees in hand. He drew Emily's attention, which gave me the opportunity both to sigh with relief at being momentarily unwitnessed, and then direct one of my nastier glares in James' direction. I didn't know why he'd taken so long to get from the elevator to the office, but I hoped it was because he was kicking himself for being a jerk. For what it was worth, I thought his eyes looked apologetic, but it wasn't worth much.

"Miss Brewer," James said to me as he passed Emily her coffee, "Miss Swan and I were just going over the in-development stuff. Most of it you've worked on, I know, but I saved one for last because I don't believe you're familiar with it. Will you join us?"

I rolled my eyes at being 'Miss Brewer'ed by him — it honestly took me a second to register that he'd been talking to me — but nodded. He wasn't usually a super formal guy, so I didn't know what throwing all these honorifics around was supposed to achieve. Possibly he was trying to sound like a proper adult, and not a twenty-three-year-old running a tech startup with daddy's cash.

Hey, if he was going to call me a bitch, I was going to be one! In the safety of my own head, anyway.

We arranged ourselves around the desk they'd been using. James sat next to me, opposite Emily, which I thought was a bit unfair on her, like we were ganging up on her or something. He seemed to be vibrating with nervous energy, like he was finding the stress of not actively being a jerk hard to handle. I wanted to put a hand out to calm him down but, for a number of reasons, decided against it, not least because he'd been a jerk to me, personally, extremely recently. With luck, Emily, who didn't know him, wouldn't notice anything out of the ordinary.

He talked us both through the project. It was pretty interesting, I had to admit, although early enough in development that I didn't see how it could be ready even for next year's round of trade shows unless we literally doubled our engineer count.

But Emily Swan was extremely impressive. I could tell she knew her stuff from the questions she was asking, and I wondered what she was doing on the agency modelling circuit with a brain like hers. On the other hand, what did I know? Maybe modelling was just more fun than coding? I shifted in my uncomfortable underwear and my tight skirt and I kind of doubted that wearing ridiculous clothing in front of hundreds of people for three days straight could be particularly fun even for someone who didn't have a nasty pinching sensation in her foreskin when she sat a certain way.

"And with that," James finished, "I'll leave you in the capable hands of Miss Brewer."

He'd been smarming at me for the last five minutes, so I kicked him under the desk. The boots I was wearing were quite heavy; I hoped I left a bruise.

"Thanks so much, Mr McCain," Emily said.

I gave him a tight smile as he left, watching him carefully to check for a limp (nope; drat), but I didn't let out the breath I'd been holding until his office door was good and closed. I felt my shoulders droop as all the air rushed out of me.

"Is everything okay between the two of you?" Emily asked.

Yeah, I probably should have been more subtle. Loudly signalling to strangers that I was fighting with my boss: not particularly professional. Idiot. "Everything's fine," I said, sounding rather too venomous for that to be believable. "He's just an arsehole, that's all."

I'd been glaring at the desk for a few seconds before I noticed Emily hadn't replied yet. I looked up and saw she was frowning. Quickly, I replayed what I'd said and swore to myself: I'd sounded like someone trying to be tactful or evasive while still labelling their boss abusive or sexually inappropriate.

I really *was* an idiot.

"Is there anything I should know?" Emily said, before I could head her off.

"No," I said, speaking slowly so I could sort out my phrasing as I went. "I just realised, playing it back in my head—" I span a finger around by my temple, as if I were rewinding the ancient reel-to-reel tape recorder my brain increasingly felt like, "—what it sounded like I was saying, and no, he's *not* that kind of arsehole. We've known each other a long time, and he knows how to get under my skin. Actually, he rather *likes* to get under my skin, and he was doing just that in the elevator on our way up here. And I'm *pretty* sure he's been acting so formal around me either as an apology or as a way of needling me further, and the most infuriating thing about him is I can't work out which."

"Formal?"

"Oh." I shrugged. "Calling me 'Miss Brewer', and all that. I've always been just 'Alex' to him." Oh, so accurate. And then another neuron fired; presumably the reel-to-reel tape in my head hit the end and started playing back normally again. "Huh. You know, if I'm to grant him the benefit of the doubt—" I said it like I was pulling glass out of my skin, "—he *might* simply have been trying to look professional. Contract engineers aside, we've never hired in anyone from outside before." I groaned. "I've been mad at him — *more* mad at him — for trying to make a good impression. Am I a jerk?"

Emily's brow puckered. "I don't think so."

She was looking at me funny; I'd said too much, or said it the wrong way, with the wrong words. I glanced down at myself and was reminded of what I was wearing; I'd dressed up as some kind of corporate ice queen — and I suspected the first impression I'd made had reinforced that, seeing as I'd come striding in, carrying coffee, wearing expensive clothes and a pissed-off look — but the matching persona didn't come naturally to me. I was, in fact, babbling.

Well. If I was going to babble, best to do so early and establish appropriate expectations. I wasn't any kind of ice queen; I was a nervy but friendly idiot. *With great legs,* my inner Ben added.

"You know what it's like," I said, feeling very tired, "when you've known someone forever..."

"Have you and he ever...?"

"Have we...? Oh!" It was like someone'd dumped a bucket of ice into my bra. "No. Definitely not. Nope. Never. Not in a million years." Getting into doth-protest-too-much territory; bloody Girl Alex. "I'm not into men," I said, attempting clarification.

Emily laughed. "Does *he* know that?"

111

"Yeah." I frowned. "Yeah, he definitely knows that."

She laughed again. "Poor guy," she said, and leaned forward, continuing in a conspiratorial whisper, "I think he's got it *bad* for you."

The ice cubes in my bra spread to the rest of my body. "I really don't think so," I said quickly.

"You said he was trying to get under your skin?" she asked, and I nodded. She laughed. "It's like being back at school; boys pinging the bra straps of girls they like." Then she frowned. "Or girls they hate. Or, uh, girls."

"He doesn't think of me that way," I said.

"What way?"

"Any way. We don't have that kind of relationship."

"Ah," Emily said. "Sorry if I crossed a line there."

"No," I said, "you're fine. He's just been... difficult lately. Asking a lot of me." Understatement. Not that I hadn't gone along with it, every step of the way, for reasons that still eluded me. "And, since it's usually only the two of us here, he's hard to escape." I smiled. "He can be sort of exhausting." She returned my smile, which was reassuring; my *ice queen* act may have fallen at the first hurdle, but my *girl* act was still in the running.

"So," she said, tapping a finger on the unopened pack on the table, "did you want to go over the materials for tomorrow?"

"Yes," I said, "but, before we get into it, I have a few questions for you, if that's okay. About trade show modelling."

"Oh?" She looked surprised.

"We couldn't book any other models to back you up," I said, and saw her expression change in response so I continued quickly, "and your boss was *very* clear you mustn't be required to work solo, so I was... volunteered. I'll be out on the floor with you. That's at least part of why I'm annoyed with him." I nodded towards James' office door.

"Ah," she said, understanding dawning.

"I'm annoyed at myself, as well," I admitted. "I gave in way too easily."

"Well, he *is* your boss," Emily said.

"I think it's more that I can't say no to him when he looks like a kicked puppy. But now, on extremely short notice, I have to be a model, and I've never done anything like it before. That's, uh, why I'm all dressed up today. Normally I just wear whatever, but James wanted me to get used to being poshed up, so before I know it I'm being shuttled around by Ben — his friend who does drag — getting my hair done and being handed all these nice clothes. I'm not even used to the makeup; the most I've ever worn before is a bit of lipstick." This was true: at school I was in an otherwise all-girl group of friends in drama class, and they thought it'd be brilliant if I played Juliet in our end-of-year production, opposite my friend Kelly as Romeo. I'd had to wear a wig that smelled of straw, and lipstick that I was pretty sure had been stolen from someone's mother. Like I said, kernel of truth, sack of lies, etc. Keeping my stories straight would be a lot easier if the only *actual* lie I was telling was about my gender, and my rusty acting talents would be less stretched if I played the dork out of her element rather than the effortless superfemme. "When I got my makeup done, Ben had to spend five minutes lecturing me on not touching my face! I've been binge-watching YouTube tutorials done by people who own more makeup brushes than I've had hot dinners. All of this—" I waved my hand over my body, "—is hard to get used to, which is part of why I wish James would lay off."

She thought for a moment. "Maybe it's only that he's not used to seeing you like this. Like a 'real' woman. That's why he's behaving oddly." She finger-quoted on 'real', so I didn't feel like I had to stand up for unreal women everywhere. "Even though he knows you're... unavailable."

I indulged a sudden urge to be nasty about him. "I think it's because he's had a longer dry patch than usual, what with us being so busy, and now, all of a sudden, he can see my legs. It's got his small brain all confused." With my thumb and forefinger I described the exact size of his brain.

She copied my gesture and lowered her hand, smirking. When I got it, I laughed, and she laughed with me.

"So," I continued, "forgetting about my jerk of a friend *and* my arse of a boss, who are, tragically for me, the same person... Trade show modelling! I've never done it before and I don't know what to expect."

Emily put a hand on mine. "You poor thing," she said.

"You mean, it's *not* a laugh a minute?"

She shrugged. "It can be fun. Kind of. Sometimes. But I wouldn't have picked it as a career."

"How did you get into it?"

"I got my degree in software engineering, decided against going postgrad, and then failed to get a job in my field. I figured I'd do the model thing while I waited for an opportunity to turn up, and hoped I'd get a chance to network while I'm at it."

I couldn't possibly have missed the question she was asking. "If this weekend goes well for us," I said, thinking quickly, "I suspect we'll be looking for at least one new engineer. If you can get me some sample code, I can pitch you to him. For a try-out."

"Really?"

"He already told me he was impressed with the questions you were asking. And after this weekend, he'll owe me one." I snorted. "He'll owe me a *thousand*. I'm pretty sure I can get him to consider you." I liked Emily already, and if she was as capable as she seemed, she'd be a lifesaver. And, I decided, while mentally rehearsing my arguments for hiring her, it'd be nice to have another woman around the office.

* * *

People (and romantic comedies) talk about *the spark,* the imperceptible but vital romantic connection between two people, and I'd always been waiting to experience it. After James suggested, in the elevator up, that Emily was my type, a small part of me expected to feel it with her.

No. Nary a spark; nary a glimmer.

I liked her a lot; I think it's not an exaggeration to say that we bonded during our few hours together in the office. We ordered James around, requested of him in our most demure voices that he fetch us cups of tea, and giggled when he delivered them (with good grace, to his credit). We discussed modelling, coding — she was impressed that I was largely self-taught — and our school days. I liked that I didn't feel I had to lie to her, except about the exact nature of my full name and the contents of my knickers; despite my femme façade, she didn't judge me for my unfamiliarity with makeup and fashion, or for my slightly sad lack of a life outside work. In return, she shared stories of late nights staring at the laptop screen, of having to cover her dark circles for modelling gigs, of the many irritations, large and small, involved in being an attractive woman taking a computer science degree and attempting to find work in the field after graduation.

It did occur to me, after she left for the evening, after we booked her train ticket with James' money — James and Ben and I were planning to take a car, along with a couple of our work-from-home engineers; Emily would meet us at the hotel — that I'd more or less offered her a job, which would have been fine except that by the time she showed up to the office, after the expo, I'd look rather different. I sat on the problem for a couple of minutes but couldn't find a solution that didn't involve breaking my promise to her, which I wasn't prepared to do, so I put it on the pile of things to think about after we survived the weekend.

I stretched, looked down at my legs, remembered what I was wearing, and realised I had another question to answer: what was I going to do about tonight? Everything'd gone by in such a rush that I hadn't thought to bring men's clothes with me to work, and that meant either going home as Girl Alex, which would involve navigating my neighbourhood and my block of flats in a severe skirt and heels combo (nope), staying at James' again (definitely not; I needed some space away from him, if only to clear my head), or booking a hotel. The final option was tempting, and I knew I could get James to pay for it — if we could get him to fetch a pair of giggling trade show models slash coders multiple cups of tea in his own office, then he was clearly in a malleable mood — but I rather wanted the comforting, boring familiarity of my own apartment. I also would have preferred not to be on the emotional hook for yet another outlandish expense from James.

"Home sweet home it is," I muttered to myself, and then had to brainstorm how I was going to get there without risking running into my neighbours while dressed up as a girl.

I was at James' office door a few minutes later.

"Alex!" he said, when I pushed it open, but I silenced him with a raised finger.

"I'm going out," I said, "for maybe half an hour, but I'll be back. Do *not* leave before then; we have to talk, James."

And I turned and left without another word, catching a satisfying glimpse of his expression on the way out.

There was a retail park just down the road from us, and it wasn't long before I was headed back to the office with a few bags of tracksuit bottoms, a t-shirt, an oversized hoodie, a pair of trainers in size 8, a pair of thick walking socks to pad them out, and (crucially) a large woolly hat. I'd gone to the most upscale store in the park, and in deference to the way I was dressed and the voice I was still using, I'd shopped in the women's department. It wasn't the most pleasant experience: the whole time I was there I was waiting for the hand on my arm, the quiet word in my ear, the security guard leading me out to the car park for the crime of shopping while crossdressed, but the whole process was ultimately uneventful.

Cheekily, I paid with the company credit card, to which I was developing a Gollum-like attachment. I decided, though, that this didn't count as a favour from James; making the walk home without twisting my ankle in heels was definitely a work expense.

I stopped in the lobby for a few minutes, to walk in circles and lecture myself. James was up there and I had to face him, for real, for the first time since the elevator, without the support of Emily or the cushion of the carefree persona I'd slipped into while I was with her.

Breathe, Alex.

I found him sat at my desk in the main office, with a bottle in front of him and two glasses already poured. He smiled as I approached. I dumped the bags, sat opposite, and deliberately pushed away the drink that was meant for me.

He said nothing. It's possible he was getting smarter.

"James," I said, sounding as tired as I felt. But then his eyebrows creased, and that was enough to explode my calm. "James, what the *fuck?*"

"Alex—"

It all burst out of me. "What *was* that, back in the elevator? I was just *standing* there, I was psyching myself up to talk to Emily, to spend *hours* with someone who had *no idea* who I really am, and you— you— you fucking *tease* me, you throw in my face that I'm— that I'm a fucking— Oh God, oh Christ, oh *shit,* James! How *could* you?" I had to clamp down on myself for a second, hugging myself around the belly, squeezing off the breaths that had started to turn into ugly, heaving gasps. I think, perhaps, the stress was getting to me a little.

"I wasn't trying to tease you," James said. "I just... forgot. How you were dressed. What was going on." His voice was as calm as I wanted mine to be. Aspirational arsehole.

"*How could you forget?*" It came out at a high pitch and almost as a single word. I hugged myself more tightly, tried to force myself to calm down. All the fear, all the stress, all the panic, all the consequences were all hitting me at once, and his stupid placid face and his stupid reasonable demeanour were causing *awful* things to bubble up inside me, things which wanted to force their way out as screams, as wild accusations, as random acts of violence more likely to injure me than damage anything or anyone I might happen to unleash myself on. I loosened my grip on my belly so I could bloody well breathe, and crossed my ankles. *Breathe, Alex,* I insisted, inside my head, over and over again. It'd been a long time since I'd felt so out of control; almost a decade, maybe, in the run-up to my parents' divorce. "I don't understand how you could just forget," I said, between wheezing breaths. "*I* can't."

"Alex, you're *not* okay," James said, reaching for me over the table. It took everything I had not to pick up the glass with his stupid peace-offering drink in it and throw it in his face.

117

He must have seen me twitch because he leaned back again and worried at his lip, his eyes locked on mine. It was, somehow, enough; his concern for me and his obvious distress broke through, and I felt the heat recede from my limbs.

"Jesus," I commented, flopping forward. I unwrapped my hands from my waist just in time to catch my head before it hit the desk. I sat there for a moment, in an undoubtedly comical position, feeling faint, unsure as to what exactly had happened to me.

He leaned forward again, and this time I didn't flip out. "You're dizzy, aren't you?"

I didn't feel up to nodding, and I was pretty winded, so I formed one of the hands holding my head in place into a thumbs-up. Miraculously, I didn't collapse onto the desk, although it got a bit close.

James nodded. "I saved you a sandwich. I nipped out to get some while you were out with Ben, and I saved you one. It's in the fridge. Want me to get it? It's egg and cress."

I flashed him the dangerous thumbs-up again.

James had found a plate from somewhere, and when he presented the paper-wrapped sandwich, with its accompanying bottle of water and packet of crisps, I almost laughed. It was so *normal.* He put it all carefully down on the table in front of me, placed a steadying hand on my back and another on my shoulder, and slowly unlocked me, helped me lean back, took my weight until the seat could take it for me.

Another normal thing. I got like that sometimes, after long sessions at work. Not from stress or hysteria or whatever the hell that had been just now, but from forgetting to eat, from working too hard, from concentrating for too long. I'd get light-headed, I'd get dizzy, and he'd help me sit back, bring me food, and stay with me to make sure I didn't fall.

God, I really was too reliant on James. A good thing he was so reliant on me, too, or I might have felt guilty.

"I'm sorry," I said, trying to look up at him and failing.

"Eat your sandwich," he said, patting my back and letting me go, "and don't think for a second that you have anything to apologise for." He rounded the desk and flopped back down in his chair, stared at me for a moment with the strangest look on his face, then downed the contents of the glass in front of him.

I took a few bites of my sandwich while I waited for him to tick over to whatever he was going to say next.

"Alex," he said, after a while, "I'm sorry. I have excuses, and you can probably guess them, but, in the elevator, I... Fuck. I said I forgot, but that's a lie. A stupid, self-serving lie. And I'm sorry for that, too. The truth is, I was feeling guilty as hell. I wanted to reassure myself that you were still *you*. If that makes sense. And I picked the worst possible time to do it. Probably the worst way to do it, too. I'm sorry, Alex. I'm sorry for being a dick, and I'm sorry for forcing you into all this. I feel like I'm making you become another person." He looked miserable enough that I couldn't find any pleasure in his obvious guilt about making me into his fun Barbie project.

"I'm not becoming another person," I insisted, as much to persuade Girl Alex as James, "I'm still me."

"But that's it," he said. "You're different. And it's not the clothes. Or it's not *just* the clothes. You're more... more *something*, I don't know. I can't describe it."

"You called me a bitch," I said. I felt like we were heading in another direction, and I needed him to address it.

"Yeah," he said, not looking at me. "I was confused and defensive and prioritising my own shit over yours, and that was wrong of me, because your shit is, especially now, way bigger and *way* stinkier than mine." I snorted, and he added, "Metaphorically."

"Just what a girl wants to hear," I said, pointing at him with the remains of my egg and cress sandwich, "that her shit is the stinkiest in the office."

"Sorry," he said, allowing a grin onto his face for a moment. It died quickly. "But look, I *am* sorry. For everything, including calling you a bitch. I'm not that guy, you know? Not any more. But I used to be." He poured out another drink. "Before you knew me, when I was, like, fifteen or sixteen, I was a shit to girls. I was a bastard little kid, and I got away with it all the time. Well, a lot, anyway. Having a rich dad and being, uh, you know—"

"Ridiculously good-looking," I supplied.

"Um, yeah," he said. I would have expected him to agree with that more emphatically. "I'm not that guy any more. And I hate myself for calling you that. I'm still sorting out exactly why I said it, but I did, and it was inexcusable. Alex, I'm sorry."

"Okay," I said. "I get it." I hated to let him off the hook, but he *had* helped me calm down, he'd saved me a sandwich, and he was drowning in guilt. Ordinarily I'd assume he was milking it a little, but there was no chance of that: he looked nothing more than really fucking miserable. "But, you know, the way to not be 'that guy' is *not to be him*." I tried to ignore the irony of me, looking like I currently did, saying that. "If you're not that guy until a woman pisses you off — or someone who currently looks like a woman," I added, belatedly, "then you pretty much still are that guy."

He nodded, and I didn't want to push it any more; if he hadn't got the message now, he never would. But I thought he had.

He poured another drink and took a sip — which surprised me because his demeanour led me to expect him to down it again — and set the glass down heavily on the table. I took the opportunity to reach forward and take his hand. He didn't flinch like I expected, which was interesting; he was starting to get used to me. To *this* me. I squeezed his hand, trying to reassure him that, while he *had* fucked up, he hadn't fucked up terminally. I wasn't going to be one of those girls who left her handbag at his place and never came back for it. Well, not yet, anyway.

'Not that guy'... It made me wonder how well I really knew him. I set a reminder in my head to email one of James' old girlfriends and ask if she left him amicably or if he lost his temper and hurt her or something. He'd met two of them through work, so they would still be in our directory; hopefully one of them would reply to me. I didn't think it likely he'd done anything to any of them, but I was beginning to understand that men show a different side of themselves to other men than they do to women, and he'd never, in all our time together, called Boy Alex anything on the scale of *bitch*. I could be charitable for now, but I wanted to be sure.

I put the thought out of my mind for now and returned to more present concerns. "Please just remember how hard this is for me," I said, squeezing his hand again. He looked so sheepish; surely his old girlfriends left because he worked too hard, right? *Shut up, Alex.* "I get that you didn't mean to upset me," I continued, a little too fast, "but I don't always have the space in my brain to sort through charitable explanations every time it *seems* like you're being a jerk." Okay. I had to let it out. "And you calling me a bitch? I think I understand what was going on with you, but you need to know: that's scary, James. I'm not just your employee—"

"—you're my *friend*—"

"—and right now I'm *also* a, um, a guy, dressed as a woman. I'm so vulnerable around you, it's ridiculous. Vulnerable to exposure and, well, physically vulnerable. I'm half your size, James, and I can't run in these things."

He looked like I'd just shot him. "...Shit," fell out of his mouth.

"James—"

"I'm... Shit. Alex. Shit." He held up his free hand, asking for time to put his thoughts together. "I'm ashamed to say," he said, hesitantly, "that I never thought of it like that. I mean, I go back and forth between seeing you as *Alex,* my friend — *not* just my employee — and as what you appear to be, right now, a woman. A fucking gorgeous one, I might add. The idea that you can be both at once — and more — has been something I've been chewing on, but I didn't think about... the unique ways you've been put at risk. That *I've* put you at risk." I could be both, 'and more'? What did he mean by *that?* "But, Alex, God, the thought of hurting you never crossed my mind... The idea that I could do it by accident, through carelessness, it's... it's *unacceptable.*" He took my hand in both of his, and waited for me to look him in the eye before continuing. "I will *never* hurt you again."

My breath caught in my throat. All I could do was nod.

"Alex?" he said softly.

"Yes?"

"That's a promise. I'll never hurt you again."

"I mean," I babbled, finding my voice again, "you didn't *hurt* me, you said something that was just kind of rude and maybe thoughtless but there's no reason to go blowing it up beyond—"

"I *hurt* you," he insisted. "And I'm sorry."

I shut myself up and nodded again, withdrawing, sitting back. He let me go only slightly reluctantly. To give my hands and particularly my unhelpful mouth something to do, I opened the bag of crisps. Prawn cocktail: he knew me well.

I offered him the bag and, true to his nature, he took three, and screwed up his nose in pretend horror as he tasted them.

"Hmm," he said, "I prefer the ones from Waitrose."

"Snob," I accused, finding a smile.

"Peasant," he replied, grinning.

We finished the bag together.

"Oh yeah," I remembered, "what was with calling me 'Miss Brewer' the whole time with Emily?"

"I thought it would help you stay in character," he said ruefully. "I got a text from Ben that was like, 'Help her,' which really added to the guilt. It was all I could think of."

"Okay," I said, "but it was kind of weird. I'm just Alex. Just me. Okay?"

"Okay," he said, broadening his smile, "Alex." Then he blinked and squinted at me, like I'd just shone a 200-watt bulb in his face. "God, Alex, look at you! How are you *doing* this?"

"You're the one who put me up to it," I said testily. Huh, 'testily'; I wondered if the word had the same origin as the name for the things that were currently shoved up inside my body, feeling vaguely hot and uncomfortable. I tried not to laugh.

"Yes, I know, but I thought you'd look, you know, *good enough.*"

"Thanks," I said. The sarcasm seemed to wound him.

"I mean, good enough to pass for, you know, a girl, a pretty girl, especially with Ben's help, but— but you're *gorgeous!*" It seemed important to him that I know this about myself.

"Thank you," I said, sincerely this time. Whatever the motivation and whatever the reason, it was a nice thing for him to say. "Look, about that," I added, "there's some stuff I don't quite understand."

"What sort of stuff?"

"I know why we need a second model—" even in my head I didn't use the term 'booth babe' any more; no matter how satisfyingly disparaging it was when I applied to myself, it didn't seem right to use it for Emily, "— and I know why we didn't ask your cousin Sophie to do it — she would literally murder you just for suggesting it, and I'm not sure how good a saleswoman she'd be, anyway — and none of the other women you know will talk to you ever again, or you wouldn't have a drawer of their stuff in your bedroom that they've never asked for." Unable quite to dispel the thought from earlier, I watched for a reaction from him as I said that; none was apparent. "So, even though it is *completely absurd,* I understand why you asked me. But I don't know how you knew I'd turn out to be good at this! I was just— I *am* just a... a fucking *guy,* James!"

He shrugged. "You don't go on Facebook much, do you? Your mum has you tagged in pictures from a school play." I groaned. Of course: fucking Facebook. He continued, "You looked really good, and in the other photos from back then you don't look much different to how you normally look these days, so... I was pretty sure it would work out."

"Fine." Not fine. "Still, though, me working the trade show is one thing. But the hair? The personal shopper from Harvey Nichols? You're laying out a lot of money on this, and I don't understand why you didn't just allocate that money to modelling in the first place. I'm sure we could've got someone even at short notice, if you'd told me you were willing to spend."

"I got swept up in the panic of it all," James said. "Emily Swan called and, suddenly—" he clapped his hands together, "—we were *out of time.* Ben suggested extensions so you wouldn't have to deal with the wig all weekend, which sounded like a good idea, so I okayed it. And then he suggested the personal shopper to expedite things, and to have someone in the loop who really understood women's fashion, and *that* sounded like a good idea, so I okayed it." He sighed and finished his drink. "It was easy to agree to it all. We wanted you ready as quickly as possible. And we wanted you safe and comfortable. And I checked, you know, yesterday afternoon, in my apartment, while you were getting ready: even for all the money in our accounts there were no models available at such short notice. Whatever magic you worked to book three girls from Hammond's, I couldn't repeat it. We were out of time. It was you or no-one." He looked away. "It was always you or no-one."

I felt like I needed some support at that point, so I reached forward and retrieved the glass he'd poured for me. It warmed my throat as I sipped it.

We sat quietly for a moment. I wished I knew what he was thinking.

"About the money," I said. "It feels a little foolish? To spend that kind of cash, I mean. With the company at such a crossroads. *Especially* on someone who isn't going to have a use for all this stuff inside a week."

He finally looked at me again. "Alex, you've seen the numbers. You *know* a thousand pounds here or there won't make a difference to this company. The stakes are so much higher than that; if we fail, it won't be because the balance sheet has an expense on it that's less than it costs to set up a desk and computer for a single employee."

"I suppose," I said. "It's... this is all so weird." I was saying that a lot, but it was true.

"I mean, yeah," James said. "I didn't think you'd go for it, to be honest. I hoped, but—"

"We both know I'm an idiot," I said. "But I mean..." I couldn't bring myself to say, 'I feel like your dress-up doll.' "I feel like you're enjoying this a bit too much. Enjoying playing around with me, I mean."

"I won't pretend it hasn't been fun," he said. "You've always been so buttoned up. Quiet. Kind of sad. I've been a bit worried about you." I tried not to boggle at that; it was news to me. "Watching you come out of your shell has been... motivating. At the restaurant, and after, in my apartment, you were like a different person. And today! With Emily Swan! You were magnificent!"

"I was terrified," I protested.

"Until you weren't. In the restaurant. Today. You're tense to start with and then you relax into it and then—" he waved his empty glass around as he searched for the right word, "—then it's like you've been this person all your life."

I wanted to tell him I never stopped being scared, but it wasn't true. Yes, my anxiety spiked when I had to do anything I hadn't done before, but, every time, as soon as I'd gotten over my initial fear of discovery, the fear evaporated. In the restaurant and with Emily. It had been strangely normal, both times, chatting, working; normal enough that I'd been able to relax and get on with it. And a string of other random people — Uber drivers, shop assistants, waitstaff — who had also responded well to me each added a tiny bit of reinforcement to my confidence. I wasn't quite at the point where I could walk up to a stranger and know for sure how they would read me, but that level of certainty didn't seem far off.

With the terror of being found out gone, the times I'd been most scared were when I was alone with James, but not because of him; because of the way I was responding to him. The way I *kept* responding to him. The way I was responding to him *right now*. With my anger boiled away and with the warmth of alcohol settling on my stomach, something of what I'd felt last night was coming back to me. I'd leaned forward in my chair — farther forward than I'd needed to just to fetch my drink — and James had leaned in again, too. We were closer, sitting on opposite sides of the desk, than we'd been in the restaurant, sitting across the table from each other.

I realised with a shock that the whole time I'd been thinking, I'd been looking at his lips.

"I won't keep pushing you to do all this if you're not comfortable with it," he said. "The hair and the clothes and everything. Like I said before, we can stop at any time." He smiled. I drank it in. "I just wanted you to have some fun."

My eyes left his face and tracked down his upper body. God, I *really* wanted to have some fun. I could just reach across the table and—

God fucking dammit, Alex Brewer! Who the hell are you lately?

I pushed my chair away and stood up, shaking my head to try to clear it.

"I'm going to get changed and go home," I said.

I think it must have looked to James like I was angry again, or maybe scared. I wasn't; I was merely giving myself emotional whiplash. He stood up and took a step around the desk, at first looking like he was going to try to touch me and then visibly deciding against it, stepping back again, dropping his hands to his side and carefully standing very neutrally. His expression was difficult for me to read.

"I'm sorry," he said again.

I wanted him to stop apologising, so before I thought about it too hard, I walked up and hugged him. It took a moment for him to hug me back, but when he did the pressure of his arms around me was wonderful.

"It's okay," I said. "I'm managing. I think... I think getting it all out just now really helped. So thank you. And you're going to *keep* helping me, aren't you?" I prompted, looking up at him. Even in my heels, I still had to look up at him; maddening.

He looked down. Our faces were so close that his breath made my lips tingle. "I promise," he said, sounding hoarse. "Anything you need."

He still looked kind of sad, so I leaned up and kissed him on the cheek. It felt different from when I kissed Ben. I lingered for a second and then, quickly, cheeks red, eyes now directed firmly away from him, I escaped with my carrier bag to get changed for the walk home.

* * *

I was magnetically drawn to James. There was no arguing with it any more. The best thing for my peace of mind, therefore, was to escape from the bathroom directly down the back stairs to the street. I texted him when I was safely away from temptation.

Alex: I'm walking home. Could use the exercise! I'll see you in the morning. Where are we meeting again?

The reply came *very* quickly. I wondered if he had me open in the app and saw my typing indicator.

James: At the office. Ben will do you up once you're here. He said the rest of it's at my apartment, already in suitcases, so I'll bring it with me, go get the dresses from the tailor, and meet you back there. I've got a car booked to take us to Birmingham.

Alex: Okay. See you in the morning then!

James: You sure you're okay walking in those boots?

Alex: No. That's why I bought new shoes. Actually, YOU bought me new shoes.

James: I bought you new shoes? Again?

Alex: You didn't see the bags I dragged in when I got back?

James: Oh. Are they sexy?

Alex: They're trainers, James.

James: Ah. Are they sexy?

Alex: Calm down.

James: :3

Alex: Don't use that emoji. Bosses aren't allowed to use that emoji. It's too enigmatic.

James: I'm :3ing in my capacity as your friend, not your boss.

Alex: Noted.

James: It's a long walk back to yours, and it's a nippy night. You sure you don't want to stay over at mine again?

I stopped walking, brought up short by the thought.

I'd stripped off all traces of Girl Alex in the bathroom, swapped skirt and boots for jogging trousers and trainers, and glared at myself in the mirror with my hoodie and woolly hat on, hair extensions hidden, makeup washed off, to try to fix in my mind the idea that she was gone for now, that it was just me. I felt somehow diminished, and unsteady on my feet. I'd had to sit on a toilet until I regained my composure.

Now that it was just me again, a proposal from James to stay the night at his place ought to have been significantly less enticing, and it was, kind of. But there was another part of me — the part that was tempted as hell and didn't see anything wrong with that — that didn't want James to see me like *this*. Not yet.

If he saw me like this, it might break the spell.

Alex: It's fine. The walk will help me clear my head, and I'd like to sleep in my BED, not on your sofa.

His next reply, his last for the night, took a long time to come.

James: Okay. Be safe. Call me if you need ANYTHING.

I stared at my phone screen for quite a while.

I walked on. It was quite cold, but I liked it. I was still a little warm inside from the alcohol, and I needed a good buffeting from the wind to help me think clearly. I let it pass through me; I unzipped my hoodie and let it chill me to the bone. I'd be like those Scandinavian guys who go out naked in the snow and then leap into a hot bath, although in my case it'd be a shower with a towel around my head because Ben had told me not to wash my hair yet.

I checked to make sure there was no-one around, and temporarily switched back to my old voice, just to hear it. Except, just like this morning, it came out as a strangled adolescent warble. I shrugged; it was probably a good thing that it wasn't so easy for me to switch my voice back. I'd have to practise talking normally again for a day or two when this was all over.

I made it back to my block without incident, nodded at rather than greeted the few people I saw hanging around, and locked my front door gratefully behind me. It'd been only a little more than a day since I'd last been home, but it felt like a lifetime.

My flat was essentially one room to live in and one room to wash in, with a cupboard and bookshelf in the small hall that connected the two. Before I forgot, I extracted the Harvey Nichols outfit from the carrier bags and hung it up in its component pieces in my wardrobe. I didn't want to imagine how Ben would react if I just slung it all in the corner in a plastic bag. I peeled the boobs off my chest and wiped them clean. I laid the handbag and underwear and boobs out on my table and tried not to look at it all.

The hot shower I'd been dreaming of was calling to me. I undressed and threw my jogging stuff on the bed, but left the hat on. I planned to wrap a towel around it so the extensions could have two layers of protection while I washed.

But the bathroom mirror caught me, trapped me as I was stepping naked into the shower. It was positioned over the sink and thus only showed me from the chest up, and I looked... strange. I shouldn't have; I'd been looking at this body, unchanged in most fundamental aspects, for years, and even if my eyes never normally lingered on it, it should have held no surprises. It shouldn't have rattled me like this.

I looked like someone had loaded me into Photoshop and fucked around with the proportions. Or like I was a long-dead actor being revived with computers for a franchise movie. I was the same as always, and I was *wrong*. I felt like if I punched the glass and shattered it and dug through the shards I might find in one of them a reflection that looked right.

I didn't know myself.

No. That was ridiculous! I was just tired. Tired and stressed and emotional and indulging unfamiliar thoughts. I was the same person I'd always been; the same *man*. Nothing had changed.

I faced myself, and it had never been so hard to do.

Slowly, very, very slowly, I reached up and pulled off the hat, dropping it carelessly into the empty bath. My hair tumbled out from under it, coming to rest around my shoulders. I finger-combed it, gently shaping it until it didn't look quite so messy.

Still not right.

I felt like I was fighting against myself, like I had only so long I could keep this up before the dizziness took me, so I obeyed any instinct that seemed like it might help. I grabbed the bath towel off the railing and wrapped it around my chest, tying it at the front, and as soon as I did so it was like my vision cleared. Like I was at the optician, trying out lenses, and they'd just switched me to the correct one.

It still took a few seconds for me to stabilise, and I gave myself that time, breathing deeply, watching my chest rise and fall under the towel. Then, moving as if in a trance, I left the bathroom, walked carefully over to my kitchen table, and rummaged in my handbag until I found the lipstick Ben stuffed in there.

I returned to the mirror and swiped it over my lips, colouring them the just-deeper-than-natural shade Ben picked out for me.

I lost control at the last moment. The lipstick clattered into the sink.

A minute or an hour or a year later I came back to myself. In the mirror I saw eyes wet and red, saw tear trails on my cheeks. I looked down and found I was leaning on the sink with both arms, supporting my entire weight on it. Suddenly afraid I'd break the thing, I let go, and glared at myself.

I wiped the colour off my lips with my forearm, tore the towel from my chest and threw it on the floor, and looked again, daring myself to react. And I did. Oh, I fucking did: with blood hissing in my ears the dizziness and the vertigo came back and they claimed me, pulled me backwards onto the tiled floor. I barely caught myself in time with my elbows and landed awkwardly on my side, taking most of the weight of the fall on my hip.

Fuck. That was going to leave a hell of a bruise.

What the hell was going on with me?

Be practical, Alex.

Questions could come later. For now, I scooped up the towel from the floor and hung it over the mirror, which left me free to relieve myself, wash my hands and face, brush my teeth, and rush out of the bathroom. Even though I was completely alone, I felt exposed in my nakedness, so I redressed in the joggers and hoodie and dove into the bed. I pulled the covers over my head, the vision of my broken body burned into me.

In the dark, it was just me and her.

The night before, I'd asked myself what I wanted. Tonight, I asked *her*. I got nothing coherent in response.

I could guess: she wanted James.

There was no denying that I was attracted to him, in a way that was completely new for me. And not just new with James; new with anyone. Last week we'd been working until late together, sharing the office, talking, eating takeout, and it had all been quite ordinary, but now just being close to him electrically charged my body. I had to force myself to walk away from him. I had a physical need for him I'd never felt around anyone before.

And all that had changed was the girl stuff.

That shouldn't have been possible! As much as I'd tried to pretend that Girl Alex was a separate personality, she was me, through and through, top to toe, just playing a role; pretending to lock her away in my head until I needed her was nothing more than trying to hide some of my wants and needs from myself, was calling them illegitimate, invalid; fake.

But it didn't matter that some of those wants and needs were new to me. It didn't change that they were *mine*. I had to face her — face myself — and ask, honestly, what I was, and what I wanted.

What I wanted was James. What I was, seemingly, was... bisexual?

So, why now? Was it really just that the girl stuff brought something out of me that had always been inside? Had I always had feelings for him but interpreted them as admiration and gratitude? I was starting to wonder if I could trust my own memory.

I wrapped myself in my duvet, luxuriating in the stored body heat that was finally radiating back to me. I put aside all my questions and made it simple for myself: I tried to imagine kissing James. I pictured him in his apartment, lounging on his couch, pictured myself walking over to him, taking him by the hand and kissing him. It was... empty. In my head, he was unresponsive, and I was barely there: a ghostly presence in my own mind.

When had I been most attracted to him? Most *aware* of him?

Suddenly I was there, I was back in the office, with him in his damnable Marks & Sparks smart casuals and me in the skirt, top and boots I'd worn today. He was in his office; I was walking up to the door. He smiled as he saw me, a warm, anticipatory smile that pulled me in. We met.

We embraced. I stood in front of him, elevated enough by my heels that I had to stretch only a little to reach him.

He put one arm around my shoulder while the other stroked my spine, and the way his fingers compressed the fabric of my top, so that it amplified his attentions across my back in a ripple of silk, was more than enough to galvanise me into action. I met his eyes, grabbed the hand that was on my shoulder and pulled it down, encouraging him to caress me as we went, until I'd guided it to my bottom. I hopped a couple of times, with the tip of my tongue held cheekily between my teeth, and he got the idea and raised me up just enough for me to kiss him. I felt his lips part, felt his tongue against mine. I could feel his body in every point of contact between us.

He gripped my bottom harder, lifted me, turned me so he could place me on his desk, knocking documents and oddments aside so I could sit unimpeded. With my hands free, I wriggled them under his t-shirt and raised it up over his head, letting it linger when it covered his face. I kissed him through the fabric, giggling at his helplessness. He took over from me, pulling the t-shirt the rest of the way off and tossing it aside, and then did the same with my top. We kissed again and I buried my fingers in his hair. He found the waistband of my skirt and slipped his hand under it as I clasped my fingers together behind his head. My legs parted to allow him closer, skirt riding up until it sat on my hips, and he pressed himself to me. I felt my breasts compress against his chest and his hands find my crotch and, finally, alone in my bed, eyes closed, heart racing, I reached down and let him touch me.

Chapter Six

Nightmares tied my duvet in a knot.

I woke, clinging to my pillow, still half in dreams, chased through mistily remembered classrooms and offices, shedding clothes as I ran but somehow still moving too slowly, tearing my skin away in wet clumps to make myself lighter, smaller. Finally I made it to my cold, dark apartment, and with barely controlled panic I shut and locked the door against my formless pursuer and collapsed into my bed, breathing hard, drenched with sweat, legs trapped in my sheets, alone, awake.

My phone, blinking darkly at me from its charging mat, informed me it was 3:51am.

The jogging bottoms and hoodie were plastered to my skin. I felt filthy.

* * *

I couldn't bring myself to get changed before I walked to work.

I'd never arrived at the office before 6am before. Sure, James and I worked overnight pretty often, especially when we were coming down to the wire on a project. It was how we'd got the latest one done, actually: with two desks pulled together and a mountain of takeout between us, huddled around the light from our computer screens like campers around a bonfire, night after night. One time, he made the comparison explicit, distracting me from a bit of code that was making my brain hurt by pulling out everything needed for s'mores. We melted them with his fancy lighter — one thing I always felt explained James very nicely is that he, a lifelong non-smoker, kept an expensive, filigreed metal lighter in his pocket all through university, solely to impress girls who asked him for a light — and tried feeding them to each other on impromptu s'more skewers (pencils). It didn't go well: he poked me several times, and I got more marshmallow on my chin and upper lip than in my mouth, which James found terribly funny for some reason.

I flushed as I remembered him reaching forward and wiping melted sugar off my face with his finger, an action that I'm sure felt very different at the time than it did now, looking back.

Anyway, my point: I might have practically camped out in the office on multiple occasions, but when it came to ordinary workdays, I had firm(ish) boundaries that started at 8:30am and included something caffeinated.

I unlocked the main door and stamped inside, hauling my ratty suitcase after me. The suitcase was mostly empty, apart from yesterday's outfit, carefully folded, and all the other accessories of womanhood that had been forced onto me. The plan was for Ben, when he arrived at probably a much more sensible hour, to fill it with my 'real' luggage; I wouldn't be needing my regular clothes on this trip, after all.

The mini-gym in the office basement also housed an even mini-er laundry room and a changing room with, crucially, a shower; I wanted nothing more than to wash off the sweat of a shameful, confusing night, in an environment that wouldn't (with any luck) do anything more strange to my head than was already happening. I headed down to the basement, hoping to find it as empty as six in the morning suggested it would be, and was glad to find I hadn't misremembered the presence of a small box of disposable shower caps with a post-it attached declaring them 'free use'.

I dumped all my crap by the treadmill, stripped, wrapped myself hurriedly in one of the branded robes that were always hanging just outside the shower room, and threw last night's sweaty clothes and the tucking knickers in the washer dryer. I stuck it on 'refresh', a setting I'd never seen anywhere else that claimed to utilise a quick wash and a spin cycle (with an RPM that rocked the building on its foundations) to deliver fresh and reasonably dry clothes in just thirty minutes. I'd always assumed it was intended for the executive in a hurry who'd slept in their work clothes, but perhaps the designers had spared a thought for the needs of panicked amateur crossdressers, too. That done, I stepped into the shower.

The hot water didn't have the invigorating effect I'd been counting on. I still felt enervated after a night of bad dreams and body horror and whatever the hell that'd been in my bathroom, and I realised that if I didn't make some sort of peace with it I'd have nothing but rough nights ahead of me, so I decided to be a bloody adult about it and ignore it all. Whenever I felt the wheels of introspection turning in my head, I would deliberately redirect them; I couldn't afford to be a mess today or at any point over the long weekend, and I knew myself well enough to know that once I got started thinking about something unpleasant, I'd have trouble stopping. Best to not start in the first place.

So I was attracted to James. So what? Plenty of people are bisexual, and I'd apparently joined their ranks. Everything else — the ramifications that my crush on him suggested might be impending for our friendship and my job, and the downright strange feelings I'd been having whenever I looked in a mirror, dressed up or not — could wait until I had the time to dedicate a good solid couple of days to going completely to pieces over them.

Finally, the mood boost I'd been looking for!

I hopped out of the shower a good deal more refreshed and optimistic than I probably had any right to be, wrapped myself in towels, threw the robe back on, and settled down to wait for my clothes to be done.

* * *

Putting on the bra and popping in the boobs was becoming routine, even with the extra step of glueing the bloody tits to my chest. I was also (reluctantly) getting used to applying the dreadful tucking knickers to my long-suffering undercarriage (reach down, push *back* with your middle finger and *up* with the fingers either side, and then pull up your underwear quickly with your other hand before your junk works out what you're trying to do to it). Unfortunately, even with my genitals jacked right up into my subconscious, I couldn't wear the new bum pads with my jogging trousers, and the old bum pads, the ones I hated but which worked with everything, were presumably still at James' place, so I felt top-heavy as I headed up to the office. I examined myself in the semi-reflective elevator walls and confirmed that, yes, horror of horrors, I had a flat butt. At least my clothes and underwear were fresh from the washer dryer (and only slightly damp) and would keep me warm until the heating clicked on at 8am.

My next task was also my biggest challenge: makeup. I wanted to learn how to do it for myself. Yes, Ben was perfectly capable of making me pretty, but he'd likely get here after James, and... I didn't want James to see a man when he looked at me. The thought of it made me wriggle with discomfort, which made no sense whatsoever — he'd known me for years, and I'd been a man the whole time (well, a boy, really; even at nineteen I struggled to identify with *man* because it never seemed right for me, like I hadn't earned it) — but the idea was in my brain and there was no point pretending it wasn't. Yes, it was a bit weird, but I wasn't going to think too hard about it until after the expo. The fallout was for Future Alex to deal with; I, Girl Alex, owed it to him to make it that far without losing my shit.

With all the complicated emotional stuff safely packed away in a box, stapled tightly shut and saved for later, I was free to focus on the practical: if I wanted James to find me attractive, if I wanted him to see me as a woman— God, that was almost as hard a word to claim as *man;* where was all this shame even coming from? *Later,* Alex. Put it in the box and start again.

James needed to see me as a woman.

Ben wouldn't be here until later.

Therefore:

I needed to make *myself* look like a woman.

Which meant I needed to learn how to apply makeup.

And then James would catch his breath when he looked at me, like he did that first day, like he did again in the lobby.

I emptied my bag out onto the desk, but all I had on me was the makeup I went home with last night: lip gloss and a powder compact. I'd thought there was more, but I must have been thinking of my old handbag, the one I'd had in the restaurant. Shit. Well, there was a local solution, if I was bold enough to try it.

Was I?

Yeah. I was. For James, and for the look in his eyes, I was.

I stuffed everything back in my bag, checked the time — coming up to 7am — and headed back downstairs to the mini-gym to check myself out in the full-length mirror.

Not bad!

With the boobs on under the hoodie I had sufficient curves even without the bum pads that I didn't think anyone would look twice at me. Yes, I had a flat butt, but I could hardly have been the first woman to lack a bit of shape. The biggest question was my face. I'd applied some lip gloss in the elevator down, but there was nothing particularly transformative about that; I could still see *me,* the face I'd known my whole life, peeking out from under all the hair. I honestly couldn't tell if I looked different enough just from the hair and the body shape, or if I would elicit comment the moment I stepped out onto the street.

"Oh, hey," said a voice, at which I'm pretty sure I didn't jump. A guy I vaguely recognised as working somewhere else in the building was standing at the entrance to the shower area, an outer layer of shed gym clothes in his hand. "You done?" he asked.

"Huh?" I said, winning a handful more prizes for my intelligence and quick wit.

He pointed past me to the cubicles. None of the basement facilities were split by sex, which I remembered with a start at the exact same moment I realised why that was a good thing for me: it meant I couldn't be caught coming out of the 'wrong' cubicle, no matter how I looked at the time.

"Are you done with the showers?" he said.

"Um, yes," I said. "I'm just on my way out."

He dumped his hoodie on the bench and took off his t-shirt, exposing a chest lightly dusted with hair and, like the rest of him, shiny with sweat. He was more slender than James but still very nicely built, and I caught his smile at about the same time he caught me looking.

Wow, Alex. Come out to yourself as bi and suddenly you start ogling every half-naked man you encounter? Granted, this one basically popped up right in front of me, but I'd thought I had a *little* more self-control than that!

"I'm Vikram," he said, holding out a hand. "I work at Williamson's, on the fourth floor." Some kind of consultancy outfit, I thought. Education, maybe? "Are you new?"

Yes, Alex, are *you new?* "Yes," I said, trying to sound self-assured and like I wasn't scrambling for a grip on this conversation. "At McCain." I took his hand and let him shake mine; he did that firm handshake thing I was so bad at.

"Ah, the software people," he said.

"That's us."

"What's your name?"

"Alex," I replied, without thinking. Shit. Would he remember me? We hadn't exactly talked a lot.

"Hi, Alex," he said, finishing the handshake. He was still smiling, so I decided I got away with it. "I hope I see you here again."

I smiled at him in return and escaped the basement, forever grateful to my parents for choosing a name that was plausibly unisex, as if they knew I would turn out to be a massive dumbass.

* * *

I made it to the retail park shortly after it opened, and after a few minutes' confused browsing in the cosmetics aisle I gave up on trying to find direct substitutes for the products I remembered Ben using on me. So I picked up a makeup gift set and a tube of liquid foundation that I colour-matched against the back of my hand, the way I was fairly sure you were supposed to. The girl behind the counter treated me with the bored indifference I always hoped for from people who worked in shops (I hated when it seemed like they were happy to see me; I knew from experience it meant their bosses were forcing them to act that way, and it was impossibly tiring to keep that up all day) and I was back at the office minutes later.

I'd been tempted to nip to the department store and pick up a nicer outfit, so James' first glimpse of me wouldn't be in the hoodie and jogging trousers, but I shelved the idea: I didn't have all that much time to try to make myself look nice, and I could well imagine the precious minutes I'd waste having a crisis of confidence over some skirt or pair of shoes.

Remembering the YouTube tutorials I'd found before, I dug them out of my search history, but I couldn't really see how the techniques they demonstrated could apply to my own personal face, so I kept looking until I found someone who not only explained every step clearly and carefully but took ten minutes at the start of the video to go through all the tools one might or might not have access to, and the proper care thereof. The only thing I didn't have was primer, but I figured I could cope without and, after a few attempts — there was a travel bottle of cleanser and some cotton pads in my handbag, thank God, or Ben — I decided I was good e-fucking-nough. I even managed some rudimentary wings with the eyeliner pencil and a ruler, and resisted the temptation to rub them into smudges out of embarrassment long enough for me to forget they were there.

Ben could, and inevitably would, redo me at the hotel, anyway, when I had to put on that awful garish dress I was trying not to think about, so I figured I didn't have to be perfect; I merely had to silence the voice in my head that panicked about James seeing me the 'wrong' way.

I was just berating myself for not having bought some nice clothes after all, when the office door opened and James walked in.

I couldn't help but smile when I saw him, but the short period between him coming in through the office front door and him noticing me, sat at my desk, grinning at him like an idiot, was one of the most nerve-racking handful of seconds I'd ever experienced. We'd made up yesterday evening, sure, but I'd all but run out of the office immediately after we hugged. He could very well have been in a mood with me.

He wasn't. He answered my smile with one of his own, and dropped the cases he was towing as I almost ran over to him. And because I was done pretending I didn't want him, I hugged him with all the enthusiasm I had inside me. Screw reticence: let him interpret my actions as he wished. When he returned the hug I tightened my grip, pleased and a little excited that he accepted my embrace so readily.

I let myself believe, for as long as we held each other, that he wanted me like I wanted him, and it warmed me.

"Hi, Alex," he said. "You feeling okay this morning?"

I was right. He'd been worrying about me. "Yes," I said.

He must have sensed something in my voice, though, because he asked, "You sure?"

"I had a difficult night," I admitted, and was pleased we were still hugging because it hid my frown as I remembered, "and a bit of a difficult morning, but..."

My pause, which I spent releasing him from the hug, relieving him of some of his bags and lugging them over to the desk in the corner we'd earmarked for expo crap, was clearly enough to spark concern. "But...?" he prompted.

I hoisted myself up on the desk, dangling my legs over the edge and remembering the fantasy I'd had about him the night before — *his hands on me, raising me up, entering me* — which I'm sure showed in my ever-present, ever-revealing, ever-irritating blush. At least my dick was securely tucked back and couldn't embarrass me further by, say, becoming inappropriately erect at the thought of him touching me that way.

"I decided to change my attitude," I said. "You were right: I'm having fun. And, yes, it's scary sometimes, and, yes, it's knocking my head about a bit. But you know what?" My speech slowed as I realised that what I was about to say was not only the absolute truth, it was probably the reason for the difficulties I'd been having that weren't just about coming to see that James was, objectively, subjectively, and under my grabby little hands, fucking *hot.* "I was fighting against it. Against the fact that I'm actually okay with it. That it's *fun* to look like this, to play this role. God," I added, "it was consuming me, and I wasn't even worrying about what it 'means' that I'm enjoying myself; I was worrying *about* worrying about what that means. You know? The thought so scary you don't even want to think it, so you don't, except you don't stop thinking about the fact that you're not thinking about it." I'd been twirling my index fingers around each other, trying to illustrate circular reasoning, and in the face of his confused frown I raised one of them to my temple and twirled it there instead. "I've been an idiot," I clarified. "I've decided to stop being an idiot and have some fun."

James' smile, now that I'd stoppered the direct connection between my disorganised thoughts and my mouth and could thus no longer disrupt his mood with unmitigated idiocy, was wonderful to see. "Good," he said. "Because I've been worrying that—"

"Don't," I interrupted. "You agreed to make this easy for me—" I hopped off the desk, fetched my handbag, and walked over to him to briefly take the first few fingers of his hand and squeeze them, "—which I *really* appreciate. Just don't do anything that'll make me regret this," I added, letting him go. "Want some coffee?"

"Oh," he said, "um, sure?" He blinked at me for a moment before adding, "I got new pods. Look in the orange bag."

I followed his pointing finger to one of the bags I'd dumped in the corner, found and cracked open the multipack, and started the machine.

"How do I look, by the way?" I asked, as it did its thing. "I know, jogging clothes and all that, but I did my own makeup this morning, so... how do I look?" I couldn't resist posing.

He took his sweet time answering me, but I resisted the urge to beat it out of him, and eventually the warring expressions on his face coalesced into the broadest smile I'd seen on him all morning.

"Really good," he said. "Like, *really* good."

I beamed at him.

* * *

It was just like old times. We lounged around the office in a terribly unprofessional way, drinking coffee, chatting about nothing, enjoying each other's company. James sat with his legs propped up on box files, and I reclined next to him in the only office chair that went back all the way (which was his; I always stole it from his office at times like this, and he always complained and let me take it anyway). All that was different was that this time I'd cheekily propped one of my legs on top of his, just above the ankles. He didn't comment, so I had no idea what he thought of it, but the small, hot point of contact seemed slowly to be gathering all my spare nerve endings into itself; it was hard to think about anything else. Unless I looked at his face, which was distractingly lovely.

Incredible how much I'd changed in such a short time. And it wasn't the physical stuff, not really. The boobs, the makeup, the hair and even the voice were all new to me, yes, but I was used to all of them by now. The boobs were almost ignorable; the makeup was just a reason not to touch my face too much; the hair was all gathered up in a clasp because it'd gotten fluffy from the moisture in the air; the voice was second nature. What had really changed was *me;* it was like I'd never felt things so deeply, with such vibrancy or urgency. I needed him and I needed him *now,* and nothing else mattered.

142

At least we were touching. Skin against skin. I luxuriated in the sensation.

Sometime shortly before nine, while we were being sensible adults and actually discussing our floor strategy — correction: I was being sensible and James was making horny comments about how tight the expo dresses were; I told him I'd kick him if he said anything like that in front of Emily, and he just grinned at me — Ben arrived, stumbling through the office door with all the grace and poise of someone who was, spiritually, still in bed. He was towing a couple of huge suitcases behind him, and I felt a little guilty that I'd had to lug only one, and one that was mostly empty, at that. Mind you, I was probably also the only one of us who'd walked in.

We both waved at him.

"Why do you two look so disgustingly relaxed?" he said. "Are you aware of the time?"

"It's not *that* early," James said lazily. "It's, like, nine."

"Yes, James," Ben said, glaring at him. "It *is* 'like' nine." He didn't do the finger quotes because he had his hands full, but I heard them anyway. "Have you picked up the dresses from the tailor yet?"

"Fuck," James said. "I'd better go."

I lifted my leg off of his, to let him out. As he left, he ran his hand along the back of my chair, casually, just to steady himself; the way his fingers brushed against the back of my neck was definitely a coincidence. I watched him leave and, feeling self-conscious, covered the smile on my face by holding up a hand and fake-coughing into it.

If Ben saw through my deception, he graciously didn't say. Instead he asked, "Alex, why is your hair up?"

I undid the clasp and let it fall as it chose. "Went fluffy," I explained.

"Oh my god."

* * *

Ben wanted me to dress nice for the journey up to Birmingham, so I demonstrated for him what I thought a death by explosive blood clot (brought on by inadvisably fashionable clothing) might look like. I told him how much it would cost to have the rental car cleaned afterwards and suggested James might take it out of his fee. He finally got the message when my (mimed) blood spurts reached his face, and relented, reluctantly packing away the skirt and boots he'd intended for me. The jeans he provided were not actually all that comfortable, but they were relatively loose and thus less likely to fatally injure me.

He compensated with a pretty but alarmingly low-cut white top, which somehow managed to keep the aftermarket nature of my breasts a secret, and a loose tweed jacket that looked a bit home counties on the hangar but worked surprisingly well once it was on me. I got to keep my trainers, after I took them off and made him compare the softness of the sole to the shoes he favoured, and his complaints about the colour were, I thought, mostly token. He swapped out my handbag for a larger, cross-body affair in black, with more pockets. I approved.

The bathroom down the hall from the office didn't have a full-length mirror, so I had to stand on a suitcase to inspect myself. I looked good, if perhaps a little angular, despite the boobs and the butt padding, which I put down to the close-fitted jacket. I said as much when we got back to the office.

"Thin is in," he said, fussing at me, tweaking the fabric at the elbows and directing me to pose, which I did with a grin and a thrill, "and you're *ever so*. If you haven't got it, flaunt it!"

"You don't think it makes me look—" and I don't know why I dropped to a whisper for this, but I did, "—like a *boy?*"

He laughed at me — rude! — and declined to comment further. I decided to read reassurance into it and let him drag me to a chair so he could fix my hair.

"I saw you two together, you know," he said, brushing and spraying. "Sitting there. On top of each other. *Touching*. And that bullshitty fake cough you did to hide the way you were drooling over him? Fooling *no-one*."

"I know," I said, wincing as he pulled on some of the real hairs at the nape of my neck, "and if you want to say what I think you want to say, you can say it."

"You won't get mad?"

I sighed. "I like James," I said. "And, yes, that means I like him *that* way. I don't know why, because I've never liked guys before, but I like him." He grinned and nudged me. "God, I *really* like him…"

He paused in the act of mutilating my head to hug me, carefully, around the shoulders. "Aw!" he said. "My little baby gay!"

"Baby *bi*," I insisted.

"Uh huh. What made you realise, in the end?"

I shrugged. "Lots of little things. I can't stop thinking about him. When he's in the room, I can't stop looking at him. When I dream, I dream about him. Oh, *fuck—*" I giggled nervously, "—do I dream about him. And earlier? When we were talking? He made the worst joke, just the shittiest joke you've ever heard, and before I knew it, I was laughing. Like, throwing-my-head-back laughing."

"Yeah," he said, nodding, "you've got it bad."

"I even leaned forward and touched his hand," I added, demonstrating. "I felt a bit silly after, but he didn't react like it was strange or unwelcome, so neither did I, and before I knew it, it felt natural. Maybe it's the dresses. Maybe when I quit wearing them, all this will stop." Wordlessly, Ben pointed at my jeans; I retaliated by pointing at my hair. One-nil to Alex. "But," I continued, "I doubt it." I smiled, dipping back a couple of days in my memory. "I know when it started. I know ex-*actly* when it started."

"Oh?"

"Two nights ago. When you dressed me up for the first time. My brain was already doing cartwheels, and I was preoccupied with learning the voice and then *keeping* the voice—"

"You're doing great, by the way."

"Thanks. So I was flustered and nervous and feeling a little silly and then *he* came back and *you* said, uh…"

"Something obscene about his dick, I think," Ben put in when I trailed off.

"Right. But before that, before you sent him off to get dry, he just... Ben, he *looked* at me. Like, really looked at me. And it was like everything that was spinning around inside me calmed down, right at that instant. And then I started blushing, and you were very rude, and he went off, and you said he was horny for me, and then we were talking and it all went away... but that was it. That was the spark." I leaned back in the chair and earned a light whack on the shoulder for taking the back of my head out of range. "The spark that started the fire that kept burning until it consumed me, last night."

"She writes code *and* poetry!"

I rolled my eyes; it's not like I had room for lyrical English skills *and* all that anxiety in my brain. "No-one's ever looked at me like that before. I didn't know what I was missing before. It didn't sink in immediately, though; I kept insisting to myself I was a straight guy. Kept finding reasons to explain it all away."

He poked me. "We've all been there."

In appreciation, I poked him back.

"So, you've really only been attracted to him these last two days?"

"Well..." I considered it. "I guess it's always been easy for him to get me to do stuff."

"'Stuff'?" I could hear the leer in his voice.

"Work stuff! You know, stay late, work on extra projects, that sort of thing. He brought me on as a favour, Ben, because our families know each other and I was kind of adrift, but then I got pretty good pretty quick, and we started working together a lot." I frowned. "I never resented the long hours because it was time I got to spend with him."

Ben tapped me on the head. "Kinda slow, aren't you?"

"Very slow," I agreed. "But then, I'm not educated like you. Actually, speaking of, you were at uni with him, right?"

He turned a wary look on me. "Yes?"

146

"I know he's not, you know, into guys, but... how hard and fast is that?"

"You mean," Ben said, "is he maybe into 'guys' like you?" I nodded, ignoring the ironic finger-quotes. "Not as far as I've ever seen, no." I tried very hard not to sag in the chair. "Not in an overt way, and not in a painfully obviously closeted way like you were, either. And he had *ample* opportunity; as you can imagine, when we went out together, guys would approach him. He turned them all down, even when he was single. He's *definitely* straight. But," he added, and I was hanging so pathetically on his every word that I perked up, "don't forget that he responded to *you* the other night. Not to just any guy, but very specifically *you.*"

I swallowed, unable to get my heart rate under control. "What do you think that means?"

"Honestly? I don't know. I *do* know he's been obsessing over you, ever since that night at the restaurant, which he insisted on telling me all about, in *great* detail, I might add." I raised my eyebrows: 'obsessing'? "You know," Ben continued, and he switched into a bad impression of James' voice, "'Do you think she'll be safe at the expo? Do you really think hair extensions will be more comfortable for him? I really pissed her off today; what do you think I should do?' God, it's been endless. Yesterday afternoon, especially. And yes, he keeps flipping pronouns; I don't know what to make of *that* at all. It's not him being enlightened; he's spent more time around queer people than your average guy, thanks to yours truly, but he still never really *got* the whole fluidity of gender thing. In *that* he is most definitely a normal straight man: 'Gender hard, sex easy; put penis in now?'"

I closed my eyes and concentrated on my breathing (and on my breasts, moving up and down in my bra). Ben's monologue had taken me on a journey, and I needed time to process it, even though it was absurd; there was no chance James was into me, was there? Surely it'd be obvious?

The tucking knickers worked extra hard for a few moments, and I shifted uncomfortably, hoping my undercarriage would pop into a configuration that didn't pinch quite so much. It didn't.

"So, um, you think I might have a chance?" I asked.

Ben frowned, thoughtful. "A week ago, I'd've said no way. But now... anything's possible."

* * *

There's no experience quite like your first ten steps after a two-hour car journey. Your first are wobbly and uncertain as your spine has to rediscover that you possess muscles below the waist; the next few steps are sore and tingly as your heart overcompensates and pumps out all the stale blood that had been sitting, unused, in your feet, and replaces it with fresh new exciting blood at perhaps twice the rate that would be wise; and the final few steps are downright dangerous as your brain finally catches up with the situation and gets mad about all the blood and oxygen it used to have. After that, if you're still upright, you're basically fine, and nothing else the day can throw at you will be a challenge at all.

So I hoped, anyway. I still had to climb into a show-floor dress I'd seen only on computer screens, and wear it in front of hundreds of people.

Birmingham was refreshingly dry compared to London. I walked a full circle around the ugly fountain out front of the hotel, stretching my legs and enjoying the way I wasn't getting rained on just for being outside.

Ben had added a second suitcase to the one I'd brought from home, and made dark enough threats about its contents that I had a horrible suspicion it contained more than just the Harvey Nicks haul. I'd have to wait to get to my hotel room to discover what horrors he had in store for me, though, because we'd travelled up with the two engineers who'd be helping us out on the show floor, and they either didn't remember me — to be fair to them, we'd only met once before, and I haven't always been a very memorable person — or were too polite to mention the boobs I'd grown; whichever it was, I didn't feel comfortable talking about dresses and tucking in front of them.

One advantage of being McCain Applied Computing's resident woman — at least for the purposes of this trip — was that Ankit ("Kit, please.") and Marcus, the engineers, insisted I be relieved of any responsibility for lugging our kit around or setting it up, so they got to go on ahead to the venue in the minivan with all the heavy stuff and my responsibilities were reduced to just picking up all our room cards from the hotel staff.

Which is when I discovered the problem.

I waved James and Ben over when they came trotting in, trailing their own luggage. I'd staked out a corner of the lobby where it looked like we wouldn't be overheard.

I had my serious face on, so James shelved all the stupid comments he'd undoubtedly been saving up, and asked, "What is it?"

"We only have three hotel rooms between us," I said. "We had six before." I spread the room cards out on the table like they were a winning hand in poker.

James' face fell. "Oh, fuck," he said. "This is my fault. I cancelled some of the rooms the other day, when we lost those two models and swapped in Ben instead of my cousin. I must have forgotten to verify how many rooms we had to start with."

I nodded, following the logic. "I'd planned to spread the three models across a single and a twin, but I get why you cancelled two rooms, if you were thinking two models equals two rooms. Why cancel Ben's, though?"

"I thought Ben and I could room together, like old times," he said, looking sheepish.

"That's sweet," Ben said, attempting to pinch James' cheek and getting fended off. "Dumb, but sweet."

"Okay," I said, tapping at the room keys, "let's think this through. We have three rooms, six people. I think it goes without saying that Emily gets her own room." They both nodded. "So, she gets the single. It's the smallest, but she won't have to share." I pushed her card away from the other two. "Which leaves us five people to spread between two rooms."

"Maybe you should have a room to yourself," James suggested.

"Lovely thought," I said, "but that would leave *four* adults in one room. It'd be uncomfortable as hell and the hotel would throw a fit if they found out. Fire regs, probably. And do *you* want to explain to Kit and Marcus why you're sharing a room with them when you're the CEO?" I resisted the urge to smack some sense into him.

"What size rooms do we have left?" Ben asked.

"A twin and a double," I said. "The twin has two queen-sized beds; the double, one king-size."

"I assume they have sofas or comfy chairs that could accommodate someone reasonably well," James mused, and I nodded; this was quite a pricey hotel, and the rooms were likely to be fully kitted out. "Clearly, you—" he pointed at me, "—need to be roomed away from both the engineers and Emily because none of them know you're not a real woman."

"Yes, and..." I started to reply, continuing from the thought I'd expected James to express, and then my mouth caught up with the rest of me and I stopped dead.

I heard Ben gasp, but if either of them said anything after that, it was lost in the static.

He's right, Alex: you're not a real woman, are you?

My knees buckled and I got top-heavy, the way I sometimes do when I'm getting overwhelmed, so before the shakes and the unpleasant noises set in, I grabbed the card for the double room off the table and ran for the elevator. God must have been looking down on me in that moment because, just as I approached, the doors opened and a woman in her late middle-age emerged, blinking slowly at me. She stepped aside to let me past but blocked the doors from closing with her body.

"Are you okay, dear?" she asked.

I had enough presence of mind to nod. "I just need to lie down," I said. I well and truly had the shakes by this point, and it gave my voice vibrato. I had no idea why James' words cut me so deeply, but they had, and all I could do now was get somewhere safe. I willed the old woman to leave, to let me go, to let me run.

"I'll be in the main bar if you need to talk to anyone," the woman said, smiling at me and patting me on the shoulder. Then she stepped away and the lift doors closed.

My reflection in the mirrored elevator walls watched me with wide and moistening eyes. It told me that I looked for all the world like an attractive young woman who'd just received some bad news. But that was a lie, wasn't it? I was a lie. A fake. A costume for the weekend, with the hair, the makeup, the tits, the voice, all of it just a convenience, part of a stupid confluence of coincidences that had put me here, in this lie, so we could sell some fucking software.

When I got to the room, I collapsed onto the bed and disappeared for a while.

* * *

"Alex?"

Ugh. That fucking name. I was starting to hate the sound of it. Grudgingly I opened my eyes. It took me a moment to orient myself: I was in one of our hotel rooms, the one with the king-size bed, which I'd thrown myself onto with all the violence I could muster. I'd had enough presence of mind to tuck an arm under my head, so at least I hadn't stained the bedsheets with the makeup I'd cried off.

God, I really had *cried,* hadn't I? My head was fucking pounding.

Ben had a gentle hand on my leg. He looked like he could wait all day for me, but I knew we didn't have time, so I sniffed — which sounded disgusting — and sat myself up.

"Hi, Ben," I said. "I know, I know; this isn't the time to have hysterics. I'm fucking things up, aren't I?"

"No," he said, "you're not. *Absolutely* not. Look, Kit and Marcus are getting the stand set up, Emily's already there, and I sent James over after her to, one, deal with anything else that needs dealing with and, two, stop him from hovering outside your hotel room door like an anxious bloody honeybee. The show floor doesn't open for more than two hours. You have time."

I shrugged, gathering myself up on the bed, knees under my chin. I wanted to make myself small. "Time for what? I don't know what I'm *doing*, Ben! I don't *know* why I'm so upset."

He stroked my cheekbone with his thumb. "I have an idea about why," he said.

I looked at him, almost afraid to ask. But what more could this weekend do to me, really? How much more could I change?

"Tell me," I said.

"This is more than dressing up for you, isn't it?" he said. "And it's more than realising you're attracted to men."

"I don't know what you mean," I mumbled, into my knees. I really didn't! "Maybe?" What else was there?

Ben shuffled up on the mattress until he was sitting next to me, and took one of my hands in his, prying it away from its vice grip on my shin. His hands were slightly larger than mine, and I flushed as I realised how much I liked being held the way he was holding me. Maybe if James didn't want me, Ben might—

"Alex..." he said.

"Sorry," I said, ashamed of my thoughts. He shouldn't be anyone's second choice. He was sweet, thoughtful, thoroughly beautiful... I turned away from him, rested my cheek on my knee and wished to disappear. "Sorry," I said again, and put into that word all the trouble I'd caused him.

"Shush. Take a moment. Sit with your thoughts."

"I don't *like* my thoughts."

He snorted. "Then talk to me instead! Tell me why it upset you so much when James said... what he said."

I closed my eyes. I was grateful to him for censoring; even the echo of the words made my chest hurt. "I'm not sure," I said. "It felt... *insulting*. Like he was judging me. And... it felt like hearing that *should* hurt me." With my free hand, I pounded on my leg a couple of times until he caught that one, too, and held me still. "It makes no sense. Because he's right. I'm not... you know, I'm not *real*."

"Oh, Alex," he whispered, "you're real. I promise."

It was my turn to snort; I'd never felt real in my life. Not until...

Not until James looked at me. And that was the crux of it, wasn't it?

I took deep breaths, and I thought:

What did I know? I knew I was into James. And I knew James was straight. Straight enough that living with a drag queen for years, spending a lot of his social time in gay spaces and having a lot of gay friends hadn't made him so much as consider experimenting with men. So, James? He liked women. And however much he might be fooled into seeing me as a woman right now, and be attracted to me on that basis, he *knew* what I was, and that therefore we had no future except as friends. Maybe he'd said it to remind himself, to clear his own head, to reestablish the borders of his sexuality in a way that firmly excluded me, no matter my mode of dress. He would never, could never, be mine.

That had to be it. It hurt enough to be it. Since Ben and I talked, back in the office, I'd so latched onto the idea that James might be into me that the reminder that he couldn't be was painful enough to make me lose it.

They say your first crush is the most intense, and I'd never been into someone like I was into James. I was starting to wonder if I'd ever truly been into anyone at all before him. Everything felt so new. So raw.

"Alex?" Ben asked quietly.

Now, it seemed like Ben was implying I was transgender. 'This is more than dressing up' was not a subtle hint, and neither were the times he'd tried — largely unsuccessfully — to educate me on transgender terminology. But I wasn't transgender, I was sure. I was... what was the word? Cis. I was cis. Cisgender. I'd run across the word online a few times since Ben introduced me to it, but a few clicks had led me to a heated argument over whether it stood for 'comfortable in skin', and I'd hurriedly returned to my makeup tutorial videos.

I chewed on it for a bit. The whole concept sounded kind of silly; no-one's *really* comfortable in their skin.

Still, after everything Ben had done for me — was still doing for me — I owed it to him to at least consider the idea. It was true that I found the whole business of looking like and being treated as a woman surprisingly comfortable, once I'd gotten past my initial terror, but I'd seen some stuff online about transgender people, and the thing with them was, they *knew*. It was practically their defining characteristic! Transgender children and young teenagers were in the news all the time, kids who knew when they were, well, kids. I was *nineteen*. If I was like them, I'd know by now; of that I was completely certain. I'd be consumed by the need to— to— to do whatever the term for officially switching genders was; get a sex change?

I didn't hate my body; I didn't like it. I didn't think about it much at all, except when forced to; when washing it, for example, or when forcing it into tight dresses and horrible tucking underwear. If I were transgender, I'd *care* more, surely?

"I think what it says about me," I said, raising my head again and feeling more confident about my conclusions all the time, "is that James is straight and I am *not* dealing well with that."

"You're sure that's all it is?" Ben asked.

"I'm sure," I said. "I know what you're getting at, but... it's not that. I'm bi, I'm into James, he's not into me, and processing all that is messing with my equilibrium." I emptied my lungs; I felt better already. "That's all!"

The very idea that I could be transgender was ridiculous. That I considered it even for a moment was just me being my usual suggestible self; like last night, alone in my shitty little flat, exhausted and stressed out and practically seeing things. Ben had put the idea in my head, my subconscious had run with it, and before I knew it, I was freaking out at my own reflection. I did stuff like that sometimes; I was a panicker.

This all started when I put on a dress for the first time, stepped briefly into a *very* different life, and confused the shit out of myself; it could happen to anyone. 'Never felt real in my life'? What nonsense! I was *fine*.

"I think you need to talk about this," Ben said.

"Thanks," I replied, "but I'm okay, and we really do need to get moving. I've got to get cleaned up, get dressed, get my face on, and get to the expo in time." I was feeling foolish for my overreaction now, and wanted to be *doing something,* not wasting more time talking about things that had been resolved to my satisfaction.

"Don't push yourself too hard, Alex. You can afford to take a little time."

"Ben," I said, "I can't leave Emily down there alone. Oh, and don't say anything about this to James, please."

He frowned. "Are you sure?"

"I'm sure," I said. I'd spent the last couple of days falling down a very peculiar rabbit hole, but now that I'd had a chance to, as it were, assess my velocity, take note of the boundaries of the warren and plan my exit, I was feeling a lot more optimistic about my future. I'd keep going, but it'd be best if I didn't come to any grand conclusions about my identity while I was still tumbling.

It was time to assert some boundaries in my head. I could have fun this weekend, sure, but that's all it was: a bit of fun, a chance to play at being someone totally different from myself. And I'd get home Sunday night, strip all this off, sleep like the dead, take Monday off because fuck going into work after a weekend like this, and I'd be back to normal.

"Alex, I don't think—"

"I'll talk to James myself. Don't worry! I just need to relax, and I'll get through this without going mad, and without driving the rest of you mad, too. If there really *is* anything to think about afterwards, and I *don't* think there will be—" Ben looked like he wanted to interrupt me, so I raised my voice and steamrollered him, "—then I'll think about it next week, in the comfort of my own home."

"I'm worried about you," Ben said.

"Don't be," I said. "Please. I got carried away, that's all. That happens with me sometimes."

He looked sceptical.

* * *

I was profoundly grateful to my past self for taking the time to go through the sample dress images and select one that wasn't too showy and wasn't too revealing. At the time, I hadn't wanted our company to look like it was run by horny teenage boys; nor had I wanted to lumber the models with anything too uncomfortable. Of course, this was before I knew exactly what 'uncomfortable' meant when it came to wearing a dress. If I could have five minutes alone with Past Me, I'd probably have suggested something that wasn't quite so tight around the waist, right before I told him to run for his life.

The dress was bright blue with yellow accents — the company colours — and while it did have a knee-length skirt, something I'd requested specifically, it also had a three-inch slit I wasn't particularly happy about. It covered my shoulders but not my arms, and the neckline was fairly high. Overall, it wasn't too bad. If you took a photo in indirect light, so you couldn't tell how weirdly shiny it was, and desaturated the colours and cropped out the company logo on the chest, it could pass for an extremely tacky church dress.

I felt very silly, but at least you couldn't see my thighs unless I sat down. It wasn't even the most revealing thing I'd worn out; that prize went to the ice queen getup.

Still strange to see myself like this.

"You're good?" Ben said. I think he was standing off to one side specifically so I couldn't see him in the mirror, so I could properly and without distractions absorb the full effect. It was working; the particular shade of blue we used was so vibrant it was giving me a headache.

"I'm good," I said. Ben had worked his usual magic with my hair and face. I looked less like my normal self than I had even after doing my own makeup, which helped when it came to getting into character.

"Good," Ben said, nodding. He pulled a long black coat from the depths of one of the suitcases. God bless him (again), it was calf-length and modest and when I put it on I looked like a femme fatale in her I-definitely-didn't-murder-him outfit. He gave me one last once-over, tidied away a couple of stray hairs, checked himself in the mirror — "Immaculate!" — and together we rushed out to catch an Uber.

* * *

The convention hall was much larger than I'd imagined. I'd seen the specs when I was organising all this, and I'd even had a visualisation up on the computer back at the office so I could approve the design of our booth, but in person (and in dress) it was quite something else. Ben and I walked past companies that had whole wings to themselves, and even though it was these very companies James wanted to court, I started to feel nervous about our place in all this. Would we even be noticeable next to these huge names?

McCain Applied Computing's spot was in a maze of booths in the small vendors section of the hall, next to a couple of companies I'd never heard of (and who I highly doubted had ever heard of us). We weren't the only ones to have models, either, which was a relief; in the Uber over I'd entertained a fear that Emily and I would be the only girls dressed like idiots on the show floor, but the two women standing at the booth next to ours were dressed as stewardesses, complete with jaunty little hats.

Hats! Drat! *We* should have had hats!

Next time.

Emily and the stewardesses were chatting, and she waved at me when she spotted us coming. Unlike me, she looked fantastic in our branded dress, but then, she was the model and I was the... me. Her wave seemed to summon James from wherever he'd been lurking behind our booth. Yeah, he looked worried; I was going to have to deal with him.

When we were close enough, Emily called my name. I joined her and the other two models at the intersection of our booth and theirs. Ben, thankfully, intercepted James and they started a whispered conversation on the other side of our booth.

"This is Martina and Kristen," Emily said, indicating the stewardesses, "and this is Alex. Alex here is a veteran; she's been modelling for... how long now?"

I could spot a prompt when I saw one. I looked at a non-existent watch on my wrist, and said, "At least forty-eight hours."

It got a polite laugh, which was enough for me. I exchanged smiles with Kristen and Martina, and briefly covered Emily's hand with mine when she grasped my upper arm in greeting.

"I love the coat," she said.

"Ben gave it to me," I said. "I had no idea he had it; I think he's trying to save me some embarrassment."

"Is it working?" Emily asked as I shucked it off, revealing myself to be just as ridiculously dressed underneath as she was.

"No," I said, and grimaced.

"You look fine," she whispered.

"Thanks. Oh," I added, "did you get your room key?"

"Yes, from Ben," she said, nodding. "He's really sweet, isn't he?"

"Yeah, he's— oops."

James had extricated himself from Ben and was coming over. "Alex," he said gravely, "do you have a moment?"

I nodded. As we walked to a spot where we could have some limited privacy, I heard Emily say to the stewardesses, "He's her boss, and they have *history*..."

"Before you apologise," I whispered to James when I was sure we were out of earshot, "I want you to know you don't need to."

"I'm still sorry," James said quietly.

"I think, maybe, that I'm still getting acclimatised to this," I said, careful to choose words that wouldn't be revealing if we were overheard. "I panicked, that's all. Ben helped me put my head back on."

He looked relieved. "I thought I'd really upset you."

I gave him a friendly punch on the arm. "I'm good," I insisted. "It was a blip. I'm over it."

"Sure?"

"Sure," I said. "Shall we sell some software?"

"Definitely," he said, grinning.

Together we headed back round to the front of the booth. I rejoined Emily, who was leafing through her pile of printed materials.

"All good?" she said. I nodded. "Great, because the doors open in two minutes."

I squared my shoulders, smoothed down my dress, and looked out across the show floor. The bigger booths were pretty quiet, but most of the smaller companies like ours were still a flurry of activity as people rushed to make last-minute preparations. I put on my lanyard, smiled at Kristen and Martina, who were adjusting their stewardess hats (of which I was still extremely jealous), and fixed my eye on the countdown clock hanging from the ceiling in the centre of the conference hall.

You can do this, I told myself. *You'll be fine. Play your role, have some fun, and then go home and never think about this ever again.*

Show time!

Chapter Seven

I got used to being out on the show floor pretty quickly. Yes, it could be boring, especially when the others at my booth were busy and I had no-one to talk to. And, yes, it could be creepy, when a guy stood too close to me and brushed his hand against my arm. But mostly it was quite fun. There were times when I felt unexpectedly glamorous, standing there in my silly dress, selling our software, posing for pictures (although we seemed to be slightly less photographed than Kristen and Martina, the stewardesses next door, for which I was thankful). And being admired by men, I had to admit, was nice. Provided they kept their distance.

Emily told me I was lucky my first modelling experience was on a relatively quiet day; Friday at the expo was a closed session, with the only attendees being representatives from other companies and a few select journalists. Saturday, when the doors opened to the public, was likely to be crazy.

She looked after me a lot, which was how I was able to enjoy myself at all. She'd whisper reassurances to me in quiet moments, she'd swap jokes with me, and occasionally she'd help me out in ways I didn't even know I needed, not until after the fact.

I got tired as the day rolled on — I might have gotten used to walking in heels by this point, but standing in them for hours on end was still a challenge — and took a break a few hours in, sitting myself down on one of the stools we had at the side of the booth. I'd not been resting for more than twenty seconds when a man approached me, came specifically for me, even though I was deliberately quite out of the way. But before he got close, Emily inserted herself between us, smiled, asked him his name and which organisation he represented, and guided him so subtly over to the other side of the booth I didn't think he noticed he was being manipulated.

After he left, she explained. "If you're sitting down when guys come over," she said, "sometimes they take that as an opportunity to get closer to you, and especially to put their hands on your legs." I shuddered; I might, as I had discovered recently, like men, but that didn't mean I wanted just *any* of them touching me. Aside from the issue of consent, I'd been in men's toilets; I knew how many of them didn't wash their hands. "Oh, they *act* like it's all casual and friendly," Emily continued, rubbing my shoulder reassuringly, having seen the look that crossed my face as I recalled the horrors of having to share facilities with men, "but all they're doing is copping a feel. And if you call them out, they act all wounded and innocent, and then *that's* a whole thing you've got to deal with. But if you're standing, it's more formal; you get that distance. They have to be that much more of a creep to try anything."

"Thanks, Emily," I said. "I never expected to be in this position. It's all so new. And still kind of disorientating." I looked down at myself. "I mean, there's never having been so dressed up before, and there's never having been so *on show* before. I feel like I should buy a taser."

"They're illegal to own for private use," she said quietly, and I stared at her for a moment. She spotted me looking, realised I was wondering what could have happened to her that she felt she needed one, and added, "Oh, creative writing assignment at school. I looked it up. But if you find a loophole, buy one for me, too?"

"I will," I said, and we both laughed the kind of laugh that comes from released tension as much as from humour. The creepy guy was gone, and it was just *us* again. Despite the dress and the shoes, I felt comfortable.

"The important thing is to keep your distance. If they get handsy, yell for security! Or for Mr McCain, when he gets back," she added, nudging me. I chose to pretend I hadn't heard that last part. "I've seen him watching you, you know. Maybe you could give the poor, lovesick thing a break?"

Emily still believed James was into me, and while I would have loved to share that belief, I knew it wasn't possible. I'd started to harden against even the idea of it, to the point that when James spent the first half hour of the open floor hovering nearby, glaring at conventioneers and practically bodyguarding me, I asked him in my sternest voice for some space. He'd looked hurt — I made myself not care; he'd get over it — and sulked for a few minutes, then made some excuse and vanished.

But I couldn't be sharp with Emily the way I had been with James.

"I *gave* him a break," I said, shrugging, forcing indifference. "He left."

"Hmm," Emily commented, sounding remarkably like Ben. It suddenly occurred to me that the two of them had probably gossiped about me while Ben was doing her makeup, and the idea was distasteful; I resolved to find him later and insert both my high heels somewhere sensitive. "Anyway, as I was saying, keep your distance, and enforce it as much as you can. If you judge it safe to shake someone's hand, that's fine; if you judge it safe for someone to take a posed photo with you, even a selfie, that's fine. But *you* make the judgements. Take as much control of the interaction as you need. And if they cross the line, don't be afraid to ask for help, from me or the boys, or from security."

"Didn't you say they'll pull the innocent act?" I asked. "What if they make a fuss and drive people away? Or get us the wrong kind of attention?" I didn't want my insecurities, my failures, to cost us business.

"One," Emily said, holding up a finger right in front of my face, where I couldn't avoid looking at it, "your safety is more important than the product, and don't protest because you *know* your boss agrees."

"I don't know about that," I said wretchedly.

"That's what he told me," she said. "Explicitly." I harrumphed at her, and she smiled at me and continued. "So that's one. Two—" she incremented the number of fingers she was holding up by one, "—while I'd love to say that in the enlightened year of our lord 2019, most of these reps' bosses wouldn't want a whole Hash Me Too thing on their hands, *some* of them definitely wouldn't. So—" she dropped her raised fingers and poked me with them, "—don't be afraid to assert your boundaries."

I reviewed my objections, decided she was probably right, and withdrew them. "Thanks. That's actually super helpful." I squashed the urge to give her a hug; she was seriously big-sistering me, and as an only child it was blowing a lot of relays in my head. I gripped her hand in gratitude instead. "Hey," I added, struck suddenly by one of my periodic bouts of self-consciousness, "you really don't think I look silly?"

"You look great!" she said, for the ten-thousandth time.

As I said, I never really thought much about my body and my appearance before, but I still had a very clear view of how I looked, and of how people could be expected to respond to me, and not even the dress and the shoes and the horrible bloody underwear could countermand that for long; I kept periodically resetting to my default view of myself as a questionably presentable and visually unimpressive dork. And, though I'd gotten dressed up and been made to look pretty before, at no other time had I been surrounded by women who were professionals at getting dressed up and looking pretty; even with Emily, back in the office, I'd outglammed her by a factor of at least five, thanks to Ben. Here, she and I were dressed identically, except she was taller, prettier, more confident and overall *more real* than me, embodying a grace and poise that seemed so far beyond me as to be unreachable. I was an imposter, suddenly all too aware of my fake boobs and my padded hips and bum, of the form and feel of my body, of its ugly, shapeless maleness.

So I kept turning to her for reassurance, and I kept not quite believing her.

My dick chose that moment to complain about its entrapment, twanging a nerve in my scrotum and causing me to flinch. Another reminder of who I really was, under everything.

You're a fake, I told myself, in the relentless voice of self-hatred, the voice I couldn't ever silence because a part of me didn't *want* to silence it, because I deserved its opprobrium, because I knew it was right. *You're a fake and a liar and James will never love you the way he could love a real—*

"Alex," Emily said gently, breaking into my thoughts, protecting me from them. I wanted to push her away and almost did, not out of any animosity towards her but because, in that moment, the idea that anyone could understand how I felt was revolting. To understand how I felt would be to understand *me*, Alex, the scrawny boy under the façade, and I couldn't ever let that happen.

"Yeah?" I replied, sounding husky. I held myself very still.

"Are you okay?"

"Yeah."

She handed me a water bottle and I took a few swigs, imagined it flowing through me, cleansing me. "Don't drink too much," she said. "You don't want to bloat up your belly in a dress this tight; it gets uncomfortable."

"Thanks," I said, forcing a smile. She'd seen my distress clear as day. There was a time I'd considered myself a pretty buttoned-up guy, but either these last few days had changed things — very possible! — or I'd always been easily readable, like an educational toy to teach kids about the perils of insecurity. At least the water had helped get my voice back under control.

"Where did *that* come from?" Emily asked, taking my hand.

"Old stuff. I'll tell you some other time." When she came to work for us and saw me in my natural habitat, she'd learn everything anyway. It'd probably explain a lot. "I'm okay, now," I said. "I think."

"Well," Emily said, leaning in to whisper, "like I said, you look fantastic."

The voice inside me quieted some; I wished I could package Emily up and take her with me everywhere I went. "I still feel silly," I said, looking down at myself and experiencing another flash of revulsion — I could see my stupid angular body clearly through the dress so *how did no-one else see it?* — which I managed to turn into an almost real-sounding laugh.

"You look *great,*" she insisted, and I repeated her words inside me, held them close. "And—" she made a show of looking around the hall, "—when it comes down to it, we're dressed fairly normal. I mean, *look* at some of those outfits. You should thank whoever picked ours."

"Um, I picked them," I admitted. "I just never thought I'd end up wearing one."

"Then thank *you.* I guarantee you half the models here are jealous of us." She snorted. "You should see some of the stuff I've had to wear at other events; crazy outfits like out of a video game. A lot like cosplay, except cosplay is usually better made and easier to move in. Tell you what, when you take your break, get out of this corner we're stuck in and have a look at the other models, see what ridiculous shit they're stuck in. Especially the big companies. Lots of money often equals lots of stupid accessories to lose. And temporary tattoos of the logo."

"She's right," Martina said from the edge of her booth. "I'd kill to be on your stand right now. Do you know how hard it is to keep the seam straight on these effing stockings? Oops," she added, as a man approaching her booth waved for her attention.

I laughed, and it was genuine this time. "Thanks for keeping me from going crazy, Emily," I said.

"No problem," Emily said, smiling. "Are you okay to cover solo for fifteen minutes? I need to pee."

I felt recharged, so I shooed her away. "Go. Go! I'll be fine. I can always yell for Kit to rescue me if someone gets weird."

She flashed me a smile and disappeared in the direction of the maze of small rooms at the back of the convention hall. I watched her go — she really did look good in the dress, despite its obnoxious blueness — and fixed in my head the fact that if this ridiculously beautiful woman thought I looked perfectly okay, she was probably right.

You're fine, I told myself. *You're fine. You're just like everyone else here. You're just like everyone else here. You don't stand out. You* don't *stand out.* It seemed like a serviceable mantra, so I repeated it as I looked out over the intensifying crowds.

A minute or so later, a boy who didn't look much older than I was trotted up to our booth. He'd been reading our signage as he approached, rather than watching where he was going, and he almost collided with me.

"Hi," I said in my customer service voice, and he took several startled steps back. "Welcome to our stand. Is there anything you'd like to know about McCain Applied Computing or our products?"

"Um," he said, and took a full two seconds to recover. His blush would have been visible from space if we weren't indoors; you could likely have spotted it with one of those heat-mapping satellites anyway, if you knew where to look. Remembering what Emily said about controlling the interaction, I took a step forward, so we were only a metre apart, but knotted my hands in front of me, to establish that this was *my* space. I smiled at him, which only intensified his blush. I wasn't worried about this kid trying anything; if it came to it, I could probably have beaten him up myself without taking my shoes off first.

"Uh," he rallied, "I read your company's promotional post on, um, Reddit? And I was interested to learn more about your software."

And that was the other thing: boys like him, who I would normally count as peers, were dying of sheer nervousness just from being near me. It was, when I allowed myself to realise it, another reminder that I was not myself, not here, not any more. I was something else, someone else, and couldn't rely on old assumptions. I held onto that, too, held it with Emily's reassurances and Ben's confidence in me, and put it all into my smile.

"I'm Alex," I said, extending a hand. He took it limply and sort of waggled it. I deliberately didn't look down to see if his trousers tented; I deliberately also did not giggle at the thought of it. My crisis seemed years in the past already. "I wrote that post. I've also had a hand in the code for most of our projects, although—" I disengaged from the handshake and shook a warning finger in what I hoped was an obviously lighthearted manner, "—I can't give you a deep dive here on the show floor. What's your name?" I added, when his only response was to swallow.

"Harry," he said, after a good long pause. I put a small bet on his having needed some time to remember his name. "I— I write for Rayleigh's Journal."

Okay, *that* was impressive for someone so young. Rayleigh's Journal was quite a big fish in the picayune-technical-details pond: a former print magazine, now entirely online, catering to the kind of technology nerd who never needs an acronym explained in the same way salmon cater to bears.

"Would you like to speak with one of our engineers?" I said, looking around. Marcus was on his break, Kit was showing someone our only demo unit, and James was presumably schmoozing people elsewhere. "They're all engaged at the moment, but I'm sure someone will be available to talk to you soon." I wouldn't have bothered for a random blogger, would have told him to come back later, but I didn't want to risk losing access to Rayleigh's readership. I was kind of curious as to what they would say about our work anyway.

"I can wait," Harry said. "You have one of the more interesting software proposals on the floor today. Um, if it works."

I smiled again, enjoying the way his eyes widened slightly when I did so. "I can assure you it does," I said. "You need a particular type of screen, but it definitely works." I'd have shown him the selfies I'd taken with the screen and lens assembly we'd cobbled together to test it out, but I didn't have my phone with me, and — I winced as I remembered, hoping it didn't show — all the shots were of the old me, anyway. Not a good thing to show someone here.

"Then I'd love to see it," he said.

"Kit can show you when he's free," I said, "or Marcus, or Mr McCain if he comes back before anyone else is free." I decided to omit the inconvenient part of the truth: "I'd show you the selfies I took with it, but they're saved on my phone and I'm not allowed to have personal equipment on the show floor."

He swallowed. I realised I'd leaned towards him a little, as if sharing a scandalous secret, so I leaned back. A laugh I couldn't quite suppress bubbled out.

I glanced back again and noticed Kit had finished showing off the demo phone. I reached back and picked it up, unspooling the wire that tethered it to our booth.

"Here," I said, "why don't you have a look at the demo unit?"

It wouldn't pass as a modern phone even in low light — it was an older Samsung model from before they started doing the wraparound screens, and we'd hacked it apart to move the camera under the screen, so it was twice as thick as it should have been — but it worked well enough. I unlocked it and paged through a couple of apps, so he could see it working unimpeded, and then loaded up the camera software and handed it to him.

"Try and find the selfie camera," I suggested.

Puzzled, he covered the place where the camera hole used to be, at the top of the phone, but he could still see his face, partially obscured by his palm. He slowly moved his finger down the screen until he finally found it, just below the centre. He covered and uncovered it, over and over, squinting at the image on the screen, looking for defects. I knew he wouldn't find any; the implementation on our demo unit was carefully tuned.

"This is incredible," he said.

"Thanks!" I said.

He jumped. I don't think he'd realised I was watching over his shoulder. I took a step back and held out my hand. Reluctantly he gave the unit back to me, and I replaced it in its cradle.

"What was your name again?" he asked, biting his lip and then hurriedly retracting his teeth. I tried not to laugh again; I'd probably break his ego into a million bits. We were cut from similar cloth, but I'd never been as terrified of attractive women as he obviously was. Sure, they mostly hadn't been *interested* in me, but that was another thing entirely.

"Alex," I said, and he nodded. I'd realised shortly after talking to my first rep on the show floor that I was giving my real name to a whole lot of people who'd now seen (and photographed) me in a dress — James couldn't have engineered a more awkward situation if he'd tried — but I decided that on the remote chance any of them ever swung by the office, I could just nip out the back and down the fire escape, or put on a really big hat or something. Perfect. Flawless. Foolproof. With plans like that, I could have been a supervillain.

He couldn't find anything else to say and Kit was still unavailable, so to stop the silence becoming any more awkward than it already was, I asked him, "So, how did you come to work for Rayleigh's?" I was curious, anyway, and it was a safe topic; one of the things we hadn't had time for was briefing me on what level of disclosure was appropriate — Kit and Marcus had been fully briefed but they were also attending as their original genders, which left more of their morning free — and I didn't want to rely on common sense and guesswork. And, when it came right down to it, I *was* just a gopher; an assistant, not a real engineer.

"Oh," he said, "um." He sat on the syllable for a bit while he thought. "I'm still at uni, so I'm only submitting the occasional article. My old project supervisor is also an editor at Rayleigh's; he asked me to work for him." When he mentioned his supervisor a look of pure joy temporarily replaced the nervously neutral expression on his face. "Part time," he added. "He couldn't attend the expo this year, so he sent me."

Well, *that* was disturbingly like looking in a mirror (minus the university education and the sweatiness). An older man, a mentor, someone he admired, asked him to come work for him, probably worked him far more hours than he was contracted for, and eventually had him attend a trade show. I was half-tempted to warn the kid to run as fast as he could, lest his editor ever look at him with a smirk and a credit card and suggest he try wearing a dress, just for a change.

Actually, I realised, narrowing my eyes, Harry might have looked quite decent if he exfoliated and wore some foundation garments. His hair was already long enough, just about, and—

Alex Brewer, who have you even become?

We discussed his university project for a few minutes — he was working on an interesting idea to do with eliminating clipping artifacts in video games; not my field, but fascinating — and he came out of his shell a little. Yes, sure, his shell was definitely still there, and I could absolutely prompt a retreat back into it if I smiled at him too much, but he was doing pretty well!

Out of the corner of my eye I saw Kit finishing up with the man he was talking to, so I put a hand on Harry's shoulder — he jumped again, which was adorable — and made to guide him over.

"Oh, er," Harry said, blushing again, "before I go, could I get a selfie? I mean, one I can keep."

I laughed. "Sure!"

He dug his phone out of his pocket and held it up, framing us on the screen. I put on my best smile, stuck one arm around his shoulders and did the peace sign with my other hand for the hell of it. He snapped a couple and I let him go.

He thanked me profusely.

"Old technology, now," I said, indicating his phone.

It took a moment for him to get what I meant, and then he laughed far harder than the joke merited. Flatterer. "Um, yeah," he said.

"It was nice meeting you, Harry," I said. "Good luck at Rayleigh's."

I guided him over to Kit, made the introductions, patted him on the back, and returned to my position at the front of the stand, clamping down on my need to laugh as much as I could.

Being able to do that to guys was *fun*.

* * *

"Alex!" Emily hissed urgently as she walked up to me, her break over. "I just ran into Caitlyn from our agency, and they've got her dressed up like a sexy cop!"

"Oh my God. Can we see her from here?"

She pointed, I looked, and sure enough, when the crowds parted, I caught a glimpse of four cops at one of the larger booths in the mid-size section of the floor; except police uniforms weren't normally quite so shiny, and the skirts generally left more to the imagination.

"Holy shit," I said. We both laughed, and I felt grateful once again to Past Me for not fucking us over with ridiculously short dresses or midriff-revealing cutouts. "God, I just saw one of them have to tug her skirt down. I feel bad for laughing."

"Don't, seriously," Emily said. "At the last one of these, she got to wear jeans and I had to be a fucking *mermaid*."

"Oh no," I said, "with the tail and everything?" She nodded and I lowered my voice. "How did you *pee?*"

She shuddered. "They had to drop a curtain around the pedestal I was on, so it wouldn't 'break the illusion'—" air-quotes and an extremely derisive tone of voice, "—and I had to shimmy out of the bloody thing right up there and peg it out the back door. At least they let me wear leggings under it."

"Wow," I said.

"I haven't seen anything quite that egregious so far today. Which isn't to say there aren't some ugly bloody outfits. Check it out: over *there*—" she pointed, "—is a bunch of girls dressed in what I *think* is tin foil, with fairy wings, advertising something to do with... steering wheels? No, I have no idea what the connection is supposed to be. I think those women *there* are supposed to be some kind of strange plastic valkyrie army. And you can't see them from here but there's a booth with like a dozen women all in the same wig and coordinated makeup and they even have different size heels on to make them all the same height; it's *eerie*. Oh yeah, and whoever's done the outfits for *that* booth has a serious hard-on for platforms, look."

I looked and saw five women who were wearing relatively simple skirt-and-jacket outfits but with four- or five-inch platform boots that made my back ache just at the thought of wearing them. I wondered if it was supposed to symbolise something, like, *Our Software Stands Tall!* or, *Reach for Success!* or, *Our Boss is a Massive Perv!*

"God," I muttered, "there are *so* many sadists in trade show costume design."

Emily shrugged. "Sadists; straight men; what's the difference?"

"I will never complain about a simple blue dress ever again," I promised.

* * *

A short while later one of the big brands announced some demonstration event and almost instantly cleared out the entire convention hall as every rep, journo and blogger disappeared in the direction of their huge, garish booth. Kit and Marcus, with encouragement from Emily and me, followed; I wasn't particularly bothered about it as I'd never been as interested in finished products as I was in the building blocks, and I knew they'd come running back in a panic if they saw anything that could trump one of our projects. Besides, the prospect of milling around in a crowd while in this dress and playing this role did not appeal. I promised the boys I'd field all inquiries in their absence. I hadn't really thought about it — understandably, I think, since I was preoccupied with, e.g., the fake breasts I was wearing — but they'd been working pretty hard, too, and being able to give them a break to go dork out over something was quite satisfying. Marcus was so grateful he said he wanted to kiss me; I suggested he kiss Kit instead, and he did, on the hand.

It was adorable.

Emily and Martina took advantage of the lull and the lack of attention being paid to us to make me practise doing 'modelling poses' — which, I maintained, don't count as *real* modelling poses if you can't stop giggling and you lose your balance a couple of times — which all coincidentally involved one hand or other stretched out, the better to keep eager businessmen at minimum safe distance (and to wield any improvised weapons that came to hand). It didn't take long for the three of us to start messing around. We did more poses, egging each other on until we were being excessively silly; we used one of the neutered phones tethered to the

McCain booth to snap pictures of each other pulling all the stupid faces we couldn't pull with other people around; we complained about our bosses. It was fun, and I felt strangely like I belonged; a novel experience, outside the office.

I was in the middle of telling the (lightly edited) story of my first overnight stay at work — James had promised to join me but hadn't, and I'd had to keep myself warm under a pile of coats — when the bottom fell out of my world.

James was on his way back, and he was wearing his best suit.

Of course he was! He'd have made a presentation to a huge company or something, and he'd have wanted to make a good impression, so *of course* he would have worn his best suit. It was just a coincidence that it was the same charcoal suit, off-white shirt and maroon tie he'd worn in my dreams. The suit that had had a supporting role in the first real wet dream of my life. I felt my junk tense in its awful prison and I clenched my teeth in response.

He was walking back to our booth and chatting with Kristen as he came.

Of course he was! Kristen was beautiful. Kristen was funny and friendly. Kristen was dressed as a sexy stewardess with a sexy little hat. Kristen (probably) didn't have a dick. She was perfect for him.

And that was a good thing, I insisted to myself. James deserved to be with someone who could make him happy.

"Alex," Emily whispered quickly, "do you want to go on your break?"

I nodded vigorously. What was the point of pretending to Emily any more that I didn't have feelings for James? I'd stopped pretending to Ben; I'd stopped pretending to myself. Did it ultimately matter if everyone knew I was bi?

Just as long as James didn't find out.

"Go, go, go," Emily said, gently pushing me out of the booth in the opposite direction.

I almost staggered as I escaped in the direction of the women's staff loos. I was fairly sure James watched me go.

174

If I held my breath, glared at myself in the mirror and kicked the bottom of the sink with my foot, I could keep from crying and messing up my makeup. I didn't want to have to find Ben and get him to touch me up, because then I'd have to admit *why* I was so messed up, and I was pretty sure he'd go right back to seeing things in me that weren't there, and I couldn't *handle* that right now.

I looked around the bathroom to make sure I was alone. When I was certain I was, I started whispering sternly to my reflection.

"You're an idiot. I know you want him to like you back, I know you *need* him to like you back, but it's not going to happen. It can't. And *you*—" I pointed at myself, "—are confusing him by running hot and cold around him. Hugging him one minute, running off crying the next. No wonder he called you a bitch."

Yes, I was still hung up on that.

"And you *are* a crazy fucking bitch, *Alex*," I hissed, really building up the venom now. "A crazy, stupid bitch! You want him, you want him like you've never wanted anyone else, but you keep asking yourself, 'Is it just because I'm in a dress right now?' as if these feelings will just *go away* on Monday morning. You stupid—" kick, "—stupid—" kick, "—stupid—" kick, "—fucking, fucking *stupid bitch.*"

Fuck. What was I doing? This was nuts. I was textbook losing it. I took a deep breath, held it, and let it out slowly, trying to imagine the awful voice inside me — the one that kept calling me a fake, the one that thought James was right to call me a bitch — pouring out of me and dissipating into the air.

"Alex," I said to myself, "talking to yourself is one of the signs of madness. There's a list somewhere. Although, huh, I *bet* whichever shortsighted idiot drew up the list didn't have an entry for putting on a dress at the behest of your boss, with whom you are hopelessly in love, and parading around a huge conference hall in front of hundreds of people."

Another deep breath.

175

...Did I just say I was in love with James?
Kick. Kick. *Kick.*

* * *

"Nice break?" Emily said to me as I returned, a meaningful look on her face that I interpreted as *I will cover for you as long as you need.* I smiled broadly at her and decided, right there and then, we were fucking well hiring her. We'd pay her all the money we wouldn't be spending at Harvey Nichols any more.

"Yeah," I said, taking up my place in front of the booth, "it really helped. Thanks."

James almost immediately disengaged himself from the conversation he was having with Marcus and rushed over to me. He touched my elbow. I let him.

"Hi, James," I said, to forestall any more apologies or anything on his part. "Sorry I had to rush out like that; the bathroom called, you know?"

He nodded and I gave him my bravest smile. "Hey," he said, "I heard you sweet-talked the guy from Rayleigh's into giving us a good write-up. Kit said he couldn't stop singing your praises."

"He just seemed kind of shy, is all," I said. "A bit of a chat, and he really blossomed." Well, maybe a little green shoot finally grew out of the ground; the kid would need a hundred women to ask him about his interests and take a selfie with him before he'd stop nervously staring at their shoulders instead of their faces. "Oh yeah, you had a meeting, right? Or something? How did it go?"

I'd decided, after I'd kicked the sink until my foot hurt, to tough it out. If James wanted to talk to other women, that was for the best; he was never going to be my boyfriend and that was just a fact. If I really did love him — another confusing question for the pile — then I wanted the best for him.

The best for him was quite clearly not me.

"Really well, I think!" he said. "The longer I talked, the more I got the feeling we have something no-one else has. Something they really want. Their rep is going to bring us a couple of devkits later; next week, you and I have some work to do to get it working with their hardware. If it does..." He finished the sentence with a huge, boyish grin, his eyes warming and crinkling.

I carefully stopped my heart long enough to kill it.

"Congratulations!" I said happily, grasping his forearm with both hands and squeezing.

* * *

A burst of visitors who'd had a drink or five at lunch and thus had been less restrained than they ought when it came to respecting my personal space (and not touching my fucking leg) had worn away at me. Emily saw it happening and, bless her soul, earned ten times her fee intercepting as many as she could, but they just kept coming. And it was wearing on her, too; by 5pm her smile had long since ceased reaching her eyes. As closing time approached, she looked like she would happily strangle and eat the next man who so much as looked at her, and I could sympathise, because I wanted nothing more than to rip off my dress and jump in a bath of acid.

I couldn't put my finger on *exactly* when it stopped being remotely fun, but it might have been around the time Kristen came back from her late break with a Coke for her and a Coke for James. I didn't want to hate her — she was lovely — so I decided to hate James instead. It was difficult: I tried to glare at him, but his tie really did bring out the deep brown in his eyes, and I couldn't help thinking about that dream. It rattled me how much I was focused on it, so I settled for trying (and failing) to ignore him.

Which compounded the indignity when he rescued me, just before the doors closed, from a particularly unpleasant blogger who persisted in taking a step towards me whenever I took a step back. His liquid lunch boiled on his breath, and he got so close I could see the sprinkle of stubble on the back of his jaw where he'd missed with the razor. He leaned in and put his hand on my thigh, coupling it with a lusty exhale I wanted to gag on, and that was when James smoothly put himself between me and him, lifting the man's hand off my leg and pushing him towards Marcus. For a moment it looked like he was going to make a fuss, but James glared at him — I think; I didn't have a good angle on James' face, and I was in any case focusing on not throwing up — and he consented to fuck off without causing a scene.

"Alex," James said, and the emotion he put into my name made me forget everything else. He'd saved me. He'd *saved* me. "Alex?"

Fuck. *Wake up, Alex!* "Yes. Hi?"

"Are you okay?" he said, looking down at me with gentle eyes. "I'm sorry I wasn't faster; I didn't see what he was doing until he already had his hands on you." The last few words were delivered in a growl I'd never heard from him before, and I realised with a start that I'd never really seen him angry. Not *truly* angry.

I bit my lip, tried not to look at him, tried not to cry. My composure had been tested to its limit by the preceding few hours and was now, in James' presence, with his fingers resting lightly on my elbow, with his body so close to mine I could feel its heat, threatening to snap. I'd been watching James for most of the afternoon, whenever I had a spare second, whenever I was sure he wasn't watching me. Obsessing over just how out of my reach he was. 'Tough it out,' my padded arse.

His grip on my elbow tightened and he led me gently behind the booth, out of sight, and asked again if I was okay, and that was what broke me. I batted away his hand and flung myself at him, wrapped him in the tightest hug I'd ever given anyone. He reciprocated instantly, and we stood there in silence, holding each other.

I couldn't have him. I couldn't. He would choose someone else and I would have to move on. But I could draw comfort from him, and I chose to do exactly that. For a little while. For as long as I needed.

I just wished I could stop thinking about the way he'd looked with Kristen. With the perfect and beautiful and actually female Kristen. I put myself in her place and my brain practically did backflips until I forced myself to remember that I was imagining the impossible.

God, I wanted a vacation from my body. I wanted to rip myself out of it and go spend time in someone else, someone who could have who they wanted, *be* who they wanted. Someone who didn't have to strap down her dick just so the man she loved would look at her.

Yeah. *Loved.* It was definite. In his arms, it was definite.

"I'm not okay," I whispered.

"What can I do?" he whispered back.

"I need to get out of here."

Barely a minute later, he was ushering me into one of the taxis out front of the expo centre and sending me back to the hotel. He'd offered to come with me, but I wasn't certain I could keep my head around him any more, and I needed the space, anyway, for the plan that was starting to form.

Because I *could* be someone else for a while. I could be the only other person I had access to: the ordinary straight boy I'd been before all this started.

In my room, I struggled out of the dress and the bra, wiped off the makeup, stashed the boobs and the hip pads at the bottom of one of the suitcases, found a neutral-looking black top amongst the clothes Ben had provided, and pulled on the unisex jogging trousers and hoodie I'd bought the morning before. I couldn't take off the horrible stretchy underwear unless I wanted to wear nothing at all because I hadn't had the presence of mind to pack anything else, but, that apart, I was ready: everything feminine stripped away, except for the hair.

It took me a moment to gather the courage to look in the mirror. I wasn't sure what I was afraid of: that I wouldn't look sufficiently different or that I would look *too* different, too much like a boy, too much like someone James couldn't love. It was a shock, then, when I finally faced myself, because I just couldn't tell any more.

Harry, the kid from Rayleigh's, had emboldened me somewhat, and after I took the selfie with him, I did so again and again, with dozens of men. I saw myself over and over in their phone screens, had the contrast between my face and theirs so drummed into me that thinking of myself as looking like a woman had become, if not natural, then a *lot* easier. But that was with the assistance of clothes and makeup; bare-faced and plain-clothed, with only my wide-eyed, terrified self staring back at me, I should have been able to assign a gender to the person in the mirror.

I couldn't.

Was it the smooth face? No; I'd been clean-shaven for years before I started trying to grow out my supposed beard. Was it the way I was standing? I shifted, tried to masculinise my stance, and immediately felt foolish. Was it the hair? I reached back and pulled it into a high pony; God help me, if anything I looked *more* like a woman with more of my face exposed.

My woolly hat was on the bed. I leaned back, grabbed it and tugged it on, gathering up all my hair and stuffing it inside, yanking the brim down until it almost covered my eyebrows. Maybe now, without the hair, without the makeup, without the clothes, the scales were tipped in favour of man, or boy, or whatever the hell I was.

Vertigo played at the edges of my consciousness; I looked away.

Fuck it, I decided.

I needed to get out of there.

* * *

My phone buzzed in my pocket and startled me out of my thoughts. I dug for it and realised as I pulled it out that I had no idea where I was, beyond 'somewhere in Birmingham'. I'd left the hotel, hair jammed under my hat, gait feeling very strange without the weight on my hips and the elevated heels, and zoned out. I supposed I had to count myself lucky I'd managed to cross roads without being hit by anything.

Whatever; I had a phone and the company credit card. Wherever I was, I could get a car to pick me up at the end of the night. The privileges of making a rich guy feel guilty about you!

Waiting for me on my phone were texts from Emily, Ben and James.

Emily Swan: Hi, Alex, it got fairly hairy out there towards the end, didn't it! I'm bingeing Netflix with my headphones on and I'm not leaving my room for anything short of a nuclear apocalypse, and I suggest you do the same. You did great today btw. See you tomorrow for round two!

I tapped out a quick reply, letting her know I was fine and wishing her a restful night. Her instant :) made me smile.

I leaned against a nearby streetlight and opened the other texts. They were essentially the same: worrying about me, wondering where I'd gone, etc. I replied to them both at once.

Alex: I've gone for a walk. I'm fine, I just needed some space. James, I'll see you in the morning; Ben, I'm taking the bed, you can have the sofa.

The last I'd heard was that James was staying with Kit and Marcus and Ben was staying with me, and I wanted to reinforce that in case there was any confusion. Ben could complain about me taking the bed if he wanted, but only one of us had spent the entire afternoon in heels. Probably. He was way more used to them, anyway.

I put the phone in airplane mode and resumed walking. I knew that if I wanted to get a drink someplace, I'd have to get my old voice back, so after looking around to make sure I was mostly alone, I cleared my throat and tried the inverse of the training Ben had me do: I hummed and sang and recited nonsense poems with a hand on my chest. Ultimately, I wasn't sure whether I could feel the resonance or not, but I sounded deeper in my head. It'd have to do.

It wasn't long before the anonymous street terminated in a bar, one of those basement places that looks like it's undermining the much more respectable establishments squatting on top of it. The chalkboard by the steps advertised 'Spectrum Night', which seemed like it meant music from the 1980s, judging by what I could hear. Still, there was probably alcohol inside, and because it was fairly early for a Friday night, the queue to get in was almost nonexistent. I decided I wasn't likely to stumble upon a better option and got in line.

I had to show the bouncer my ID to get in — a perennial Alex problem — and he did the usual double take. I sighed and wearily held out my hand so he could give my driving licence back.

"Have a good night... sir," he said. Sarky bastard. How would he like it if he was nineteen but looked like he still had to wear a school uniform?

* * *

It occurred to me as I waited to be served that all I'd eaten that day was a cereal bar from a box Kit had passed around, so when the woman behind the bar asked my order, I stuck with a light beer. I wasn't planning on getting drunk, and it'd be easy to overshoot with so little in my stomach. She handed over the bottle and I found a table as far from the speakers as I could.

God, it was nice not being looked at. I unzipped my hoodie a little and sat back in my chair, enjoying the anonymity and sipping from my bottle. Sure, I was a little out of place in my tracksuit bottoms, like I'd gone out drinking straight from a run, but for some reason I didn't feel bad that literally everyone else in the bar was dressed more garishly than I was.

I found myself swaying gently to the music. It was something by Madonna, but not one of the few songs I knew well, so I was saved the embarrassment of half-consciously mouthing the lyrics. I stretched out my legs and wiggled my toes inside the trainers — no heels! room for my toes to move! — and drained my bottle.

Despite the noise, I felt quiet. Almost at peace.

I was on the verge of closing my eyes when someone put another bottle down on the table in front of me. A dark-haired, fair-skinned someone.

"Mind if I sit down?" she asked. "I brought another beer as payment."

"Sure." I returned her smile and accepted the beer, taking a swig as she sat down opposite me.

"I'm Vicky." She had a Manchester accent, if I was any judge.

I shook her outstretched hand. "Alex. Just visiting town." Whoops; there I was, telling my real name to yet *another* person I was meeting as a— Oh. Wait. I was a man right now. Easy to forget.

"Hey, same." She grinned at me, took a long drink from her own beer and propped her head up on her other hand. "So why are you here tonight?" she said. "And all alone in this bar?"

"I had the longest day," I said, "and I needed to get away from *everyone* I spent it with. So as soon as I got back to the hotel, I took off the, uh, the suit, put on the most comfortable stuff I could find, and just... started walking." I shrugged. "This is where I ended up."

She laughed. "That sounds familiar. I spent the entire afternoon travelling, which is bad enough, and with my boss, which is worse. First chance I got, I escaped, looked online for places that seemed okay, and came here." She looked around the place. "But it's kind of empty, and I'm bored, and you looked bored too, so..." She was right; the bar wasn't exactly rammed. It wasn't much past 7pm, though.

"I hadn't even noticed there weren't many people here," I admitted. "I'm only half awake. I feel like I'm jet-lagged, even though I only came up from London."

She smiled.

I felt obscurely like I ought to make a move on her, if I really was out tonight to reclaim my identity as a straight man, but the thought of it was unpleasant. Besides, I realised as I interrogated the impulse, it wasn't as if I was trying to be a generic straight guy, was I? I was trying to be *Alex*. And Alex had zero experience starting things with women. What would he even do? Lean forward, smirk, say something corny like, "What's a nice girl like you doing in a place like this?" and then get a drink thrown in his face?

No. Best not to ruin Vicky's night and make an arse of myself in the process.

Besides, Alex's dating history consisted almost entirely of women who had approached *him*, so on that front, I was doing quite well. Quite Alex.

The realisation prompted such a rush of relief that I found myself smiling inanely at her, and had to cover my subsequent embarrassment with my beer bottle. It didn't hide it that well — it was much narrower than I was — and she giggled at me. I blushed and, the ice thus broken, we moved on to small talk. She was a photographer — which dispelled my nagging worry that she was a tech blogger or something, in town for the expo — originally from Manchester but down from Newcastle for the next week or so. I obfuscated my own story a little, specifying that I was from London but glossing over exactly why I was in town. I told her I was being dragged around by my boss, too, and needed a break from him.

Vicky leaned closer to me as we talked, but I found myself leaning away from her. I didn't know why. Something about our conversation was making me uncomfortable, but I couldn't put my finger on exactly what. I considered that maybe it was just that I'd grown so used over the course of the day to pushy men grossing me out that I wasn't prepared for a conversation in which I had to inhabit the man's role, and as I thought about it, I shuddered. The very idea of being *anything* like the man James rescued me from!

James...

Fuck. Getting off the point. I shook my head, hoping to clear it.

"Are you okay?" she asked, pausing her account of a photoshoot back home in Newcastle that had gone horribly wrong.

I smiled. "I'm fine," I said, "but I'm sorry, Vicky; I'm just really tired and I'm getting a little loopy. I think I should probably go back to my hotel room."

"Sorry," she said, "I'm boring you."

"No!" I insisted. "Absolutely not. I just think that what I need more than anything else is to sleep for, like, a million years. And probably what *you* need is someone who won't collapse on the table mid-conversation."

I went to zip up my hoodie and she pulled out her phone. "You want to exchange emails?" she asked. "I'm here a few more days."

"Sure." She was nice, and fun to talk to, if I could just get over myself. She gave me her email address; I had to turn airplane mode off to send her a quick message, and I winced when the voicemail icon lit up. "I bet a tenner that's my boss," I said, showing her the notification. "Wish me luck."

"Good luck!" she replied, sounding genuine. We shared one last smile and wished each other a good night. I went outside to wait for my Uber and listen to my voicemail; she stayed at the bar, presumably to look for a guy who wasn't as much of a mess as I was.

* * *

I puzzled over the encounter all the way back to the hotel, but no matter how much I thought about it I couldn't identify exactly why talking with Vicky had felt so strange. Yes, sure, my initial conclusion — that I was uncomfortable occupying a man's role after the day I'd had — *seemed* sound, but it fell apart as soon as I pointed out to myself that one day of interacting with people as a woman does not cancel out an otherwise unbroken nineteen years of being a man/boy/baby (adjusting for age).

What else could it have been, though?

Perhaps it *was* just that I was tired.

The Uber driver left me alone with my thoughts, obviously sensing that I was struggling with the mysteries of the universe; I gave her five stars.

As soon as the car pulled away, I whipped off the woolly hat and shook out my hair, checking my reflection in the nearest window to make sure I looked appropriately womanly (my conclusion: uhhhh, maybe?). Back in territory where I was known solely as Girl Alex, I felt self-conscious and exposed. I hurried back into the hotel, taking the stairs up to my room rather than the elevator to reduce the chances of running into anyone. I'd not had the door shut behind me for a minute before I had the bra and the boobs back on. I felt safer that way.

I didn't put the bum pads back on, though. I'm not a masochist.

I sifted through my luggage for a new top, discarding a few I wasn't keen on before locating one that seemed practical and called to me for some reason. It was off-white and short-sleeved and much more obviously feminine than the one I'd worn to go out. It also had a high neckline, which I decided would be helpful for keeping my not-currently-glued-on breasts in place, and a slight flare to the lacy bottom seam that I hoped would flatter my unpadded hips. I was struggling into it when a knock at my door kicked my adrenaline into high gear.

"Just a second!" I yelled, pleased I'd slipped back into my girl voice without issue.

I finished pulling the top on and making sure all my various parts were still in place, and examined myself in the mirror as quickly as I could. No makeup, but no facial hair either. My hair looked... messy, like it had spent hours under a hat, but I didn't want to brush it out as I still wasn't confident I could do so without ruining the extensions, so I found a clip and put it up, teasing out a few locks to frame my face.

I stood back to check out my figure. It was unexciting without the bum pads on but it probably passed. I wondered for a moment whether to switch out my jogging bottoms for jeans or a skirt or something, and was just snatching up something long and pleated — I belatedly remembered Ben calling it a 'broomstick skirt', which was delightful — when the door banged again.

"It's James!"

"I'm coming!" I shouted, practically leaping out of my trousers and into the skirt, billowing out the folds with one hand while I dug in the bag on the table for lip gloss with the other. I gave my lips a quick coating, rubbed off the excess on the back of my hand — and then cleaned my hand on the discarded joggers — and gave myself one last look: the skirt's pleats and layers loaned my lower half a little of the shape I normally relied on padding for, and my face looked... decent.

I knew nothing could happen between us, but it didn't mean I couldn't look nice.

I blew my reflection a kiss and giggled.

James, it turned out when I opened the door, was dressed casually. He'd swapped his suit for a teal sweater and some of those comfortable-looking trousers I thought might be called chinos (I have never been, like I said, a fashionista; after a few days' pummelling from Ben I was probably much more up to speed on women's fashions than men's). He looked *amazing*. I stepped aside to let him through, beaming up at him like an idiot.

And I mean *up:* without my heels on, he towered over me.

"Did you get my message?" he said, watching me carefully as I closed the door.

I nodded. His voicemail had been pretty light: he'd wished me a fun night out, reminded me to stay safe, insisted I call him if I needed any help, and suggested I get a lot of sleep to prepare me for the chaos come morning. I winced, remembering that Saturday was set to be 10:30am to 6pm on the show floor; a full day being pawed at didn't appeal.

But *this*... This appealed. After the confusing encounter with Vicky, seeing James again solidified it beyond all doubt or denial: I wanted this man; I loved him. Accepting the knowledge, making it part of me, was like a drug high (or what I assumed a drug high was like; I'd been a sheltered teen). I wanted to kiss him, touch him all over, look pretty for him—

"So?" he continued, and I almost gulped as I realised where my thoughts had been headed. "*Did* you have a good night?"

"I had a short night," I said as he sat down on the edge of the bed and kicked off his shoes, generously reducing the height difference between us by nearly a centimetre. I sat down next to him, rejecting instantly the idea of sitting on the sofa or anything stupid like that. I hoped, as he loomed close, that I didn't need the full makeup job to look right, that just the clothes and the boobs and the hair and the quick swipe of lip gloss was enough, because if I made an excuse and popped into the bathroom for fifteen minutes and came back fully prettied up, I'd have to have a conversation I wasn't ready for. "Went for a walk. Went to a bar." I looked away, and added shyly, "Met a girl."

"And how did *that* go?" he asked. I couldn't detect anything but honest curiosity in his voice. Another unwelcome reminder that he thought of me exclusively as a straight man.

I shrugged, affecting indifference. "It was... awkward? She was nice and everything. She approached me, bought me a drink, and we talked. But it felt—" I frowned, searching the memory, "—unnatural. Not like the situation was unnatural; *I* was. Me. I felt artificial, like I was faking it." *Careful, Alex; you're getting dangerously close to telling the truth, here.* "And, you know, I was tired, so I made my excuses and left."

"Maybe you're not cut out for the lesbian lifestyle," James said. I hit him. Not hard, just a tap on the arm. I hadn't even really meant to, but something about the joke really hurt. "Sorry," he added.

"I wasn't there, you know, like *that*," I said, struggling with the words, trying to find ways to talk around the elephant in the room (or the two elephants in the room; my tits). "I kind of... took it all off. I went out as, uh, as the *old* me." *Please don't picture it please don't imagine it please don't think of me as* him, *not yet, not ever, I'm begging you...*

"*Oh,*" James said. A lot of emphasis for a single word.

"Yeah." I didn't know which I was more ashamed of: that I'd gone back to being my old self prematurely or that I still felt strange about having done so. It was undeniable that I hadn't felt truly comfortable until I got back to my room, and I wasn't certain I could put that sensation entirely down to the fear of discovery. Though that fear was growing the more I thought about it; it had been foolish in the extreme to show *his* face in a city he'd never visited before, but in which *she'd* been seen by hundreds of people.

I wanted comfort and I wanted reassurance, and I knew where to find them: I leaned against James, covering the last inch or so between us and resting my head on his shoulder. He responded instantly, with an arm around me.

"I'm surprised," he said slowly, "that you went to the trouble of putting it all back on again after."

"All what?" I asked. "Oh. Right. Yeah, I put the boobs back on when I got back here, and put on a skirt. You know, in case anyone came to my door? I'm supposed to be a girl here, after all," I added, scolding him.

"No..." he said. He was looking at our reflections in the mirror and seemed puzzled. "I mean, all the makeup and stuff."

I frowned. "I didn't." God, I wished I had, though. "I mean, when I heard it was you, I put some lip gloss on, but—" I shut myself up as soon as I heard what my idiot mouth had said, hoping James hadn't noticed.

"You're not wearing anything except lip gloss?" he said, looking down at me.

"Nope," I said, looking up at him, confused as to why he thought I was.

"Which you put on *after* you knew it was me at the door," he confirmed.

Shit. Rumbled. "I do have to look nice for the boss."

He laughed, but didn't stop looking intently at me. "You do, you know," he said. "Look nice."

I blushed and then, thinking quickly, closed my thighs more tightly together, because his eyes were so wonderfully, deeply brown and his arm around me was so firm and my body was definitely responding to him, and I didn't want my trapped prick getting any ideas. Why hadn't Vicky done this to me? Why hadn't Emily or Martina or Kristen? Why was my sexuality so determined to imprint on the least practical of all possible choices?

"What's up?" James asked, reading me like an open and deeply insecure book, as usual.

"Oh, um," I said, stalling for time, throwing my gaze around the room. "I just wondered why you're alone tonight. Or... alone with *me*. I thought you'd be out with Kristen."

"Kristen?" he said, surprised. "Oh, yeah, I mean, she asked, but I'm..." he trailed off, then rallied, "I'm not here to meet women. Except in a professional capacity."

I blinked, feeling stupid. "You were talking to her..." I muttered, only half-aware of what I was saying. "I thought you were interested."

He was silent until I looked back up at him, at which point he made sure we were looking into each other's eyes and said carefully, "No."

Jesus Christ. It wasn't *fair* to say something like that with so much conviction! That was the kind of thing that could have given me *ideas.* I swallowed, light-headed, and bumped my head against his shoulder again.

"You okay?" he asked.

"Yeah," I replied, and sought refuge, again, in an incomplete truth. "I haven't eaten anything much today, that's all. It just hit my brain."

A sudden manic grin lit James' face. "We can solve that," he said. "Room service!"

* * *

He charged it to the company. Decadent!

We sat nearish but not right next to each other on the bed, him cross-legged, me with mine tucked underneath me, and a spread of food in front of us. I'd put down a towel, just in case. We hadn't ordered anything too heavy, so it was mostly sandwiches, but James hadn't been able to resist ordering a single serving of chocolate cheesecake.

I ate happily.

"So," James said, with his mouth full of sandwich like some kind of disgusting child, "what was it like being out as a guy again?"

I poked him. "I have nineteen years' experience being a guy, you know," I said. "I've only been doing *this* for a few days."

"It felt weird, though, right?" he prompted. My face, open book, etc.

"Yeah," I admitted. "Really weird."

He grinned. "As weird as that first evening in the restaurant?"

"Weirder." I paused to think, and he let me. "In the restaurant, I was with *you,* you know? I know you and I trust you, even though I probably shouldn't." His grin widened. "But with Vicky—"

"Her name was Vicky?"

"Yeah. I didn't say? With you, it was like I had training wheels on. You knew about me, and you were there specifically to support me and help me, so even though it was new and scary as hell, it could only go *so* wrong. Despite your complete freakout when we first got there."

190

"Oh yeah. Sorry about that."

"But with Vicky, the training wheels were off, and I was rolling down the hill at top speed. When I thought she might be coming on to me I felt *completely* out of control, like I was headed right towards somewhere I didn't want to be."

"You think she was coming on to you?"

I shrugged. "She bought me a drink, unprompted. I'm not great at spotting the signs, but I'm pretty sure that's a big one."

He was quiet for a minute, thinking. I took the opportunity to demolish another sandwich.

"How did you, you know..." He looked awkward. "How did you go back? To 'guy mode'."

"Big hoodie. Big hat. Deeper voice."

He squinted at me, trying to imagine it. It made my skin crawl. "Stop that!" I squealed, and almost threw my half-finished sandwich at him.

"Sorry. I was just picturing you, at a table, in a bar, looking like..."

"Looking like *what?*"

"Do you think, maybe, that Vicky might be a lesbian?"

Well. *That* gave my brain a kick.

"What do you mean?" I said slowly, but if he answered my question, I missed it; I was connecting the dots in my head. I hadn't been *sure* I had chest resonance when I did that quick voice practise in the street; I could have just sounded like a woman with a deeper voice. And yes, I'd shoved all my hair under a hat, but as I'd finally acknowledged to myself, I had to have a fairly feminine face to pull off all this modelling stuff in the first place, and with no facial hair to tip the balance in the other direction, and gender-neutral clothes...

And the bouncer made a thing of calling me 'sir' *after* seeing my licence.

"Mother *fucker,*" I said.

James was grinning at me again. I really did throw my sandwich this time.

***

I saw the funny side eventually. I'd gone out as a man and fucked it up *completely.* A part of me wondered why I wasn't more bothered about that, but mostly I was just embarrassed. I couldn't stop seeing myself walking over to the table in that bar, in my jogging clothes and woolly hat; my imagination kept inserting a try-hard swagger I'd never knowingly attempted in real life, and it made me feel like an idiot. And I had to admit that if I'd screwed up being a guy so thoroughly in front of a complete stranger like that — James called it a 'male fail', which was cute — then it did sort of suggest that I really didn't need the whole makeup shebang to look nice for James.

"Don't worry about it," he said. "If you really miss it that much, we'll rediscover your manhood together when all this is over. We'll go out together and you can go on the pull. I'll be your wingman."

"No thank you," I said quickly. Maybe I'd feel different when all this was over, but the thought of going out with James and us both going home with different people was heartbreaking. "I was never any good at that, anyway," I said. "The old me's batting average is pretty terrible."

He smiled, looking thoughtful. "You keep saying stuff like, 'the old me'," he said. "What's up with that?"

"It's just the way I've been thinking about it. It's easier to stay in character if I don't think about going back. When I do, I get kind of..." I waved a hand around my head. "It's like vertigo? I'm just trying to concentrate on one thing at once, here. And I think tonight just reinforced the wisdom of that position."

"Maybe you shouldn't..." James started.

"Shouldn't what?" I asked when he trailed off, but after looking intently at me for a moment he shook his head.

"Wanna split the cheesecake?" he said.

"Sure," I agreed, more than pleased with the subject change. Talking about my sex life with him was kind of unpleasant.

He split the cheesecake into two halves and looked expectantly at me. I spread my arms out, to say that he had the only fork and I wasn't going to eat with my hands. He smiled, sliced off a piece, and held the fork out.

I wasn't going to let a cue like that go unexploited. I leaned forward and ate the cheesecake right off the fork, keeping eye contact the whole time and clenching my stomach to keep myself from laughing.

He ate a piece himself and offered me another one, which I ate the same way. We alternated until the cheesecake was all gone. I'd have loved to have said it was delicious, but I honestly had no idea what it tasted like.

* * *

"Where's Ben?" I asked. "I thought he was staying here tonight."

We were lying on the bedsheets, looking up at the ceiling. I'd taken my hair out of its clip and shaken it out, hoping the frizz had calmed down a little, but I wasn't all that bothered if it hadn't; I was too full and content.

"He found another room for the night," James said.

"He paid for one?"

James laughed. "Alex, you're adorable!"

I wasn't going to stand for that. "What?" I said, and batted at him.

"He met someone," he said in a patronising tone.

"Oh." I giggled. "Good for him."

"Speaking of rooms," James said, "I should go join Kit and Marcus so I don't wake them up, stumbling in after midnight."

I blinked sleepily. "Midnight? What time is it?"

James pointed at the alarm clock on the bedside table. The time was literally right next to my head; it was 11:52pm. I felt, as usual, a bit stupid. I put it down to intense tiredness this time.

"You don't need to go," I said.

Silence from my left for a few seconds. "Are you sure?" James asked, sounding serious.

I yawned, one of those huge ones that makes your toes stretch. "Yeah," I said when I was done. I was having trouble keeping my eyes open. "Just don't molest me or anything while I'm all vulnerable. I got enough of that at the expo today."

"Wouldn't dream of it."

I must have drifted off for a few minutes, because when I came back to consciousness James had taken off his sweater to reveal — God *damn!* — a very well-fitted white t-shirt, and was wandering aimlessly around the room while he brushed his teeth. Just innocently ambling around as if he wasn't casually showing me how ripped he was.

"Oh crap," I muttered when I got enough of my shit together to stop staring. "I need to brush my teeth." He reached out an arm and helped me up, and I staggered into the bathroom.

By the time I got done I was even sleepier, and decided against trying to change into pyjamas, both because I'd have to get naked in front of James and because I wasn't convinced I could change clothes without falling down. So I just kicked off my skirt, left it where it fell, and climbed laboriously back into bed.

James was dithering in the middle of the room.

"Shall I take the sofa, then?" he said.

"You'll be cold," I said, patting the pillow next to mine. "Just remember what I said about not molesting me and we won't have any trouble."

He took off his trousers and got in the other side without further hesitation. I was glad: I was starting seriously to fall asleep and all this talking was getting tricky. I rolled over to face the wall, arranged my arms under the pillow, and let my consciousness drift away.

"Alex," James said, bringing me back after what could have been a few seconds or a few hours. I liked the way my name sounded on his lips. I might have genuinely liked my name for the first time ever because of him, and I wanted him to say it again and again and again...

"Mmm..." I said.

"You know," he said, "maybe you don't like thinking about going back because, deep down, you don't want to go back."

"Mmm…" I said. I couldn't concentrate on what he was saying. I just wanted to make agreeable noises so he'd let me sleep.

"You said you were having fun. Could it be more than that?"

"Mmm…" I said.

"You think maybe a part of you wants to stay this way?"

I rolled over to face him. He was still talking, and even though I wasn't able to pick out individual words, it was enough to keep me awake.

"Shush," I said, trying to place a finger over his lips and missing. "Go to sleep…"

"Goodnight, Alex."

The last thing I remembered was James smiling at me.

Chapter Eight

I woke to a tray of coffee and what turned out to be Marmite toast being laid carefully on the bed next to me. Carefully I unglued my eyelids and inspected my surroundings: James, already up and dressed — although, looking more closely, he was wearing the same shit he had on the previous night, minus the sweater, so I deducted some points — was handing out breakfasts like a benevolent toast god.

Just looking at him was still a pleasure, and brought with it a cascade of memories. I'd fallen asleep watching his face, listening to him mumble, thinking of him; is it any wonder I dreamed of him again? Over and over, at work, in his apartment; in the elevator at work, in the bathroom in his apartment; kicking aside the desk in his office and having him press me against the window, knocking over the bar in his apartment and having him push me down into the thick carpet; he kissed and touched and caressed me in every way possible, and I saw it all, felt it all as I looked at him.

It felt good to not be afraid of it any more. It felt good to not be ashamed. My desires for him were mine; I claimed them; I wanted them, and even if they couldn't ever be reciprocated, I could luxuriate in their recollection. A vulgar, excitable, hungry side of me had awoken after being asleep my whole life, and it wanted to be *fucked*.

"Hi," I said, pushing myself up the headboard with my elbows, being careful not to rock the tray. I managed, through the application of much diligent shuffling and two adjustments to the position of my breakfast — James helped — eventually to shove myself into a loose approximation of sitting up, and smiled at him, wondering if any of my powerfully focused attraction towards him was visible on my face, and if so, how much.

"Hi," he said, smiling broadly, keeping one hand on the edge of the tray just in case. I could feel the back of his hand against my thigh through the duvet, and I'd never before cursed a few thin layers of fabric and fluff with such vehemence.

"Hi," I repeated. I was pleased to note that my tits, which I had forgotten to take out before falling asleep — 'forgotten' in large, bold-type scare quotes — had stayed in my bra and hadn't, for example, migrated upwards and attached themselves to my head like earmuffs. One of them was a little out of position, so while maintaining eye contact with James, I nudged leftie with the inside of my upper arm until it fell properly back into its cup, next to rightie. Damn things! How much more convenient it would be to grow my own! If they were real, they probably wouldn't try to escape. "Hi," I said once more.

James laughed. "Hello, Alex. Would you like to try any *other* words this morning?"

I scowled at him. "No. Gimme coffee."

Miraculously — he *was* my boss, and there I was ordering him around again — he retrieved the mug from the tray and placed it into my waiting hands, although given that to do so he had to remove his hand from where it had been connected directly to my thigh and thus my entire nervous system, duvet be damned, I still considered it, overall, to have been a bloody stupid request on my part.

At least it was hot and plain black, exactly as I liked it; the perfect caffeine delivery system. I slurped.

"What time is it?" I asked. I'd woken up still talking in head voice, although I sounded a bit like I'd been gargling thumb tacks; I wondered if going back to a male voice would involve speech therapy or testosterone injections or a carefully timed kick in the balls or something.

"Seven thirty," James said, retrieving his own coffee and drinking deeply. I had no doubt it was full of milk and sugar and chocolate sprinkles and cinnamon sticks and basically like having caffeinated dessert for breakfast. No wonder he spent so much time working out. "So you're in no rush to get ready. Ben won't even be here for an hour or so."

I nodded and continued slurping. "Thanks for the coffee," I said when I came up for air.

"No problem. I've had two cups already."

Huh. "How long, exactly, have you been awake?"

"About an hour."

I took a final deep draught and mock-glared at him over the rim of the mug. "And you didn't wake me?"

He sat down on the mattress next to me, with one leg curled up. It put his *whole damn thigh* in contact with mine; or it would have, if I'd done the sensible thing and thrown off the covers at my first opportunity. I tried subtly to press against him, anyway.

I think he waited until I was so distracted by his presence to reply, solely so I would fail to control my reaction, because when he said, "You're cute when you're sleeping," I stopped breathing for a moment. "I couldn't bring myself to wake you," he continued, smiling indulgently as I struggled for oxygen, "until it was absolutely necessary. And I figured you'd want a little time to ramp up before Ben gets here and starts fiddling." He wiggled his fingers, to indicate the dark and unknown arts of feminine beauty. "Besides, I had some notes to type for my meetings today, and you're *very* distracting. God, Alex, I have so many meetings today!" He pressed a hand against his chest to emphasise the enormity of the sacrifice involved in having actually to do some work; I, having finally recovered, simply rolled my eyes at him. "I suppose I have only myself to blame, since I spent half of yesterday in *other* meetings, schmoozing and kissing arse so I could get some face time with the big guys; I should have slacked off, like you."

Oh, we were being cheeky, were we? Two could play at *that* game. "If you really want to feel hard done by," I said sweetly, leaning forward so that my artificial cleavage only just didn't spill out of my top, "you should go to those meetings in a dress."

His eyes flicked downwards. *Gotcha!*

"No thank you," he said smoothly, as if I hadn't just caught him looking at my aftermarket assets. "There's only one of us who can pull that off, and it's very much not me."

True.

He fetched me a second cup of coffee, and while I poured it down my throat, he returned to his notes, leaving me with no choice but to be responsible, a good employee, a competent assistant, etc., and check my emails. I discovered I had a reply from one of James' exes, which put my heart into overdrive until I finished skimming it and found nothing damning. Rereading it with more of an eye for detail, she said more or less exactly what I'd hoped she would: he was perfectly nice the whole time she knew him and never abusive or unpleasant, but he'd been far too absorbed with work and consequently rather boring to be around. Plus, he constantly cancelled dates because he was busy. Sounded like the reason *my* last girlfriend left, except with me there'd been an undercurrent of bedroom ineptitude.

Well, more like a current. An overcurrent. A raging tide, perhaps; a tsunami of sexual incompetence.

But I'm cute when I'm sleeping, huh? No girl had *ever* said anything like that to me. Few had ever had the opportunity.

I tapped out a quick reply, thanking her, and with an obscure feeling of victory over the girl — to whom I would be, when I got over this unbecoming moment of extreme smugness, extremely grateful — I backed out to the email list and poked through mundane work stuff. "Oh, hey," I muttered, thinking aloud, "Harry's asking me for some official quotes."

"Harry?" James asked, turning around from his perch at his laptop and sounding strangely neutral. "Who's that?"

"Who's who?" I said, projecting guarded innocence, just to see the look on his face. When his eyes widened, I added, quickly, "Just kidding. It's the boy. You know? From Rayleigh's?"

"Ah. The one you were... friendly with."

"Friendly *to,*" I corrected. "He was just so nervous! It was adorable. Hmm. Lots of praise for me in this email." I was done teasing James; now I was reminding him I was still an excellent frontline employee, even when hampered by a dress that restricted movement down to my knees. "Although he spells my name with a *y*. Curious."

We thought for a second, and then we both said, "*Half-Life*," at the same time.

"A retro gamer," James said.

"Not necessarily," I said. "The whole series is basically the cereal box prize for opening Steam." And the games were old enough to be playable on office PCs. Not that I'd ever wasted time like that. Not that I'd ever caught James trying to place portals so he could ogle the main character from *Portal 2* when he was supposed to be working. "It's flattering, but I'm *way* too pale to be Alyx."

"*I'm* not," James said.

"Wrong sex, though," I said absently, starting my reply to Harry's email.

James gasped, mock-insulted, and when he had my attention he posed, so I could see him in profile. God, what a profile. "You don't think I could pull off Alyx Vance?"

I put my phone down on the bed and squinted at him, pretending to consider it. "No," I said, "I don't think so. Hair's too short."

He made an irritated noise and returned to his work. I returned to mine, emailing with one hand and eating lukewarm toast with the other. I shuffled around on the bed until my back was vertical and brought my knees up to keep me in place while I worked; a mistake, as it turned out, because my junk took the opportunity to remind me I hadn't taken the stupid knickers off before I went to bed. I'd spent the entire night with my testicles rammed up inside their little one-car garages. Probably the end of any chance I had to have kids.

"Ouch!" I muttered, wriggling against the pillow.

"You okay?"

"Oh, just a little twinge in my back," I lied. "Heels all day, you know? It'll be fine. If I *ever* wear them again after this weekend, I'll make sure I do six months of yoga first."

"I would count it as a business expense," James said graciously.

"Oh?" I said, instantly suspicious. "Is that because you want to get me in heels every time we have something to sell?"

He smirked at me. "I wouldn't say no. They make your legs look *so* good."

He was lucky I'd finished my toast or he would have ended up with Marmite in his eye.

* * *

James spent about twenty minutes getting ready, and while I could well have been annoyed with him for not showering while I was asleep — I was going to have to rush a little to be ready for Ben in time — I got to watch him wander the hotel room half-naked, and the only price I paid was having to suppress the occasional full-body shudder inflicted on me by my junk. If I hadn't known better, I'd have thought James was showing off on purpose, the way he walked up, glistening with shower water and wearing only a towel, to ask my opinion on something he planned to raise in one of his meetings.

I had immense difficulty controlling myself.

Finally, for the good of my sanity (and the health of my poor, distressed genitals), he left, giving me a whole twenty-five minutes to get ready. It was lucky my hair didn't need a wash, or I really would have been late.

All I had to do was get undressed.

I wasn't looking forward to it. A night in the tucking knickers followed by a morning of constant arousal had left me both flustered and increasingly concerned about the state my junk was going to be in when I released it. I stood there in the bathroom, shower water warming and heart beating fast, psyching myself up. Eventually the tension and the need to piss became too much, and I pulled down my knickers in one smooth motion.

It was as if I'd just stabbed myself in the crotch with a carving knife.

"Fuck!" I yelled, and slapped a hand over my mouth, because I could feel myself winding up for a full-power scream and I didn't want to deal with a noise complaint from the suite next door. With my other hand I slowly and carefully pulled my component parts loose, tearing them away from the skin they'd been stuck to by sweat and pressure. As I worked, I kept up a stream of personally very helpful muffled swearing and pathetic whimpering.

Washing myself was going to be unpleasant. I'd never been especially fond of interacting with my genitals at the best of times, and this was making a decent play for being the worst of times, at least as far as my cock and balls were concerned. I contemplated skipping the shower and just putting on a fresh pair of tucking underwear and ramming all my junk right back up there, to teach it a lesson, but for the first time in days I succeeded at a wisdom roll. Besides, I was kind of sweaty, and the odour wafting up from my bruised and insulted penis suggested I'd probably clear out the conference hall if I walked in there without first giving myself an unpleasantly thorough scrubbing.

I peed, wiped, winced, and stomped my way into the shower, walking like a cowboy.

* * *

I found Ben waiting for me when I left the bathroom. He tapped at his wrist, and I growled at him. Yes, I was running late, and yes, I knew it, but there was no way I was going to tell him *why*.

The truth was that I'd had a couple of minor crises while I was showering, and they took time to resolve.

1) When I went to wash my chest, it felt weird as hell, and I managed briefly to convince myself there was something horribly, medically wrong with me until I realised I'd just gotten used to having the breasts on;

2) When I was almost done, I spotted James' underwear, which he'd left on the towel rack, and that sparked thoughts of him wandering around in his towel, which sparked something else entirely in the parts of me that had previously been strapped down for their own good, and I'd had to deal with *that* before I could properly finish washing;

2a) Dealing with it was a mixture of exciting and shameful, and I had to have a little cry, after.

I was glad I had, though, no matter how unpleasant it felt to masturbate. I briefly imagined what might have happened had I ignored it and marched back into the main room with a prominent erection under my robe only to find Ben waiting for me, and in my subsequent dizziness, I fell onto the bed.

"You're late," Ben said unnecessarily. I didn't have the energy to respond verbally because I was still busy dying in an embarrassed heap on the bed, so I just gave him the finger. "Rude," he commented, and I elected to ignore him for the next little while.

He started clattering around the room, making noises consistent with unpacking torture devices from the suitcases.

"Hey, Alex," he said, "why is James' sweater on the sofa?"

"He must have left it behind."

"Oh?" Ben said neutrally. "James was here last night?"

"Yeah, he stayed over," I replied, without thinking about it.

Whoops.

I sat up just in time to witness the expression on Ben's face morph from glee to stern disapproval. "And you made him sleep on the *sofa*," he said. "Shame on you!"

"No," I corrected him, "he slept in... my... bed..."

Engage brain before opening mouth, Alex.

"He—"

"It wasn't like that!" I said quickly. "He came to see me after I got back. We ate room service, and by the time we were done, it was late. I didn't have the heart to kick him out. We didn't *do* anything."

"Pity."

I would have yelled at him, but he looked genuinely sorry for me.

"Yeah," I agreed, "but what can I do about *that?*"

I must have looked even sadder and more pathetic than usual, because Ben stopped setting up his work area and came over to give me a hug. I leaned into it, imagining him briefly as James before remembering why I'd decided that kind of thing was a dick move. Once I switched back, once I was... what I used to be, I'd have to ask him for dating tips.

He indulged me for a moment, and then led me over to the cushions he'd put down so he'd have somewhere comfortable to sit while he got me ready. I wondered, as he sprayed my hair and painted my face, if the memory of James holding me during the night was from a dream, or if it had really happened.

* * *

I exchanged greetings with Kit and Marcus, who were finishing laying out all the stuff they'd had to pack up from our booth the day before, waved to Kristen and Martina, and accepted a friendly nudge from Emily, who waved a bag of jelly babies at me. I took one.

"Have a handful," she said. "Stops you from getting a dry throat from talking but doesn't make you have to pee."

I took three more.

Now that I was back on the show floor, I was a lot more relaxed about the prospect of another day at the expo. Perhaps it was because I'd fallen further into my role — it'd been a strange relief to put on the absurd, bright blue dress again, to slip back into the foundation garments and the heels, to see this creature I'd christened Girl Alex come to life again in the mirror, to inhabit her — and perhaps it was because I'd gotten some half-decent sleep. I trembled as I remembered exactly who I'd spent the night with, and gave myself permission to think for a few more seconds about how James had smiled at me as I fell asleep.

On cue, James appeared from the staff door nearest our booth, talking with a woman I recognised as being from one of the larger companies, the ones that had spent Friday circling small outfits like ours looking for buy (or buy-out) opportunities. He saw me looking and smiled at me. I smiled back. He shook hands with the woman, walked over, and got me in a shoulder hug. I leaned in, pressing my head against him. He was warm and pleasingly firm. My compliments to his gym membership.

"Hi, Alex," he said, looking down at me. I liked wearing heels around him, because I didn't have to look up as far. *And* he'd said they made my legs look good.

"Hi, James," I said breathily. I was absolutely aware of how I was coming across, but I didn't care any more. If I had to be honest, and I decided I'd used up all my credits when it came to lying to myself, I was enjoying playing the part of Girl Alex. Especially around James.

"You look nice," he said.

"Thanks!" I said, preening. "Better than I did first thing this morning, huh?"

"About the same," he replied, smirking. I stuck out my tongue at him and pirouetted away from under his arm. I was getting good in heels, and it was fun to show off a little. He spread his arms, pretending to look disappointed, and I winked at him.

"So," Emily whispered, amused, "you gave him a break, then?"

"A very small break," I whispered back, feeling a little giddy. She laughed. I glanced back over at James, and he returned my wink.

"Five minutes!" someone yelled above the general hubbub, and I cleared my head. Software demonstrations *now,* indulgences *later.*

* * *

Saturday on the show floor turned out to be less tiring than Friday had been. There were more people in the hall, but mostly they were members of the public, who flocked mainly to the larger stands. We still had a fair amount of foot traffic from bloggers and publications that were interested in the esoterica the smaller booths were showing off, but even then, they were mostly of the can-I-have-a-selfie-with-you variety, so I didn't have to spend much time explaining our software solutions in detail and I could just pose.

By midday, James had vanished to some meeting or other and Emily had gone on her break, so I was dealing with the small queue of selfie-hungry attendees on my own. I was getting pretty good at it, too: beckon them in, stand next to them and wait for them to arrange themselves, smile, wait for the click, encourage them to move on immediately after; next! Marcus, who was taller even than James, was covering for his boredom by playing bouncer, standing intimidatingly close by with his arms folded. It was sweet of him. He'd catch my eye every so often, and we'd share a smirk.

I'd just dispatched the last of a diminishing queue when I heard the clip-clop of approaching heels and sighed with relief. As accustomed as I was to herding horny men, talking with the occasional woman was still preferable; I was getting tired of hover hands. I'd almost started my welcome spiel when the face recognition circuits in my brain clicked on, and I went cold.

It was Sophie. James' cousin. Sophie fucking Lincoln-fucking-McCain. The one he'd originally asked to do hair and makeup for the models, before all the *everything* happened and he enlisted Ben instead. What was she doing here?

I tried not to show my nerves on my face. She knew me. Not the *me* I was being at that moment; the old me the boy me the real me, the who-the-fuck-*ever*. She knew me.

"Oh my God," she said as she approached, her voice as unrestrained as I remembered it, "you have *no* idea how long it took me to find this booth. This place is *huge* and this map—" she brandished one of the pamphlets they were handing out at the front doors, "—is fudging *useless!* I swear I've been confronted with more useless gadgets and gizmos than I *ever* want to see in a *million* years. Hi!" She extended a hand to me. I took it, trying not to cringe. She'd visited the office several times, had even gone out to dinner with James and me, but didn't seem to have recognised me so far. "I'm James' cousin. Is he about? Mr McCain, I mean."

Yeah. I was going to have to talk to her.

I knew I sounded different. Those first two days, when I'd been learning to find and maintain head voice, I'd listened to myself repeatedly. I'd gone from strained, adolescent shrieking to a voice that sounded enough like a woman's that no-one felt it necessary to comment. What I couldn't tell was if I sounded different enough to my old self that someone who'd met me before would be able to tell it was me. My face, apparently, was not immediately recognisable; what about my voice?

I had no choice but to reply, though, not unless I wanted to try communicating telepathically, and my track record there was appalling. I pitched my voice as high in my head and as close to the front of my mouth as I could, and said, "Mr McCain is in a meeting at the moment. He shouldn't be long."

"Oh, yes, that's fine," Sophie said. She pulled out one of the stools from under the booth, narrowly avoiding yanking down half the display with it, and sat. "It was originally going to be me who did your makeup, you know," she added, squinting at me, "until dear Jamesy decided he'd rather have his mate from uni do it. Seems he did an okay job, though."

I was offended on his behalf. 'An okay job' indeed! "You mean Benjamin?" I said, defensively lengthening his name (more syllables equals more professional, my panicking brain decided). "Yes, he did me. Emily, too. She's the other model."

Sophie nodded. "Well, I decided I wanted a holiday anyway — I was *frightfully* bored, you know — so I thought I'd come see his whole setup." She waved a hand at the booth she'd almost destroyed. "See what he's doing with the family money. Mum never shuts up about it, you know."

I hadn't had much exposure to the extended McCain family. My mum knew James' mother of old, and James' father visited the office occasionally, but beyond that, all I knew was that James' decision to borrow a small sack of Daddy's cash to try to make a name for himself in technology was mildly controversial in an extended family that, on Sophie's side of it, tended more towards silly hats and horses.

"So, what's it like?" she asked before I had an opportunity to comment. "Booth babe-ing?"

I coughed delicately. "It's 'trade show model', not 'booth babe'." For some reason, I'd taken a strong dislike to the term. "And it's mostly smiling for photographs, answering extremely simple questions, and showing off the demo hardware." I shrugged. "Today it's almost entirely smiling for photos."

Sophie was still squinting at me. "You know, this is the *craziest* thing," she said, "but I feel like we've met before."

I was running through possible non-incriminating answers when a hand that didn't belong to either of us appeared in front of me, clutching a bag of jelly babies. Emily, back from her break. I'd been so focused on looking and acting unrecognisable for Sophie that I hadn't heard her walk up.

"Hey, Alex," Emily said. "Got you your own bag so you'll stop thieving mine."

"*Alex?*" Sophie exclaimed. "Alex blooming *Brewer?* I *knew* I knew you!"

"Excuse me," I said to Emily, and took Sophie by the arm. She didn't resist; she was busy absorbing all the ambient energy in the area, like an aristocratic elementalist, building up to yell something incriminating at ear-shattering volume. Through clenched teeth I whispered, "Sophie, would you please come with me?"

I frog-marched her out through the staff door and into the women's toilets. I checked the stalls to make sure they were all empty and then risked a look at her, preparing for an explosion of anger, of disgust, of *something*.

She wasn't angry or disgusted. She was giggling. "Al— Alexander, this is the *ladies' loos!*"

Top marks for observation. "Would you like to take this to the men's?" I asked, gesturing at the clothes I was wearing.

"God— God— *Why?*"

I leaned against a sink, feeling suddenly tired. "Long story. The short version: the models we booked fell ill and we couldn't get anyone else at such short notice."

She barked a laugh. "So you just... *decided* you'd replace them? Just like that? And what about the other one? Is *she* a—?"

"No!" I said quickly. The last thing anyone wanted was Sophie trotting back out there and trying to look up Emily's skirt. I thought Emily, especially, would be against it. "It's just me. And *I* didn't decide; it was James' idea."

It was Sophie's turn to have to prop herself up. She was laughing so hard I thought she'd collapse, so I offered her an arm, and she let me hold her up until she recovered.

"God," she said. "Let me look at you."

I didn't know what else I could do, so I took a step back and did one of the poses we practised the day before.

"Ben does good work," she said critically. "Of course, he wasn't exactly working with Chris Hemsworth to begin with."

I shrugged, unable to counter that. Chris Hemsworth, in addition to his movie-star body, had a distinctive and masculine face, whereas the best you could say about mine was that it was a nicely inoffensive oval shape.

"You said it was James' idea?" she asked. I nodded. "Hah! You know, he showed me that photo? On Facebook? From a school play or something? He kept talking about it afterwards." She drummed her fingers on her chin. "I *bet* he was just waiting for his chance to have some fun with you."

"He's been kind," I protested. "He hasn't made fun of me." She raised an eyebrow. "Okay, he's made fun a little. But mostly he's been kind."

"So," she said, leaning forward, continuing her inspection, "what's it like? Life on the other side of the fence?"

"It's the same, but the shoes are less comfortable. And men are more annoying. Like, exponentially more annoying."

"You're not... *bothered* by this?"

"By the men? God, Soph, I'm *extremely* bothered by—"

"No, no, I mean—" she gestured at me with a hand that seemed unable to stay still, "—all *that*. The clothes! It *must* bother you."

"Why? They're just clothes." Oh, I was bothered, but not particularly by the clothes. "It was unusual at first, but I got used to it pretty quickly." I decided not to mention the whole bisexual thing, or the whole being-in-love-with-Sophie's-cousin thing.

"Incredible," she breathed. "How do you do the voice?"

"Ben taught me. It's like singing, but you talk instead. It's not that hard." Okay, I was showing off a little. I was proud of my voice. It felt *good* to speak in, and it was extraordinarily satisfying to have someone recognise what an achievement it had been to come so far in so little time.

Sophie looked... the only word for it was *enraptured*. "Alex, this is bloody brilliant!" she said, a little too loud. "I mean, you're a *guy*—"

I shushed her, and to her credit, she allowed herself to be shushed. "Please be careful," I said. "No-one can know about this. Emily, the other girl, she doesn't know; she thinks I'm just a tomboy or a butch or something, which is how I explained having to get used to the heels—"

"—and your attraction to women," Sophie interjected, nodding thoughtfully.

"Um. Yes. It's only James and Ben who know. Not the expo organisers, not the other engineers, no-one. So, please, tell me you won't tell anyone? Or fuck up my pronouns? Or call me 'Alexander' again?"

She gave me the look that said *you're an idiot*. I was used to that look from James; it was genetic, apparently, on his father's side. "I know what to call a queen when she's in her frock, dear. This is *far* from my first rodeo. Let's be clear, though: who, exactly, do Emily and the engineers and everyone else *think* you are?"

"I don't know about Kit and Marcus," I said, "but Emily thinks I'm a soft-butch geek girl who never dressed femme until this week. And, yes, like you said, I told her I was into girls."

"What, you just came out with it?" Sophie said, grinning.

"She thought James was looking at me," I said. "I told her there was no chance, because we were old friends, he's my boss, *and* I'm not into guys."

"*Really?*" Sophie was intrigued. "*James* has been looking at you?"

"No, nonono," I said. "She *thought* he was. She saw things that weren't there."

"I see. Anything else?"

I wanted to bash my head against the bathroom wall, partly to get some relief from the idiotic things I kept saying, and partly to see if any genuinely useful information that Sophie really needed to know fell out of it, but I suspected I might look crazy if I did.

"I don't think so."

"Well then, come *on,* girl," and she beckoned at me as she started to leave the bathroom, "we need to get you back to your *stage!*"

I had a horrible feeling this was all going to end with her calling me 'fierce'.

* * *

I let her lead me back to the booth. As we exited the staff door onto the expo floor, I spotted Emily talking to James; I dreaded to think what she was telling him. She caught my eye and raised her eyebrows, and because I was just behind Sophie and thus invisible to her, I mouthed *James' cousin* at Emily, and waggled my finger next to my head.

"James!" Sophie exclaimed as we approached the booth. "How *dare* you try to keep me from your expo! It's such a... such a..." She looked around the local area, which was practically empty; Kristen and Martina were the only other people around, and they were both pretending to read some of the advertising bumf that was piled up around their booth, presumably so they could eavesdrop on us while maintaining the appearance of innocence. "Such an *exciting* event," Sophie finished, failing to convincingly fake sincerity. I wanted to golf clap.

"Hi, Soph," James said, sounding tired. "What are you doing here?"

We arranged ourselves around the booth, with me propping myself up against one of the sturdier bits. I needed the support; I was feeling quite light-headed, because I was certain Sophie was planning to milk the situation for all the delicious awkwardness she could squeeze out of it.

"I'm *here* because I wanted a holiday!" Sophie said, putting on an air of wounded innocence. "And I wanted to see—" she poked him in the chest in time with her words, "—my beloved cousin. But you weren't here, and I ran into *Alex* instead!" James closed his eyes; I felt a silent camaraderie with him, and pushed down on the temptation to sidle over and hold his hand. "It took me *ages* to recognise her, James; what *did* you do to her?"

I hoped I was the only one who could hear the slight, delighted emphasis she put on the pronoun. I tried to get into the spirit. "He made me put on a dress, the bastard," I said.

"Oh, sweetie," Sophie said with mock concern, "did it hurt when you were turfed out of your Birkenstocks and dungarees and forced into normal clothes for once?" Undoubtedly, that was the first image that came to mind when Sophie imagined a lesbian.

"You call this 'normal'?" I tweaked the fabric on the skirt. "Save me, Soph; I look like an idiot!"

"You should make *him* wear the dress next time," Sophie suggested, with such a gleam in her eye I wasn't entirely sure it was a joke. I hummed to myself, looked him up and down, pretended to consider it.

I had no idea what Emily thought of this little display, but I could guess, judging by her quizzical expression. Fortunately, James had finally rebooted his brain.

"Hey," he said, "don't encourage Alex to be mean to me. She doesn't need the help." He stepped closer and gave me a comradely tap on my bare upper arm.

"No, but I appreciate suggestions," I said.

213

"Soph," James said, "why don't you and I go to lunch, and we can leave Alex and Emily to do their jobs?"

"You don't want to come with us, Alex?" Sophie asked, leaning around her cousin.

"I can't," I said. "I've got to mind the stall with Emily."

"Then lead on, James!" Sophie announced. "Show me the sights and sounds!" As she and James passed by, she said in something closer to a normal voice, "Emily, it was just *wonderful* to meet you."

"Likewise," Emily managed.

James threw the both of us a backwards wave as he dragged Sophie away. The last thing I heard her say was, "So, how *did* you get Alex to dress up? Was bribery involved? Blackmail?"

I closed my eyes, put my full weight on the sturdy bit of the booth again, and let the nervous energy drain from my body. I wondered if I could get James to subtly and with great tact put her on a train to France. Or on a rocket to the moon.

"That was an experience," Emily said, propping herself up next to me and bumping my shoulder with her upper arm. "Is she always like that?"

I gestured back and forth, from the empty space where Sophie had been standing, to Emily. "Emily; Sophie Lincoln-McCain, James' cousin. Sophie; Emily Swan. And, yes, she's always like that. James was too, a bit, Ben said, in his first year of uni. Sophie's always been off in her own world. Comes from being—" I put on a dreadful accent, "—terribly, terribly rich, *dahling*. Everything's a game; everyone's just *mahvellous* fun."

Emily nodded, and nudged me again. "She said you usually wear Birkenstocks?"

"I wear sandals to work *one time...*" I griped.

"I don't know, I think they'd suit you. Not with that dress, of course, but—"

"*Alex?*" said a voice.

God, I was getting tired of people saying my name as if they'd just discovered me floating in their soup. Emily's body was partially obscuring

214

whoever it was, but unfortunately for me, she stood quickly aside, bringing me to face my accuser.

It was Vicky, the girl from the bar, staring right at me, lowering an expensive camera and frowning.

Oh *shit*. I'd hoped never to have to test James' theory that Vicky-from-the-bar thought I was a woman, and I'd certainly hoped not to have to do so in such a public place. I tried my hardest not to duck back behind Emily again, even though I really wanted to.

"Alex," Emily whispered, suddenly aware that something might be up, "are you okay?" I nodded, hoping that I was. Poor Emily; she signed up for an ordinary trade show job but got stuck babysitting a crossdressing idiot who was making a credible run at the world record for most nervous breakdowns in a long weekend.

Vicky stopped close enough that she could speak quietly but far enough away to allow me an exit if I really needed one. Thoughtful. "I'm sorry," she said. "I didn't mean to startle you."

I tried to regain my professional composure. "It's fine," I said. "It's just that I'm easily startled right now. It's not your fault. I'm having some circumstances. Lots of them. All at once." I tried to mime it with my hands, but mostly I flailed.

"Do you have a few minutes?"

"I wish I did," I said, "but I don't." There was a large-ish group of people hanging around in the middle of the show floor, looking like they might head in our direction once they'd gotten their bearings. "I should help Emily cover the stand. Oh, this is Emily, by the way. Emily, Vicky."

Emily smiled. "Vicky, huh? Hi."

"Hi," Vicky said briskly, and turned back to me. "You're sure you can't talk?"

"It's been so busy," I said, doing my best to sound rushed off my feet and hoping Vicky wouldn't notice how relatively sparse the area around the booth was. "And Sophie's still knocking around. I don't want to inflict *her* on poor Emily without me there to protect her." I wasn't being as generous as I sounded: I didn't want Sophie collaring Emily on her own. I wasn't convinced she'd hit the correct pronouns every time if she wanted to talk about me, and she would *definitely* want to talk about me.

"Sophie?" Vicky asked.

"*Long* story."

"Then why don't you tell me later?" she said. "You're staying locally, right? Which hotel?" I named it. "Same. Meet you in the bar, seven o'clock? Just for an hour or so; I still have work stuff this evening." She rolled her eyes at that, and I offered a nervous smile in return.

"Sounds good," I said.

"Good." Vicky nodded decisively. "Um, would you mind?" She waved a hand towards the both of us and raised her camera. "I need to get some pictures of the stand...?"

Emily and I obliged with our product-demonstration poses. Vicky snapped a couple of shots, got a close-up of the demo device as I held it for her, nodded and smiled at me, and headed off with the man who was presumably her boss for the next booth.

"I'm never modelling again," I said to Emily, as soon as they were out of earshot.

"I said the same thing after *my* first time," Emily said. "I had a complete 'mare. Although that was mostly 'just' men being unpleasant. I didn't have any real drama until some guy from uni saw me on a booth babe website."

"There are booth babe websites?" I asked, the undeniable wisdom of all my recent decisions weighing heavily on me. *So* many photos of me in a dress, immortalised on the internet. She nodded. "Oh. Shit."

"It didn't go well," she said. "For *him*. I got him back *good.*"

I was about to ask for more details when Marcus tapped me on the shoulder — it was a good thing I'd seen him approach out of the corner of my eye, because I was so jumpy, I might have lamped him otherwise — and wordlessly handed me his phone. It was James.

"Alex?" he said. The grumpy noise I made into the handset was obviously sufficient to confirm my identity, because he continued, "Sophie has agreed to leave you alone for the rest of the weekend—" I sighed in relief, "—*if* you agree to have dinner with us tonight."

"Do I have to?" I whined.

"I think, overall, you probably *want* to," he said.

"Fine," I said. "I'm having drinks with Vicky at seven, so make it eight-ish at the hotel restaurant."

"Vicky..." James said, obviously having trouble remembering.

"From last night?" I prompted. "Before you came over to my room? At the bar?"

"Oh," James exclaimed, as Emily's eyebrows tented, "*that* Vicky. Did she call?"

"She appeared," I said flatly. "Here. At the expo. She's a photographer, and apparently we — Emily and I — are among her subjects."

He laughed, and if he were physically present, I would have kicked him in the ankle with my pointy shoe, but he wasn't, so I just had to use my imagination and put my trust once again in my psychic powers. "So, uh, was I right about her?"

I sighed. "I honestly have no idea."

"Oh," James said, sobering up. "That could be awkward."

"Yes," I said. "That could be extremely awkward."

"Take your phone," he ordered, "and have my number ready to call, so it's the first thing on the screen when you unlock it. I'll be at the bar with *my* phone out in front of me. Not close enough to overhear you, so you can talk about whatever you might need to talk about without worrying what I might think, but close enough that if you dial my phone, I can be over at your table by the second ring. I won't even pick up. I'll just run."

"Um, don't you think that's going a little far?"

"Remember what I said about your safety? I won't risk it. You're not just a woman here, which is dangerous enough. You're a— Look, if she finds out you were a guy and threatens to hurt you..."

"She won't," I said. "I'm sure."

"I'm not," he said, and hung up.

217

"Jesus," I commented, staring at Marcus's phone. I waved it at him, dumbly, and he came to collect it.

"Okay," Emily said, "so, Alex. You met a girl at a bar? But then *James* came up to your room, not the girl? I'm sorry, but I'm *way* too curious about this to mind my own business."

I explained, keeping it as brief as I could and altering some of the details. I tried to suggest that I'd been too tired the previous night to get a decent read on whether Vicky had been coming on to me, not that I didn't know which gender she'd read me as. A ridiculous situation to be in, but my life was just like that now, apparently.

"And James is going to be at the bar to, what, protect you?" Emily said, puzzled. "Or because he's jealous and wants to check out the competition? You know," she added, "I think he's right that she's into you; it took her about five seconds to ask you out."

"It's just drinks," I protested. "And only for an hour."

"Still."

I made an unhappy noise. At this point I wanted a friend much more than I wanted a hookup from Vicky, no matter how attractive she was. And I really didn't want to be thinking about this when we still had photos to smile for and men's hands to avoid. To that end, I tried to encourage a subject change. "So, what did you do to that guy? The one who saw you on the booth babe website?"

Emily looked a little put out but consented to tell the story: he'd threatened to tell everyone from her hometown, her parents, and so on, and he was quite aggressive and unpleasant in his messages, so she screengrabbed everything and sent it all to his mother, who had some choice things to say to him about respecting women. I pictured the guy's face when he realised his mother knew what he'd been up to, and it forced a laugh out of me, breaking through my stress. After that, whenever we had free time between attendees, we began swapping dating horror stories; I didn't have to be careful about genders when it was my turn because Emily already thought I was a lesbian, or a bi woman who preferred other women, so my personal disasters went more or less unedited.

Overall, I was sufficiently diverted, both by Emily and by my bag of jelly babies, that I was spared too much time to myself to worry about whether Vicky *knew*, and what her intentions were.

* * *

I blessed Ben down to his cotton socks for spending so much of James' money at Harvey Nichols. I had the contents of our suitcases spread out on the bed, looking for something nice; if Vicky was going to expose me, then I wanted at least to look like I knew what I was doing, like I knew how to dress, like I was authentic (even if I wasn't). I couldn't put my finger on the precise origin of the impulse and didn't have time to question it, so I just went with it, eventually picking out a matching floral print silk top and midi skirt, paired with a small white shoulder bag and an absolutely gorgeous pair of white leather sandals that, despite the one-and-a-half-inch heel, felt like they were kissing my feet.

I'd taken off the garish show floor makeup and done my best to replicate one of Ben's more subtle efforts. I was still terrible at eyeliner, though, so I mostly didn't bother with it except in the outer corner. I vowed to practise when we got back to London.

In the end, I was pleased with the results. The clothes fit me perfectly, obviously — well, they fit me with the padding around my chest, hips and bum provided by Ben's little accessories — and were beautifully made, and all the good parts of my hair were extensions put in by expensive hairdressers; it would have been a waste of James' money if I *hadn't* looked amazing. Reassuring, but also frustrating and upsetting, like there really *was* nothing real about me, like I was mere artifice, created by money (and animated by anxiety). When this was over, I decided, I was going to go shopping by myself, for myself, and see if I could still make myself look good when someone of ordinary resources (me) was the most I had in my corner.

I retrieved my phone from where I'd left it on the bed that morning, checked the time and my messages and emails, and made sure it was on the contacts app with James' details open before I locked it and threw it in my bag. One last glance in the mirror to make sure I still looked good — was I becoming vain? because I lingered for a moment, admiring myself — and it was time to go.

I wondered if Vicky, assuming her intentions tonight were good, would send me a copy of the photos she'd taken at the expo. As a memento.

* * *

Vicky was waiting for me outside the bar and smiled when she saw me. I couldn't detect a hint of vindictiveness in her expression, and I scolded myself for doubting her intentions. She was dressed casually: blue jeans, white trainers, and a white blouse with a print pattern of tiny parrots on it. Her dark hair was pinned up and she was wearing, if I was any judge, very little makeup.

Instantly I felt overdressed — another thing that was becoming a habit! — but she didn't comment. I let her take me by the arm and lead me to one of the more private corners of the bar, where we were instantly accosted by a waiter.

"Just an orange juice, please," Vicky said to the waiter. I asked for Diet Coke, and when we were alone again, she explained, "I shouldn't drink; I have a strategy meeting tonight and then tomorrow I have to be on the other side of the city, bright and early."

"It's fine," I said. "I'm not drinking either. I'm meeting my boss later — hence the extreme dressiness — and I'd rather be awake for it."

"Well," she said, "you look incredible."

"So— so do you," I stammered, and busied myself inspecting the table. *Smooth, Alex.*

"Thank you," Vicky said warmly.

As I was analysing her words — did 'you look incredible' mean 'incredible for a girl' or 'incredible for a crossdresser'? — the waiter glided smoothly past our table and dropped off our drinks. I wrapped my lips around the straw and drank some Coke, taking a moment to look around the bar.

There was James, fiddling with his phone, ignoring his beer, positioned so he could see us out of the corner of his eye. True to his word, he was too far away to hear our conversation. Unless he'd installed a listening app on my phone...

Paranoia gives you wrinkles, Alex, chanted my inner Ben.

"It's dreadful that both our bosses have us busy so late," Vicky said.

I snorted. "Mine's not exactly a work event. I almost wish it was. He's making me have dinner with him and his cousin, Sophie."

"The Sophie you didn't have time to talk about earlier?"

"The same. She's not a bad person, she's just... She's a lot."

Vicky choked on her orange juice. "Wait; your boss isn't trying to hook you up, is he?"

"Not with his cousin," I said carefully. "Definitely not." Perish the thought. "I agreed to come mainly so she wouldn't spend all afternoon hassling Emily and me while we were trying to work."

"Speaking of work," she said, "you're a booth babe!" She looked like she'd turned over a rock and found a winning scratchcard underneath.

"Trade show model," I said. "And when you said you're a photographer, that meant..."

"Technical photography, today," she said, grinning. "Shooting the 'exciting' new devices for a tech website — and the pretty ladies standing around holding them up — and tomorrow is more of the same, but offsite. Monday, I get an actual day off, and then Tuesday we're shooting for a local fashion designer. We're contractors: if you can't afford a full-time staff photographer, you hire us."

"Sounds more interesting than modelling," I said. "Although that's not what I *really* do."

"Modelling's just the day job that pays the rent?"

"Actually, the day job's why I'm here. I'm a professional computer dork, but two of the models we had booked got sick at the last minute..." I ran through my spiel, inserting the usual lies. I wondered how many more people I'd tell the *My Fair Lady* version of my week to by the time it was over, and laughed, having just realised why Ben had found it funny I'd chosen to recite 'the rain in Spain' while I was training my voice. "I'm sorry I didn't tell you about it last night," I said, when I was done.

"We didn't exactly talk for hours," she said.

"I know, but I thought about it and deliberately didn't tell you." I frowned. "I made the decision to lie about it. Or omit the information; whichever. Like I said, I'm not a model, not professionally, and I came into *this* with some... preconceptions I had to drop. I guess I was worried about other people holding the same views."

"Then you're forgiven," Vicky said, smiling. "But you don't owe that kind of information to a random hookup. Which is," she added, raising her half-finished glass to her face so she could look at me over the rim, "what I was trying for last night, by the way. Looking back, I'm not sure if you were clear on that."

I giggled. "Yeah, I picked up on it."

"And you can stop doing the perky straight girl voice if you want, since it's just us here," she said, dropping the coy look and smirking.

I coughed to cover my reaction. I'd almost forgotten that when we met, I'd been attempting to speak in a man's voice; incompetently, it would seem. "I would," I said, "but I have dinner with my boss soon and switching back and forth is... hard on the throat."

"I get it," Vicky said. "It's tricky for me to get my employee-of-the-month shtick back sometimes, too." She nudged me with her free hand. "We should form a support group; we can't be the *only* exasperated queer women here this weekend."

Shit. God damn fucking *shit*. Here she was, opening up, speaking to the shared experiences she thought we had... and here I was, lying to her. Lying and lying and lying, from the moment I walked into the bar in my expensive skirt and my designer shoes and my fake hair. She thought I was a girl, someone like her, someone she could relate to, and she was completely and utterly wrong. I hated all this bullshit, these barriers I'd been forced to erect. I just wanted to *talk* to people, to be around them without fear of discovery, without the terrible awkwardness of attempting to be a guy and suddenly having no idea how to pull it off. Two evenings of mistakes in a row.

I'd always been good at talking to people, but there was something different about it now. Something deeper, something I wanted to grasp and never lose. Something I was *going* to lose, unavoidably, after the weekend. Suddenly I could build connections with people, real connections, and though they were shallow and fleeting, they felt more real than friendships I'd had that had lasted *years*.

"Oh God," Vicky said, picking up on my reaction. "I'm sorry. If you're not gay or bi or anything, I'm—"

"It's not that," I said quickly. "It's... it's more."

She leaned forward on the table. "More?"

"More," I whispered.

"Alex..."

That *fucking* name. "I don't know what I am," I said.

She waited for me to look at her, to make sure I could see she was smiling kindly, and said, "Is that why, last night, you looked very much like you wanted to kiss me, and then you immediately made excuses and ran off?"

I ran through stories, ways to explain it, truths to avoid and lies to spin that would *keep the secret* and I hated myself for it more thoroughly than I'd ever hated anyone or anything. "I used to believe I was attracted to women," I said, and with the hand below the table I mauled the seat fabric as hard as I could, "and only women. It was one of those facts of life, like: 'My name is Alex, I have two eyes, two arms and two legs, and I like girls.' One of those things you never think about."

"You *never* thought you were interested in guys?" Vicky said. "Not even when you were young? Well, younger? The whole comp-het thing?"

"Never. Not until a few days ago. Not until..." I sighed heavily. "Not until my boss."

"Oh. Oh shit. And now you're here, out of town, *in a hotel*—"

"Yep," I said. "Last night, when I met you, I was still telling myself it wasn't real, that I wasn't into him. That I was still the same g— girl I always thought I was. And then we got talking, you and me... and I felt like a fraud. A total and utter fraud. Like I'd just ripped up the corner of my painting and it said 'Joe Bloggs' on the back instead of 'Michelangelo'. Bloody counterfeit girl." I shook my head. "I still feel like that. Right now." She reached a hand across the table, but I didn't take it. It would make things worse, I was sure. She wouldn't want to touch me if she *knew,* and I felt that knowledge, that certainty, suffuse me. "I'm sorry. I'm sorry. I shouldn't have talked to you..."

"It was me who talked to you, remember?" she said. "I sat at *your* table last night."

Her kindness was awful. "I'm sorry anyway," I said.

"What happened with your boss?"

I stared into the memory. "Like I said, he asked me to fill in for the models who got sick, and his friend dressed me up like I've never been dressed up before, to see if I was capable of, you know, walking in heels, avoiding flashing people getting in and out of cars, that kind of thing."

"Did he teach you how to talk proper? Like in *My Fair Lady?*"

"A little bit, actually." Why did everyone get psychic powers except me? "So we went out to dinner," I continued, ignoring her gentle grin, "and got a bit drunk, and he kissed me, and..."

It was time to face up to the other part of it. The conclusion I'd been avoiding coming to. The obvious truth.

"...and I've never felt anything like it before," I finished. "Not ever. Not even close. I was thinking, for a while, that maybe I'm bi and never figured it out... but now I'm thinking, what if I'm— what if I'm *straight?*" I almost said it the wrong way round. "What if I'm straight and I have been all along? And then as soon as I think *that,* I start worrying all over again that *none* of it is real, that it's just the whole modelling thing. Dressing and acting the part and getting swept up in it. Because otherwise it'd mean I'd been wrong about myself my whole life." I gave her an apologetic smile, and finally laid an arm on the table where she could get at it. "And that's the mess you bought a beer for last night. I should pay you back."

"Don't," she said, and patted me on the hand. "And I get it, I do. The first girl I was interested in, when I didn't know I liked girls at all, was a bit of a hurdle for me. Took me a long time to realise what was going on in my head. And it turned out to be kind of a disastrous relationship! But she helped me come to terms with my bisexuality, and now it's just a part of who I am. Of course," she added after a moment, "he transitioned after that and now he's a guy, so maybe if he'd been the *only* 'girl' I could have kept fooling myself that I was straight, but then I met Faiza and we dated for four years, so."

I got stuck on a word. "'Transitioned'?"

"Yeah, he's a trans man. And," she added, gesturing with her nearly empty glass, "he didn't work *his* shit out until he was twenty-two. How old are you, Alex?"

I blushed. "Nineteen."

"*Nineteen?*" Vicky looked scandalised. "God, it's a good thing we didn't do anything. Look, do you know how many people have themselves completely figured out at *nineteen?* Like, three smug bastards in the whole country, per year. I hate them."

"He really didn't figure himself out until he was twenty-two?" I asked urgently. "He didn't *know* he was trans?"

"No?" she said, puzzled. "He had some stuff happen, said it 'cracked his egg', which is a term trans people use for when they come out to themselves, when they realise who they are."

"He just... worked it out one day?" I swallowed, as if my sudden dizziness were a condition of the inner ear and not the result of every assumption I'd ever made about my life collapsing around me.

"He said, up to that point, he'd been unhappy and uncomfortable with being a woman, and he sort of low-key hated his body, but he didn't put two and two together until something happened." She shrugged. "I don't know the details; I saw it on Facebook. We had a bad breakup, like I said."

"I thought they always knew..." I muttered.

Vicky reached for my hand again, but I withdrew it, feeling suddenly so delicate that the gentlest touch might shatter me.

"Are you okay?" she asked.

"No," I whispered, and closed my eyes.

* * *

"Alex?" Vicky said gently.

Trans people knew from birth. Everyone *knew* that! They were 'born in the wrong body'! That was why that phrase even existed, right? Transgender people *had* to have the self-knowledge to understand that they'd been wrongly sexed, or else how would they summon the courage to change it? How would they know?

But Vicky's friend didn't figure himself out until he was even older than I was. And that one fact, quietly stated, had just thrown a wrench into the workings of my carefully constructed denial.

What did she say? He 'low-key hated his body'; he'd been 'unhappy and uncomfortable with being a woman'. If I applied those two concepts, suitably gendered, both to my own life and to the whirlwind of the last few days, what exactly would I get out of it?

I gripped the edge of the table.

Steady, Alex. Steady.

When it came down to it, had I always thought of myself as a guy solely because I'd always thought of myself as a guy? Was it nothing more than inertia? Had my entire identity rested on circular fucking reasoning? Hell, the one thing I knew for certain was that I'd spent nineteen years being as wrong as it was possible to be about my sexuality, which raised the chances that I could be wrong about anything and everything else by quite a lot.

What would it be like when I went home, when I stripped off the tits and took out the extensions and returned to how I used to be? I tried to imagine it, and nothing about it pleased me. I'd be the guy again, the one I'd tried and failed to be in the bar the night before. I'd grow more and more into him, every week, every month, every year, trying and failing over and over to find a connection with someone and understanding too late that you *can't* make connections when you're broken; not properly, not reliably, not in the way I was suddenly coming to understand I might always have been broken.

"Alex?" Vicky said again.

I looked up. "Sorry," I said. "Kind of went somewhere for a second there."

"Yeah," Vicky said, still looking worried. "I thought you'd blown a fuse."

"Blew a couple, I think. Look, Vicky..." I swallowed. Took a deep breath and let it out. Drummed my fingers on the table a little. Not so much stalling for time as giving myself a moment to understand that, yes, I was going to say it. I was going to make it real. "I've got to tell you something. I've never told anyone before, and it's pretty huge, actually, and you're this lovely girl I met just last night and it's not fair to you that it has to be you but it *has* to be you because there *is* no-one else, no-one I can trust to be objective, or *sub*jective, or whatever's required in this situation, and—"

"Alex," she said, having somehow spotted that I was losing focus. "Tell me."

"I think I'm trans," I said.

And the most wicked thing about finally allowing myself to think it, to say it, was that I felt like an idiot for not properly contemplating it that very first night I dressed up and went out. The first night I spent time with James, as... well, as *me*. Hardly a coincidence it had also been the night my long-simmering crush on him finally intensified enough that even I could spot it.

I'd told myself it was the clothes. Something about the way men and women (or people who look like women) interact. Something about our friendship or my poor romantic history or... or whatever. But I'd been looking too hard at what James and I had between us, the spark that I *couldn't* deny for very long, to think much about how I felt when we were apart. How I felt around other people, people who I wasn't in love with.

I got along so well with Emily... I bonded so quickly with Ben... How could it just be the clothes?

Because it wasn't the clothes, was it? Not intrinsically. It was how people responded to me when I wore them.

People treated me like a woman, and I loved it.

No, not even that. People treated me like a woman, and I felt *real.* And in doing so, they showed me I'd never felt real before in my life.

"Go on," Vicky said gently.

"It's been bubbling under the last few days," I said, monotone, "but I just thought it was, I don't know, the novelty of it, the new environment, the— the *clothes*... God, I'm an idiot."

As I spoke, I argued with myself:

If I were a real trans person, I wouldn't have questions, I'd just know.

Vicky's friend didn't know.

Yes, but then he had a revelation, and he did.

A revelation? What do you think *this* is, idiot?

"Vicky," I whispered, "how do I know if it's real?"

She bit her lip for a second, examined me. "I don't know loads about this stuff," she said, "but I do know you don't need to decide if it's real, or if it's right for you, straight away. I know you can take your time and think it through, that just asking the question is enough for now. And," she added with a grin, "now I also know a high proportion of the lesbians I approach aren't lesbians at all, but trans men who haven't worked it out yet."

"It's not like that," I said. "If I'm trans, and that's *if*... then it's not in that direction."

"What do you mean?"

I took a deep breath before I continued. "Alex is short for Alexander. I'm a... I'm a boy. A guy. A *man*." I growled the last word; it had never felt so poisoned on my lips.

"Oh," Vicky said.

"Yeah," I said.

"*Oh,*" Vicky said.

"Uh-huh," I said.

"To be clear, you *don't* mean that you're a trans man."

"No."

She touched my hand again, and this time I let her. "I'm sorry, Alex, but I just can't see it. You're so... natural like this." And then she frowned and retracted her hand and I thought for a horrible moment that she'd finally realised what I was saying and become disgusted, but she continued, "Shit. Well done, Vicky."

I matched her frown. "What?"

"That was a pretty insulting thing for me to say, don't you think?" She repeated herself in an unflattering parody of her light Mancunian accent. "'You're so natural, Alex, I could hardly tell you're a...'" She shook her head. "You know what I mean."

"Oh," I said. "Yeah, I suppose so. Didn't occur to me, though."

"All I meant was, I look at you, I talk to you — hell, I try to pick you up — and I can't believe you *ever* thought you were a man."

I sniffed. "I thought exactly that for nineteen years! And then, all of a bloody sudden, my boss gets me in a dress; five minutes later, I'm blushing down to my *knees* when he kisses me. And I'm more comfortable like this than I ever was before. I can talk to people. Really talk! And it feels right and— and— and *normal* in a way I've never felt. But I've been fighting it. Like last night."

"Last night? You mean, like, *at the bar* last night?"

I nodded. "I was at the expo all day. I'd been like this—" I waved a hand at my outfit, "—all day. And it was making my head spin. So I put the hair extensions under a hat and I tried to get my old voice back and I went out. As a guy. As 'Boy Alex'. I told myself I was just getting too involved in the role I was playing, that all I needed was to be a straight man again and I'd get my head back on."

I could tell Vicky was trying not to laugh. "You mean, last night you were trying to be a *man?*"

I smiled. "Yeah, I know. And the daft thing is, that's basically how I always used to look. Just with scrappy stubble and a different voice. And not usually a hat."

She squinted at me. "I still can't see it."

"Good," I said with satisfaction. "Wait; you're not angry?"

"Angry?"

"I mean, you came onto a... guy."

She rolled her eyes and held up a finger. "Okay, first of all, I told you I'm bi, right? I like guys, girls, nonbinary people; I really don't care as long as they're pretty." She incremented the finger count to two. "And second of all, it doesn't seem like you're *actually* a guy. Inside."

I shook my head. "I really don't know." How *could* anyone know? All I had was... suggestive evidence.

"Alex, I think guys, actual guys, they *know* that. Someone asks them, 'Are you a guy?' and they're confident about their answer."

"Maybe. I never thought about it before this week. It just— I just *was*."

She smiled. "You think most straight guys would be comfortable doing what you've done this week? Wearing that? Being a *booth babe?*"

"It's just a job," I mumbled, embarrassed.

"Oh, no you don't, young lady," she said, slapping me lightly on the forearm. I looked at her, stunned. "I am *literally* watching you think yourself back into the closet. And I know it when I see it, because I did *exactly* the same thing when I first realised I liked women. I lost a year of my life to that shit and fucked myself up good and proper. I'm not watching it happen to anyone else. I am going to give you—" she reached into her bag, retrieved her purse, took out a business card and started writing on the back of it, "—the address of a website I found when I heard my ex transitioned and I wanted to know what was going through his head. And you're going to go there, *tonight,* and read what the people there say. And maybe talk to them about your own story. Okay?"

I was helpless in the face of an attractive person giving me instructions. It was how I ended up in a dress in the first place. I put the card in my bag;

it looked like she'd written a subreddit URL on it. At least there I was on familiar ground.

"Okay," I said, smiling.

Vicky squeezed my arm. "This is normal, you know," she said. "Lots of people transition. You're not alone." She glanced at her phone. "I have to go, but before I do, I want you to promise me you're going to go to that website and you're going to talk to a trans person."

"I will," I said. "I promise."

She got up, and pulled on my arm until I got up, too. She hugged me, and I hugged her back.

"You be careful, okay?" she said. I nodded. She pulled away from me for a second, and then kissed me on the lips, softly and briefly. "Enjoy your dinner."

I smiled. "Enjoy your strategy meeting," I said.

"That," she said, "is absolutely guaranteed not to happen."

Chapter Nine

Vicky reminded me one more time to be careful and left for her strategy meeting. As I watched her go, I admired the way she filled out her jeans but realised as I did so that I wasn't imagining what it would be like to kiss her, undress her, or do any of the things I'd always tried so hard to do with women I found attractive; instead, I wondered how those jeans would look on me. I'd need the bum pads, of course, to even hope to do them justice; without my little helpers, Vicky's butt was a hundred times nicer than mine was.

I was envious of her! Perhaps a little attracted to her, sure, but mostly I wanted what she *had,* who she was; I didn't want *her* except as a friend.

Had I always been envious of women, and called it desire?

Another blindfold comes off. How many more before I was done? I told Vicky I thought I was trans, and while I was still unsure, it felt like I was *this close* to seeing clearly for the first time. I just needed a little time...

Lost in thought, I didn't notice James walking up until he stepped right into my line of sight. He brought me back to reality: I was still standing right where I had been, leaning against the table, hugging my belly, staring blankly at the double doors Vicky had left through.

"I presume it went okay," James said teasingly, "if you already miss her so much."

"Hmm?" I said, still not entirely among the living. I replayed what he said and detected a touch of sourness in his voice, despite his pleasant tone. "Oh. No. It's not that." I shook my head absently, as if the action might dislodge a few stray thoughts. *Was* I trans...?

"You kissed!" James said.

I focused on him properly for the first time. "You watched!" I said to his frown. "You said you wouldn't."

"What I said was," he replied, "that I wouldn't *listen*." He tapped me on the nose, which startled me. I was still slightly behind events; my mind was working overtime behind the scenes and had allocated only a few measly brain cells to important things like *listening to your boss* and *standing upright*. And they weren't doing a very good job, either! They were probably the brain cells that normally dealt with unimportant things, like remembering how to spell *antidisestablishmentarianism* and retaining the ability to ride a bike.

I shook myself again. I needed to be present. I had a lot to think about, for sure, but right now I had an evening to survive, and it would probably require all my attention to do so.

James had sat down, so I followed suit, returning to my seat and finding a new glass on the table in front of me. He must have brought them with him. God, where had I *gone?*

"If you *had* listened to us," I said, "you'd know it was the furthest thing from a romantic kiss." I sniffed the contents of the glass: rum and Coke, like he told me he used to drink at the cheap bar at uni. "She was being kind. Reassuring me. Giving advice. In case you hadn't noticed, I'm a *little bit* of a mess."

"*You're* not a mess," he said enigmatically, and sipped his rum and Coke. Before I could ask him what the hell he meant by that, he added, carefully and steadily, "What sort of advice?"

I knew that tone. He used it when he was talking to soon-to-be or just-recently-become ex-girlfriends. On the phone, generally. Neutral, polite, incurious, flat.

He was pushing his emotions down. Why?

"She helped me think about something," I said carefully. "Something pretty big."

"And?" he pressed. "What is it?"

I didn't want to get into it with him, not right here in the hotel bar and especially not before I'd had a chance to properly think it through. I'd spent the last few days like that, bouncing from situation to situation, and it wasn't doing me any good; I had to slow down, take some time to myself and read up on things, like Vicky suggested.

"Just some stuff. I want to think about it before I talk about it."

"But you can talk about it with her?" he said, frowning again.

"She brought it up." Was he upset with me?

"Hmm," he said. Yeah, he was upset.

His hand was resting on the table next to his glass. I took it. He flinched a little, which was disappointing; I'd hoped we were past that. I massaged his knuckles until he looked at me again.

"I promise I'll tell you," I said, "if you give me a little time?" I tried a reassuring smile, and I could have sworn his pupils dilated.

"Um," he said. His face lost all the signs that he was controlling his expression, which was good; it meant he was coming out of his studiedly neutral mode. "You can't tell me what it's about? Not even a little?"

"Patience."

He was still looking at me kind of strangely, so I had some rum and Coke and let him look.

He looked for a *while*.

"James?" I prompted, after he'd been quiet for perhaps a minute. "Are you okay?"

He bit his lip — actually *bit his lip!* — and once again looked at me without quite looking at me, his eyes searching all of me that was visible. "Yes," he said. "Sorry. Soph said something to me earlier, and it bothered me a little at the time, but before long I was so busy with work, I didn't have a chance to think about it any more. And then, when I was sitting over there, watching you... it came up again." He tapped a finger on his temple. "Now it's all I can think about."

He went quiet again, so I had a bit more rum and Coke and propped my chin on my wrist, the better to look at him properly. I was tired, and the bit of my brain that was usually pretty good at decoding James when he was being mysterious apparently needed new batteries.

"So," I said, when it seemed like he was going to spend another full minute staring at my neck without saying anything, "what did she say?" It was either prompt him or give him that kick I'd fantasised about earlier, but I liked my white sandals a lot more than the heels I wore on the expo floor, and they weren't anything like as tough; I didn't want to break them against his stubborn calves.

"Hmm?" he said, which very nearly made me kick him anyway; he could buy me a new pair if it came to it. Three pairs, actually. In multiple colours. "Oh," he continued after a moment, "it's really nothing I want to talk about right now." He sounded suddenly more confident and James-like than he had the whole evening.

As much as I wanted to yell at him, to drag from him whatever it was Sophie said about me, I *had* just insisted on keeping my thoughts to myself, which, fuck. Fair's fair. Fair's bloody fair.

I disguised my sigh as a deep breath, and said, "Let's agree to give each other time to think. If we're *both* stewing on something, then we both get some peace and quiet to work on it. Okay?"

He smiled. "Okay."

"And that's assuming either of us can stay awake long enough to think about *anything* tonight. I've barely eaten today; I think a full restaurant dinner will send me straight to sleep."

"Oh shit," he said, laughing a slightly forced laugh, "I almost forgot about dinner with Sophie."

"Lucky you," I said sourly. "It's been on my mind for *hours*. But let's agree, yes? To put our stuff, whatever it is, on the back burner until we've survived dinner? And talk about it with each other only when we're ready?"

I was still holding his hand — I was a little amazed, in retrospect, that he hadn't ripped it away from me during his crisis, but I supposed he needed all his brain power for being obfuscatory, the same way I needed all mine for staying awake (and for keeping scary and confusing thoughts properly taped up in the box marked *for later)* — and he took advantage of that, pulling suddenly on me and nearly throwing me off balance, and lancing me with his most punchable smirk when I met his eyes in astonishment.

"Ow!" I protested.

"Got you," he said, and I knew what he was doing: puncturing the moment, releasing the tension. Teasing me. It was the kind of thing he'd do occasionally at work when I got too involved in a difficult problem. Still annoying, though.

"Sod."

"Sorry." He wasn't sorry. He released me, waited for me to rearrange myself, and continued, "You're right, though. Let's just have a nice— let's just have an *evening* with my cousin, and deal with our shit later."

"Right," I said, nodding and sorting the evening into two categories with my hands. "Dinner with Sophie; dealing with all our shit."

"By the way, you look fucking *amazing*."

I knew it would be impossible *not* to blush at that, so quite sensibly I didn't try to suppress it. Instead, I turned my head slightly so my reddening cheek would just about be visible through my light foundation. I wanted him to know the effect he had on me. It was important. I wanted the dream. For a few more hours.

"Thanks," I said. "I thought I'd try to make myself look nice tonight."

"For Vicky?"

I flicked my gaze up to meet his. "No. Not for Vicky." Yeah, I was being more intense than usual, but I needed him to know. This was for him. For me, yes, far more than I expected, but for him, too. I'd chosen this: picked the outfit, done my own makeup, been pleased with the results. I wasn't going to deny it any more. This was part of me now.

"Do I have Ben to thank for..." He waved a hand, indicating the whole of me, toe to top.

"Nope," I said, grinning. "I mean, his shopper bought the clothes, *obviously*. But I picked them out, did my face, all of it. By myself. I think I'm getting pretty good."

He nodded. "*Really* good."

The tension was back, but it was different this time, and I revelled in it. It wasn't just that I liked being looked at by James, although that was part of it; it was nice simply to forget all the questions about my identity and my future, to be in his company, to be the pretty girl with the handsome boy, to throw myself into the role with everything I had. And it was so different to how it used to be with him. We were more careful around each other and yet more apt to touch. I didn't mind, though. Quite the opposite.

I looked into his eyes and knew, unequivocally, what I wanted. What a fucking *rush*.

His phone alarm chimed, and we both sighed. It would have been nice to live in that moment a while longer.

"Dinner time," he announced, standing up and, as an apparent afterthought, draining his glass. I left mine half-finished on the table. I was already flirting with exhaustion, and the vaguest hint of a buzz from the rum was as close as I wanted to get to being drunk.

I still wobbled when I stood. James caught me, stepping into the space beside me and looping his arm around my waist, taking all my weight. It was like steadying myself on a crowbar. I let my feet sort themselves out, but I also let them take their time because he had his arm around me, and as far as I was concerned, he could leave it there forever if he wanted.

"Forgot I was wearing these for a second," I explained, leaning against his body so I could lift up a foot and waggle it. Also, incidentally, showing off my sandals (and my calves).

"I thought you were used to the heels by now," James teased, keeping hold of me and looking exactly where I wanted him to (at my legs).

"I'm used to them, for sure," I said. "But I'm forgetful. And *super* tired."

"Do you, um, want any help getting to the restaurant?"

There was no way I wasn't going to say yes. Helpfully, it was true that I could use some assistance; it also meant he'd keep touching me.

"It couldn't hurt," I said.

He released me, but before I could be disappointed, he presented his arm to me like a gentleman. I linked arms with him and let him lead me out of the bar.

* * *

Sophie's reaction, when she saw us walking arm-in-arm into the restaurant, was contained entirely within her eyebrows. But between them they did a *lot* of work. I wondered if James had to persuade her to keep her voice down in polite company, but then I remembered: the rich are trained to be decorous in restaurants; it was only in the wider world, among the plebs, that they really let rip.

She stood as we approached, opening her arms and walking towards us. James let me go — I didn't stagger — and Sophie and I embraced and exchanged cheek kisses, and goodness me if I didn't hope against hope that the skin on my face was still smooth and unstubbled; I cringed at the idea that just touching me would be enough to break the illusion.

She stepped back and looked me up and down and I tried my best to look normal.

"You look fantastic, Alex!" she said, with apparent sincerity.

"You too," I replied. "I *love* your dress. Oh, and your *shoes!*"

"Thank you!"

She really did look good. She was overdressed for a mid-priced hotel restaurant, but then, so was I. She wore a midi dress, similar to the one I'd worn that first night, but more flattering, in black, and with a likely price tag in the hundreds of pounds at least. She paired it with a simple but stunning pair of black sandals with a crisscross pattern up her calves and spike heels of sufficient height they made me wince. They also made her taller than me.

I still thought James was the better-looking of the two, though, even discounting my bias. He was wearing another suit from the Very Pricey collection by Georgio Expensivo (I'm a fashion ingénue but I learn fast). Thankfully, for the sake of my delicate equilibrium, it wasn't the star-of-my-wet-dreams charcoal suit; this one was navy blue, with a matching tie over a white shirt. I felt a familiar stab of lust, gazing at both him and his tailored clothing — accompanied by a stab of pain from my much-abused dick, letting me know, in case I'd forgotten, that it was jammed up against my body and not having the greatest time — but I was also a little sorry for him that his options were limited, in such an environment, to various flavours of fitted suit, while I got to be wrapped in silk.

Sophie had gotten us a spot at the edge of the dining area: three soft-backed chairs around a circular table, so we could be equidistant from each other. She gestured towards the chair that backed against the wall and, walking perilously unaided for the first time in an hour or so, I made it to my seat without falling down or even visibly wobbling. I appreciated the wall behind me — enough people had scared the shit out of me over the last few days by poking or tapping on me from behind that I was beginning to want a portable one to take with me everywhere — but it did mean I was effectively boxed in by McCains on both sides.

Well, Sophie was a Lincoln-McCain. Same difference.

"Alex, you really are adorable!" Sophie gushed, when we were all in place and she could make a proper start on embarrassing the shit out of me without disturbing our fellow diners. "How long did all that take you?"

"Give her a break, Soph," James said. I appreciated his intervention — I'd already lunged for the breadsticks and was busy chewing — almost as much as I appreciated the pronoun. It was nice to hear it from him.

"I *am* giving her a break!" she insisted, with an emphasis on the 'her' so slight I'm not sure anyone not listening for it would have detected it. It rather spoiled the high from James gendering me that way, though. She directed her attention back to me. "Who picked out that *gorgeous* outfit for you, Alex?"

"I did," I said, taking refuge from her inspection behind a breadstick.

"And those *curves*," she said. "Are they *real*? I thought I detected a *hint* of—"

"Sophie!" James whispered. "Remember what I said?"

She sighed. "Yes. Yes, James, I bleeding well remember."

"What did you say?" I asked.

"He *said*," Sophie announced, "that you were having a hard enough time of it without *me*—" she placed an innocent hand on her chest, "—causing a fuss. So I should 'lay off'. But you're doing so *well*! Nobody would *ever* know—"

"*Soph!*" James hissed.

"—you'd never modelled before," she finished smoothly.

"Well, I haven't," I said, "and however relaxed I might appear to be, I've been running *kind* of nervy all weekend, so a little consideration would be nice."

"Fine," she said, dialling down the attitude just a little. I didn't know what had gotten into her; I was used to pushy Sophie, but tonight she had an undercurrent of something I couldn't identify. It was making me antsy. "I just think it's a little *unfair*," she continued, "that you look so *good*, considering, you know..."

She left the dot-dot-dot hanging. I picked it up. "Considering what?" I asked sweetly. "And in what way is it 'unfair'? What advantages do you think I have? How much did *you* risk when you put on that nice dress this evening?" Bloody Little Miss I Can Just Throw On A Dress And Look Stunning; I had a perverse desire to pull out a boob and throw it at her.

"I just hope my *cousin* remembers what I said," she said, turning her smile on James. I wanted to intercept that smile, like a bodyguard jumping in front of a bullet.

"Yeah," James said, "I remember." Under the table and out of sight he took my hand. Squeezed it. Stroked me a little with his thumb. I took it to mean that she was referring to the thing he hadn't wanted to talk about earlier, and that I shouldn't pursue the subject at the table. I was about to squeeze his hand in return when he abruptly released me and directed all his attention conspicuously at the menu.

"Are you ready to order?" the waiter asked. I flinched; he'd somehow managed to sneak up on me despite being in my direct line of sight. Either this place sent their waitstaff to a better class of stealth combat school than Pizza Express did, or I was even less alert than I thought I was.

I tried not to be annoyed with the waiter. I just wanted to get the whole dinner over with and hide in my hotel room for a while. I had some serious thinking to do, and this was both holding me up and increasing the likelihood that I'd pass out as soon as I got back to my room. I didn't want to have to get through another whole day with such a heavy question hanging over my head.

"Not just yet, thank you," James said, switching smoothly into Rich Guy Mode — he sat up straighter and I swear I heard a little beep in his head as the Polite Bullshit circuits clicked on. He flashed a professional smile for the waiter; gone in a second and utterly insincere. "May we have a wine for the table while we decide?" He scanned the wine list and named a bottle, which turned out to be worth more than my best pair of (men's) shoes.

The waiter nodded and melted back into waitspace.

James immediately leaned forward on his elbows and glared at Sophie. "Can you *please* just be nice?"

"I'm just making observations!" she protested.

"Make yourself useful," James said, "and observe the menu. It's getting late and I'm hungry."

We all studied the menu. James and Sophie were, I assumed, getting more out of it than I was; they discussed the options with the confidence of people who knew what the hell they were talking about, while I squinted at my copy and wondered what a 'tomato concasse' was, and what you did to cabbage and apples to make a 'jus'.

When the waiter returned, bearing wine — James did his tasting routine — I ordered the chicken, confident in my deduction that the 'frites' it came with were something I'd be reasonably happy putting in my mouth. If only there were pictures...

And then my bladder sent an interrupt to my brain; it had just got done working on my Diet Coke and needed attending to.

"If you'll excuse me," I said to the table, code-switching (badly) into Posh, "I must use the ladies."

Before I'd even stood up — putting all my faith in the one-and-a-half bread sticks I'd wolfed down to keep me properly upright and respectable — James had pushed back on his chair, creating a space between him and the table, inviting me through the gap. I smiled gratefully and manoeuvred myself past him, trying to conduct myself with an impeccable level of dignity instead of, for example, smacking him in the face with my arse. If I denied I didn't take at least *some* pleasure from pressing my legs against his as I climbed over him, I'd make a liar out of myself, and when he touched his hand against my thigh to help steady me, I almost passed out from the thrill of it.

I was halfway to the bathroom when I saw Sophie following me, that same tight expression on her face. There was nothing I could do about that except perhaps run screaming out of the room, and at no point over the past few days that I'd contemplated that had I actually followed through.

"I have to ask," she said, as soon as the door to the ladies' closed behind us, "do you even *have* an Adam's Apple?"

"*Jesus,* Sophie!" I said, as my heart jump-started into a full panic. I checked under the stalls and discovered that I'd got lucky: either we were genuinely alone or the women in the stalls had sensed incoming drama and lifted their feet out of view so they could listen in without distracting us. "Are you *trying* to get me beaten up? What are you *doing?*"

I would have loved to wait for her answer, maybe pinned her with a searching and stern look, but I was desperate for a piss and still needed to disassemble my complicated underwear before I could relieve myself. I picked a stall and slammed its door, much harder than I intended. I think I made my point, though.

"What am *I* doing?" Sophie asked, aggrieved. "What are *you* doing?"

"What do you even mean?" I snapped. "I'm just trying to get through this fucking expo!" Lift up skirt, lift up bum pads, pull down knickers — *fuck, too fast, holy shit that hurt* — and relax. *Aaaaaah.* "If you have a problem with me, please *say* what I did to piss you off. I can't handle the suspense. Not on top of everything else."

"I can *see* you flirting with James," she said, entering the stall next to mine.

If I hadn't already been pissing, I think that might have jump-started me.

"Sophie, we're *friends*," I tried. "We've known each other for *years,* for fuck's sake. He's probably spent more time, total, around me than anyone apart from Ben and his immediate family. We're just... close."

"You walked in arm in arm!"

"Oh, you noticed, did you? I'm *tired,* Sophie. I've been on my feet all day, and then I had a thing with a friend, and now *this...* I should have been in bed watching TV at seven sharp, not still clattering around the hotel. He was helping me walk. That's all."

"Convenient," she sniffed.

"Don't forget, I've only been wearing heels a few days."

"Alexander *Brewer!*" she said, wielding my full name as might a fae. "I saw you *touching* each other under the table! And at the expo, you were *all over him.* Admit it! You can't claim there are *reasonable explanations* for any of that."

I wanted to bite something, but the only things nearby were all native to the ladies' loos, and I'd catch something horrible if I tried to cram any of them in my mouth. Over the last few days I'd learned, to my surprise, that women's facilities weren't necessarily any cleaner than men's; the queues were just longer.

In the absence of anything else to take out my anger and my fear on, I picked Sophie. "You know what?" I said. "*Fine.* You're right. You're *so* fucking right, Soph: I'm into him. And I think I always have been. Your cousin's *hot* and he's *kind* and when he puts on a suit, he looks like the second coming and the rapture all at once. You know what that makes me?

Still not his type." My eyes started to sting, and I blinked rapidly; I did *not* want to mess up my eye makeup in front of her. "James is straight, Sophie. He's fucking straight. He made it all the way through university rooming with a gay man who is, frankly, absolutely gorgeous, and who also, I remind you, wears dresses from time to time; five days with me in a skirt is child's play. If anyone was going to turn him gay, it wouldn't be me and it wouldn't be now, if that's what you're so bothered about."

"Jesus," Sophie said, hesitant, "I'm not— I'm not *bothered*."

Now I *really* wanted to bite something. "You *sound* kind of bothered to me, Sophie."

She went silent. I used the reprieve to finish my business and clean myself so I could strap everything up again.

"Fuck," she said quietly. A surprise: Sophie didn't swear, as a rule. "Fuck, Alex. I'm sorry. I'm stupid."

Okay, *now* I was confused. I finished arranging myself, flushed and exited my stall. Sophie was still in hers, but either she was the world's stealthiest pisser or she was just sitting there with her dress hitched up, doing nothing. I washed my hands while I waited for whatever was coming next.

"I'm protective," she said after a good long while. "Not without reason, but... Look, do you have any family around your age?"

"Not really," I said. "I have a cousin who's twelve. That's it."

Sophie snorted. "That's about the age gap between James and I," she said. "Our families are very close. I watched him grow up. Watched him grow distant from his parents. Watched him escape."

"Escape?" I asked.

"You've met his father?"

"Yeah," I said. "He's... a lot." My mum knew James' mum through the church. Always kind, always generous, always had a big bowl of something delicious for the harvest festival. When she married James' father and moved away, they stayed in touch, but it wasn't until I started at McCain Applied Computing that I finally met his dad.

245

I hadn't spent much time talking to him, but I'd come to think that if you were tight for space in the dictionary, you could replace the entry for 'benevolent sexist' with a picture of Henry McCain. I didn't imagine he was an easy man to have as your relative, if you happened to be a woman.

I heard a flush, and a moment later Sophie emerged with messed-up eye makeup. She was suddenly every girl I'd ever seen who'd had a breakup, or got some bad news, or had otherwise been upset. Dark smudges on her cheeks.

"Fuck, Sophie—" I said, completely unprepared for Sophie to be so *ordinary*.

"It's okay." She sniffed, wetly rearranged some awful alchemy of tears and snot in the back of her mouth, and spat in the sink. "I'm just protective of James, like I said. Rather stupid, really, since he's managed what I never did, which is to just step away from all our family *bullcrap*. All the expectations, all the obligations... even the money, sort of. I admired him for that. Built up an idealised version of his life in my head. And then, when I saw how you two behaved around each other..."

"I'm not who you want for him?" I suggested. It hurt.

"It's not that!" She sniffed again. "I promise it's not that. We talked about you at lunch, you know. I rather confronted him, I'm afraid. Told him you were *way* too easygoing and receptive to all this, and he was just taking advantage." I went cold. That sounded too much like what *I'd* said to James, back at the office when I was angry as hell with him. "He insisted he was trying to help you through a difficult time," she said. "Told me till he was blue in the face that's all it was. And that was it, Alex; he was *too* defensive."

"You *were* accusing him of—"

"He wasn't defensive of himself! It was all about *you!* He was defending *your* honour, talking up *your* virtue. Went on and on about how kind you are, how sweet, gave it *all* that. The way he talks about you, Alex..." She sighed. "I think he loves you."

"Um," I said, and slumped against the wall, dizzy.

"But not as a man," she continued. "I kept going on at him about that, calling you *he,* reminding him who you are, because that was the point I started to think you might be manipulating him—"

"*Manipulating him?*" I interrupted. I couldn't help it.

She smiled weakly at me. "Alex," she said, "look at yourself. Look at this whole situation! You're wearing expensive clothes *he* bought for you, hair and nails he paid for, and you're *way* too good at this for it to be your first time." She looked away, at the floor, at the sink with the remains of her gross snot bomb in it; anywhere but at me. "I told myself you were after his money or his company. And... and it sounds *really* stupid when I come to say it out loud."

"To be clear," I said, "I've never done this before. Any of it." I flapped a hand at my dress, my shoes, my face. "I'm a complete rookie. Apart from that bloody school play, the first dress I ever put on was the one Ben gave me, and that was a test to see if I could do this *at all!* I'm *really* not a— a—" Words failed me.

"An *en-femme fatale?*" she asked, grinning damply. If there was a joke there, it was beyond me. "Never mind," she muttered.

I was still stuck on something. Something *quite* crucial. "Why do you think he loves me?"

"Like I said, he was defending you. He kept correcting me when I talked about you as a man. Over and over. 'Show her some respect!' That kind of thing." She frowned. "He got quite angry about it."

Shit. That was it? "That's just—"

"Don't say it's just for your safety," she said sharply, pinning me with a glare. "It's *not* that. Yes, your safety is important to him, but it's so much more than that. It's—" she waved a hand in the air, as if scrolling through dialogue options, "—it's important to him that he thinks of you as a woman, Alex. It's important to the way he thinks about you, and it's important to the way he thinks about himself. Because you're right; he's straight. And he's falling in love with the woman he sees when he looks at you. And that *scares* me. Right now, that scares me."

"Because I'm not a woman?" I said bitterly.

"Aren't you?" she said, and *that* made me glad I had a wall to support me. Sophie seemed suddenly far more insightful than I'd given her credit for, despite her tendency to leap to dubious conclusions. "You're not like any man I've ever met. And this isn't the first time I've thought that about you. It *is* the first time I thought it in this... exact context, though. So the question, Alex, is what *are* you?"

"Soph," I whispered, "I don't know." I kicked my expensive heels against the restroom floor. "All my life I've been this, you know? Well, not *this*—" I laughed hollowly and gestured at myself again, "—but what I was the last time you saw me. I never questioned it. Never had a reason to. Always thought of myself as just a normal guy. A normal *straight* guy. And then, suddenly, dressing like a woman, talking like a woman, being *treated* like a woman... Fireworks in my head, Soph. Big damn explosions going off, and I'm a tiny little prehistoric creature who's never seen fire before. And that's without even getting into the fact that I really am, I think, in love with James. I'm asking all these questions about myself I never even knew to ask, and I'm having to do it while spending all day in a stupid outfit being *pawed at* by greasy men. It's... it's *terrifying*, Sophie."

She whistled. "Wow."

"Yeah," I said. "*Wow* doesn't even begin to cover it. I know I'm not like most men, at any rate — it's been pointed out to me that 'most men' would be pretty fucking uncomfortable doing what I've been doing — but that's about as far as I've got. I'm setting aside some time later tonight to have a really good think about it."

"*Fuuuudge*," Sophie said, doing terrible damage to the vowel. She slumped against the opposite wall. "I'm so sorry, Alex. I walked into this whole complicated situation and stuck my size sevens right where they could do the most damage. Making assumptions." She kicked backwards at the wall. "I've become my mother. I've bleeding well become my mother! You know why I'm twenty-nine and still single? Because my mother was a total b-word to *every* guy I brought home when I was young. There was always a reason: they didn't make enough money; they were 'too rough'; they were 'disrespectful'. I got away from her eventually, but I internalised a lot of what she said. So says my therapist." She pulled an exaggerated grimace. "I *thought* I was just a danger to myself. Turns out I'm also projecting all of it onto James. But, Alex, I have to know—" she pushed away from the wall and grabbed me gently but firmly around my upper arm, "—if you're going to hurt him."

I looked her right in the eye and told her one of the few things I knew for certain: "That's the last thing I want to do."

"Good," she said, and let me go. "Look, you've obviously got more going on in that head of yours that I realised. I thought it was like a game to you. And then when James was really obviously infatuated..." She trailed off, shaking her head.

"You thought I was playing with him," I finished for her. "I'm not. And I get it: you don't want him hurt. But—" and this was the point where I had to confront the whole of it, "—you say he's falling in love with the woman he sees when he looks at me?" She nodded. "Jesus," I commented, and lost control of my knees. Sophie grabbed me again and supported my weight. Held up by both McCains tonight.

Well, Sophie was a Lincoln-McCain.

"You really didn't know?" she asked, smiling softly.

"I didn't," I whispered. "I mean, I thought, maybe, but it was such a dream. I didn't want to hope."

"I suppose the question is," she said, "whether the woman he sees in you is real or not."

I closed my eyes. "She might be."

"Good enough for now," Sophie said, and gave me a quick embrace before carefully letting me go, one hand at a time, the way one might detach oneself from a particularly wobbly vase that could smash itself to bits on the floor if balanced incorrectly. "You'll figure things out before you let anything happen between the two of you, yes?"

"Yes," I said, as firmly as I could manage.

"Good girl." She sighed heavily, which seemed to indicate the end of the heavy conversation, and regarded herself in the mirror. "Fudge. I really made a mess, didn't I? Of you, of James, of my face..."

"*And* you gobbed in the sink," I pointed out. It had been weighing on me.

"Sorry. Habit. Girls' school."

"That's not an explanation."

She shrugged. "Put enough girls in one place for long enough and they're *at least* as gross as boys. You wouldn't know, I guess."

"No," I said, a little coldly, "I wouldn't."

"Oh. Crap. Sorry."

I smiled. "Hey, I missed all the boy stuff, too, I think. Missed everything."

"That's so sad, Alex!" she said, hugging me again.

"Hey, woah," I said, pushing her off and laughing, "don't get your snot on me!"

She grinned and pulled a soft case out of her bag. "So help me fix it?"

"I mean, I'm still practising," I said. "But sure."

* * *

"The key to dealing with men," Sophie explained as I repaired her mascara, "is to keep them off-balance. If he thinks we've been talking about him, he'll feel like we've got him on the back foot."

A few women had come and gone while we worked on her face, limiting our conversation a little, but by this point we were alone again, and Sophie was taking advantage of the privacy to dole out some advice, 'woman to probable woman'.

"We *have* been talking about him," I pointed out.

"Mostly about you."

"Seems a little unfair."

"No," Sophie said sternly, holding a finger up in my face. "There's *way* too much power on his side right now. He's your boss, he's got money, he's straight…"

"Is he?" I asked, closing the mascara and handing it back. "If he's into *me,* how can he be straight?"

250

"Because he sees you as a woman, Alex." She punctuated my name by bonking me on the head with the mascara. "Whether you *are* or not is something you need to work out, but as far as he's concerned, you are. So you need to take control of the situation and slow things down a bit, at least until you've had your big think."

"Okay. How?"

"You've seen the way he looks at you, right?" she said. "I know I have. I bet every time you touch him, he gets a semi. So for now, *stop touching him*. Don't take his arm, don't hold his hand, and, for the love of little green apples, Alex, don't stick your bottom in his face."

I blushed. "He—"

"I *know* he basically invited you to do that." She closed her eyes and spritzed herself with setting spray. "He's a man; he's controlled by his knob. If you're going to join Team Girl—"

"That's not a given," I interrupted.

She looked at me like I'd grown a second head and I was letting it say really dumb things. "*If* you're going to join Team Girl, you need to learn how to be the adult in the room. Don't take the opportunities he puts in front of you, no matter how much you want to. Ease up on the physical contact until you get the time you need to think about—" the door to the restroom opened again, reducing us once more to communicating in code, "—about what you need to think about."

"Okay," I said. I *had* been indulging myself without any clear idea of where I was taking things, I suppose because I hadn't believed we *could* go any further than just flirting. "You're really okay with, um, me and him? If that's how it works out?"

"I'm okay with it if it's what he wants — if it's what *both* of you want — and if it's real. But I mean it: if you break his heart, I'll be mad at you. And you don't want me mad at you; I can be very annoying. I learned from my mother and she's the best. So—" she marked every word with a wag of her finger, "—don't break his heart!" She narrowed her eyes, inspected me closely. "I don't think you will."

We walked out of the restroom arm in arm and James practically jumped out of his seat when he spotted us. With the way we'd been before we left, he probably expected us to emerge covered in nail scratches, with makeup smeared, clothes dishevelled and hair sticking up. We shot him identical sweet smiles as we approached, and he rolled his eyes at us.

Sophie helped me back to my seat via the non-James route, which was a sacrifice, but a necessary one. If she was right, if James really was attracted to the woman he saw in me, I owed it to him and to myself to figure out if she was real before I acted on it.

I needed a barometer. I needed to talk to trans people.

* * *

I got through the meal on autopilot; I had far too much to think about to actually taste my food. James tried to touch me a few times, just casually, but I fended him off every time, smiling to let him know it wasn't out of malice. It must have got through because after a while he concentrated on his dinner.

I escaped as quickly as politeness allowed, picked up a Red Bull from a vending machine on the way through the lobby — I'd had only one glass of wine, but along with the half-finished rum and Coke and my encroaching exhaustion it was enough seriously to impede my concentration — and leaped for a closing elevator door, almost colliding with the man inside.

"Oh hi!" he said, in a tone that reminded me of grabby conventioneers. I checked him out in the mirrored elevator wall. Early forties, probably, and thus far too old to be directing a hopeful leer at a nineteen-year-old woman.

"Hi," I said, trying to inject as much finality into the syllable as I could.

"Which floor?" he asked, with his hand hovering over the panel so I couldn't hit the number myself.

"Fourth," I said. Something inside me — the same part of me that was calling me an idiot for getting into a lift without checking its contents first — made me lie. I could always hop down a flight of stairs when I got out.

"Ah!" he said, delighted. "Same as me."

Naturally, I said to myself.

"My name's Frank," he said. "I'm here for the expo that's in town."

Naturally times fucking two. "I'm here meeting my husband," I said, having decided to let the part of me that thought the rest of me was a dumbass control my mouth, on the basis that it could almost definitely do a better job.

"Ah," he said again, considerably more crestfallen this time. Were men always this obvious? Or was it just the creeps? *Who hits on someone in a fucking lift?*

We rode the elevator in silence after that. I started second-guessing myself immediately, telling myself I was being rude to a perfectly normal man who was being perfectly nice and perfectly innocent and — I checked — was staring at my arse in the mirrored wall.

When we got to the fourth floor, I stepped back to let him out first, and then hit a number on the panel as soon as I was free to.

"I forgot something," I said. "Have a nice evening."

The doors closed on his sad little face.

Did I really want to be a woman, I asked myself as I waited for the elevator to spit me out at the correct floor, if that was the sort of attention I had to look forward to?

* * *

I set myself up at the tiny desk, the one with the lighted mirror, and arranged in front of me my work laptop, my Red Bull, Vicky's card, and my encroaching sense of despair. I couldn't get the encounter with the man out of my head. He'd looked at me and looked at me and *looked at me,* in a way I'd thought I was used to after two days at the expo. But in a confined space, with no-one else around, it had been very different.

"Don't lose heart," I said to myself. "Just learn from it."

Talking to yourself again, Alex.

I booted up the laptop, tapped in the URL Vicky had given me, and settled down to read.

Half an hour later and I was no closer to an answer. Sure, I'd discovered that essentially everything I thought I knew about trans people was wrong — and, yes, many of them *hadn't* realised they were trans until they were my age or older, which was a big kick in the face to my theory that I couldn't be trans because I hadn't known all my life — but I was having difficulty applying their experiences to my own. I'd just come to the conclusion that I needed to register a throwaway account so I could talk directly to someone, when my phone screen lit up with an email notification.

It was Vicky, forwarding the photos she'd taken of me at the expo. I opened one.

By this point I'd seen myself in mirrors, car windows, reflective walls, and the phone screens of random guys as they took selfies with me, but something about this photo was different. I was *there,* chatting with Emily — Vicky must have snuck some candid shots when I wasn't looking — and I looked so perfectly at ease it made my heart ache. In a daze I thumbed through the other photos, and they were all like that: there stood a normal woman, albeit in a very silly dress, and she looked like she belonged. She looked *real.*

I'd always hated looking at photos of myself. They always made me feel uncomfortable, like I didn't belong in the picture, like the photo had been digitally edited somehow. I *thought* I was just another self-conscious nerd who didn't like having his picture taken; I *thought* everyone who wasn't supremely confident in their own appearance felt like that. But seeing these photos instantly recontextualised every other photo of myself I'd ever seen.

It turned out it *wasn't* normal for your skin to crawl when you see yourself.

There goes another blindfold...

I had to talk to someone.

[-] donut_appreciator

dude that's the most egg thing I've ever read in my life

[-] random_throwaway_484357

'Egg thing'?

[-] donut_appreciator

you don't know what an egg is???

okay so an egg is basically a trans person who doesn't know they're trans yet

there's a whole subreddit for memes, you should check it out, you'll probably find it insufferably relatable

anyway you're like making this big post about how basically you've been living as a woman for like three whole days now and you've never felt so comfortable or accepted in your life

and immediately after laying all that out you're like "help I don't know if I'm trans or not"

and that is the most classic egg move ever

more so than most actually

like with most eggs it's like they're looking wistfully at girls or boys or enbies or whichever and wishing they could be like that but then they immediately write it off as perfectly normal curiosity

like that's the main feature of being an egg

in your head you turn very obviously trans thoughts and experiences into "well that's just how everyone feels"

"every man hates being a man and secretly wishes they were a girl, that's just what 'be a man' means" sort of thing

but you actually TRANSITIONED three days ago and you're happier than you've ever been and you're STILL finding excuses

there's a big flashing neon sign in your face that says YES YOU ARE TRANS and there are like musicians and singers and backup dancers all on the theme of YOU ARE A GIRL and you're looking at the whole stage show like "yeah but what if I'm not???"

[-] random_throwaway_484357

But I'll be going home in less than two days and taking all this off.

What if when I do that it feels okay? What if I'm fine being a boy again?

[-] donut_appreciator

dude you can't even say "man" you have to say "boy" and I think that's pretty diagnostic of how you feel about your agab

[-] random_throwaway_484357

What's my agab?

[-] donut_appreciator

never mind

look the point is

do you WANT to go home and be a "boy" again?

or is that just what you feel like you SHOULD do?

[-] random_throwaway_484357

I have no idea. Both?

[-] donut_appreciator

okay well first of all FUCK "should"

if all of us did what we "should" do then I'd be a miserable girl still living with my mum and spending all my time playing video games in the dark

instead of being a happy guy living with my dad and spending all my time playing video games but with the curtains open this time

(I'm recovering from top surgery)

"should" is the word we use when what we NEED conflicts with what other people WANT from us

except from what you said it sounds like the people around you are pretty chill with the idea that you're a girl

so the biggest obstacle here is you
and "should"

[-] random_throwaway_484357

But that's the thing, what if when I stop doing this I realise I was just caught up in the novelty of it all? In the way dressing and acting like this makes me feel?

[-] donut_appreciator

how does it make you feel?

[-] random_throwaway_484357

Happy, I think. But that could just be from getting out of my rut.

[-] donut_appreciator

you're making excuses

it's a funny thing, when people treat us as who we really are, it tends to make us happy

and when WE let OURSELVES be who we really are, it tends to make us happy

bottom line:

IF there were no obstacles in your way, no-one to tell you what to do or who to be, if you could just flip a switch and be a woman forever, would you do it?

don't think just answer

[-] random_throwaway_484357

Yes.

[-] donut_appreciator

https://urlshorti.fy/2tx34

Fuck. Was I really so certain? When he asked me about going home, being a boy again, my answer was pretty rote, and it felt like from his reaction that I'd got it wrong, so maybe this time I just said what he wanted to hear?

No.

Alex.

For God's sake.

What did Vicky say? What did this Reddit guy just say?

No more excuses.

Face up to it.

I closed my eyes and once again tried to picture myself returning to my life as regular old Alex, and it was easy enough. I saw his flat, cold and small and lonely. I saw his job. I saw him returning to his old, friendly relationship with James.

I saw his routine. I couldn't see his *life*.

And that was it, wasn't it? I'd never actually had a life, to speak of. I coasted into my job and then I stayed there, and I realised as I thought about it that I had no plans beyond 'keep working for James'. Sure, I always imagined that one day there'd be a girl who stuck around, but it wasn't like I *wanted* that. It was just the done thing. So I'd do it. Like moving a game piece around a Monopoly board: follow the instructions, pay bills, pass Go. Over and over, round and round, in ever more dizzying circles.

I pitched forward in my chair and almost hit my head on the desk. Jesus. I was describing a fucking nightmare.

So, what was the alternative?

I pictured myself remaining as I'd become, committing to it, living as a woman for real, and suddenly a future unfolded in front of me. I found myself imagining day-to-day life, getting caught up in the details of how I would redecorate my nasty little apartment, of where and when I would go shopping. I imagined hanging out with Ben and Sophie and Emily and, yes, I definitely imagined a relationship with James, as unlikely as that still seemed despite Sophie's claims. I saw a life. Sure, I'd have to get treatment or whatever, but if trans people managed it— if *other* trans people managed it, it had to be doable.

I followed the link. It took me to a webpage with the title, *So your egg cracked. What now? (UK edition).* It laid out the paths to treatment like they were three marathon runners, from slowest to fastest. Slowest, with a timetable of at least four years before treatment could start and a warning that it could be years longer still, was going through the NHS; I dismissed that immediately. In the middle, at up to six months to treatment, was a guide to arranging an appointment with one of a small brace of private doctors. Fastest, at a couple of weeks and with a handful of warnings attached, was going online and buying the requisite medication from an overseas pharmacy.

Did I want this? Did I *really* want this? Because it looked from the link that if I did, I could just bloody well do it.

[-] random_throwaway_484357

Thanks for the link! It's all still pretty overwhelming though.

[-] donut_appreciator

well I mean you don't have to make any decisions right away

but remember

even if right now you're lucky enough to be able to pass with just some makeup and rubber tits, that WILL NOT LAST

unless you have a condition that makes you insensitive to testosterone, which is possible but far from guaranteed

but otherwise YOU WILL start to masculinise sooner or later

it happens to almost everyone

it's probably already happening for you in little ways, the T is insidious like that, for girls

I started testosterone at 18 and I wish I'd started earlier

[-] random_throwaway_484357

So I'm basically sitting on a ticking clock?

[-] donut_appreciator

more like a ticking time bomb

a ticking T bomb!

[-] random_throwaway_484357

Haha.

[-] donut_appreciator

there!

that's proof you're a trans girl

trans girls love puns

[-] random_throwaway_484357

Is that really a pun?

[-] donut_appreciator

trans girls are also pedants

[-] random_throwaway_484357

You think I should just buy the medication online?

[-] donut_appreciator

it's not ideal like at all

ideally you'd have someone take your bloods and work out an exact treatment regimen for you

and then you'd come back every six months for more blood tests to make sure you're not over or under dosing

but what ACTUALLY happens for most trans people in this country is we just get put on the same dose as everyone else and then blood tests happen later

so if you buy off the internet you're not ACTUALLY doing anything the NHS wouldn't do for you, you just don't have like the official rubber stamp to get your HRT for cheap at the local pharmacy

[-] random_throwaway_484357

But wouldn't it be safer to see a doctor who can diagnose me? I need to know I'm not about to make a terrible mistake, surely?

[-] donut_appreciator

lol

seriously: lol

ask any british trans person on here

the diagnostic procedure comes down to, "do you have a persistent wish to live as the opposite gender" which is what I asked you earlier but with the word persistent in it

[-] random_throwaway_484357

Oh.

[-] donut_appreciator

yeah lol

also they ask you a load of invasive questions about how often you wank

thing is

no one has a foolproof machine they can point at you that goes beep if you're trans

like in some countries they have a thing called informed consent where you just sign a piece of paper saying I understand what I'm doing now gimme hormones

so in buying off the internet you're just doing that really

I understand what I'm doing and here's some money now gimme hormones

anyway going on HRT is diagnostic in itself

if after a couple months your mood has worsened and you feel like shit all the time and you don't like the changes that have started in your body you can just...... stop

[-] random_throwaway_484357

You really can just stop HRT? There's no side-effects or anything?

[-] donut_appreciator

yeah

your body will take over hormone production and start pumping out testosterone again

depending on when you stop you might have like slightly bigger nipples but a couple of months isn't enough time to like give you a supermodel body

[-] random_throwaway_484357

I can't believe it didn't occur to me I could just try them out. I've been thinking of this as a huge, life-changing decision.

[-] donut_appreciator

yeah it's really just a load of little ones

imo the life-changing decision has already been made

you said yes before

you know what you want

you know what you need

now you just have to get past your doubts

* * *

I was reading the section of the website that covered the effects I could expect from HRT — softer skin, some breast growth, a fleshier butt, but no help with my voice or facial hair — when my phone chimed again. This time it was a text from James.

James: Hi. Mind if I come up?

Alex: Sure.

And then I took a very deep breath and slowly composed another message.

Alex: You can bring your overnight bag and something to sleep in, if you'd like. Since you were so well-behaved last night.

If he wanted to talk, I wanted to listen, with no time constraints.

His reply took longer than I'd like. **Five minutes then,** he wrote, **to get my stuff together.**

Okay! Five minutes to prepare. I closed the laptop lid so I could inspect myself in the mirror; I still had makeup on, and it was still mostly fine. I stood up, looked in the full-length, and decided the clothes I'd worn for dinner, while gorgeous, were rather too formal for... for whatever was about to happen. We'd promised to tell each other what was going on inside our respective heads, and I didn't want to be an immaculate Harvey Nicks-clad goddess for that. Even though, thanks to Sophie, I had a fair idea of what might have been bothering James, I still wanted to be approachable and maybe not flaunt my fake curves quite so much.

I dug out the not-terribly-comfortable jeans and top combo I'd worn for the journey up from London and quickly got changed. I didn't bother with shoes or socks. But when I checked myself out in the mirror, I still felt a little dressy. It took a moment for me to identify why, and I was just wiping my lips on the back of my hand when James knocked.

On my way to the door I noticed I was practically skipping. I took a deep breath, calmed myself, and opened it.

James was carrying his suit jacket and tie over one arm. His shirt was unbuttoned at the top, and I had to bite my lip to stop myself from focusing solely on the little scruff of chest hair that was visible.

He looked downcast.

"What is it?" I asked urgently. I reached for his free hand, intending to lead him into the room, but he jerked away from me. "James?"

"Sorry," he said.

I tried taking his hand again, and this time he let me. I closed the door behind him, led him over to the bed, and sat him down. He kept looking at the floor.

"James," I said, "what's going on?"

He was silent.

"James?" I repeated. "Please look at me."

When he finally met my eyes, all I saw in him was utter despair.

Chapter Ten

I put him on the bed and I stood in front of him and I worried. James kept looking at me for brief seconds and then looking away again. He'd stare at the floor, at the door, at his own reflection, and then back at me. After a while I gave up on asking him questions and just sat next to him, which compressed the mattress under us and pushed us closer together than I intended, but when I checked on him he didn't react, so I didn't try to move myself away. I stayed with him, rubbed his spine gently, two fingers up and down, barely making contact. I wanted him to know he was welcome here, he was wanted here, and he had all the time in the world to make up his mind to speak.

From where we were sitting, I could see both of us in the mirror, and when he wasn't paying attention, I scrutinised his reflection as much as I could. It wasn't *likely* I could suss out what was wrong just by looking, but it was better than doing nothing.

He wasn't drunk: his eyes were bloodshot, but that had to have been from crying, not alcohol, and the tear stains on his cheeks backed me up; he also didn't smell like he'd had much more than just the wine we'd had with dinner and the rum and Coke beforehand.

I'd never seen him like this. What could have happened to upset him so much? Had Sophie said something? Was this my fault?

Or had something *truly* awful happened?

"James," I said, suddenly panicking and imagining terrible things, "please tell me what's wrong."

"I shouldn't," he whispered, and I felt my throat dry out in sympathy; he sounded like a man dying of thirst. I let him go for a moment, dropping back on the bed and reaching behind me for a water bottle. He took it wordlessly and drank, and I returned to stroking his back.

"Why shouldn't you talk?" I asked as gently as I knew how.

"I'll make it worse," he muttered. "That's all I do. All I've *been* doing."

"What do you mean? Was it something Sophie said?"

"It was something I did."

"Tell me. Please."

He drained the water bottle and threw it carelessly at the waste basket, missing by a mile. "I was feeling so good about myself," he said eventually. "So proud. About us. About our company." He often referred to it like that: as ours. As if it weren't his name on it, his money in it; I just worked there. It was nice of him anyway.

He didn't say anything else, seemed exhausted by that small confession, so I tried encouragement. "You should be proud!" I insisted. "We've done really well."

"*You've* done well," he said, strangely bitter. "You've done great. All I've done is the rich-boy dance for people impressed enough by my name and my accent to give us a shot. But you've been out there—" he waved a careless arm in entirely the wrong direction, "—going above and beyond for us."

"It's nothing more than Emily's done," I said. She didn't get anything like enough appreciation. She'd had to fend off the exact same crap I had, and she'd done so while shielding me from the worst of it *and* effectively training me.

And backwards! an irreverent part of me added. *In high heels!*

The point was, none of that stuff was in her contract, and I'd be angling for a huge bonus for her as well as the tryout at work. At least I wouldn't have to worry any more about her encountering a boy wearing my face when she turned up at the office. That would have been embarrassing.

James grunted his acknowledgment, chewed on the inside of his cheek for a moment, and said, "She didn't have me... pushing her."

Oh crap. This *was* about what Sophie said to him.

"You didn't—"

"I did!" he interrupted. "I pushed and I pushed and I pushed." He shot me a sad smile. "You know, I loved spending time with you here last night. And I loved dinner together tonight. And we've been on the go so much I haven't ever given myself time to think about *why* I had such a good time. And... there's all the other things, too."

"What things?" I pressed.

"I abused your trust."

"James, you've never—"

"You called me out, remember? When I got Ben to take away your clothes that first night, because I wanted you to 'get more into character'." I'd never seen finger quotes articulated with such contempt before. "I took away your agency and you called me on it, and you were right." He almost smiled. "You're always right. But I didn't do it to help you. That was just what I told Ben. The real reason was just... selfishness. Like with *everything* I do."

"What—?"

"You work for me," he said quietly, pulling away from me and shaking his head, "and what do I pay you? A pittance. A fraction of your worth. But when it's something *I* want... it's like there's nothing I won't consider." I tried yanking on him, to bring him closer to me again, to emphasise as much as I could that I thought he was talking nonsense, but he was like a rock, and I could no more have moved him than I could have picked up the bed. "Hair extensions," he continued, glaring at himself in the mirror, "clothes, shoes... I *threw* money at this." He broke eye contact with himself and, finally, consented to be pulled back my way. "You're the most incredible person I've ever met, Alex, and I've been taking advantage of you. Not just this week, either. Always."

"That's not true, James," I said, reaching out for his hand and, when he tried to take it away from me, keeping hold with as much force as I could muster. "It's *not*. When you hired me, you didn't just give me a job, you gave me a *life*. Everything after that has been more than I ever thought to expect. Seriously." I leaned around, tried to put myself in his field of view. "And this? The modelling thing? The girl thing? You asked. I said yes. We both agreed it was necessary for the company."

"Just a flimsy excuse," he hissed from between gritted teeth. "Just a stupid idea of mine based on nothing more than..." He trailed off, and in my hands his palm flexed. "And you! You just... went along with it. Because you are kind and helpful and good and— and—"

"James."

"You didn't have to parade around like that. We could have made do. I saw you on the expo floor; you could have sold our software wearing a *sack*. We didn't need to do this to you. It was all just... my vanity. My ego. All because I wanted it. Because the rich boy's so used to getting what he wants he's started treating people like toys. Because he— because *I* can't tell a favour from a game from a— a ruinous fantasy."

I'd decided to let him talk himself out, but he sort of ground to a halt. It was like he switched off, like his self-loathing had overwhelmed all his other functions and left him without conscious control over his body. He slumped.

"None of that's true, James," I said, pushing my voice as far to the front of my mouth as I could and hoping I sounded as sympathetic to him as I did inside my head. "None of it. Do you think I've been having a bad time? Because I haven't. Once I got past my inhibitions, I—"

He erupted, pulled his hand away from me. "You shouldn't have *had* to!"

I reached for him again, pulled him back, reclaimed him, started stroking his fingers one by one. It seemed incredibly intimate, but I didn't care. He needed me. "It's good that I did," I whispered. "I'm glad that I did."

He nodded, slowly, thoughtfully, and started responding to me, turning his hand over in mine, taking its weight, and gently massaging my palm with his thumb. I closed my eyes for a second, revelled in his touch — until suddenly he dropped me and stood up from the bed. When I opened my eyes again, he was standing over me, shaking. "Sorry," he hissed.

"What for?" I asked, standing up. I got right into his space, looked up at him, made him look down, made him acknowledge me. "Are you sorry for being kind to me?" I stepped forward again. Close enough to feel his body heat. "Are you sorry for helping me through all this? Or—" I decided to risk it, "—are you sorry for holding my hand? Sorry for being gentle with me? For touching me at all?"

He staggered backwards a little, and for a moment I was worried he might fall. But he was just reasserting his space; a space that didn't include me.

"I would have done it again," he said, monotone. "Made choices for you. You called me out and I stopped, but I wanted to keep doing it. Wanted to take control. Wanted to mould you. I would have taken your agency away any way I could, just to make you stay like this." He turned his back on me and I had to strain to hear him. "Before we started this, I thought it was going to be how it used to be with Ben, back at uni, when he'd do a show and I'd come along and we'd hang out together, have a laugh, but... Alex, as soon as I saw you, I forgot *all* of that." I stepped around him, manoeuvring carefully around the edge of the bed so I didn't fall, and sat on the end of the mattress, just about able to see his face. "It was like an electric shock. You know? You touch an exposed wire and suddenly your heart's beating faster than it ever has before and your skin is on fire and everything's... tingling. Shit. I'm stupid. This is so fucking stupid."

"James—"

"You don't understand, Alex," he said, turning back to me again, leaning against the wall by the bathroom door and looking about ready to slide down it, to come to rest at its base and never move again. "You don't *know* what shit I would have pulled. I got you in the wig and the clothes and then we went out to eat and you looked *so good,* and then I got you in the extensions and then— then, fuck, that *outfit* you wore to the office, that one damn near fucking killed me, and so then *of* course I got stupid and confused and said awful things. And then I saw you out there with Emily, Emily the professional model, and I realised... Alex, I realised I wasn't looking at her at all. I was looking at you. I couldn't stop looking. And all the time there was this voice, getting louder and louder, and it was saying, 'Never let her stop. Never let her go back.' I couldn't help listening, Alex."

I knew what he meant about the electric shock; I was feeling it now. This seemed like everything I wanted to hear... except it was coming from a man who was ashamed to say it.

He called me *her,* though. That was something I could take solace in, no matter how the rest of this went. To James, I was *her.* I didn't know why the pronoun had ever bothered me. Except, maybe, it had been prodding at wounds I didn't even know I had.

"James," I said, "you didn't do anything."

"But I wanted to. So much."

"But you didn't," I repeated. "And look at me; I've been having a great time!"

"You're just lying to be kind," James muttered. I shook my head firmly. "Sophie was right," he added, after a few moments of silence.

"Did she say you were playing with me?" I suggested, knowing full well she had. "Taking advantage of my, uh, compliant nature to push me into doing things?"

"She was practically quoting you, Alex! Said I was enjoying myself at your expense. Dressing you up like my own personal Barbie. Which is what *you* said!"

"Yes," I said, pushing through whatever he was about to say next and just bloody swallowing my irritation — at him for being so stubborn; at myself for saying something so foolish, so long ago — "I *did* say that, and

270

then we *kept talking,* James! We kept talking and we moved past it. And you said..." I shook my head as if that would dislodge the memory. Everything prior to today was getting fuzzy, like I was trying to recall decisions and mistakes made by someone else, someone who didn't have all the information. But I remembered one thing clearly enough: "You said I was becoming something more than I was. And I've been thinking about that ever since you said it." Not necessarily consciously; my subconscious had been ten steps ahead of the rest of me the whole time. "You were right, James."

"But that's just it! You were *you,* you were *Alex,* and then I came along and turned you into something *I* wanted, out of pure selfishness."

There was only one way to derail his destructive — not to mention inaccurate — train of thought, but to do it, I'd have to flip the coin and find out: was he really, genuinely attracted to me, and struggling with it for whatever reason, like Sophie said? Or was he simply getting overwhelmed by his guilt over coercing someone financially dependent on him into a dress, for his own amusement or gain?

"You know what Sophie said to me in the restroom?" I said. "She asked me point-blank if I was going to hurt you." He had something to say about that but I carried on, talking over him, and after a few words he let me. "She asked me if I was playing a game with all this. She thought I was manipulating you! She even said—" I paused for a quick breath; the stress of this was definitely getting to me, "—she said she was worried because she saw you *falling* for the woman you saw when you looked at me." There. Now the idea was out in the world. I'd thrown it down between us like a live grenade: *James is attracted to Alex.* Yes, you didn't have to read James' actions especially generously to come to the same conclusion, but there *were* other possibilities. So it was time to clear it up, once and for all.

He said nothing.

Shit.

Fuck it. I needed him to know everything anyway. No matter how he felt about me. "James," I said, leaning back a little on the bed so I could steady myself, "you were right. I was just Alex. And I barely existed. You *know* I've had nothing in my life except work. And a handful of relationships barely worthy of the name. And... and *you*." I swallowed. My mouth was dry and my throat was aching, but I couldn't stop. "You showed me another way I could be. You showed me *this,* and whatever your reason for proposing it, whatever stories you're telling yourself about how selfish you are, I'm grateful. I'm so grateful I want to lean out the window with a megaphone and tell the whole *city* about it!" I pushed up again, leaned forward, elbows on my knees. A little closer to him. "You know what the amazing thing is? The ridiculous thing? The total fucking miracle? It turns out this is *me*. This is who I am. This is who I always want to be. Old Alex? *Boy* Alex? A holding pattern. A dead end. A pit I never would have climbed out of because I didn't even know I was in it." I smiled at him, desperately hoping I was getting through to him, because I had no other cards to play. "Until you. And this whole deeply silly, incredibly wonderful booth babe thing."

"Trade show model," he corrected in a whisper.

"You're damn right," I said. "You found me, James. You threw me a rope and you pulled me up and you showed me what happiness is. You found *me*."

"What do you mean, 'I found you'?" James asked. He was staring at me now with an intensity I'd never seen in him. A hunger.

"I mean," I said slowly, "that I was just a— a—" I remembered something the donut guy on Reddit said, "—an empty shell. No, an egg, waiting to be boiled. Hatched. Cracked? No. Shit. I don't know how the metaphor's supposed to work. *James.* What I mean is, I'm not going back. Not after the expo; not ever. The old me is gone for good." His eyebrows were still knotted; I wasn't being clear enough. Time to stop being oblique. "I'm not taking out the hair extensions and I'm keeping the dresses; sorry about the damage to the company credit card. And I'll buy my own pair of tits just like these until I can grow my own. I need this to never stop."

"What are you saying?"

"James, I'm trans. Transgender. I'm a transgender woman." My tongue got stuck on the word. "I'm a trans woman. I think I always have

272

been, but I never knew. I thought all the things missing in me, in my life, were things everyone dealt with. I just assumed it was the way things were supposed to be. Until this." I met his eyes. "Until you. I'm a girl, James."

There. It was finally out there.

James ruined it, naturally.

"But I still pushed you, because *I*—"

"No!" I interrupted, raising my shut-the-fuck-up finger. "You said it yourself! You said it was like I was a different person. And that was half right. But it's more like I wasn't a *whole* person before, and now I am. Thanks to this. Thanks to you! So *if* you were pushing me, and, sure, I'll grant that it's possible you were, it's because you saw something in me I couldn't yet see for myself."

"Don't make me out to be so noble," he said, still miserable. "*Just last night* I was trying to tell you not to switch back. And I wasn't being kind. Just selfish."

I frowned. "I don't remember that."

"You were falling asleep. And I was lying there thinking about you, and about what I wanted, what I was coming to need. So, like an idiot, I started... suggesting you might not actually want to go back to how you used to be. And you—" a smile captured his face despite his misery, "—you rolled over and shushed me. I'm fairly sure you didn't hear a single thing I said. And right up to that point, I thought I was in as deep as I could get. But then you just lay there, looking at me, with your eyes almost completely closed, and you were *so* beautiful, I couldn't help myself. I started... fantasising about what it would be like if you'd always been this way. Or if you never had to change back." He looked away again. "More than fantasising."

I almost hiccupped in surprise. "James Ian McCain!" I exclaimed. "Are you saying you *masturbated* to me?"

His cheeks burned red, and a part of me liked letting him be the one who was embarrassed for once. The rest of me simply hated seeing him so miserable.

"It wasn't the first time," he admitted.

I stood up, took his hand again and led him back to the bed. I sat down and he did the same, but he put more space between us than I wanted, so I pushed up against him and wrapped an arm around his waist.

"Is that why you're feeling so guilty?" I asked. He didn't say anything. Damn; he was going to make me lay everything out, wasn't he? Not just trivialities, like the seismic shift in my self-concept, but the *really* embarrassing stuff.

"You know the first night?" I said quietly, unable to believe I was about to tell him what I was about to tell him. "After the whole thing when you had to measure me, when I went to get changed and you fell asleep on the sofa?" He nodded. "Do you remember kissing me?"

He groaned. "I thought I dreamed that," he said.

"Nope. I was covering you with a blanket and you leaned up and kissed me. I didn't really process it at the time and you were mostly asleep so it was this whole sloppy mess, but even so, it was the first time a kiss ever made me feel *anything*."

"Sorry," he said.

"Afterwards," I continued, ignoring his entirely pointless apology, "I slept in your room. In your *bed*. Everything around me smelled like you and I loved it. I fell asleep thinking about the restaurant, thinking about the kiss; thinking about you. And I was primed as hell because not half an hour before, you'd had your hands all over me. I dreamed of you touching me. James, I dreamed of you *fucking* me." He'd twisted almost out of my grip and was just staring at me now. "And the next night, alone, at my place, I kind of... made the dreams happen myself."

"What do you mean?" he asked, unable to look away from me.

"I'm going to have to say it, aren't I?" I sighed. "I wanked over you, James. I fantasised about touching you, about you touching me. I imagined you hoisting me up on your desk, sweeping all your crap out the way and finger-fucking me right there in your office." I grinned at him. "And you were so *good*. I mean, at the time I was too confused about what the hell was going on to really understand why I was doing it — and why I needed to imagine myself as a woman to get off on the idea of being with you — but I knew I desperately needed to do it, and I didn't want to stop."

James looked like he was trying to form words, but couldn't for some reason.

"All I want," I said, "when I'm around you, is to touch you, and for you to touch me."

"Um—" he started, but I interrupted him because I needed him to know the truth in the simplest possible terms.

"James. I'm a woman. And I'm in love with you."

* * *

I don't know what I expected. Probably near the bottom of the list, especially considering the way James had been since he'd shown up at my door, was for him to burst out laughing.

"Oh my God—" he gasped out, between wheezes.

"James," I said, juggling options as to whether I ought to be mortally offended or mortally wounded, "I'm serious."

"Oh no," James managed, "I totally believe you. I don't know why I'm laughing!"

I needed to take charge of the situation. I started running one hand up and down his spine again, to calm him as gently as I could. With my other hand I took his, which was in his lap, and squeezed it.

Gradually he got control of himself.

"Fuck," he summarised.

"Yeah," I said.

"All this time," he said, breathing hoarsely between the odd word, "I've been looking at you, talking to you — fuck, lusting after you — and feeling guilty, and then feeling confused because I've never been even *slightly* bi, and then feeling double confused because it didn't seem like I was into you in a way a guy would be attracted to another guy, so then I was thinking of you as a woman and feeling guilty *again* because, in my head, it was *me* making you do that..."

"Believe me," I said, "it's been similar inside my head." I let his hand go so I could finger-quote. "'Why am I so attracted to James?' 'Why don't I hate dressing like this?' 'Why don't I fancy Emily or Vicky or Sophie?' and especially, 'Why am I dreading going back to being the old Alex?' What a fucking rollercoaster." I sighed. "What a pair of fucking idiots," I added, unable to stop myself from giggling.

"I can't believe we've just been chewing over all of this completely separately," he said. "We're supposed to be friends, but—"

"Let's make a deal," I interrupted. "Next time one of us starts going crazy, we bring the other one into the loop early, so we either go nuts together, or we figure it out together."

"Deal," James said.

"Oh my *God*," I said, flopping backwards onto the bed and stretching my arms out past my head, allowing myself a moment to feel nothing but joy.

James loved me.

James *lusted* after me.

I shivered as I stretched, and wondered which was more delightful.

When I got done with my arms, I steadied myself on my elbows and arched my back, stretched out my feet, wiggled my toes. I ran through a whole routine, and it was only when I'd finished that I realised he'd twisted around to watch me.

Well, shit. I'd been *so* undignified.

The flush on my cheeks matched the grin plastered all over his face, and when he was sure I was lying normally again he lay down next to me, facing the ceiling like I was. In my space again. Or I was in his.

If I touched him, would he be okay with it?

I thought quickly.

James was attracted to — lusted after! — me-as-a-woman. I, obviously, was extraordinarily attracted to James-as-James. But what did it mean for *us*? Was he attracted to me as a *trans* woman? As someone with a currently unmodified body? Or did his mental picture of me involve all the traditional fleshy accoutrements of womanhood? Could I, to be blunt, get naked?

I didn't know. Maybe he didn't, either.

Take it slow.

We were still staring at the ceiling, so I felt around for his hand and took it in mine, finger by finger. I pressed my arm against his, up to the shoulder. An unambiguous gesture: we'd declared our attraction to each other, so he was unlikely to be under any illusions as to my intentions; I wanted to touch him. I'd said as much.

He squeezed my hand, and in companionable silence we lay. For about two fucking seconds, because suddenly it wasn't enough.

I let go and rolled over to face him, took a second to enjoy being so close to him — I could get lost in those eyes, Jesus Christ, I really could — and then, purely for the purposes of keeping my balance and with zero ulterior motive, put my arm across his chest and my head against his shoulder.

I felt his smile.

"Alex?" he said.

"Yes?" I replied, imbuing the word with as much innocence as I could manage.

He tensed, just a little. "Um. Nothing."

Fine. It was up to me to take the initiative, then. To *grasp* the initiative, to stroke it, to— *Jesus, Alex, calm down.*

I put more of my weight on his chest, pushed up on my other arm and, feeling like I was about to take the biggest risk of my life, darted in and kissed him on the cheek. His stubble tickled my lower lip, and while I'd kissed men on the cheek before — James and Ben both — the experience was still delightfully novel. I kissed him again on the jaw, ran my lips gently over a few centimetres of skin. I let myself rest against him for another few moments and then rolled back onto my side into a position where I wasn't reliant on his body to support me. I watched him carefully, trying to guess his thoughts; although I was completely certain that what I'd just done was okay, that it was something we both wanted, a part of me, deep in my core, was getting worried.

He propped himself up on his side so we were facing.

"Alex Brewer," he said, quietly and teasingly slowly, "what *do* you think you're doing?"

Screw it. "This," I said, and closed the distance between us quickly and fluidly, caught him before he could react, and kissed him firmly on the mouth. He made an almost inaudible sound, and I tried to pull away to see if I'd misjudged the situation horribly, but his hand found the small of my back and pulled me in closer, trapped me in his arms. He kissed me back.

He tasted like wine and rum and Coke and coffee.

James snaked his other hand under me and pressed on my hip, rolled me over so I was on top of him. The hand on my back started making its way downwards, his fingers slipping under the waist of my jeans. For my part, I steadied myself on the mattress and I kissed him and kissed him and kissed him.

And then, as I wriggled around on top of him, I realised that the firm pressure against my inner thigh was, in fact, his burgeoning erection.

In my surprise I broke the kiss. I sat up, still on top of him, straddling him and wobbling a little. He made quickly to support me and I giggled.

"What?" he asked, smiling but confused.

"Um," I said, pointing crotchward with my eyes. He didn't seem to get it, so I repeated myself more firmly: "*Um.*"

"Oh!" he exclaimed, finally realising just how much dick he was pushing into my leg. "Sorry," he added sheepishly.

I leaned down and kissed him on the lips again. Just a quick peck this time. "Not looking for an apology," I said. "It's nice to know I merit a proper stiffie."

"It's not the first time," he said. "If you've seen me walking funny recently, that's probably why." He caught me as I tried to rise and kissed me again, and I snorted; and what a dreadfully attractive thing that was for me to do while he was kissing me!

I pulled away, just far enough that he'd have to pull me back or come up to meet me himself if he wanted to continue the kiss, and locked my thighs so I wouldn't topple over, freeing one of my hands to touch his body. I knew it well already — the times I'd seen him topless or in a tight t-shirt were burned into my memory — but my fingers didn't. Keeping eye contact with him the whole time, to make sure I'd know if he took a dislike to anything I was doing, I ran my hand down his neck, along his clavicle and down his chest and stomach, biting my lip to help control myself. He was the perfect combination of hard and soft, with just enough muscle for me to feel it, overlaid with supple, lightly haired skin.

I took my time, but eventually I made it to his crotch. He still had an erection, and I thrilled at it, but, God, the thing was *massive!*

Okay, so it was probably a pretty normal size, but it was my first dick, so it didn't have any competition; it was massive in a field of one. Through the loose, thin material of his trousers, I massaged his penis and felt it twitch under my fingers.

My own dick, trapped in my underwear, responded in kind with that not entirely uncomfortable mixture of pleasure and pain. Unfortunately, it meant something else to me now, too.

Fuck.

I almost fell off his lap.

James reacted instantly: he took my weight, held me tight, steadied me. He sat up, slowly and carefully. Made sure I had my balance back. And then, with a strength that startled me, he practically lifted me off his lap and deposited me on the bed next to him, keeping a hand on my shoulder in case I wobbled again.

"You okay?" he asked.

"Not really," I said, trying to swallow away the thickness in my throat. "It's, um... shit. Difficult to talk about."

He smiled for me, ran a concerned finger down my cheek, and took my hand. "You can tell me anything."

I nodded, swallowed again, and decided that I'd better just keep ripping off those band-aids. "The times when I've fantasised about this," I said, "I've been a woman. A *normal* woman. And that's how I want you to see me. But we've known each other for so *long,* and you've known me as a *man* for so long..."

"Alex, what's wrong?"

"That," I said, pointing at his crotch. "It's natural and normal for *you* to have one. It's... Fuck, it's *good,* James, and it's hard for me not to want to— Shit. Getting off-topic." *Jesus, Alex! Control yourself.* "When I was touching yours, I got excited and mine... paid attention. And in doing so it reminded me in a way I couldn't ignore that I'm *not* a normal woman, and there are parts of me I've always, the more I think about it, actually kind of hated, and even with everything strapped down and the boobs on and the hair and everything, the real me is still under here, and while you're touching me all I can think is that if you see *me,* if you touch me, if you even think about me..." I waved an arm, frustrated; I still wasn't *saying* this right!

He caught my arm. "You think your womanhood is so fragile it can't survive without the clothes?" he asked quietly.

"I don't know," I admitted. "I've known who I am for so little time. I don't have anything worked out. And *you!* James, I fucking *love* you! And what you think of me is *so* important to me it's difficult to unravel it from how I think about myself, and right now I can't get the picture out of my head of me, naked, really and truly naked, in front of you, and—"

"You think I won't see you as a woman any more?"

I nodded, and he smiled softly, hooked a hand around my neck and made me lean towards him to receive a kiss so gentle I could barely feel the pressure of his lips.

"Nonsense," he said, when he released me, and I slowly returned to something approaching upright. "The moment I started seeing you as a woman, days ago now, you stopped making sense to me as a man. You don't know how hard I had to try to think of you as your old self. And I tried, Alex, I really did, because I knew how hard I was falling for you, and I knew how temporary it had to be. Or I thought I did," he added, deepening his smile and cupping my cheek. "It got harder and harder until, in the end, I had to give up. I figured I'd just... see what happens when we go back to the office next week. But I knew it'd never be the same."

"How so?" I couldn't imagine it; if I'd decided to go back, to take all this off, to re-embrace my so-called manhood—

He interrupted the half-formed thought. "Because I realised it's never felt like being with another guy with you. *Never.* When you started working for me we got *so* close, so quickly, and in such a different way than with Ben or any of my other guy friends, and I never properly interrogated the feeling. But I can see it now and it's so clear to me. You've always been a girl, Alex. And I've *always* been drawn to you. It's just that when I looked at you, or when you looked in the mirror, neither of us knew quite what we were seeing yet." He let go of my face and cheekily booped my nose. "And now, knowing everything, I see a woman. Being reminded of certain facts about your current anatomy isn't going to change that."

I forced myself to breathe. "It's that simple, is it?"

"It's that simple. And—" he smiled broadly, and I got the feeling that if I'd looked even a little less fragile in that moment, he would have picked me up and whirled me around the room like the heroine in an old musical, "—good *God,* am I glad it is! Not just for you — although mainly for you — but because I can stop beating myself up about it! So I owe you thanks: the bruises were getting a bit much."

I sat forward. "Bruises? Where—?"

"*Metaphorical* bruises," he corrected me, and pushed me back. "But your concern is appreciated," he added, in a mocking tone.

"Sod," I told him.

"So, to sum up," he said, briefly adopting his Business Meeting voice before dropping it to continue, "I know what you have and I know what you *don't* have right now. It doesn't change how I see you, and it doesn't change how attracted I am to you. Which is, by the way, *very.*"

I couldn't stop the giggle from getting out, and I'm pretty sure I blushed again. "Thanks, James," I said, and bumped against him.

"Tell me," he said, reaching back across the bed and retrieving two more water bottles, "what's it like? Being suddenly and yet always a woman?"

"It's confusing," I admitted, cracking the seal on the bottle he handed me. "So much of this is new to me. It's like..." I thought for a moment, looked for a way to put it into words, as much for my own benefit as for his. "It's like I'm opening all the doors and windows in my apartment at once and seeing daylight for the first time, and it's *wonderful,* but it's not just the light I can see; suddenly I can see exactly how dusty and dirty and broken all the stuff in my flat is and has always been..." I frowned. The metaphor was getting away from me.

"I get it," he said. "You mean, you're still *you,* but now you're looking at things through new eyes. Everything's recontextualised."

"That, and I really hate my shitty apartment," I said. "I think you're getting this faster than I am, to be honest."

He smirked. "Hey, I've been hoping you'd want to stay like this for days now. I, uh, did a little reading online."

Oh God. "Oh God."

"Sorry," he said, not sounding remotely sorry.

"You probably know more than I do, then," I said. "I chatted online with a nice trans guy who helped me sort through what I wanted, in the big picture sense. And that was really useful. But since then all I've done is skim a 'what next' FAQ. I have lots of questions for myself about surgery and lifestyle changes and stuff that I haven't even begun to consider."

"I imagine you're thinking of doing something about...?" He didn't finish the question, but pointed down with his eyes, the way I had earlier.

"I'm still sorting out how I feel about it, I guess," I said. He smiled at me, encouraging me to keep talking, to pick my way through this topic at my own pace. God, it was nice to talk about this stuff out loud, to someone else, and not simply stew about it inside my head. Because inside my head was where I kept all my idiocy, and even sensible thoughts got corrupted if they spent too long in there. "Right now I hate it. My prick and everything to do with it." Prick: a horrible word for a horrible thing. "Which you probably guessed. And, thinking back, I've never really liked it much. Never liked to touch it, never liked to use it." I laughed bitterly. "And I think I might have just clued you in on why I could never keep a girlfriend."

"Poor Alex," he said. "I'm glad I don't have any competition, though."

I groaned. "I do! *How* many women have you been with?"

"None like you," he said. "None who know me like you do." He pulled my top up a little and started stroking my exposed belly with a finger. It was nice. "So if you hate it," he continued, "do you think you'll get rid of it?"

"I don't know," I said. "I do wonder how much of hating it is bound up with how I don't like my body at the moment. You know that first night when I went back home alone? I tried to shower but the moment I saw myself naked, really naked, without the... the helpers—" I poked myself in the tit, "—I felt *super* weird. I couldn't shower after seeing that. Just threw all my clothes back on and dived under the covers. Didn't want to be naked any more. Looking back, that was a pretty big clue."

He surprised me with another kiss on my cheek; I'd been staring at the ceiling again and didn't see him come in. I smiled and reached over to kiss him back before he could escape. We stayed like that for a few moments, gentle pressure on each other's lips, but I let him go in the end. I wanted to keep talking. Keep thinking.

"If I liked my body more," I said, "it's possible my feelings about it might change. Or they might stay exactly the same! I don't know how I'm going to feel about *anything* once I'm on hormones."

"You're going to do that?" James asked. "For definite?"

"Yes," I said firmly. "It's the one thing I'm sure about. I was *this* close to loading up an online pharmacy when you knocked. You can go through the NHS for them but apparently it can take years." I made a face which James echoed. "And you can get them from a private doctor, which is much quicker but pretty expensive and it still takes a while. Buying them online's quickest."

He frowned. "Won't you need blood tests and stuff?"

"Yes," I said, "but that's not as urgent as stopping what's left of my male development in its tracks." I shuddered; I'd let quite a bit of venom creep into my voice. Feeling so strongly about something was kind of new to me. "The trans guy I spoke to said I'm sitting on a ticking T bomb, and the more I think about it, the more it freaks me out. I'm getting away with it now — obviously — but I know it can't last." I held out a hand, examined it, imagined it growing thicker, becoming hairy. "It's irrational, but I suddenly feel like at any second I could just... change. It's terrifying."

He pulled me into a hug, and I leaned into him. "I still think blood tests are important," he said. I was going to protest, but then he added, "Your health is important, Alex. What if you bought hormones online, but we got you in to see a private doctor as soon as possible? I can, um, help with the cost."

I think my eyes bulged out of their sockets. "You'd do that?" On the one hand, I was handing him even more power over me; on the other, he had money and I didn't. And it wasn't like I was anything but ride or die for James now anyway.

He laughed. "Of course! What can it cost? A couple of thousand pounds?"

"I think more like a couple of hundred," I said sheepishly. Rich boys!

"That," he said, breaking the sentence up by kissing me again, "is more than fine."

* * *

We hugged for a good long time. My little freakout had drained all the sexiness out of the room, but just being in the same space as him, lying with him, holding him, it was *all* special. I didn't need to be rubbing up against him to delight in his presence (although I couldn't pretend that part hadn't been pretty good, too, until my little episode). He was gentle with me, held my hand, drew idle shapes on my arm with his fingertips, planted the occasional kiss on me. I, for my part, simply clung to him like I'd never had a boyfriend before. Which, yeah.

James wanted to make plans for my treatment but I asked him to leave it until morning. I knew what I wanted, and when I examined my anxieties with all the rationality I was able to bring to bear (not loads), I knew one night wouldn't make a difference. I also didn't particularly want to move from where I was lying.

But time caught up with us in the end.

"Don't wanna go to sleep," I said childishly, my voice muffled by the way my head was buried in his chest. "I like this too much."

"Sorry," James said. "We have stuff to sell tomorrow."

"Sucks," I mumbled. "I hate capitalism."

"Go clean your teeth," he ordered.

Reluctantly I extracted myself from his embrace and plodded off to the bathroom to clean my teeth, inspect my hair, stare blearily at myself in the mirror, wonder how dark my under-eye circles would be in the morning, et cetera. I was halfway done when James entered the bathroom, carrying his overnight bag.

He was naked except for his boxers.

Jesus...

I think I dribbled some toothpaste down my chin. The man was a fucking demigod; I had no idea what he saw in me. Maybe it was just that I was easy to tease: he grinned like the Cheshire Cat when he saw the effect his naked body had on me. Thank God I still had the tucking knickers on or I would have drilled a hole in the wall.

I wanted to hurl my toothbrush at him but my vengeful instincts were calmed when he stood next to me at the sink, loaded up a toothbrush of his own, and kissed me on top of my head before he started on his teeth. Mollified, I leaned against him and finished up. Bless him, he even handed me a towel when I got done washing my face and was still blinking water out of my eyes, and when I finished drying myself he wordlessly handed me a tube of moisturiser.

Yeah, fine. I'd keep him.

I couldn't resist running a hand across his back on my way out of the bathroom.

Alone in the main room, I shucked off my jeans and top and dumped them on the floor. I didn't mean to leave them in a crumpled heap — Ben would have words, I was sure — but I caught sight of myself in the mirror, almost naked but with the tucking knickers and the bra still on, boobs still nestled in the cups, and it started me thinking. When I started taking hormones, how would I change?

I examined myself critically. I had pretty narrow shoulders but my hips were even narrower — it's why Ben loaned me the pads in the first place. The website had been clear that not everyone gets wider hips, but with the rest of me likely to fill out somewhat — I could expect a bigger butt and thighs and probably a rounder belly — it would hopefully be enough to balance out my shoulders even if I did retain my current lower proportions. I was trying to imagine what home-grown breasts would look like on my frame when an arm wrapped around my waist, taking me by surprise.

"Hey, beautiful," James whispered into my hair. "Come to bed?"

Suddenly self-conscious, I tried to pull away, but he held me firm.

"James!" I protested.

"If you're thinking anything other than, 'James thinks I look incredibly sexy,'" he said, "then you're so very, very wrong."

"I look weird," I said, frowning at our reflections. His masculinity emphasised my androgyny, and I felt scrawny and unfeminine. I cursed my past self for not somehow having had the grand revelation a couple of years earlier; if only I hadn't been so dense for so long, I could already have been the right shape to entice and keep a man like James.

"You're beautiful," he insisted.

I turned away from the mirror, choosing instead to look up at his face, in case it made it easier to believe him. It certainly made it easier to kiss him.

"Thanks," I said. "I don't believe it, but thanks."

He put both arms around me and lifted me again — I was starting to think he just liked doing that — and put me down on the edge of the bed.

"Then believe this," he said, looking down at me and smiling. "Looking at you, right now, all I want is to touch you, and for you to touch me."

He was a charming little bastard, I had to give him that, even if throwing my own words back at me was a dick move. But I forgave him, kissed him again, and let him entice me into bed and pull the covers over us both. He turned out the light and gathered me up under one arm, which he cinched around my belly. I fell into the divot we were making in the middle of the mattress and arranged myself so I was facing away from him, and he let me wriggle and fidget until we were spooning and then kissed me on the back of the head.

"Goodnight, Alex," he whispered, and kissed me again.

I covered his arm with mine, squeezing it against my stomach.

"Goodnight, James," I replied, and gradually drifted off, guided into sleep by the gentle in-out rhythm of his chest against my back.

Chapter Eleven

Another version of me, a younger, more naive and considerably stupider version of me, had set my phone to wake me at seven in the morning, and so it did, blasting some pop song I was vaguely familiar with and dragging me out of pleasant dreams into my, for once, even more pleasant reality.

"Taylor Swift," James muttered.

I batted weakly at my phone until it shut up and he fell immediately back to sleep, unconsciously dragging me closer with the arm that had been wrapped around me all night. I pressed myself against him, drew animal comfort from his warmth. I was going to stay there forever, I decided; I'd never woken up in the embrace of someone I loved before, and I deserved to indulge myself.

And, God, yes, I loved him. I absolutely did. More, probably, than I had before, as if a night in his arms had deepened my devotion, opened my heart to him to an extent I hadn't thought possible.

I'd told him everything and he accepted me. He loved me. And he didn't even love me despite it all; he just loved me, simply, clearly, without complications or conditions.

I wriggled under his arm, feeling a primal need to burrow into him, to pull his arm more tightly around me. I never wanted this beautiful, sweet, mildly infuriating man to let go of me. He moaned happily, dumbly, thoroughly and beautifully unconsciously, and I lay there a while, gently stroking his fingers. His warm breath moistened my shoulder; his morning erection poked my butt. I arched my back, trying to extract myself from the ministrations of his dick while still maintaining full-body contact with the rest of him, but it didn't work, so I reached down and slipped his penis back inside the lining of his underwear, resisting the temptation to snap the elastic against his skin. I tried not to linger on the task, lest he wake up with my fingers on his boner and start getting ideas.

It was too early for ideas; too early even for vague concepts. I wanted nothing more than to stay in bed until my brain finished assembling something approaching a usefully conscious mind out of the Lego bricks of id, ego, superego, newly acquired knowledge about dresses, generalised embarrassment, and the detailed files a small but dedicated part of me was putting together about the way James' dick had felt in my hand.

I let myself drift.

Gradually I woke up enough to realise my feet were cold, so I gathered the sheets around me from where they'd bunched up. A vague memory presented itself: at some point in the night I'd overheated, but rather than wriggle out of James' embrace, I'd thrown off half the covers. Once again, I had to give unconscious Alex more points than regular Alex; of the two of us, she continued to make the better decisions.

That pronoun again. *She.* I was still getting used to it. It felt good, though. Felt right.

She. She. She.

How had it taken me so long to come to such an obvious conclusion? I was a woman, and it was the most natural thing in the world.

I was a woman in love!

I was a woman who needed to pee.

Fucksake.

Grudgingly, I levered James' arm off of me, slid out from under it and gently lowered it onto the mattress. With any luck I'd be able to get all the way out of bed without waking him. I took a moment to admire his sleeping body — and to wipe a little drool off his chin; adorable — and escaped to the bathroom.

* * *

I brushed my teeth and pissed at the same time. I'm a multitasker.

* * *

My junk was sufficiently sweaty after a night in the horrible tucking underwear that I decided I needed a shower as a matter of urgency, lest James wake up and smell something untoward. I finished taking off my underwear and my extra body parts, laid my bra and boobs carefully on the shelf by the sink, and looked down at the red marks around my crotch where the knickers had dug into the skin.

Hmm. Ugly.

I gingerly touched the very end of my battered and sore dick, and the light contact with just my foreskin was painful enough that I let out a hiss. But I had to pull the damn thing back from where it had stuck to the rest of me, and had to free my testicles from the mysterious internal cavern I'd been pushing them up into, so I gritted my teeth and renewed my efforts.

It was like peeling chewing gum off the sole of your shoe.

I really, really hated the tucking knickers. It was dawning on me that I'd have to wear them, or something like them, for the foreseeable future, and the thought was the most unpleasant one I'd had since I finally came out to myself. Maybe I could get fast-tracked for surgery if I told the doctors I really, really hated tucking?

Maybe I'd just wear loose skirts for the next couple of years.

It occurred to me that I was already treating the inversion of my dick as a foregone conclusion; was I really so certain I wanted rid of the thing? I looked down at it again, dangling uselessly between my legs and throbbing with residual pain, and decided, yeah, probably. Apart from anything else, if I wanted to wear, say, the corporate ice queen outfit again, it would find its smooth lines quite spoiled by a crotch-height bulge. And sure, while my brief foray into the transgender subreddits had turned up a few girls who didn't tuck and were proud of it, I didn't think I could ever be one of them; my self-confidence had come a long way in a short time, but given where I'd been starting from that just meant I was finally beginning to approach normal people's level of daring.

Best to know one's limits (and hide one's penis).

And there were other reasons to want it gone.

I turned on the shower and ducked under the water, and had to immediately clap a hand over my mouth as hot water hit my ailing junk and I very nearly screamed.

Yeah, buddy; your days are *numbered.*

* * *

I kept the shower cap on the whole time. Going another day without washing my hair was pushing it a little, but I still hadn't had time to read up on how to care for my extensions. Once I was out of the shower and relatively towel-dry, I took off the cap and, feeling slightly childish, spun it around on my finger before aiming it and firing it across the room towards the waste basket like a rubber band. I laughed at my immaturity, turned around to fetch my things from by the sink, and caught sight of my reflection.

Oh yeah.

That was still me.

Flat-chested, angular, shapeless. I gripped the edge of the counter, steadied myself, forced myself to face my mirror self.

Him.

292

The pronoun warred in my head with what I saw and what I desperately wished I could see. *He,* the man in the mirror, glared back at me, and I reminded myself that *he* was still *me,* that I was nevertheless still a woman, still defiantly and definitely a *she,* and if that was the case then so was the mistily hazy and half-visible *girl* looking at me. I made myself look at her. Redefined her as much as I could.

I knew now why I'd always hated mirrors.

She was still looking at me, so I decided to reassure her.

"It's going to be okay," I told her, and found a smile on her face, brief but brave. "You know it will be. You're going to *fix* all this. You're not going to look this way forever."

And then she burst into near-hysterical laughter, because she and I had both realised that this probably counted as the most insane thing I'd ever done; a considerable achievement considering my activities over the preceding few days. She looked beautiful in her laughter, carefree and innocent, and I felt suddenly protective of her.

That's you, you idiot, I reminded myself.

I nodded at her, covered her nakedness with a robe, and left the bathroom to discover James snoring noisily. In my absence he'd rolled over onto his back and was filling the room with sounds that an impartial observer might perhaps have considered unpleasant. I didn't care. It was sweet.

I blew him a silent kiss, fished a fresh bra and knickers out of my suitcase as quietly as I could, snapped a hair tie around my wrist, and returned to the bathroom with the alcohol and the glue to clean and reattach my tits. I used the bra to help me position them, but when they were stuck properly in place I took it off again, the better to see *me.*

So much better. The woman in the mirror grinned broadly at me and I grinned back. Rubber tits: a cheat code for my self-image. This would be me soon enough, and that other body, the one I'd been neglectful in charge of, the one I had inexplicably chosen not to stuff with estrogen at the first opportunity, was just a temporary affliction. The fake boobs warmed quickly to my body temperature in the steamy bathroom air, a process that always helped them feel like a part of me. I couldn't help giggling as I remembered thinking, a mere day ago, how much more convenient it would be for the whole modelling thing if I could grow my own, and suppressed a scowl as I realised I should never tell anyone I'd ever thought that or they'd start calling me an egg again.

Back to the mirror. My hair didn't look *too* bad, but I pulled it up into a high pony anyway, posing, tilting my head this way and that, trying to decide if exposing my temples was enough to reveal me as a man. Shoving all my hair under a hat hadn't manned me even slightly, even though I'd been trying really hard at the time, and neither had any other hairstyle I'd attempted over the last few days, but my paranoia was nothing if not proactive.

Having finally accepted myself as a woman — and thus having also accepted that passing as one on a full-time basis was going to be a thing I should probably keep half an eye on, for safety's sake, if nothing else — I wasn't the greatest fan of my hairline, but I realised as I moved my ponytail this way and that, shifting the hair around on my head, that it wasn't all that bad. I hadn't started receding yet, thank goodness, and while it was a little farther withdrawn at the temples than I'd prefer, it was probably still inside the normal range for a cis woman.

Yeah. Probably safe. Probably fine.

My paranoia, though, still made me tease out a bit of a fringe, to frame my face and hide my temples. I inspected myself again, decided it was good and tied the ponytail, blasting myself with a spot of hairspray as an afterthought. I wouldn't look quite as glamorous as I had on Friday or Saturday, perhaps, but the pony would help hide the extent to which my hair needed a good shampooing.

I frowned at my reflection: a few beard hairs were starting to poke through, reddening the skin around them. I fought against another wave of vertigo — every part of the whirlwind makeover Ben had dragged me through was starting to come apart — and took a deep breath. The hairs *weren't* permanent; they were going to be dealt with just like everything else. Lasers and electric needles and the like, which didn't sound pleasant but which would be infinitely preferable to allowing anything to grow out of my face below the eyelashes ever again. So I glared sternly at myself and set to dealing with the hairs, taking care to moisturise thoroughly after, lest Ben give me the same look he'd turned on me when he discovered I hadn't been moisturising my legs.

As an afterthought I also moisturised my legs.

* * *

Hot breath on the back of my neck broke my concentration. I looked around from the laptop and there was James, leaning down behind me; gloriously, wonderfully, deliciously naked.

Well, naked except for his underwear, damn him.

"Hi," he said, smiling.

"Hi," I replied. He stood up and I kept looking at him, craning my neck back as far as it could go so I could keep him in sight. He took the prompt and leaned down again, over me this time, and kissed me on the lips, his face upside down relative to mine and slightly comical for it. I laughed into his mouth and he threatened to pull away, so I reached up and yanked on the back of his neck, keeping him in place. I was under no illusions about who had the power in this situation, but he consented to be controlled and I pressed up against him, kissing him and kissing him and bloody well kissing him.

God damn, he felt good.

I caressed the scruffy hair on the back of his neck. I scrunched my fingers into his skin. I wriggled in my chair, straining to keep myself in place and starting to ache in unpleasant places until he took charge again, pulled away from me and pecked me quickly on the forehead before placing a hand on the back of my head, under the ponytail, and pushing my head back into a more ordinary, less painful position.

He crouched down next to me; I delicately massaged my neck.

He tapped at the laptop screen. "Is that...?"

"Yeah," I said. The website I had open, an online pharmacy, was the one the FAQ had suggested. I'd loaded the recommended drugs into the shopping cart and had been waiting for my courage to build up enough to make the 'process my order' button properly clickable.

Still crouching, he leaned against my bare legs. I'd started to get dressed when I came back into the room but had gotten only as far as slipping on a top before being seized with the need to start making things *happen* in my transition. My sore dick, my flat chest and my facial hair, all were signs that my biology was going to keep working against me until I got my shit together. But when I'd sat down, looked everything up and filled the cart, I'd gotten scared.

The FAQ said to expect doubts. People on the subreddit said to expect doubts. Common sense said to expect doubts. But somehow, boiling away inside me, *my* doubts seemed more profound; not mere cold feet but confirmation that I was wrong about everything, that I was deluded, that I was about to make a mistake, that I was really a man and had been all along.

Around James, though, my doubts were easier to deal with. I anchored my certainty in him, reminding myself that he'd seen the woman in me before I had. She was real; she was *me*.

"'Cyproterone acetate'," he read off the screen, "and 'estradiol valerate'. Hormones?"

I nodded. "And an anti-androgen."

"You're definitely going through with it, then?" he said, doing that neutral thing with his voice again. I wondered if he was still feeling guilty about having 'made' me do all this.

"Yes," I said, trying to sound more certain than I felt.

"Good," James said, squeezing my bare thigh.

Good, I repeated inside my head. *Good. Good good motherfucking good.* He wanted this for me.

Maybe that was what I had to tell my doubts. Maybe the question of who I 'was', really and truly and metaphysically, was one I could explore at my leisure, with James as my partner, and without the time pressure imposed by, say, growing older with testosterone still dominating my system. Maybe the question that was important was, what do you want, Alex Brewer?

Do you *want* to be a girl?

Yeah.

Yeah, I fucking did.

I reached forward, clicked the button and let out a long, tired breath. It was done. The first step. The machinery of international mail would drop the damn hormones in my lap; until that happened it was out of my hands. The guy on Reddit was right — as were the handful of other people who'd commented after I'd gone to bed — transition really was just a whole lot of little decisions, very few of which were final.

"You okay, Alex?" James asked, frowning up at me. I must have been showing my emotions on my face again. Damnable habit.

"Just cold feet," I said, as much to myself as to him. "I want this. I really do. But it's hard not to worry if it's right for me, or—" and a whole other worry presented itself, unwelcome and bright in the front of my mind, "—about how people will react. God, James, I told Emily she should try out for a job with us, and that means I'm going to have to tell her the truth, and—"

"Alex," he said quietly.

"Yes?"

He didn't say anything else, not yet; instead he stood, pulled me out of the chair and into his arms, and I fell into him, let him take my entire weight. I was overwhelmed. It was finally dawning on me how much everything about my life was going to change, and while I wanted it — needed it — it was *so* intimidating. He encircled me and I hugged him back as hard as I could, not even noticing I was crying until my cheeks wetted.

"I'm proud of you," he whispered. "I'm so proud of you."

"Oh, James," I said into his shoulder.

"*Alex,*" he replied.

I loved it when he said my name.

"I'm scared as hell," I admitted, my voice small and almost inaudible.

"That's because you're wise as well as beautiful," James said, punctuating his praise by tightening his embrace. "Change is scary, even if it's change for the better, and you're looking down the barrel of a hell of a lot of it." He relaxed his hold and leaned me back so he could look me in the eye. "But you won't be alone. You have me." He laughed, deep and confident, and the desire he suddenly inspired in me was almost enough to chase everything else away. "You've got me. And you've got Ben and Soph. And Emily will be fine with you, I'm sure. We'll be a united front. Emily, Sophie, Ben and me. Especially me. Me most importantly."

I nodded. He was right, of course. "Yeah," I said, unable to think of anything more useful to say.

He drew me back in. "Whatever happens, I'll be right there with you. All the way."

I buried myself in him.

* * *

I don't know how long we stood there like that, holding each other. He stroked my spine, whispered quiet reassurances, and I just leaned into him, made him my world. He let me have all the time I needed. He would have held me all day in his arms if that was what I required. We could have missed the last day of the expo, missed our ride home, overstayed our hotel booking, hell, the whole city could have burned down around us and he would have kept hold of me. Until I was done. Until I was okay.

Eventually I was. Eventually I felt clear. Unafraid. I pulled back, smiling, flushed, happy, revelling in my luck in finding someone I loved who was already in my life, who already knew me inside and out and who was worthy of my love, of my devotion. I wondered if that would help when I told my mum about myself: I already have a man, Mum, and he's *wonderful*. She might not have a heart attack.

I put her out of my mind for now, bounced on my heels to gain the height I needed, and kissed my man.

"Thanks," I said.

"Any time."

"I'm sorry I'm a basket case."

"As long as you're *my* basket case."

"For as long as you want me," I said, and for a moment my belly clenched again; I wasn't quite able to dispel the fear that he'd drop me as soon as a *real* woman came along, and—

I cut myself off. Paranoia was unhelpful, no matter how talented I was at generating it. *And it's 'cis woman', you dork,* I remembered. I was exactly as real as any other woman. I *was.*

Eventually I might properly believe it. Until then, just having James believe it was good enough.

He looked down at me again, smiling gently. "Do you still mean everything you said last night?" he asked. "Not just about transitioning; about me? About us?"

I met his eyes. "Every word. Even the stuff I said that made me sound like a complete idiot. Maybe especially that stuff." I blinked, and braced myself. "Do *you* still mean what you said?"

He kissed me again. "Yes," he said. "Even more so now than I did last night."

* * *

James, claiming he was 'cold' or some nonsense like that, had put a t-shirt on, against my protestations. I told him he was making an unwise decision, that he should walk around in just his underwear for his health, but he saw through my clever ruse. He'd kissed me — possibly to shut me up; he was nothing if not devilishly cunning — and sat me back down. Made promises about coffee.

I watched him fight with the coffee maker and I pondered. James' reaffirmation of his interest in me, and his promise to stand by me throughout my changes to come, had done a lot to reassure me. So my facial hair was going to grow back and my extensions would eventually need to be removed and my unadorned body would still be waiting for me in every mirror; so what? I had *him*. And in a few weeks, I'd have hormones, too.

It was the last day of the expo, so by the time evening rolled around I'd be back home in London, having left this strange little bubble I'd been living in the last few days, utterly altered in so many ways — or, I supposed, simply and finally cognisant of the person I'd always been — and I'd have to face living in the *real* world as a transgender woman.

But I wouldn't be alone. He'd *promised*.

James put a cup of coffee down on the desk in front of me and I blinked, startled; I'd zoned out. He'd been talking to me, I realised, and I'd completely missed it.

"Thanks, sweetie," I said, and he snorted.

"I'm your sweetie, am I?" he asked, leaning over me again.

I nuzzled into his arm. "I'm trying out pet names. I could never make them work before. You know, with girls. They always felt kind of stupid when I said them."

"And now?"

"I'm not certain about 'sweetie'," I said, frowning, "but the concept is sound."

"Good to know." He kissed me on the top of my head and straightened up again. "You're still feeling okay?"

I nodded. "Yes. Just zoning in and out, you know? There's a lot to think about. And, by the way, I missed everything you said before, 'Here's your coffee.' Sorry." I put my best apologetic expression onto my face.

"I didn't say that, though."

"Damn. Educated guess."

He rebuked me by bonking me gently on the shoulder. "It's fine," he said, pretending great insult. "You don't have to listen to me; I know you only want me for my body, not my intellect."

"Would that be so bad?" I asked sweetly.

He managed almost a full second of glaring at me before he ruined it by laughing. "I asked," he said, once he had something approaching a straight face, "if you wanted to get a blood test organised for next week."

"Why so soon?" I asked. I'd ordered what the FAQ promised was the usual dose given to newly transitioning trans women, and I'd assumed that would be that until I worked my way through the system and eventually got to see an actual doctor about it.

"I had a thought," he said, "so I did a bit of Googling." He coughed delicately. "A bit *more* Googling," he added, brandishing his phone. I rolled my eyes; he could be dangerous with that thing. "So what I was thinking was, you look like a girl, right? You pass so well you were able to hang out with *models.* It was incredibly easy for you. Yes, okay—" he held up his free hand to forestall the various complaints and remarks and other colourful commentary I was assembling, "—not *actually* easy, not with the hair and the shopping and putting up with Ben and everything—"

"—Ben's a sweetheart—"

"—but, Alex, a bit of hair? A bit of makeup? And a dress? And suddenly you look like a woman? That's not *usual,* Alex."

"It works even without all that stuff," I said quietly.

"Yeah. Your Casanova attempt at that club."

"Not just then. The first morning, after we went to dinner and I stayed over..." I sighed, feeling silly. "I borrowed some of your exercise clothes and got a car to work. No wig, no makeup, no dress. Just me. And the driver called me 'love'."

He smiled and kissed me again. "You see? If all it took was a simple... mental adjustment for people to start seeing you as a woman—"

"And a shave," I interjected.

"And a shave, sure, but, Alex, that was all it took for *me* to start seeing you that way! God, Alex, looking at you *right now,* with no makeup and your hair up... You're fucking gorgeous. And a hundred percent woman. No doubt in my mind. Or in, uh, other parts of me."

I looked away. I felt obscurely bad about that, like I'd been handed a gift I hadn't worked for. "Yeah," I said. "I don't really understand how that works."

"I mean," James said, warming to his point, "you never really saw yourself before. Not properly. I think you didn't want to. I know you always thought you looked younger than your age, because you were always complaining about it to me and I always went along with it because it seemed like it bugged you so much, but... okay, hear me out: I think you might have an unusual hormone profile for a, um, for an assigned male your age." Yeah, he'd definitely been looking stuff up unsupervised. "It might just be low testosterone, or it might be something else." He shrugged. "Or it might be nothing at all; you might just be like this."

"It's not like I have any siblings to compare myself with." My father aside — and I preferred not to think about him when I didn't have to — I didn't have *any* male blood relatives that I knew about.

"Exactly."

"So you think I should have a blood test to establish what my base levels are?"

He nodded. "Before you start on HRT, preferably."

"How long would that take?" I didn't want to wait any longer than I had to.

He held up his phone again. "Like I said before, although I suppose you weren't listening—" I mouthed *sorry* at him and he bapped me gently with his phone, "—I was doing some reading and I came up with a plan. Subject to your approval, of course."

"Let's hear it, then."

"What I'm thinking," he said, scrolling through a document he'd obviously been surreptitiously working on, "is that you get a blood test to establish your baseline first thing next week. We can get you on my health plan more or less instantly, and they'll want to see you for an opening checkup, anyway."

"You can get me in that soon?" I asked.

He looked at me like I'd questioned the roundness of the planet. "Yes?" he said, and then his expression cleared and he shook his head. "Right. NHS. Waiting lists and such. I forgot. Sorry." Rich boys! "Yes, if we get you on the same coverage as me, you'll be able to see someone next week, guaranteed. They won't be able to prescribe for you, though; you'll need a specialist service for that, so the internet hormones are still a good move. We'll get you tested for all this—" he showed me the screen and thumbed through a list of words that looked distinctly medical, "—and we ought to have the results well before your pills come. Once we have all the information, if your hormone levels look significantly different to *these*—" he showed me the screen again; fucking hell, he had *charts and diagrams,* "—then we consult a guy on Reddit called 'the hormone wizard' and ask for advice. But if you look normal for your, um, assigned gender, then you can start the standard regimen immediately." He put the phone down on the desk. "Now, the private gender clinic usually responds to booking requests within forty-eight hours, so by Wednesday we should have a date for your first appointment there, and..." He trailed off. "You okay, Alex?"

I gripped my reassuringly solid coffee mug. "I'm a little dizzy," I admitted.

"Sorry," he said. "I'm going too fast, aren't I?"

"No!" I said quickly. "I *want* to go fast. It's just... a lot of information."

"You don't think I'm taking decisions out of your hands because I think I can make them better than you can?" he asked.

"What? Is that—? That sounds like a quote."

"Just something an ex told me," he said. "I'm trying to watch out for it."

"I'm grateful," I said, "so don't worry about it. I think it's probably better for me to have your... organisational assistance." I grimaced. "You saw what I was like just ordering the pills. My hand would've been hovering over that bloody buy button forever if you hadn't intervened. Can you imagine what it'd be like if I had to book appointments unaided? Speak to medical professionals of my own free will? I know *exactly* what I want—" and I did, I bloody well did, and my doubts and my fear could all go hang, "—and I'm *still* liable to panic over each and every step. Your help is invaluable." I smiled softly. "Much like the rest of you."

"Alex," he said, "I'll help as much as I can. As much as you'll let me. I'll be overbearing and bossy and insistent and *extremely* annoying but I want you to promise me: if I start pushing you to do something you don't want to do, or even something you don't want to do *yet*, you'll tell me. Right?"

"I will," I said.

"And that doesn't just apply to transition stuff. It applies to everything. If I push too far—"

"I'll tell you," I said, trying to sound confident.

"Alex, I got *unbelievably* lucky that what I want from you happens to coincide with what you want for yourself, but I'm *very* aware that—"

"I *promise*," I said, interrupting again. "I won't do anything I don't want to do. No matter how insistent or charming you are. For example..." I set my coffee down on the desk, leaned over and kissed him. "There. I wanted to do that."

"Did you now?" he said, grinning.

"Yes." I kissed him again, but this time he caught me before I could lean away and kept me pressed against him. He stood me up, pulled me away from my chair; I think it fell over behind me, but I wasn't sure. My attention was elsewhere: the man still hadn't put on any trousers.

"Is there anything *else* you want to do?" he whispered.

The hand on my back slipped under my top, and the sensation of fingers on bare skin galvanised something inside me. I stood up on my toes, kissed him again, and put both my hands behind his neck, linking them.

"Yes," I said.

I pulled on him and he came with me and we staggered sideways towards the bed, repeatedly almost but not quite kissing each other, foiled by our clumsy conjoined gait, until we both hit the mattress at the same time and fell, laughing, onto the duvet. As soon as we were settled I pulled on him again and kissed him. God, I never wanted to let go of him. I kissed him messily and urgently, pushing against his body with my own. I felt myself react, down there, inside my knickers, but I was ready for it this time and it didn't deter me; instead of backing off I escalated, reaching down, slipping a hand inside his underwear.

I was pleased to find his penis already standing to attention, and I began firmly to massage it.

"Alex, are you sure?" he asked, and I answered him with another kiss. I released his head and pulled off his t-shirt, marvelling at the way it slid across his chest. Leaning away from him, I was rewarded with the sight of his naked upper body, and it ignited me further. I continued to stroke his dick, delighting in the way it felt under my fingers; not like mine, somehow, although I couldn't say in what way. Except that it was larger, more fun to play with, and hadn't been recently abused with horrible knickers.

His eyes widened; I took advantage of his hesitation to kiss him again, and then with gentle pressure on his shoulders I guided him back to the edge of the bed, making him sit up. He watched me, wondering what I was planning.

What I was planning was this: I kissed him on the lips, then on the chin, then on his clavicle, and on and on, down his chest and stomach, smothering against his belly my amusement at the way his body hair tickled my chin. I stayed there a while, enjoying his warmth and his scent, before leaning away from him, climbing down off the bed and, without breaking eye contact, kneeling. I put my thumbs inside the elastic of his underwear and pulled it down.

I hadn't been prepared for what the sight of his dick would do to me. I'd been thinking I'd give him a handjob while looking lovingly into his eyes or something, but seeing the thing bare and erect electrified me in a way I'd never known was possible. Before I even thought about what I was doing, I'd leaned forward and taken it into my mouth.

It tasted salty and perhaps a bit stale — he hadn't showered yet — but, honestly, it was pretty okay. It filled my mouth and then some; I couldn't take all of it, not without involving my throat, and I was already getting warning signals from back there so I settled for letting my hand do some of the work. I massaged the base of his penis with my fingers while I licked and caressed the tip with my lips and tongue. Judging by the noises James started making (and the way his hips started twitching), it was the right approach.

I laughed as I thought back to the Alex who started the week. I suddenly wanted to nip back in time and tell him he'd be finishing up the weekend with his boss' dick in his mouth, just to see how he'd react, and I realised why James and Ben had had such fun gently teasing me the last few days. Oblivious Alex *was* sort of adorable.

It felt good to think of him in the past tense, though.

James was stroking my cheek with the back of his fingers, and it brought me back to the present, back to the penis I had in my mouth. I tried pressing my tongue up a bit and rubbing the head of his cock against the roof of my mouth, and the man actually *gasped*. So I did it again.

I was making him happy, and it was fucking amazing.

My own dick quirked in its tight little trap, but I didn't care about it any more, about whether it was something I wanted as part of me, about whether it was something I loved or hated or was indifferent to; I was too far gone. I reached down and started stroking myself through the fabric of my underwear, tugging on the base of my penis to free it from its foreskin and thanking God and Ben that while the tucking knickers might have been tight and uncomfortable, they were also made of soft, silky material. There was just enough friction to provide pleasure and just enough give to keep it from being painful, although with my few remaining coherent thoughts I suspected I would have been gleefully rubbing on myself even if my dick had been encased in sandpaper and bound with barbed wire.

My cock stiffened and flexed and I moved with it, my whole body responding.

James had one hand in my hair now, bumping up against my ponytail and rhythmically pushing against my neck. I took it as a guide and kept time with him, firmly stroking his dick at the base and at the tip with my fingers and my tongue. James let out a noise I'd never heard from him before, and his other hand dug nails-deep into my shoulder. He pulled on my head and shoved his dick farther into my mouth. Too far! I didn't want to gag, so with all my strength I pushed back, and when I was comfortable I splayed my hand around the shaft of his penis and used my finger and thumb to shorten the length that could be forced into my mouth. I wouldn't normally have been strong enough to push against him, even with both arms and from my advantageous position, but he was trembling and intermittently weak; it was enough.

He kept squeezing and stroking my neck and shoulder and I kept up my ministrations in rhythm with his, rubbing myself through my underwear and hoping there were as many sparks flying through his head as there were through mine, and we kept that up for a while; eventually, though, the pressure started to build in my spine and I couldn't stop myself from going faster, becoming almost frantic, and he accompanied me, one hand on the back of my head and another finding purchase wherever it could, stroking my face, playing with my hair, occasionally supporting him when it all got too much.

Locked together, we moved as one.

There was another noise, pitched higher than before, and it took me a second to realise it had been me; I'd been moaning and whining even through the impediment of his dick. Involuntarily, hungrily, and free of the concern that he might accidentally shove himself all the way down my neck, I unclenched my throat and jaw muscles, and my movements became looser, more relaxed, but still in time with his.

I was still rubbing on my own dick, through the underwear, and my need for release was becoming more and more urgent. James' leg was right there, bucking and twitching away, so I pressed up against him, used his motion to guide and reinforce me, and the pressure in my back became heat, a spreading warmth that concentrated in my head, my chest and my crotch. I arched my back, leaned forward, took him as far into my mouth as I could — in that moment I would have swallowed him whole without thought — and my knickers wetted and my knees lost strength and my whole body quivered. I had to stop myself from resting and luxuriating in the release because I still had James in my mouth, and somehow it made my orgasm warmer, slower, more intense.

I pulsed as I pulled away from him just far enough to run my tongue the length of his dick, all the way from the head to the base, taking him once again fully into me.

James started making quiet, low-pitched noises, faster and faster. In my orgasmic glow, they were the sexiest thing I'd ever heard, and now that I was as spent and as happy as I thought I'd ever been, I was free and able to extract every bit of pleasure I could get out of him, and I did, with everything I had. Moments later he shuddered, gripped me tightly again, and ejaculated.

I was so surprised, I swallowed it.

* * *

We lay side by side on the bed. James had flopped back after we disentangled ourselves, and inched up the bed until he was comfortable. I'd followed him, acutely aware as I went of the wetness in my knickers and hoping I didn't accidentally rub any of it on him, but I couldn't especially bring myself to care. In my haze I wanted nothing but to cuddle, and if I got any of my ejaculate on him, well, I'd just swallowed his entire load, hadn't I? Fair's fair.

"Oh my *God*," James said after a while, his voice lazy and breathy.

"Was I okay?" I asked. Performance anxiety after my first blow job; hurrah.

He made me wait a few agonising seconds, and then said, "It was *beyond* okay, Alex."

"Good," I said, and kissed him on the cheek. "Never done that before."

"I wouldn't have known." James leaned away enough to look at me and, still sounding a little stoned, added, "I feel we should do you now. Um. If you want."

I blushed. Absurd that I could manage to be embarrassed under such conditions, but I was talented like that. "I did myself," I said. "During."

"Oh. Really?" He sounded almost disappointed.

"Really." I giggled. "I'm *so* wet."

I wasn't prepared for him to reach down and touch me, but he did, placing three of his fingers over the front of my crotch, over where my dick would have been if I didn't have it tucked back. He flexed his fingers and explored until he found it, returned to its normal state, floppy and flattened; considerably stickier than usual.

308

He smiled at me and I tried not to look surprised. He didn't seem to have even the slightest problem with touching me down there. God fucking bless him.

And then he blinked and withdrew his hand quickly and for a horrific moment I panicked, but he put me right. "Sorry, Alex," he said. "I shouldn't have just *grabbed* you like that. I should have asked—"

"James," I said, relieved and happy once more, "it's fine."

"Still. I should have asked."

I couldn't stop the question. That last part of me really needed convincing, I supposed. "You're okay with me... down there?"

"What?" he said, confused. "I don't understand."

"With, you know—" I dropped into a whisper, "—my penis."

He blinked again, and then smiled broadly. "Alex," he said, "I meant what I said. I want *you*. All of you. And since apparently I have to be—" he took a deep, exasperated breath, "—*ludicrously* specific, I will add that that *includes* your penis. But, also, in the interest of being, like I said, very specific and hopefully preempting any mad ideas that might enter that head of yours—" he poked me on that head of mine, "—that *also* includes whatever else you might *or might not* decide to get installed down there."

"Really?"

"Really. Although," he added, his expression turning wry, "I do feel bad I didn't even notice you were masturbating while you were down there."

I kept a beaming smile focused on him while I reached behind me for a pillow with which to beat him. He really was going to have to stop feeling guilty all the time about such random things. "Yes," I explained, "you're definitely an inattentive lover because I was doing extra stuff to myself *completely out of your line of sight.* It's fine, really." I took advantage of his momentary relief to attack him with my pillow, but he intercepted my hand, so I just kissed him instead, squirming a little; all the movement — and James' fingers — had caused the dampness to spread across more of my knickers, and I was starting to feel rather uncomfortably wet. "Besides," I added, "just touching it is one thing, but I don't know if I'm ready for, um, uh—"

"Got it," he said, rescuing me from myself. "We could always try...?"

His complex mimes were opaque to me, but I was pretty sure I knew what he was getting at all the same. "Anal?" I guessed. He nodded and had the good grace to look embarrassed himself. Ever since I'd started presenting as a woman I'd gotten to see over and over again the sheepish, unsure, delicate side of James that I'd only glimpsed before, and I liked it: he was tremendously cute when he was flustered. "Between the heels and the tucking underwear I'm walking funny enough, thanks," I said. "Maybe when we get back home?" Apart from anything else, I needed time to hit the internet and figure out the mechanics of it. I knew nothing about anal sex, but millions upon millions of people did it, so it had to be pleasurable to be on the receiving end.

James looked like he wanted to say something else, but his phone alarm went off. "Fuck," he said, reaching over to silence it. "Time's gotten on. We need to be responsible adults, I'm afraid."

"Ugh," I commented. "Don't wanna." I licked my lips. "Hey, James, do we have any orange juice? I have this strange taste in my mouth and I have no idea how it got there."

He hit me with the pillow.

* * *

"Where's Ben, anyway?" I asked James while he showered. I'd rinsed my junk, found a clean pair of underwear, and finished a whole bottle of horrifically expensive orange juice from the minibar. Now I was just hanging out in the bathroom. "Shouldn't he be here by now to make me look pretty?"

James stuck his head out from behind the frosted shower glass and made a show of looking me up and down. "Like you need *any* help with that."

310

"I'll have you know I degrade without professional assistance. Like Cinderella. I require regular ministrations from a drag queen."

"A 'performance artist in the medium of drag'," James corrected, muffled again by the shower. From the sound of his coughing, I think he got water in his mouth while he was trying to be clever.

"I'll go text him," I decided, and left the bathroom to do just that. James started singing while I was gone, so I popped back into the bathroom to tease him for his choice of song before I texted Ben. Taylor Swift again.

Ben's reply was prompt: **Sorry. Running late.**

It's fine, I replied. **I'm getting ready now.**

I chucked the phone on the bed and returned to the bathroom just in time to see James getting out of the shower, which was entirely the sight I'd been in there for in the first place. Naked, glistening, stepping out into a room misty with water vapour, James looked like someone out of one of those movies that make teens form violently opposed shipping factions, and I wanted nothing more than to leap on him. Time was not on my side, however, so I made do with giving him a kiss and a towel.

"Ben's running late," I said, when we were done, "so I'm going to make a start on my face."

"Okay," James said, and pecked me on the lips as punctuation. "I'll be out in a minute."

I slipped the third and thankfully final show dress out of its bag and regarded it for a moment. It was just as horrifically bright blue and shiny as the other two had been, and I sighed at the thought that I had another whole day of standing around wearing the thing, becoming once more a talking, posing avatar for James' company (as much as he insisted, very sweetly, that it was *ours*). Still, it was the last day, and I had to admit there had been moments where being a trade show model had been pretty fun. I laid the dress on the bed and caught myself feeling almost wistful as I turned away from it.

And then it was time for the foundation underwear. I started with the bum pads, but this time I watched myself put them on, compared my body before and after, imagined my real self curving that way. The thought was thrilling.

Except I might never curve like that. I might always have narrow hips, from what I'd read. And, damn it, that was okay! I pulled the pads down again and examined myself in just my knickers, thinking that I wouldn't necessarily mind too much if I didn't fill out.

I felt realigned, like I'd come to an accommodation with my body. It would change, and that was good, and it wouldn't necessarily change in all the ways I hoped, and that was fine. And maybe, with the knowledge that it *would* change, it wasn't so awful to inhabit right now.

Then again, it might just have been the post-orgasmic glow.

In the reflection, the clock on the bedside table caught my eye and reminded me that I didn't really have time for introspection. Grumbling to myself, I pulled the pads back up again, allowed myself another moment or two to pose in the mirror, and then finished dressing. I was sponging foundation around my jawline when James appeared, wearing suit trousers and a shirt which he had, to his credit, not yet fully buttoned up.

"Hey," he said, and kissed me on the top of my head.

I waved him away. "Hi. Now go away and let me concentrate."

In the makeup mirror, I saw him frown. "I thought you were supposed to use a brush for that."

I brandished my blender at him. "You know how long I've been doing my own makeup," I said. "Brushes are advanced class. But anyone can do *this*." I spotted a smudge by my nose and got to work on it. "Almost anyone."

He left me alone after that, and ten minutes later I had what I thought was a creditable impression of Ben's makeup job from Friday and Saturday. Perhaps a little iffy on the fine details, but I didn't think I looked like someone who was *completely* clueless.

I stood up and showed myself off to James, who hadn't managed so much as to button his shirt.

"How do I look?" I asked.

"Wonderful," James said, putting down his phone and favouring me with a generous smile.

I took a step toward him. "Good enough for the show floor?" My confidence faltered. "I don't want to look like crap next to Emily."

James stood up and came over so he could inspect me properly. "Definitely good enough," he said. "You look amazing."

I couldn't help smiling. "Thanks," I whispered.

"Aren't you going to let your hair down?"

"Oh, uh, yeah," I said. "No. It kind of needs a wash, but I don't want to fuck up the extensions, so I put it up. Do you think it's okay?"

James nodded. "Absolutely," he said, with feeling. "You look... kind of sexy, actually."

I took another step forward, erasing the distance between us. "Just 'kind of' sexy?" I asked with a grin.

"Okay, very sexy," he said, putting a hand on each of my shoulders to stop my advance. "Makes you look like a hot librarian or teacher or something."

I laughed. "Did you, by any chance, have a crush on one of your teachers?"

"Yes." James smiled. "Miss Burgess. My Maths teacher. She wore her hair in a pony just like that, and she had these little sweaters..." He trailed off.

"Buy *me* a little sweater," I said, standing on tiptoes so I could be closer to his face, and continued in a sultry whisper, "and I'll make you solve equations."

I went in for the kiss at that point, but we were both dissolving into giggles at the bad-romance-movie sexiness, and it was kind of sloppy. He kissed me on the forehead instead, and I nuzzled against him.

"I love you, Alex," he whispered.

I looked up at him again. "I love you, James," I replied, and we kissed properly that time. I didn't even register the sound of the door and I didn't think James did, either.

"Hi, kids," Ben said. "Alex! You're glowing."

"I'm sorry to have to tell you," Ben said, "but your makeup is a mess. I'll need to redo it."

I frowned. Wordlessly, Ben guided me to the chair at the little desk and handed me the remover pads. "I thought I did okay," I said, trying not to sound disappointed.

"Oh, no," Ben said, "you did *fine*. But I still have to fix it because *after* you did fine, you let that one over there kiss your lipstick all over your face."

That One Over There paused in doing his tie long enough to say, "Hey!"

"Congratulations, by the way," Ben said, smiling. "I was wondering when you'd get over yourselves."

"Oi!" I said, and kicked him. I didn't have my shoes on yet, so mostly I hurt only my toes. "Don't reduce my voyage of personal discovery to 'getting over myself'."

Ben trapped me with a look. "That night? The first time you saw each other? I knew more or less how this was going to turn out. The rest of it is just... details."

"Oh, uh, yeah," I said, "speaking of details. And please don't say, 'I told you so,' or anything like that, okay? Because there's something I want to tell you." Ben looked at me; I couldn't meet his eyes.

"Yes?" he said.

Deep breath. "I'm transgender. I'm going to transition."

He sat back. "Thank. Fucking. God."

"You knew?" James said, sitting on the edge of the bed. "Why didn't you tell me? Or *her?*"

"I knew *something* was up," Ben said to James. He looked back at me. "No straight cis man wears a dress as well *and* as calmly as you did. But I couldn't tell for certain if you were gay, trans, secretly into crossdressing, or just sort of 'gender-interesting' or something. And I didn't *tell* either of you—" he waggled a finger at James, "—because you can't rush this kind of stuff." He frowned. "I did hint at it, though, as openly as I dared. Tried to open her mind a little. But if I'd been any more direct I might have chased her right back into the closet, and that's how you create iron eggshells." He tapped me on the knee. "Would Wednesday's Alex have responded well to me telling her straight out I thought she might be some flavour of trans?"

"Wednesday's Alex was full of shit," I said. "So no, probably not."

"Well then."

That sentiment would have earned Ben a hug but I was worried I'd mess up my makeup again, so I settled for smiling and blowing him a kiss.

* * *

Emily linked up with us in the lobby while we waited for the Uber, saving me from the conversation Ben and James were having over my head; both of them were excited and both of them were taller than me, so I let them babble at each other while I rested in James' arms, content and relaxed. I spotted her as she emerged from the elevator and headed over to meet her, praying that I'd managed to disentangle myself from James before she noticed. I wasn't sure I was ready for the conversation it might prompt.

"So," Emily said, walking with me to the other corner of the lobby and making the syllable do a *lot* of work, "*that's* new."

Damn. I felt my whole body blush again. "Yeah," I said, and I knew as I said it that I wasn't going to be able to stop smiling. I could hear my happiness in my voice, in the inflection every word takes on when you can't prevent the corners of your mouth from twisting upwards. "We got together last night."

"Bit of a turnaround for Little Miss I'm Not Into Guys, huh? How was it?"

I was jealous of her long coat; I'd forgotten mine, and between the dress and the blush I was easily the most colourful thing in the lobby.

"He came up to my room last night," I said, "and he was, um, in a bit of a state." I quickly thought over how I could explain it without, technically, lying. I knew I wanted to come out properly to Emily before she started working for us, but I also knew I didn't want to do it right there and then. I wanted a warm-up. A run-up. Perhaps a sports drink and an energy bar and a coach to yell encouraging things at me. "He was feeling awful about how he 'shouldn't' like me the way he does—" she grinned at my rabbit ears around the word 'shouldn't', "—and *I* was feeling awful about always avoiding the topic. So we talked. And *talked*. And eventually decided that, yes, actually we *are* both into each other and we are also both idiots. He, um, stayed the night," I added, my blush intensifying. I was, at this point, probably purple. "We didn't, you know, *do* anything until this morning, though."

Thinking back on it, it was hard not to melt. No-one else had ever made me feel a fraction as energised; no-one else had ever made me so *hungry* for them. Just thinking about him made me ache to put my hands on him again... I started to stiffen in my underwear, and quickly changed the subject.

"But that's not what I wanted to talk to you about," I continued briskly, as if I hadn't just briefly paused the conversation to picture my boss naked. "Are you still interested in coming to work with us as an engineer? We're going to need good ones more than ever."

"Are you serious?" she said. "Yes! Fuck, Alex, absolutely yes."

We spent the rest of the wait for the Uber discussing the sort of work she'd be getting involved in, the length and nature of the trial period, whether she'd have to sign an NDA (probably) and whether the boss was likely to hit on her, too (probably not).

As if summoned by name, James appeared. He put his arms around me from behind and I sank into him. I pulled his arms tighter so he surrounded me, which pulled the already snug fabric of the dress tighter, which pulled on the hip pads, which pulled on the tucking knickers, and what I'm getting at here is that between us we started a chain reaction inside me that I regretfully had to put a stop to before I ripped his clothes off right there in the lobby and got us arrested.

I pushed his arms away, twirled around to face him, and nipped up to kiss him on the lips before he could register his surprise.

316

"Hello," he said, when I let him talk again.

"Hi," I said.

"Good morning," Emily said, reminding us both of her presence.

"Whoops," I mouthed to James, and turned around to smile an apology at Emily. She winked at me.

"What I came over to say," James said, sounding a little flustered, "is the car is here."

* * *

Between the four of us we were too many for the back of the car, so we banished James to the passenger seat in front. I, as the shortest and smallest, naturally got put in the middle, crammed between Ben and Emily and thoroughly uncomfortable. I pulled the lap belt as loosely over myself as I could, not wanting to put any more pressure than I had to on the area between the hemline of my dress and the top of my padding; I still hadn't quite recovered from my bout of James-related lust in the lobby. I'd have to be more careful what I let myself think about, at least until I learned some self-control.

I finally understood why so many people at school had seemed so uncontrollably horny; I'd been nonplussed at the time, simply not understanding why they let their libidos take them over so completely, but it turned out I was exactly as bad when I met someone who flipped all my switches. Worse, perhaps.

Shame it had to finally happen for me while I was pretending to be a professional adult. I thought of boring, unsexy things. Self-control sucked.

"Miss Swan," James said, leaning around to look at the three of us, "did I overhear you and Miss Brewer discussing the arrangements for next week?" Great. 'Miss Brewer'd again; Mr McCain was in a cheeky mood.

"You did," Emily replied. "I'm really looking forward to—"

She was interrupted by a strange, tortured rumbling sound, which after a few moments resolved into an unmistakably gastric growl. We all

317

identified the source at roughly the same time and turned as one to look at Ben.

"Sorry," Ben said. "I missed breakfast."

My belly, reminded of the existence of food, echoed his. "Same here," I said.

Ben grinned at me. "Yes, I imagine you were rather too busy to squeeze anything in."

"Oh, she ate *something*," James said, with a grin that was somehow even more filthy than Ben's. Even so, I wasn't sure exactly what he meant until Ben leaned forward and clipped him round the ear.

"Behave," Ben said.

"She had quite the appetite for—" James managed, before Ben hit him again.

I hugged myself and looked very carefully at my exposed knees. Emily nudged me and asked in a loud whisper if I wanted her to take James out back of the expo and shoot him, which prompted a round of protests from James and more violence from Ben.

The Uber driver took our bullshit in companionable silence, but rolled her eyes sympathetically when she saw me looking at her in the rear-view mirror. I rolled mine in response, and gave her five stars.

* * *

Sunday at the booth was characterised by short periods of intense activity interspersed with long periods of boredom, like a war but with slightly sillier outfits. The expo was winding down, with most of the journalists and reps already having succumbed to the weight of booze and takeaway food they'd consumed over the long weekend.

"Did you really go down on him?" Emily asked me, between groups of attendees.

"I didn't mean to," I said. "I was just kind of, you know, kissing him, and I got a bit excited, and it was, you know, *right there.*"

"Alex, where were you kissing him that his dick was 'right there'?"

I shrugged, biting my lip, and when she nudged me I grudgingly admitted, "Just, you know, places."

"You're glowing, you know."

"I know," I said wretchedly. "Ben already tortured me with that."

"It's adorable."

"It's all the embarrassment. I swear I've blushed more in the last week than I have the entire rest of my life. It doesn't help that teasing me is apparently James' mission in life."

"Are you two officially together now? Like, a couple?"

"I think so," I said, frowning. We were, I was certain. We hadn't said it, hadn't actually called ourselves *boyfriend and girlfriend* — wow, that was a weird word to apply to myself; the latest of many — but it had been implied in the strongest terms. "It's not been said out loud," I added. "But he loves me. He said that, for definite." I thought about that moment some more, dwelled on it, and my apparent outer glow was joined by an inner one.

"That sounds pretty certain, then," Emily said, giving me a quick one-armed hug. "Welcome to dating men! Expect aggravation."

I shrugged. "I'll just kick him every time he's a jerk until he gets the message."

"Sound methodology." She grinned. "He's looking at you, by the way."

I turned around, and he was. He was on the phone, and waved me over as soon as he saw I was facing him.

"Can you talk to Soph?" he said, when I arrived.

"Why?" I said warily, but he didn't reply, just wordlessly held out his phone. I took it. "Sophie?"

"*Alex!*" she shrieked, mercifully moderated by the phone's speaker. "James told me *everything!*"

"How much of everything?" I leaned on James; he put his arm around my shoulder.

"You had *sex!*" she yelled, so loud her voice was slightly clipped by the limited bandwidth of the connection.

I sighed. "Yes," I said. "Yes, we did." James squeezed me; I appreciated it.

"That's wonderful!" she enthused, and then she turned more serious. "So that means it's final, right? You're a girl, yes?"

"Seems that way."

"You're going to transition?"

"I think I already have," I said. "I just need the medical stuff to catch up with me. But yes—" I looked around to make sure I wasn't likely to be overheard by anyone but James, "—I'll be transitioning. Already ordered the hormones and everything. And before you ask, I'm not going to break his heart, Soph. Not unless he breaks mine first." I looked up at James and he made very reassuring facial expressions down at me.

"Good. Now, I wanted to ask you something." Oh God. "I'd like to get to know you properly, if you're going to be my cousin-in-law. Cousin-in-law? Is that the term? Anyway. I wanted your permission to come stay awhile, down in London."

I blinked. "Oh, uh, sure, I suppose, if James agrees, too."

"I do," James whispered.

"Don't worry," Sophie said, "I'll get a hotel. I'm sure you two will want your privacy."

I hadn't thought my blush could get any deeper, but it turned out that repeatedly talking to people about my sex life could manage it. You could have fried a whole breakfast on me.

"Um, thank you," I said.

"What are you going to do about James' family?" Sophie asked. "They've already met you as, um, 'Boy Alex'."

"Fuck," I said. "One crisis at a time, maybe?" James frowned. I mouthed 'family' at him, and he grimaced.

"Sorry!" she said quickly. "Yes, of course. James never sees his dad unless his dad imposes on him, anyway, and I can't imagine his mum will mind."

"Oh God," I realised. "I still haven't figured out what to tell *my* mum." This is what living in a strange, Birmingham-based alternate universe for a few days does to you: it becomes easy to make yourself forget about all the little inconveniences of life, like a mother who might object to you growing breasts.

James kissed me on the top of my head. It was ridiculous he could still do that even with me in heels.

"If there's anything I can do, let me know," Sophie said with apparent sincerity.

"Moral support," I said firmly. "Be there for me when I have to see people for the first time, so it's not just me and James?"

"I'm at your disposal, darling. Oops, must go!" she added. "I have to see a lady about a thing before I leave Birmingham."

The line went dead before I could say goodbye. My shoulders sagged with released tension; even on the phone, Sophie was a bit much. I gave James his phone back and slumped against him.

"What am I going to do about my mum, James?" I whispered into his shoulder. The thought was getting scarier the longer it lingered in my brain, and for some reason I couldn't dismiss it like before. Probably because we were going home soon. Reality was starting to intrude.

"We'll work it out together," he said, and kissed me. "Do you need to take a break?"

I shook myself. "No," I said. "I'm okay. And I'll *be* okay."

"Good," he said, and kissed me again. "And sorry about before, in the car. I'm just a little giddy, that's all."

I smiled at that. "I am, too," I said. "And you don't need to apologise. I can cope with a little teasing, as long as you understand that next time you crack a joke at my expense, I'll kick you in the knee."

"Understood."

* * *

By the end of the day I was so tired I could barely stand. The three days of the expo, the swept-off-my-feet madness before it, and the sudden changes

I'd undergone had all formed into a gigantic weight that was pressing down on me, and I wanted to sleep for a hundred years. Preferably next to James.

I leaned against him as we watched Kit, Marcus and Ben take the stand apart. Emily, looking almost as tired as I felt, was slumped on a stool next to Kristen and Martina and three other women Emily knew who'd been working at a booth on the other side of the hall. They were sharing the last of Emily's jelly babies and various other small treats, and between them they'd dumped a pile of discarded shoes like a funeral pyre. Kristen saw me looking and smiled. I gave her a little wave.

I'd kept my own shoes on, uncomfortable though they were after so many hours on my feet; I needed them so I could lean on James and not end up with my face in his armpit.

Despite my exhaustion, I felt at peace. I'd met myself for the first time, really gotten to know myself, filled in all the missing parts of my personal jigsaw puzzle. Sure, I had a journey in front of me, and quite a long one, but I had people who had promised to help me, I had a boyfriend who drove me crazy (in several different ways) and, most importantly, I finally knew what the hell I was going to do with my life.

In general.

In broad strokes.

Okay, fine: I was still an idiot swept along by circumstances and doing my best to keep my head clear; I was just a girl idiot now.

Now and forever.

"Weird weekend, really," James said. He was slowly stroking my bare shoulder with his fingers.

"You know," I said, "I thought if the expo went really well for us, if we found a big buyer for our software, there was a possibility this weekend could change my life. I never expected... this."

"You're happy, though, right?" James said.

I squeezed him. "Happier than I've ever been. I didn't know it was possible to be so happy."

"Good."

We watched the boys continue to dismantle the stand.

"You'll come with me to the doctor, won't you?" I said.

"Of course," James said. "I want to share this whole process with you. I mean, not to the point of joining in, but—"

I laughed. "You'd better not," I said. I didn't like the idea of James becoming a girl. I wanted him to stay exactly the way he was. Except perhaps with fewer clothes on.

I felt him take a deep breath. "So," he said, "when we get back to London, do you want to come back to my place?"

"Sure," I said. There was nothing I wanted at my flat, anyway; just a cold, empty bed, drawers full of clothes I no longer needed, a life I no longer wanted.

"I mean, do you want to come back to my place to stay?" he said, with an embarrassed little cough. "Permanently. I can, uh, clear out some space in the wardrobe and everything."

I leaned away from him so I could look him in the eye.

"James Ian McCain," I said. "Are you asking me to move in with you?"

He looked away, at the empty spot where our booth had been, where Ben and Kit and Marcus were dragging boxes of equipment out towards the doors, chatting, laughing.

"I mean, if you want to," he said awkwardly. "Do you want to?"

I stood on tiptoes, my heels popping out of my shoes, and whispered in his ear, "Yes."

The End

Epilogue

Reality hit pretty hard. I'd known it was going to — it was all I could think about on the car ride home — and I'd tried my best to prepare for it, but crashing out of the otherworldly bubble of the expo and returning to London was always going to be challenging. At least I was a girl now.

The last leg of the journey home was etched particularly powerfully into my memory. It was dark by the time we got back to London, and watching familiar scenery flow past while my new self looked back at me from my reflection in the window was surreal. It felt like a eulogy for my old life. *Alexander Brewer, we remember him sort of fondly.*

The first few days back were too busy for me to have much of a chance to think. Monday morning we went over to my flat and got rid of most of my belongings, lugging clothes and things in huge trash bags down to the dump or to the charity shop on the corner, depending. We also called James' clinic, got me on his plan and got me in for a blood test that afternoon. And Tuesday was moving day: we loaded up a rented van with everything that remained, and even though we'd thrown out, donated or — in one case — burned a lot of my stuff, there was more left over than I expected. It took the whole morning; the afternoon we spent shifting some of James' things to a storage unit, so I'd have room for my clothes and shoes and my handful of sentimental items.

I'd had, up to that point, no idea James even *had* a storage unit, and was amused to find that it was enormous, temperature-controlled, and contained a grand piano! I sat on it and posed — we took pictures — and I whined to him that we could have kept more of my stuff.

"What stuff?" he'd asked me. "The broken laptop, the collection of ugly ties I've never, ever seen you wear, or the men's dress shoes that were made, I couldn't tell exactly, from either plastic or cardboard?"

Yeah. He had a point. I gave him a little kick, anyway.

That night, then, I was officially moved in. I hung up all my clothes — thanks to Ben and his personal shopper friend I had perhaps a dozen outfits, though only three or four would really qualify as casual — set up my work laptop and my trinkets and keepsakes on an antique bureau in one corner of the living room, and collapsed on the couch with James.

We put the telly on and we hugged. It was perhaps the lowest-intensity evening we'd yet spent together as boyfriend and girlfriend, and it was, in its own way, just as special as our other, more excitable nights.

And then, on Wednesday, he went into work. He did so without waking me, the sneaky bastard; he left a handwritten note on his pillow that read, *Have to do work things! Will spare you the details. Rest up, beautiful.* I couldn't be mad at him, and not just because he also left me five Xs on the bottom of the note and a thermos of coffee. Yes, I liked work — and, more to the point, I liked working *with him* — but I was also exhausted. Exhausted from the expo, from my series of increasingly radical personal revelations, and from carrying multiple bags of men's trousers to the charity shop. Over the last few days my body had been getting increasingly insistent about the need for me to stop, please, for just one bloody minute.

So I consented to stop. For one bloody minute. Which was when the trouble started. Counting from almost exactly a week before, my whole life as a girl I'd been going a mile a minute, and now, suddenly, I wasn't. And when you still have everything in the world to do for your transition but no way to take it in both hands and accomplish it for yourself, when all you have is time, you can *really* torture yourself.

The day started well enough. I went through my morning routine; my new one, my girl one, the one I was still optimising. I showered and washed my hair, which was something I could now do without assistance and without fear that I might wreck the extensions; Ben hadn't been as precise as I'd liked about how to care for my new, longer hair, so on Monday I'd called the salon and spoken to Warren, who'd been exaggeratedly relieved that I was keeping them. "Taking those *gorgeous* locks out so soon would have been a *sin,*" he told me, and I'd looked at myself in the mirror as we talked and speculated that perhaps the greater sin was the amount of scalp grease that had built up; I itched. With Warren's guidance I'd gone online and bought the right kind of shampoo and conditioner and hairbrush, and replaced the crappy little hair dryer James owned, which had clearly been nicked from a hotel. We'd found it all in Amazon boxes outside the apartment door when we returned from emptying out my old flat.

Washing and drying and dressing myself, styling my hair, and painting my face — for practice — took enough time that it was almost eleven when I sat down on the couch, put the telly on and started, fatally, to think.

That was when the dread *really* set in.

Because when I showered I'd put my hands all over myself. When I dressed and did my face I'd had to look at myself. And all I could think about was that, underneath it all, beneath the clothes and the makeup and the hair, I was still the same thing I'd always been.

Just a boy.

A state which was suddenly horrific.

I hadn't put on the tucking knickers that morning, and that was a mistake; my junk felt like a foreign object, bonded indecently to my body and clumped ugly between my legs. I hadn't bothered with padding of any kind, so the jeans felt loose and shapeless. And the hair on my face had grown back just enough to be difficult to shave; I'd pressed hard enough on the tricky part around the chin that I'd cut myself.

My artifice had come almost completely loose. What had that guy on Reddit said? That I was sitting on a 'T bomb'? In the silence, I could hear it tick.

I had to *do* something!

Fuck it. I was transitioning, wasn't I? That meant there actually *were* things I could usefully do. I didn't have to just sit around and remain uncomfortably *male*.

I checked the order status of my hormones. Payment processed, not shipped yet.

I checked the website for James' clinic to see if my blood test results were in yet. Nope.

I searched online for local hair removal places. I found a lot of them, dozens in central London alone, and the sheer number was so overwhelming I settled for calling Warren at the salon again. He recommended a place that was reasonably close by, and I got a consultation booked in for a week on Thursday. A week on bloody Thursday! Obscenely far in the future.

I checked the order status of my hormones again. Still not shipped.

Finally, to put the cherry on top, Mum called. She called and I was so grateful to have another focus for my attention that I forgot I didn't sound like her son any more. Fortunately, my hindbrain, which was looking out for the rest of me, stopped me before I could say anything incriminating — like, "Hi, Mum!" — by slapping a hand over my mouth, and when I removed it I pretended, sheepishly, to be a coworker.

"Do please ask him to ring me back," she said, and I kept myself from audibly reacting to the pronoun by kicking the couch. "It's been so long since we spoke."

I promised to find 'him' and hung up, just barely resisting the urge to fling my phone at something. And then I did the only sensible thing I could think of: I blanked my mind. I put everything aside — fear of impending masculinisation; fear of how my mother would react to me; fear of what awful things could be happening in her life that she would *call* me instead of just sending a message on WhatsApp like usual — and occupied my hands instead. I walked calmly to the bedroom, fished out a skirt, a clean pair of tucking knickers and the more tolerable set of pads, and kicked off my jeans. I hummed to myself as I got changed because, as Ben kept telling me, the more I used my voice, the better I'd sound, and I'd been virtually silent so far this morning. Then I put away the jeans and threw the ordinary knickers in the hamper, and I cleaned.

I cleaned the bedroom — James' side of the bed had somehow accumulated more pairs of socks than there had been days since we returned — and the bathroom. I did the dishes and ran the vacuum around the living room. I found homes for the bottles of (undoubtedly horrifically expensive) liquor James always left out on the coffee table. And after everything was done, I checked my makeup to make sure nothing needed touching up, poured myself a small glass of the fruity drink James had given me that first night, and knocked it back in one shot.

I even did the thing where you breathe heavily afterwards, even though it went down like bottled silk.

And *then* I sat down on the couch again, retrieved my phone and messaged my mum. I considered taking off the makeup and tying up my hair and trying to get my old voice back so I could video call her, but I didn't want a rehash of my adolescent squawking while talking to Mum.

That was an excuse, obviously, but a good one; relevant and important. The truth was that I didn't want to take even the tiniest step backwards. My mother was a problem I'd have to deal with at some point; the calculation as to when exactly that would be was something I was happy to leave for another day. I'd get through this, talk to her about whatever she wanted to talk about, and find myself some breathing room.

I didn't want her to know the new me until the new me was sufficiently different from the old me. That felt... important.

Alex: Hi, Mum! Emily said she picked up my phone?

Mum: Emily! Who is she, Alexander? A girlfriend?

Alex: A coworker.

Mum: I didn't think you had those. I thought it was just you and James. That's what you said before.

Alex: We're trying something out. What's up, Mum?

Mum: Oh, it's nothing, really.

Alex: MUM.

Mum: I don't want to worry you.

Alex: Mum, you KNOW that those are the six words in the English language most guaranteed to make someone panic.

Mum: It's your father.

Shit. Of course it was. Dad had been a problem long before the divorce; distance and — on my side — a rigidly enforced silence unfortunately hadn't seemed to slow him down one bit. He had his girlfriends and he had his drinks but he never, despite somehow holding down a decent job, seemed to have money.

I wondered how much of James' money it would take to get him to leave Mum alone for good.

Alex: What does he want now, Mum?

Mum: Nothing much. Help with some bills.

Alex: Sooner or later you're going to run out of money, Mum, and then where will he be? More to the point, where will YOU be?

Mum: He's still my husband, Alexander. And I still care for him. Even with his problems.

And there it was. There it always was. Divorce papers and me at twelve years old screaming at him to get the fuck away from my mum may have moved him out of the county, but Mum still thought of him fondly, even though I was certain Dad no longer cared for her in the slightest. I was pretty sure he'd never cared at all.

I wasn't going to push, though. She didn't need me trying to tell her, yet again, to shut him out. Especially because I was worried that if she tried to assert herself, he might escalate.

Alex: Did you send him the money yet?

Mum: Yes.

Mum: He stopped by and I just felt like I ought to.

Mum: I'm sorry.

Alex: You don't have to be sorry, Mum. Fuck, I'm the one who should be sorry.

Alex: Sorry for leaving home. I shouldn't have left you all on your own.

Alex: I'm also sorry for swearing. I'm a bad son.

Mum: Alexander, I'm so glad you're out there working! You needn't apologise.

Mum: But you shouldn't swear.

I hated to call myself her son, but that's what I was to her. For the moment. And I wanted deeply to tell her, but it wasn't right to do so over bloody WhatsApp, and I didn't want to call her, already sounding different, and have to navigate that, all while she was dealing with the fallout from my dad making himself a problem yet again.

But I *should* have come out to her. I knew it. It's not just that it would have made things easier, but it might have brought us closer, might have bridged the gap of polite but confused misunderstanding that had always existed between us. And, God, I wanted that gap closed. I'd always thought that if Dad wasn't around, Mum and I might have been closer. But when the trouble started between them she slammed shut like a clam, protecting herself, and I learned to be independent, and we lived more like acquaintances than family, especially when I was a little older.

And I'd had other reasons to keep to myself, of course, reasons I never truly understood until very recently.

We made small talk for a while, but I could tell she was withdrawing, having made the confession she'd wanted to make over the phone, having admitted to falling for Dad's shit *again.* And my heart wasn't in it, either. Resentment was beginning to bite at my replies, causing me to have to retype and rethink several times so I didn't come across as mean. Because I was pissed off! I'd barely gotten to be a girl for a week and already my unaltered body was reasserting itself and now my old life, with all its old problems, was clawing at me.

I just wanted clear air. A little time. Nothing more. Time to get my bloody hormones; time to laser off the damn facial hair; time to get my shit together. Time to get used to my new self. Time to feel comfortable.

Time in which to be a bloody *girl*.

What a selfish desire.

James found me in a ball of tears when he got home, and he swept me up and kissed me and held me and wiped my cheeks dry and showed me how much he loved me.

* * *

The hormones shipped that night. At two in the morning. I cried all over again when I got the email, and hugged James, who made very sweet noises in his sleep as I clung to him.

* * *

I went back to work on Thursday. It was best for me to be around people, I decided. James especially.

We'd also formally hired Emily. Trial basis, limited access, NDAs, et cetera. Sorting it out had been much of what James had been doing at work the day before, without me. Today, since I *insisted* on coming in with him, my job would be to get her set up with her work laptop and desktop, get her signed in on the appropriate projects, give her the tour, let her pick out a mechanical keyboard from the pile, and so on. I was pretty certain he was giving me something so simple to do because he didn't want me working too hard and getting (more) stressed, but I was too happy about it to be irritated with him for being manipulative; I wanted to be around people, like I said, and Emily was already one of my favourites.

I was nervous about seeing her again, though. Getting dressed that morning, I felt more male than ever, more angular, more unattractive, and I couldn't shake the feeling that she'd see right through me. So I went thicker on the foundation than usual, in case any of my resurgent facial hair showed up as shadow, and I agonised for long enough over which clothes to wear that James felt the need to surprise-attack me from behind with a hug and a smattering of kisses, just to jolt me out of my stupor. He did, however, also whisper to me that whatever I chose, I'd look beautiful, which was appreciated. I poured my worries into his waiting hands and he helped me pick an outfit that didn't make me look like I was trying too hard, or like I had shoulder blades that could cut cheese.

I didn't necessarily think Emily would react poorly to finding out about me, but it had to happen on *my* terms. For now, I needed a simple, calm day at work.

"Alex!" she squealed, as I rolled into the building with James, fashionably late but, hopefully, fashionably dressed. She was leaning against a pillar in the lobby and talking to Marcus, whose presence at the office had, I'm sure, absolutely nothing to do with it being Emily's first day.

She was dressed reasonably casually as well, thank God.

She collided with me and hugged me, squishing my rubber boobs into my chest. I had a moment to worry that she was close enough to my face to see something on it she didn't like — from her position far above it; why did everyone have to be so much taller than me? — and then she was leaning away from me and beaming.

Reassured, I said, "Fancy seeing you here."

"Thank you," she said. "Thank you bloody *thank you*. You have *no* idea how satisfying it was to call Hammond's and have them take me off the roster."

"Aw," Marcus said, walking up behind her, "you're not going to model again?"

"Never say never," she said, shrugging, "but not for a while. I'm going to spend a whole *month* in comfy shoes, Alex! A month! Um, assuming this works out, of course."

"It'll work out," I said, and leaned around her. "Hi, Marcus!"

"Hi, Alex," Marcus said, standing up from the faux-leather chair and waving to James and me. "Hi, boss. Just came in to pick up the new keys." He brandished a flash drive and then dropped it into his messenger bag.

"But we don't switch security keys for another two weeks," James said, with apparent innocence. Emily, still facing away from Marcus, smirked.

"Always be prepared," Marcus said. "Lovely seeing you again, Emily. I'll tell Kit you said hi."

"Please do," she said, and watched him leave with amusement. "So, Alex," she continued, turning back to me, "show me to my desk."

It didn't take long to get her set up, and the tour took even less time. McCain Applied Computing had a perennial option to take up the lease on the remaining free office space on our floor of the building — a family reputation for reliability and filthy richness preceded James in all things — but we'd yet to need it. We didn't even use half the rooms we were paying for, with only one of the three main spaces being in regular use. James had already promised me an office of my own as we expanded, which put paid to the fantasies I'd had of moving permanently into his and taking dictation while wearing a miniskirt and a tight blouse, but which did allow me to extend the tour slightly by showing Emily the empty and dusty space I'd eventually occupy.

I was going to have a bar and it would have nothing but that fruity liquor of James' I liked so much.

Back in the main room, I got her logged in on her new account and got her computers set up, and that was that. She set to familiarising herself with our systems and I, to stave off boredom and thus the possibility that I might start *thinking* again, offered to pop out and get sandwiches for the three of us; there was less than an hour left until lunchtime, after all.

None of the servers at the sandwich shop seemed to recognise me, even though I used to pick up lunch there at least twice a week. Encouraging! Or perhaps it just said something less than flattering about how memorable Boy Alex had been.

When I returned to the office, with my plastic bag from the sandwich shop and an elevated mood, James rushed up to meet me, pulling on his overcoat and kissing me in one complicated manoeuvre.

"Alex," he said, "Got to go out. I'm so sorry. Follow-up from the expo. Very sudden. Back soon." He kissed me again. "Love you!"

"Wait!" I hooked my hand into his elbow before he could leave. "Take your sandwich," I commanded. "You haven't eaten yet."

"What did you get me?"

I gave him a look. He *always* got the same order from the sandwich place. "Ham and egg on wholemeal, with pickle and mustard."

"English mustard?"

I gave him another look. I'd had a long time around James to build up a whole repertoire of them, and one of the good things about makeup was that it made my looks more striking. "What is this, my first time?"

He took the wrapped sandwich out of my hand and ran for the stairs, blowing me a kiss through the closing door.

"He's so cute," Emily said.

"He kind of is," I agreed, walking over to her desk and looking for a patch of clear space in which to drop the sandwich bag. I had a little trouble — she had various folders open and documents scattered, and she'd set up the laptop next to her desktop — but in the end I simply scraped up all the paperwork and dumped it on a spare chair.

"Hey!"

"No more work," I said, unpacking her chicken salad sandwich and my egg and cress. "Lunch."

We ate in silence for a while.

"So, Alex," she said, after she finished her first half-sandwich. "I know I said it already, but I'm really serious about it, so I'm saying it again: thank you for this."

I swallowed before replying. We might both have been dressed casually — me in the jeans Ben got and a sort of billowy green top, her in cargo trousers and a logo top that looked like it had been crafted out of a much larger logo top — but I still didn't want to look slovenly in front of the professional model, which is why I was dressed in casual clothes from bloody Harvey Nicks and why I made sure I wasn't going to spit egg and cress at her when I spoke. "Thank *you,* Emily. I couldn't have made it through the expo without you."

She bit her lip and looked away from me for a second, frowning at something on her laptop. "Actually," she said, "there's something I wanted to ask about."

"Oh?" I couldn't see the screen, but since she'd been deep diving into our project database I assumed she'd spotted something in our tangled web of code, some strange and inadequately commented cluster of commands I'd left squatting in the depths of the codebase. James said my contributions to our projects were like biblical angels: inexplicable and a tad frightening, but they got the job done.

"Yes," Emily said, nodding to herself. "Um. Yes."

"Yes?"

"Right. So. I was going through the files for the camera project? The one from the expo? And there's a folder of, um, test photos on the network. You can really see how the software came along, actually, with how the pictures start grainy and then get clearer and clearer and—"

I had to stop her before the creeping chills gave me frostbite. "Test photos?"

Silently she turned her laptop to face me. I didn't exactly remember the picture on the screen — until recently I didn't like looking at myself, and that extended to the test photos; fortunately, for my part of the project, I hadn't had to engage with them much — but I remembered the night we took it: it was barely two weeks ago. We were on the home stretch and mucking about late one evening, posing for selfies with our takeaway dinner. In this one, James and I were both in the frame, facing the camera, lips pursed, cheeks almost touching, connected by a single noodle dangling between our mouths. It'd been James' idea.

Hello, Boy Alex. Remember all that shit you used to let grow on your face?

Emily was leaning on her wrist, her elbow on the desk by the laptop screen, and the effect was very much as if she were framing the photo. She was smiling, with a slight frown, and seemed more puzzled than pissed off. I very much hoped she was, anyway.

"That's you, isn't it?" she said, and I was so surprised I just stared at her and blinked for a while. I'd been expecting her to ask if the guy on the screen was my brother or my cousin or something, and I'd half-prepared responses along those lines. I even had a few excuses in mind to explain my brother-cousin's absence, because there was no way I was going to let my life descend into the kind of farce that seemed inevitable when you had to pretend to be, for example, two different people. The way she asked the question was strange, too; like she didn't even need the confirmation, like she could tell from the way I reacted. Like she was planning to base her judgement of me on *how* I responded to the question than what combination of fact and fiction I chose to reply with.

Fuck it.

"Yes," I said, pleased to have kept my voice steady.

"It's recent, isn't it?" Another non-question; the file was clearly timestamped.

"Yes." Words of one syllable; very doable.

"The million-dollar question, then," she said. "What's going on, Alex?"

"Which do you want? The long version or the— I'm sorry, but could you close the laptop or turn it away from me or something? That's... weird to look at."

"Sure," she said, closing the laptop. "And I'd like the short version, please."

"I'm trans." The *really* short version.

She nodded. "I'm not going to say, 'I couldn't tell,' because I'm pretty sure that after a whole weekend of guys pawing at you, you already know that *no-one* can tell, and it's rude as hell to say, anyway. But I *am* confused, because Marcus and Kit talk about you like they only just met you last week, but the pictures on here go back almost a *year,* and—"

"I think you need the long version. You want the long version?"

She nodded. I gave her the long version. To begin with, she didn't say much, just nodded, smiled encouragingly and sipped her coffee, but when I got to the part about dressing up for the first time, her composure broke and she snorted. And then her eyes went wide and she clasped a hand to her mouth, carefully swallowed, and slowly returned her paper coffee cup to the table. She'd come close to spilling it and, by the looks of it, even closer to spraying coffee all over her new work laptop (and me).

"You're kidding," she said hoarsely. "You have to be kidding! Alex, please tell me you're kidding."

"What about?"

She waved a hand wildly. "Everything! You really never so much as wore a skirt or anything before, what, a week ago?"

I nodded. "I think I told you exactly that when we first met." I decided not to mention the school play for now. It would only complicate things.

"I remember," she said, smiling. "But I just thought you were, I don't know, some kind of farm lesbian."

"Nope," I said. "Just a guy. Or I thought I was, anyway. Look, Emily, I'm struggling to get a read on how you're reacting. Is it... Am I... Are you okay with me?"

"Shit. Yes. Alex. Of course I am. Sorry; I should have said. I think it's great that you're trans and I'm amazed at how fantastic you look considering you're still pre-everything. You *are* pre-everything, right?"

"I am."

"Bloody hell. But yes, I'm *more* than okay with you. I think I'm just overwhelmed because... because it's all so bananas!" She chewed on her lip for a moment. "You make *sense* now," she continued, nodding to herself. "Everything you said, the way you were. I get it. I get why you were so nervous. Why everything seemed so new. And, holy shit, I get why you were so hesitant to admit you wanted to kiss your boss!"

"You're really fine with it?" I was struggling to believe my first coming out — Ben, James and Sophie aside — was going well, considering I hadn't prepared for it in the slightest. I'd had vague thoughts about assembling a PowerPoint presentation; clearly, it wouldn't have been necessary.

"Of course I am, Alex! I'm— I mean, my friend is— Damn. I'm falling over myself here." She took my hand and squeezed it. "One of my friends is trans. Just like you. I mean, okay, she didn't come out to herself while modelling a bloody dress on a bloody stand at a bloody trade show, but, you know, everyone's coming out story is weird in its own way, right?"

That seemed suggestive. "Do *you* have a coming out story?"

She shrugged. "I'm bi. Kissed a— a girl in a school play." She coughed, suddenly embarrassed. "I was, um, not supposed to. But she'd been giving me these looks all the way through rehearsal, and one thing led to another. Radical reinterpretation of *Romeo & Juliet.*"

"Why is there always a school play?" I asked the heavens.

* * *

Emily and I went over my entire life's story over the course of the afternoon, and if she laughed at rather too much of it for my comfort, in doing so she helped me appreciate the humour in my abrupt transformation. She also, through her friend, knew an awful lot about hormone therapy and trans surgeries, and she helped guide my expectations around, for example, just how much arse I was likely to grow.

"Get on progesterone," she said, towards the end of the afternoon. "Order some tonight, so it has time to come. Wait until you've been on the estradiol a couple of months, and then start taking it." She pointed a finger in my face. "No arguments."

"What does it do?" I asked.

"Do you *want* good breast growth?"

"No arguments," I confirmed.

"And I can ask my friend where she gets her estradiol. Hers is injectable; most people find it works better."

I asked if she had any other suggestions and she said she was fresh out, but she did say she'd get her friend to send me an invite to a discussion server for British trans people my age, who'd be able to assist me with any further questions.

"They'll also fulfil any unmet needs you might have regarding visually unusual pornography," she added.

James returned to the office around 5pm, just as Emily and I were getting ready to go our separate ways. He caught us hugging, so to ensure he didn't feel left out, I went over and hugged him, too. He reciprocated with just one arm; he was holding what looked like two garment bags in the other. I tried not to frown at them, and he grinned at me.

They turned out, when Emily was packed off to the tube station and James and I were alone, to contain one of his suits and an ankle-length black evening dress.

"I called Ben's personal shopper," he said. "She says congratulations, by the way."

"On which part?" I asked idly, examining the dress.

"Both parts: becoming a girl for good *and* landing a hot boyfriend."

"I'll ask Ben to tell her thanks." I could have gotten pissy about Ben outing me to someone without my consent, but her services had been requested back when I was loudly insisting to everyone who mattered that I was a man. I decided that as long as she didn't call me an egg while I was within earshot, I wasn't going to care. "This'll look great with my tennis shoes," I added, holding up the dress.

"There's another bag out in the corridor. Dress shoes for me and thee."

"Thoughtful. What's the occasion?"

James spread his arms. "You are!"

He explained in the Uber, while I checked my makeup as best I could in the low light of the autumn evening: our other recent dinners out together had both been compromised somehow, whether because they were early enough in my personal journey of discovery that I could barely walk in heels or because James' cousin decided to have a go at me in the restroom. He wanted an evening that was just ours, and he wanted me to feel special.

And, honestly, it worked. The car pulled up to a much higher class of restaurant than I was used to, and as we swanned through the front doors — and as he whispered to me that, yes, my makeup looked *fine* — I felt even lighter on my feet than the three-inch heels made me. Because, while it might have been showy and it might have been silly and it might have required me to dress up *again,* it showed in as tangible a fashion as possible that he cared about me, that he loved me, that he wanted me, and that he wanted to be *seen* with me. And after the day I'd had, I kind of needed that.

We were tasting the wine and waiting on our main courses when I broke the news that Emily had found out about me.

"She was cool?"

"She was cool."

"Not even a hint of not-cool-ness?"

"Not even a hint."

"Because I could fire her, Alex. Seriously. She'd be out on her arse tomorrow."

"James! It was fine. *She* was fine. She, uh..." I looked around, then leaned forward to whisper. "She knows another girl like me."

"Not exactly like you, surely." He contemplated his wine for a moment, swirled it around in the glass such that it almost spilled over the rim. "No-one's exactly like you. You're unique, Alex. That's why you're so special."

He said the last sentence in his fake-sincere voice, so I shot him my most plastic smile. "You're so sweet."

"I mean it!"

I giggled at him. My glass-and-a-half of white was already starting to go to my head. "I know." I sighed, and sipped a little more. "I really do love you, James," I said. "I keep having to pinch myself to make sure it's all real. Sometimes I almost wonder if I died a week ago, and this is what heaven is: getting to be the person you were always supposed to be; getting to be *with* the person you were always supposed to be with. And then I get hit with another ball of anxiety and I think I'm in hell instead."

341

He reached over the table and took my hand. "Is this the same thing as yesterday?"

I nodded. "I'm scared something will go wrong with the shipment, or that the blood test results will come back and there'll be a problem with me taking hormones, or... you know. All of it. My brain is extremely good at inventing problems."

"Nothing's going to happen with the blood test," he said. "And if the shipment does go missing... What else is all this money for? We order some more. From three different places, just to be sure. It'll be fine, Alex."

"That helps, but, James, it's not *just* that." I thought for a moment. "It's the thing with Emily. It rattled me. It went fine, sure, but she was in the office for, what, thirty seconds? And she found old pictures of me. So now I'm worrying about what *else* might be out there, what else I might have forgotten about that's waiting to out me at the wrong time or to the wrong person. I checked, you know, and my face is on two booth babe websites, at least five blogs that I could find, and it's probably on Twitter, too. All it takes is for someone I went to school with to recognise me..."

He squeezed my hand. "So what if they do, Alex? They'll know, just like I do, what a remarkable, wonderful, beautiful woman you are. And if they think they know something different, they're wrong."

I frowned at him. "It wouldn't be... professionally damaging for you to be seen dating a trans woman?" Yet another thing that had been eating at me.

His eyes widened; clearly it hadn't occurred to him. But then he smiled. "I can't see how it would be. But who cares if it is?"

"James—"

"Remember what you told me the night you came out to me? That up to now there'd been nothing in your life but work?" With his free hand he tapped himself on the chest. "What do you think *I've* been doing the last few years, Alex? Because it's not living the rich playboy lifestyle my extended family expected of me, I promise you. I've been coming into work just as early as you—"

"—almost as early—"

"—and leaving just as late—"

"—almost as— Hey!" He'd tickled the inside of my wrist to interrupt me.

"I can see a future for myself now," he said, after I wriggled out of his grasp, "and I hope it's not presumptuous to say that the future I see heavily involves you, all the way to the end."

"Not presumptuous," I managed to reply, despite my dry mouth. Too much white wine.

"I want to be your boyfriend," he said. "I want to be, in the fullness of time, your husband, if you'll have me. I *also* want to work hard and make a name for myself separate from my dad's, yes, but on its own, that's empty. Only with you does it mean anything."

Did James McCain just say he wanted to marry me?

I made an incoherent noise.

"You're more important than anything else," he said.

I made another noise, even less intelligible than the first.

A fond smile curled one corner of his mouth. "You're so pretty when you're flustered," he said.

This went on for a little while, but I was eventually saved by the arrival of our food, and as we ate I watched him, listened to him, touched him under the table with my toes, feeling safe, feeling secure, and all the while wondering what he'd look like in five years, ten, twenty, and where we'd be, what we'd be doing, together.

* * *

The next six-ish months went smoothly, more or less. I came out to everyone else at work via the deliberately unexciting route of dropping a note on the network. At James' suggestion I added a photo, so people who'd barely interacted with me would have at least some idea who I was, though I refused to add the caption *James' smoking hot new GF*. It didn't take long for the first engineer to find it, and the congratulations started pouring in.

It was nice.

Kit was particularly excited to discover that the mousy, quiet little code gopher, coffee fetcher and engineer wrangler he'd seen around the office from time to time — and exchanged friendly insults with on the company chat server — was the same person as the glamorous and beautiful (his words) trade show model he'd gotten to know, and when in the course of telling him my whole story over a cup of coffee I mentioned that Ben did drag, he asked if I'd seen his show. I had to admit that I hadn't.

And that was how I ended up (briefly) on stage, two nights later, nervously waving to Ben's audience while he said into his microphone, "Isn't she gorgeous? This bitch cracked her egg *two weeks ago!* Hands up, who wants her genes?"

It was also how I saw Kit and Ben snogging in the dressing room after.

Sophie's threatened visit came a little while after, though she couldn't stay long and we made a mutual promise to spend a whole week, just us girls, when our schedules aligned. She did, however, stay long enough to look in my closet and get snooty about the clothes I'd been filling out my wardrobe with. She appointed herself my official stylist, browbeat Ben until he gave up the contact details for his personal shopper, and from then on ensured I had a steady enough supply of expensive clothes that James and I had to make an emergency IKEA trip for an extra wardrobe and a place to keep all the shoes.

The big contract did not, in the end, come through, but a complete technology purchase for the camera software did, and we spent a frantic week sanitising our code (and deleting all photos of me from the archive). The amount of money McCain Applied Computing earned from the sale was enough to keep us in wacky new software projects for as long as we could keep thinking them up.

Somewhere in the middle of all that fuss, I started on hormones, and three months after I came out to myself, I finally saw a specialist doctor. The diagnostic process was everything donut_appreciator promised it would be, but it got me the rubber stamp I needed to get my next batch of pills from the local pharmacy. I had to keep ordering my progesterone online, though, and the girls on the chat server Emily put me in touch with kept nagging me to try injectable estradiol.

Vicky stayed in touch. At one point she sent me some very excited messages from Italy, where she'd been sent on business; she'd met a lovely Italian girl and thought there might be something there. Four months later, her updates had only increased in sweetness and regularity, and in her most recent message she innocently raised the topic of how I'd feel if someone, hypothetically, at some undecided point in the future, asked me to be a bridesmaid. My answering squeal was so high-pitched that James pretended to check the battery in the smoke alarm.

Emily and I became almost like sisters. She was like that from the off, of course — without her support I would probably have been arse-patted to death by a legion of lusty tech journalists — but when she found out about my whole deal, she decided I needed a crash course in surviving womanhood. She wasn't going to tell me *how* to be a woman, she insisted, since no woman is the same; instead she would teach me the skills I needed to navigate the world as a woman. Some of it I'd already guessed, being both an advanced student of human nature and having been in the presence of lustful, drunken men while wearing a short dress, but some of it was non-obvious, at least to me. She also taught me how to do my hair.

To celebrate my official coming out, Emily got me a mug painted in the colours of the trans flag. It had text in the central white stripe that read, *I drink coffee because I can't stand T!* She also got one for James that said, *Assigned sex? Don't mind if I do!* He immediately declared it too precious to drink out of and put it on a shelf in his office. We thanked her for the mugs and she showed us hers; it said *Best Girl Ever (we have proof)* on the side and was so stained from use that the original internal colour was undiscernible. Months later, mine was close to sharing its fate.

James and I grew even closer. I hadn't thought it possible, but through his tireless support, boundless enthusiasm and extremely firm pectoral muscles I built strength of my own, the kind of strength you can possess only when you have a true partner. He bought me anniversary flowers every month; I, for my part, learned to care for them.

And then there was Mum.

We didn't talk all that much before I came out, and the only thing that changed in the months after was that I felt ever more guilty about it. I pretended to have a problem with the camera on my phone so we couldn't video chat and I hinted very hard at a new relationship keeping me busy. I wanted to tell her about myself, but there was always *something* happening, and it was never *quite* the right time, and the months just kept rolling on. I did make sure Dad hadn't come back for even more money and tried once again to convince her to cut him off entirely. She seemed a little more receptive than usual, which I put down to him having asked for a particularly large sum this time.

Christmas came and went. The office decorations were more lavish than I expected — the company was flush and so was James, and that meant an enormous synthetic tree and little gift bags for all the employees — and we weren't, for once, celebrating in the brief break between work and more work, so the whole holiday was rather languid. James took the opportunity presented by having the whole company in one place and *not* working our knuckles to the bone to formally announce to everyone that he and I were an item, and that any concerns regarding professional ethics should be directed to the HR department. Which was the cue for me to raise my hand: I was the HR department.

Kit threw a Christmas cupcake at me. I mimed writing him up on an invisible notepad.

And then, in the new year, when everything was tidied away and work was back to what passed for normal, James told me one Saturday morning that it really was time we told our parents about us.

* * *

"I was thinking of throwing a party," he said, carrying on the conversation as if I had any chance of usefully participating, as if I wasn't suffering a sudden attack of intense anxiety at the thought of coming out both to

James' parents and my mother *and* disclosing our relationship at the same time. "What do you think?"

I shook my head until a reply fell out. "Another one?" I didn't know why *that* was what came to mind. Maybe I just picked the easiest thing to think about. "Didn't we have one, like, three weeks ago? A little thing called Christmas?"

He pulled at me and for a moment I resisted him, preferring to stay sitting ramrod straight in the middle of the bed, making a terrified divot in the mattress. But he was very persuasive and it was quite cold in the bedroom, so I settled back into his embrace and he kissed me on the forehead as a reward. "This'll be early Feb," he said, and that helped a bit; he wasn't dropping this on me as a next-day thing. I let some of the tension unwind from my shoulders. "The excuse would be that we're celebrating the anniversary of the founding of the company."

"Excuse?"

He poked me in my dangerously exposed belly. I'd rounded out a bit since starting hormones, and he loved that my stomach was softer and squishier than before. And I loved that he loved it. I also loved that I didn't need the pads any more, and that I could tuck for all but the most revealing of clothes with just an ordinary pair of stretchy knickers. Still needed the tits, though.

Well, perhaps I didn't *need* them. They were more like comfort tits.

"Yes," he said as I squirmed. "Excuse. The *real* reason will be so we can introduce you to my parents with lots of other people around. They're less likely to make a scene."

"A scene? You think they might make a fuss?"

He shrugged. The motion bobbed my head up and down. "I think Mum'll be fine with it. She'll be happy I've finally settled down. Dad... He's unpredictable."

"Then why *now?*" I whined.

"Because," James retorted. Iron-clad. I nudged him to make him clarify, and he kissed me again before he did. "Look, you can't keep claiming your phone's busted, and you're aching to tell your mum, I know."

"Not *aching*—"

"Alex. I know you."

"Yes. Fine. Aching. Aching in all my bones. And she *should* know. I hate keeping her in the dark about this. I want to be her *daughter...*" The thought that I was, to her, still her son was one that occasionally woke me, caused James to take me into his care in the middle of the night.

"You will be," he whispered.

"I love you," I whispered back. He kissed me yet again.

"I was thinking," he said, pivoting away from me so he could look at me directly, gauge my reaction as he spoke, "we'd invite her up a few days before the shindig."

"Shindig?"

"We could have a quiet little gathering, right here, just you, me and her. And then, once the deed is done—"

"You say that like it's going to be so simple," I muttered.

"—we can ask if she wants to stick around for the party. Get her a hotel or something. Or have her stay here; she could have this room and we could take the sofa bed."

"We have a sofa bed?"

"It's the one near the bar. It pulls out. I plan ahead, Alex. It was one of the first things I bought when I moved in."

"Oh, so Ben could stay over?" I knew Ben hadn't officially moved to London until almost a year after James did, but he visited a lot.

"No," James said, smiling. "He always slept in the bed with me. Best friend privileges," he added, his grin broadening.

I tried to ignore the image that popped into my head — it was *very* difficult; they were both extremely attractive men — and said, "So, we have Mum stay here, I do the girl thing; then we do your parents at the party, hopefully with my mum as backup."

"Yes."

I nodded. "I like this. I mean, I *don't* like this — I hate it, actually, and I'm so scared of it that just the thought of it makes me want to turn myself inside out — but getting her out of that lonely house for a while... It's good. I like it." I put on my most whining voice, one which I'd become exceptionally good at after all the practice. "I *guess* I can tell her I'm a girl."

"Good," James said, and kissed me again. "Proud of you."

* * *

The day before she arrived, I cleaned the apartment top to bottom.

* * *

We had a plan. Mum was coming up on the first post-rush-hour train into Victoria, and James was meeting her there with a car so she wouldn't have to navigate London public transport. This was a compromise: I'd initially suggested she take the tube, and she recoiled so hard I could have sworn I felt it, even though we were communicating by text. James then suggested we call a car service and have them meet her, but she didn't want to travel with someone she didn't know, so the final decision was that I would wait at home, fretting and triple-checking my appearance, while James went to fetch her in a rental.

I looked myself over for the *n*th time: I looked as plain as I could manage without actively hating myself. Thanks to Sophie and Emily's combined efforts I had a hell of a wardrobe to sift through, and I'd wanted to pick something that said I was unambiguously not *Alexander* any more while not, like, glamming so hard I'd give her a heart attack on-sight. I picked out a pair of dark blue jeggings and paired them with a cami in light pink and a white, near-translucent blouse, which I wore open. In a fit of insecurity about the realness or otherwise of my body I'd left off the rubber tits and worn instead one of my small collection of padded bras, which did the best it could with what little I had.

I put my hair — which was about half-mine now and cared for exclusively by Warren at the salon — up in a loose pony, and I left off the makeup. My skin, while moisturised and exfoliated and pampered as much as I could manage, looked like shit, but that couldn't be helped: I was on monthly laser hair removal appointments, and I'd never been so prone to zits and redness.

Honestly, though, I decided the crappy skin and the fading spot on my chin would help sell the impression all the better: this is real, this is me, and even if you see me at the party with my hair done and my face painted and wearing clothes that flatter my shape, this is still what's underneath: a girl.

Call it personal growth, but by this point I was almost believing it myself.

And then I heard the door opening, so I wrenched myself away from the mirror in the bedroom and prepared to make my entrance.

* * *

"This is such a lovely apartment," Mum was saying to James as I breathed in and out behind the bedroom door and wished I'd worn the damn breast forms; I was so *flat*. "So much nicer than his old one."

"Yes," James said, audibly uncomfortable, "I like it."

"You're so good to pay him, James."

"It's not like it's charity," James said, too quickly.

"Oh, I know," Mum said awkwardly. "It's just..."

"Alex does amazing work. We couldn't have sold our last project without... uh, without Alex."

I winced; James clearly hadn't thought that sentence through, and he'd ended up having to execute possibly the least graceful attempt to avoid a gendered pronoun I'd ever heard. He needed rescuing, and in that his inelegance was my redemption: a desire to save him from himself overpowered my fear, and I pushed open the door.

"Hi Mum," I said.

It took her a second. I was glad James was holding onto her by the arm, because it meant he could catch her when she staggered, could guide her to the couch and lower her gently onto a cushion.

"Alexander?"

I'd let it slide for now. "Yes."

I walked over to her from the bedroom, reining in my hip wiggle as much as I could — a side-effect of learning to be a girl while also learning to be a model, and of growing an arse — and sat carefully opposite her, on the nice little armchair we'd got a short while before Christmas so I could have somewhere near the standing lamp to read my books without having to use the light on my Kindle. I'll fully admit that I picked out and positioned the chair and got into reading at least partly because I liked the thought of curling up by lamplight in an oversized sweater and smiling coyly at my boyfriend over the pages of some bodice-ripper, but the way it worked out was that James used the time I spent reading to play video games, and I found myself getting into science fiction rather than romance.

I smiled at my mother. Gently, like picking flowers.

She smiled back.

"Your phone's not broken, is it?" she asked. I shook my head, still smiling. Unable to stop smiling. Becoming convinced there might have been something wrong with my face. "And is this... permanent?"

I tried to reply, but it was like my throat was glued shut. James, psychic that he was, had a bottle of water in my hand before I could finish miming my request for it, and I downed half before I tried again.

"Yes," I said. "It's permanent."

"You chose this?"

I shrugged. "I've always been this, Mum. I just never knew before. They don't exactly do workshops about it at school."

"Are you... happy?"

I forced that smile back onto my face, but it was more natural this time. More real. "I am."

"Because that's all I want for you, Alexander, sweetheart—"

"Actually, Mum, would you mind just calling me Alex?"

She smiled again, with a generosity I remembered from the fleeting moments of closeness we'd enjoyed when I was a child. "And that's short for...?"

"Alexandra, specifically." That was what it said on my new bank card.

"Of course, Alexandra, dear."

"We all just call her Alex," James said, having apparently decided that this was the most appropriate moment for him to reassert his presence.

"She's beautiful, isn't she?" Mum said, stumbling a little over the pronoun but visibly pleased to have caught and corrected herself in time, and that was too much for me, that was what got me out of my seat and had me pulling her up from the couch to embrace her properly, to touch her for the first time since she arrived, to hug her for the first time in... God. Over a year.

I hadn't realised how much my former self had kept people at arm's length. My string of failed relationships with women was testament not only to the fact that I was, and all along had been, a straight woman, but also to my withdrawn and isolated nature. Good at dealing with people professionally; bad at being a person intimately. James had been the first person in nineteen years to break through my barriers, and I felt sudden immense sorrow that I'd never understood that the reason I was never close with my mother was... *me.*

I squeezed her so hard she squeaked.

"Sorry," I whispered.

"Whatever for?"

I let her go and sat down next to her. Held her hand. "For being absent, I suppose. When I worked it out — who I am; what I am — it was in a... highly unusual situation, and since then I think I'm not only playing catch-up on almost twenty years of girlhood that I missed, but on everything else I missed, too. Every week I spot another missing piece of the life I could have had. And I'm sorry, Mum, but it's only just now I realised that one of the major missing pieces was... you. I should have been your daughter, Mum, and I hope you can see me as that now, but I could have been a better son."

She reached for my cheek and pinched it, the way she had when I was a kid. "Don't be silly," she said. "Now, I don't know anything about, well, anything much! But I *do* know about blind spots. I know it's hard to see something that's always been there. If yours was you, or your sex or your gender or however you want to think of it, mine's always been your father." She cocked her head at me, thinking. "We were both preoccupied, I'd say," she continued after a short while. "Except I was supposed to be the adult. Supposed to have more of a grasp on things. So—" and she frowned at me suddenly, "—don't ever go thinking you were a bad son or a bad daughter or— or *anything*."

I kissed her on the cheek. "Thanks, Mum."

"You really are beautiful," she said wistfully. And then she muttered to herself, "Good grief, I have a lot of reading up on things to do."

"I have a book," James said. We both looked up to find him returning from the kitchen with a tray of tea — I hadn't even heard him make it — and a hardback. The spine read, *True Selves: Transgender People in Their Own Words.*

"When did you get that?" I asked.

"The day before I suggested we invite your mother up."

I shook my head. The man was unstoppable.

"This is you, then?" Mum said, gingerly taking the book and holding it out with her finger over the word 'transgender'.

"That's me," I said.

"Then thank you, James." Mum slipped the book into some dark recess of the bundle of supermarket bags-for-life she took with her everywhere, and then turned back to me. "So, Alex, I want to hear everything."

"I'll tell you everything," I said, "but first, Mum, are you okay?"

She blinked. "Am *I* okay?" I nodded. "I mean, yes, I think so, but I'm not sure what you mean."

"Are you okay *with me?* Because this *is* me, now. Forever." I wasn't sure that I'd made that clear enough. I'd said 'permanent' before, but Mum and Dad's marriage had been permanent, until it wasn't. And, hell, I just needed the bloody reassurance.

She smiled at me again. "Sweetheart, I have to say that I'm not really all that surprised. I mean," she continued after I frowned at her, "it was a shock, to be sure, but... Alex, you were always a delicate little boy. Careful. Meticulous. And sad. I worried, when you were younger, that you might inherit your father's tendencies, but you were quite his opposite. So then I worried that you were unhappy, and I think I had good reason to. So, yes, I think I became okay with it — with you — the moment you told me you were happy."

I had to hug her again. Just for a moment.

"Actually," I said, withdrawing and holding out a hand, "I have more than one reason to be happy."

James, on cue, stood up and took my hand, and I leaned back into the couch cushion, enough for him to bend over and kiss me. We kept it chaste, which was, personally, a tremendous sacrifice — just his smell, his aftershave mixed with his natural scent, was enough to get me going most days — and when we were done, I looked back at my mother.

"Ah," Mum said. "Oh, my. My, my, my."

"And it's not my apartment," I added, dropping all the bombs at once. "It's ours."

"My, my, my."

"Mum?"

"Yes, dear? Oh, sorry." She narrowed her eyes, looked up at James. "Do you love her?" Again with the slight hesitation over the pronoun. She'd get there.

"I do, Mrs Brewer," he said. "Sincerely."

She nodded to herself. "Then that is all that matters."

"Actually," I said, "it's not *quite* all that matters. You see, we're having a party on Saturday—"

"A little office shindig," James put in. I wished he'd stop saying that.

"—and James' parents are going to be there. And we're going to... formally introduce me. And us. As a couple. That's what we are, by the way: a couple."

"I understand," Mum said.

"I'd love for you to be there, if that's okay."

"Oh, Alex!" She took my hand, raised it up between us, clasped it between her palms like a precious stone. "Of course I'll be there!"

* * *

The advantage of having a lot of rented but unused office space is that when you throw a party, you don't have to cram fifty people into a space normally intended for ten. The disadvantage is you have to spend a whole morning chasing spiders with the Hoover.

Mum helped. She insisted; she wouldn't be left at home in the apartment, indolently watching television, when there was work to do! So she met Emily and Kit and Mark and was delighted when Ben popped in to drop off a case of audio equipment and a kiss for Kit. First, a transgender daughter; now, the transgender daughter's gay coworkers? Mum was becoming *quite* cosmopolitan. She also made us assist her with the crossword when she took a break.

Sophie was the first member of the extended McCain clan to arrive, and when she came bounding in through the front door shortly after lunch, she was trailing a wheeled suitcase of the sort that I still had mild PTSD about. My fears turned out to be justified when she dragged me into a side room and showed me what she'd brought.

"It might not fit," I protested as she held the sky-blue dress up against my body. "I've grown in a few places."

"It'll fit," she said confidently. "I had James refresh your measurements last week." I made a noise that I was pretty sure had only heretofore been produced by enraged gazelles, and she grinned at me. "He says you're a heavy sleeper. And look," she continued, before I could gather enough brain cells to mount a counterattack, "the neckline will flatter your bosom and show off your cleavage."

"I don't exactly have a bosom, and I definitely don't have cleavage."

"You will. I brought bra boosters."

There really was no escape.

The party arrangements were a simple affair, once everything was cleaned and fumigated and all the dust and spiders had been chucked out of the windows for the pigeons to deal with. Our usual office space was for coats, bags, luggage, and general detritus, and we'd set up the other two rooms as loud and quiet areas, with a sound system and bar in the loud room and plenty of seating in the quiet one. It wasn't exactly glamorous and it was more than a bit school disco, but we'd put it together ourselves, and that was what mattered. James hated the atmosphere you got at posh, catered parties; too much like every formal event he had to attend growing up, he said.

And now I was cowering in my sky-blue dress and my nominal new office, staring at myself in a hand mirror and fretting.

"You look wonderful," Sophie said, running a hand down the small of my back, smoothing out the material.

"No, *you* look wonderful," I retorted, because she did, as usual.

"You've got nothing to worry about," Emily said.

"Emily," I said, "I have *so* many things to worry about. For example—" I hefted a padded tit, "—what if I have a nip slip?" The dress was *really* quite low-cut.

Sophie slapped at my hand. "Stop playing with those!"

"You won't have a nip slip," Emily said.

"I'll find a way," I muttered, and went back to glaring at my reflection. "God, I swear I can see beard shadow..."

"Alex," Emily said, sharply enough that I looked away from my face for a moment, "you know how at the expo you were so pretty, guys kept diverting from other booths just to get a picture with you?"

"That's not how I remember it," I said, and Sophie whacked me lightly on the arm.

"Right now, you're prettier."

Sophie nodded her agreement. I did my best to convince them otherwise, but I was outnumbered, overruled and frankly still inexperienced at the whole *girl* thing, and had inevitably to accede to their increasingly emphatic reassurances. My heart wasn't really in it, anyway.

I did get Soph to stop beating me up, though.

God, I loved them both. And a sensible part of my brain knew they were right: estrogen suited me, and it'd done pretty wonderful things to my face, even if my chest was lagging behind.

The three of us stepped out together and began to mingle.

* * *

I knew I couldn't avoid an encounter with James' parents for very long. Yes, sure, the whole purpose of the party was for me to meet them — meet them *again,* since I'd encountered both of them in my previous form — but that didn't mean I had to be enthusiastic about it. Didn't mean I couldn't hide behind Marcus when I saw them enter the room.

James collected me in the end, smoothly guiding me out of the shadow of my coworker and into the middle of the room, where his parents awaited.

"Hah! Look at you!"

Henry McCain. Tall, wide, almost as pale as I was, and artfully tailored into a suit that could have purchased all the organs in my body with just the change in its pockets. His voice carried even more than Sophie's, and I could feel every word through the soles of my feet.

My eyes, though, were as new as the rest of me, figuratively speaking, and this was the first time I'd looked at James' dad with a full awareness of who I was. And, God damn him, I saw it. I saw what James' mother doubtless saw in him. Yes, he was blunt and rude and sexist in an unapologetic and supposedly benevolent sort of way, but I bloody well saw it: that strength, that confidence, that protectiveness.

I buried that realisation in the deepest recesses of my brain and resolved never to dig it out.

"Hello, Mr McCain," I said, in the clearest and steadiest tone I could manage, thankful for all my months of voice training and the double I'd knocked back while I was in hiding. "It's lovely to see you."

"Call me Henry, love! Or, if what I hear about your relationship is true—" and, horrifyingly, he winked at me and nudged James with his elbow, "—call me Dad!"

I smiled. "Henry, then."

He barked a delighted laugh, and then leaned closer to address me in what counted, for Henry McCain, as a whisper. "I hear I pay your wages, love! Indirectly, of course, through loans and handshake agreements and whatnot, but—"

"We're independent now," James said. "We'll have made your accounts whole in the next—"

"Keep it, lad! Keep it. For a rainy day. Or—" he returned to his 'whisper' and wiggled a finger between us, showing off his wedding ring, "—a giant rock!"

"Dad! That's misappropriation of—"

"I'm sure it is. Now." He straightened up and looked me right in the eye, and I attempted to straighten up with him. Our relative heights made it a little comical. "Worked with my son long, have you?" I nodded. "Well then, I'm sorry I missed you! I have a hell of a memory for faces, dear girl, a *hell* of a memory, and I'm certain I wouldn't have forgotten one as lovely as yours. James! You treating her right?"

"Yes, Dad," James said, sounding momentarily like a teenager who'd been asked to do the dishes.

Deirdre, James' mother, took my hand and held it up between us, and I was struck by how little she'd changed since the last time I'd seen her, years ago. It'd always been clear that it was her, not James' father, who gifted their son his looks, and hers hadn't aged a day. She'd contrasted her dark skin with a floral-printed dress in oranges, yellows and greens, which faded to pale peach just below her knees and complimented my blue ensemble so neatly I wondered if she and Sophie had coordinated their efforts. She kept her hair short, her makeup simple, and in the low light her eyes sparkled as she favoured me with a knowing smile.

Far, far too knowing.

"Alex, is it?" she said, and I knew I was busted. "Why don't we have a little chat?" She looked up at her husband, and added, "Just us girls."

"Yes, yes," Henry McCain said. "I need to talk business with James, anyway. Come, lad, and show me what you call Scotch in this bloody city…"

"Hi, Deirdre," I said sheepishly, when we were alone. I knew better than to call her 'Mrs McCain', at least.

"Alex, Alex, Alex," she said, "what *are* we going to do with you?"

I blushed. "That's sort of the question before the court. The court being, um, you and your husband."

She hesitated for a moment, and then rolled her eyes and reached out to squeeze my shoulder. "Oh, Alex. Were you worried we wouldn't accept you?"

"Um. Yes?"

"Silly girl. If James has chosen you and you've chosen him, then that's the end of it. And I was *always* fond of you. And— Oh! That's wonderful; I *just* realised."

"What's that?"

"Your mother and I are going to be related now," she said. "Goodness, is *that* why she's been avoiding me so far this evening? She's been deep in conversation with that tall girl from your office for the last half-hour, and I was just thinking about becoming offended…"

"You know how terrible she is at keeping secrets."

"True." And then she released my shoulder and poked it. "But, Alex, you've *got* to start being more careful! You've been transitioning for how long now?"

"Six months," I said, wondering where she was going with this.

"And you just *show up* to a party all dressed up, walk up to Henry and me—"

"—actually, I was kind of dragged over to you—"

"—and without a word, you're just a girl? Alex, *think* of all the ways that could have gone wrong!"

I attempted a smile. "But... it didn't go wrong, right?"

"Oh, Alex," she said again, and kissed me on the cheek. "Just be more careful in future, okay?"

I decided not to tell her that on practically my first night as a woman I went for a walk, at night, in a city I didn't know. It seemed like the kind of confession that would get me poked again.

We talked for a little longer — Deirdre reassured me again that she was nothing but delighted to discover that her son had settled down with such a sweet girl — and then we were joined by my mother, gin and tonic in hand and Emily on her arm. Emily and I exchanged smiles and Mum swept me into a hug that I had to push quickly out of.

"Mum, the dress!" I hissed. Sophie had lectured me about wrinkling it. There'd been slides.

"Oh, sorry, dear!" she replied, and then gasped with the exaggeration of the inebriated. "Wait," she added, "does Deirdre *know?*"

"Deirdre knows," Deirdre said. "You're going to be mother-in-law to my son."

"Gosh, yes," Mum said, gesticulating with her glass. "He's *besotted* with her. And so am I! She's beautiful, isn't she?"

Deirdre shared a glance with me and then looped an arm around Mum's waist to support her. "Peggy," she said, "how much have you had?" My mum frowned, apparently counting in her head, and Emily held up four fingers. "Oh, *Peggy.*"

At least it wasn't only me James' mother talked to that way.

Deirdre, Emily and I helped Mum over to a chair at the side of the room, and I crouched down in front of her, carefully managing my dress the way Emily showed me.

"Mum," I said, "what's up?" She wasn't normally much of a drinker, and I was worried my coming out had triggered some awful coping mechanism, long hidden from me but always present.

Her next words dismissed my worries, however, and helpfully replaced them with whole new ones. "I got a message from your father," she said. "Yesterday, like you suggested, I told him the bank of Peggy Brewer is closed. He sent me all sorts of invective, of course; you know what he's like." I nodded. I really, really did. "But I ignored him and he went silent after a while. Until about twenty minutes ago." With trembling fingers she reached into her bag and extracted her phone. She fumbled the unlock code twice, so I took it from her and entered it myself and there, on the screen, was a series of text messages from Dad.

They weren't pleasant. The upshot was, he was coming here. Tonight.

And he knew about me.

"Shit," I said.

"I'm so sorry, Alex," Mum said, but I shushed her, brushed her hair out of her face, patted her on the arm. She didn't need to be sorry; I should have dealt with my father a long time ago. Forced him out of Mum's life somehow.

"What's going on?" James asked, and I looked up to find him standing over us, drawn by our anxious little huddle. I showed him the phone. "Christ," he said.

"How does he even know about the party?" I said.

James shrugged. "The event's on Facebook. Sorry, Alex."

"That's probably how he knows about you, too," Emily said. "People haven't exactly been careful with their photo tags."

Fucking Facebook. Again.

"Okay," I said. "So everyone's already here, right? We can just shut and lock the door, and—"

"Nice, thought, babe, but a bit late," James said. He stood quickly and started walking away from us, and as I stood up to follow, I heard a commotion coming from the main office, just about audible over the music. Moments later, the music stopped, and I heard a voice I hadn't heard in person in years: my father.

I followed James out to the main office, aware of Deirdre and Emily behind me, helping my mum back to her feet. When I rounded the corner I found James running up to join Ben and Kit in restraining my Dad, who was himself clearly drunk and enraged.

As soon as he saw me, he pointed at me and shoved harder against Ben.

"*You!*" He yelled. "You turned my *wife* against me, you little—"

"She's *not* your *wife!*" I shouted, and my dad actually winced. Head voice: it can get really fucking loud if you push it.

"Quite so!" Henry McCain bellowed, startling me. I looked quickly backward and found him standing with Mum and Deirdre, with Mum steadying herself on one of the desks that had been pushed to the side. "A divorce is a divorce. Know when you're not wanted, man."

"Michael Brewer," Mum shouted, her original Estuary accent creeping in, "I believe I told you what you can go *do* with yourself!"

I looked at Dad, who was struggling against the combined grip of James, Ben and Kit. "In how many words?" I asked.

"I told him to bugger off and never talk to me again, Alex."

Henry McCain clapped his hands. "Good for you! Always said he was rotten."

"Fuck *you,* Mr High and Mighty," Dad yelled.

"You don't deserve a woman like Peggy," Henry McCain said, advancing on him. "You never did. Drinking and spending and gadding about with other women. That's not how a man behaves!"

Dad laughed. Bent over in the grip of the men restraining him, he laughed the bubbling, grotesque laugh of someone who has had far too much to drink and doesn't care what anyone says or does to him any more.

"A man!" he shouted. "A man! I'll tell you who's a *man.*" He pointed at me again and my brain turned to ice. "My *son* over there. My son in his fancy fucking frock, all painted up and looking like a—"

"Shut *up!*" I yelled back at him, walking forward to stand next to Henry McCain, who I knew was looking down at me but who I'd had to put on the back burner for the moment. I'd deal with my fucking father first, and then I'd deal with being outed. It wasn't like I hadn't been about to out myself, anyway. "Mum told you she was done with you, didn't she?

She told you to piss off out of her life, so you decided to have a drink and make it everyone's problem."

"No," Dad said. "I saw *you,* cavorting around in all those pictures. Dressing up like a fucking girl! *You're* the problem, *Alexander.*"

"That is *not* her name!" Henry barked, and when I looked up at him, astonished, he leaned down and whispered, "It's Alexandra, now, isn't it? Your mother's still calling you 'Alex', so I assumed—"

"Alexandra, yes. But Alex is fine."

"Nonsense. Alexandra's a wonderful name. You barely even have to change your signature. *Very* clever." Straightening up just as my Dad started yelling again, Henry cut him off, his booming voice effortlessly drowning out my father's. "Now, listen here, Michael. As much as I didn't like it, as long as Peggy was content to keep you fed and watered, you were her business. But she cut you off! And now you're *here,* at my son's party, making yourself, as your daughter pointed out, everyone's problem. Mine included. And you *don't* want to be *my* problem!"

"He's my *son,* not—"

"I'm your daughter, Dad," I spat. Positioned next to Mr McCain, I was under no illusions as to which of us was the more intimidating, but I liked to think I partially made up for my diminutive stature with sheer anger. This man in front of us, this pathetic excuse for a father, could have done so much good. He could have seen the isolation in his child and tried to help; he could have seen the loneliness in his wife and been there for her. He did neither, choosing to cheat, to lie, to waste our money, and eventually to leave.

And when he left, he didn't even have the decency to stay gone.

"We're going to call the police," I said, "and have you *removed.*" I didn't especially like invoking the police, but it was probably better for everyone concerned for them to deal with Dad rather than us. "And then we're going to go to court and get a restraining order."

"You can use our lawyers, love," Henry McCain muttered.

"We have so many..." I heard James say, somewhere behind me.

"We have a roomful of witnesses," I continued, "and bank statements that show your *continued* drain on your ex-wife's finances. We even still have the documents from the divorce that include a letter from her doctor that shows—"

"Oh, dear," Mum said. "I didn't know you knew about that."

I turned around. "Sorry, Mum. I went snooping when I was fifteen."

"That's okay, Alex."

"Or," I said to Dad, as Mum, with Deirdre's support, came up behind me and took my hand, "you can leave right now and never come back. Never bother me again, never bother Mum again, never even speak to anyone in this room again. Go back to whatever life you've been living. Do whatever you want to do. Just do it away from us. Okay?"

"Please, Michael," Mum said. "Just go."

"And if it wasn't clear," Henry added, "everything the little lady just said comes backed up by *our* people. I'm sure you wouldn't enjoy lawyers and private investigators digging through your life, would you, Michael?"

"Fuck you," Dad said, but it was clear that the fight had left him, that the consequences of his actions were finally seeping through his thick skull into his alcohol-sodden brain. I'd have loved to think it was my words that turned the tide, but Henry McCain was a man who could summon an army of lawyers at a moment's notice, whereas my most impressive assets still didn't fill out an A-cup without assistance.

A few volunteers emerged from the crowd to help Kit and Ben escort my father back down the stairs and out the door, so James could be with me, could make sure that I was okay, could hold me up when the adrenaline crashed, and it was a good thing he was there because almost as soon as Dad was out of my sight, my knees buckled and I almost fell.

* * *

The front office became an oasis of calm for our two families. Emily had taken Sophie, who'd come running in just as everything was ending, and gone back to the party, and James waited for Kit, Ben and the others to

364

return and then locked the door. Deirdre and Henry nipped around the corner for more drinks — and a lemonade for Mum — and then it was just us, sitting in our glamour on office chairs, coming down from near-disaster.

Well, okay. Maybe it had never been that bad. Had Dad found out where I lived or tried to accost me on a normal day at work, I might have been in trouble, but he picked the one night that I and my mother were surrounded by people who could pin him down and keep him down indefinitely.

He always had been an idiot.

"Come stay with us for a while, Peggy," Deirdre was saying, and my mother was silently nodding. I hoped this would mean she'd finally move out of the old house and start fresh somewhere new.

"God," I said, "I'm so sorry about this."

"Don't worry about it for a second," James said.

"Quite right," Henry said.

I shook my head. It felt heavy; the alcohol was definitely starting to sink in. "I should have told you, Mr McCain— Henry. You shouldn't have had to find out from my bloody *dad*."

"Nonsense!" He knuckled me gently on my forearm. "This'll be a story to tell the grandkids."

"Oh shit," I muttered. "*Kids*. Henry— Deirdre— I can't—" It hadn't even occurred to me that it was something I should worry about. I was still a month off my twentieth birthday, and starting a family had hadn't even been on the horizon for me. But *of course* James' parents would want grandchildren, and *of course* James would, too, at some point, and I just couldn't—

"Alex, sweetheart," Deirdre said gently, breaking through my destructive thoughts before they had a chance to properly get going, "don't worry about that for now."

"But I can't have *kids*," I protested.

"Don't be daft, girl!" Henry said. "Kids are easy! I suppose it *is* a shame you can't carry them yourself, but I'm sure your mother would tell you it's not the most pleasant experience in the world. When you decide you want some, we'll just ask around, find some young girl who needs the money, maybe she wants to get an education or a kitchen extension or whatnot, cover her in gold, and bang!" He clapped his hands together. "Nine months later, you have yourself a child."

"Or you could adopt," Deirdre said.

"Or you could adopt. See? Simple."

I nodded and tried to internalise it. Simple.

The conversation moved on, and I let it swim around me for a while, drinking my fruity drink, resting my hand on James' thigh, until a thought arrived in my head and, as per usual, spilled immediately out of my mouth.

"I don't understand how you're so okay with me," I said. "I mean, all you see in the papers about trans people is the bad stuff we're supposedly all guilty of, and—"

"Ah," Henry said, and sniffed dismissively. "The papers."

"We don't read them," Deirdre confided.

"We just get briefed on their contents. Convenient. Anyway, I knew all about transsexuals and transgenders *long* before the hacks started making a fuss about you lot." Henry settled back in his office chair, arms folded. "Old chum of mine, Percy, his daughter turned out transsexual. Came to him a few days after her twenty-first, told him she was actually a man, been one all along. And Percy, he forbade it. No chance, he told her, no way, no how he was going to tolerate anything like that from his daughter. So she left, just up and left, and now he's a strapping young lad. Ran into him at the motor show a year or so back. Works with electric cars. Good move! It's a growing industry." Henry leaned forward and steepled his fingers. "And Percy doesn't have a daughter *or* a son any more. Complete fool." He looked at me and I tried not to flinch. "Alex, you're a lovely young girl. I already know from James that you're a hell of a worker and from your mother that you're a good person. Whatever else you have going on is none of anyone's business except yours and my son's."

"And that's that," Deirdre said.

"Thank you," Mum said on my behalf, because I was too busy reeling from Henry's little speech.

"No need to thank me," Henry said. "Just decent behaviour. Now!" He slapped his hands on his thighs, stood, and held out both hands, one for his wife and the other for my mother. "I think we should give these two lovebirds some time to themselves, and I, for one, could murder another drink. Are you coming, ladies?"

The three of them ambled off, discussing what investments my mother could make if she sold her current house and bought something cheaper, farther north and coincidentally much closer to the McCain estate, and the last thing I heard from them was Henry insisting that electric cars were, in fact, just the ticket.

"Holy shit," James muttered. He grinned at me, shaking his head. "My family."

"*My* family," I countered.

And then the pop song that had been playing on the speakers in the other room abruptly stopped, and in its place were piano chords picking out a simple melody. I didn't recognise the song at first, but when the lyrics started I realised it was one I'd definitely heard before.

James laughed, easily and sweetly, and stood. He took my hand, lifted me out of my chair, and let me rest against his chest.

"Nat King Cole," he said as the song played. "Dad always plays this for Mum."

"That's sweet."

"I think he's playing it for *us* now."

"That's... intimidating?"

"He approves."

James hooked his hands behind my back, drew me closer to him, and started swaying gently to the music. A slow dance. Suddenly that electric feeling was back, that feeling I got when I *needed* to put my hands on the man I loved and I needed to do it *now*.

I resisted temptation and instead leaned back a little as we danced, so I could look into his eyes.

Never before has someone been more unforgettable, the song went.

"I can't believe it's over," I said, towards the end of the song. "Mum knows. Your parents know. Even Dad knows, and apart from him, everyone's..." I couldn't finish the sentence. I still couldn't understand how they were all so fine with it.

"They're like me, you know," James said. "They knew you before. Loved you before. And they could tell you weren't quite complete. We're all just happy you're *you* now."

"That makes—" I counted, "—five of us. I think."

He squeezed me. "I get the best deal, though. I get to do *this.*"

"Nuh-uh," I protested, leaning my head against his chest again, feeling his heat against my cheek. "I got the best deal. Me."

"You know," James said as another, more upbeat song started up, "it occurs to me, you haven't told *everyone.*"

I frowned at him. "I have!"

"Don't you have a cousin?"

"James—"

"She has a right to know."

"James—"

"We can throw another party next month, just for her."

"James," I said, "shut up."

And I pushed up on my toes and I kissed him, and he kissed me back, and everything else was forgotten.

ABOUT THE AUTHOR

Alyson Greaves is a white trans woman who lives in a very small flat in a very large city. She can be found online at twitter.com/badambulist, where she releases chapter-by-chapter updates for her fiction and complains about her bad shoulder.

ACKNOWLEDGEMENTS

Thank you to Benjanun Sriduangkaew for her help with cover design and general encouragement. Thank you to my friends, for agreeing with me that going back to rewrite this story was a great and not at all incredibly time-consuming idea. And thank you to my wife, for putting up with me.

Made in the USA
Las Vegas, NV
20 June 2023